Martin Edwards is a lawyer by day and a crime writer and aficionado by night.

Mysterious Pleasures

A CELEBRATION OF THE CRIME WRITERS'
ASSOCIATION'S 50th ANNIVERSARY

EDITED BY

Martin Edwards

A *Time Warner* Paperback

First published in Great Britain in 2003 by Little, Brown
This edition published in 2004 by Time Warner Paperbacks

reprinted 2005

This collection and introduction copyright © 2003 Martin Edwards
Copyright notices and acknowledgements on p. 495
constitute an extension of this page.

The moral rights of the authors have been asserted.

A CIP catalogue record for this book
is available from the British Library.

ISBN 0 7515 3692 X

Typeset by Palimpsest Book Production Limited,
Polmont, Stirlingshire

Printed and bound in Great Britain by
Bookmarque Ltd.,
Croydon, Surrey

Time Warner Paperbacks
An imprint of
Time Warner Book Group UK
Brettenham House
Lancaster Place
London WC2E 7EN

www.twbg.co.uk

Contents

Foreword

All right, I'm biased. But it seems to me that there is no greater accolade that any writer can be paid than to be described as a fine storyteller. And that, of course, includes winning the Booker prize!

The Crime Writers' Association, by the very nature of what its members do, positively overflows with fine storytellers. And there is probably no purer form of the art than a short story, with the tight disciplines its length necessarily imposes.

In this latest CWA anthology, editor Martin Edwards has yet again assembled a marvellous collection of such offerings, this time with a rural theme.

Storytelling is an ancient craft, almost as old as man himself. Before we could write or read we told each other stories verbally, many of which entered into folklore and were passed on from generation to generation. For myself I always think that short stories are rather like mini-crossword puzzles. Among the many skills required to produce them effectively is a quite extraordinary degree of precision. There can be no loose use of adjectives or rambling descriptions. Instead every idea must be cut to the bone, while every character has to jump off the page after no more than a sentence or two at the most, and yet the plot must unfold before the reader in such a way that both its construction and its relation seem quite effortless.

It is a wonderful privilege to be able to tell stories. On a good day I would even go so far as to say that it's a thrill. It can also, hopefully, be a thrill to read them.

Within the pages of this book are some of the best, written by writers at the very top of their craft. I am more than proud to be introducing their work, which is actually something of a master class, and equally proud that they are all members of the CWA.

Hilary Bonner, Chairman, 2003,
Crime Writers' Association

Introduction

This anthology celebrates the Golden Jubilee of the Crime Writers' Association by bringing together stories from illustrious crime writers of the past fifty years. It also traces the development of the genre, from the classic era of Leslie Charteris and Margery Allingham to the present, with contributions from household names such as Ruth Rendell, Dick Francis and Colin Dexter. Finally, there are no fewer than eight stories – those by Dexter, Reginald Hill, Robert Barnard, Lindsey Davis, H.R.F. Keating, Peter Lovesey, Val McDermid and Ian Rankin – which have been specially written for this collection.

Three stories come from writers who were around in the early days of the CWA: John Creasey, whose brainchild the Association was, Cyril Hare and Allingham. Sixteen are contributed by winners of the CWA Cartier Diamond Dagger; inaugurated in 1986, this recognises a lifetime's achievement in the genre of crime writing and is the Association's highest honour. To complete the book, we offer a selection of work from some of the most eminent contemporary writers to have been awarded CWA Daggers.

The stories represent the rich variety of crime writing over the past half-century. They offer a mix of classic detection, expert police procedurals and psychological suspense, coupled with fiendish cunning and wit aplenty. Several of the sleuths who appear in these pages have become legends, ranging from that giant of the Golden Age, Allingham's Albert Campion, to Wexford, Rebus and Dalziel and Pascoe. And, in a story which reflects the lighter vein of crime fiction, Marcus Didius Falco makes a highly unorthodox appearance.

Today the CWA is one of the UK's leading literary organisations, known worldwide as the originator of the Dagger Awards. Full membership of the Association is limited to published writers of crime fiction or fact, and many members come from overseas; associate member-ship is available to those involved professionally with the genre, including publishers and agents. The annual Dagger Awards ceremony is a glittering event and each year a fresh anthology of members' latest work, unified by a guiding theme, is published; this year sees the appearance of *Green for Danger*, a collection of crime stories set in the countryside.

But the origins of the CWA were humble. John Creasey, as energetic in person as he was prolific in print, invited twenty-odd crime writers to a meeting at the National Liberal Club on 5 November 1953. A dozen people attended and agreed to found an association 'to raise the prestige and fortunes of mystery, detective story and crime writing and writers generally'. Creasey became the first chairman and Ernest Dudley (famed in those days for his 'Armchair Detective' radio shows) was appointed as public relations officer. Michael Gilbert pointed out that, in essence, the CWA could be either a trade association or a social club; the choice was easily made and to this day the conviviality of CWA social occasions remains legendary. Within months Creasey proclaimed a massive rise in membership, conveniently omitting to mention that of the then sixty members, one third happened to be Creasey himself under his many pseudonyms – there is nothing new in the black art of 'spin'.

Creasey was full of ideas; at the outset he proposed that he could be shut up in a glass-sided box during a public exhibition on crime writing, a box within which he could be seen starting a book which he would complete before the exhibition closed (he was a frighteningly fast writer). That suggestion, sadly, came to nothing, but later a crime quiz took place at the Chamber of Horrors in Madame Tussaud's; when a spotlight was moved, the model on the guillotine began to melt and its nose fell into the basket. Agatha Christie was principal guest at the first CWA gala luncheon and the first 'Crossed Red Herring Award' (now the Gold Dagger) for the best crime novel of the year went in 1955 to Winston Graham, today best known for his Poldark novels. In the early years, most activity centred around London, although members kept in touch through a newsletter, *Red Herrings*, which remains an important and occasionally controversial forum for debate. Nowadays the strength of the CWA lies in a large number of active regional 'chapters', which have occasionally published their own anthologies, and the Association reaches out to the wider world through its own website.

Of course, the CWA benefits enormously from the prestige of its most famous members, but Christie herself put her finger on the secret of long-term success in a letter to Julian Symons: 'What you want . . . are the up-and-comings.' The CWA encourages new entrants into a tough profession by running a national competition for crime fiction by unpublished writers. The John Creasey Memorial Dagger is awarded to the outstanding debut crime novel of the year and it is noteworthy that many past winners of the Creasey (examples in the 1990s include Patricia Cornwell and Minette Walters) have gone on to enjoy sustained success.

The pleasure of compiling this anthology has come partly from the delight of discovering wonderful stories written long ago and from reading the equally enjoyable manuscripts that arrived via post and email. It has also come from the encouragement and support I have received from everyone who has been associated with the project. My thanks are due to the CWA committee and its past and present chairs, Lindsey Davis and Hilary Bonner, and to Hilary Hale, editorial director of Time Warner Books UK, herself a CWA member and experienced anthologist, whose commitment to this book has been enormously important. Most of all, I am grateful for the generosity of the contributors, not just those who put their latest novel aside for a while to write a story for the benefit of the CWA, but also to the agents, rights-holders and family members of deceased contributors who have helped to make the book what it is. There could be no better evidence of the esteem in which the CWA is held, and the gratitude which so many have for its role in forming lasting friend-ships between those who write and love crime fiction.

Martin Edwards

Mysterious Pleasures

MARGERY ALLINGHAM

One Morning They'll Hang Him

It was typical of Chief Inspector Kenny that, having forced himself to ask a favour, he should set about it with the worst grace possible. When at last he took the plunge, he heaved his two hundred pounds off Mr Campion's fireside couch and set down his empty glass with a clatter.

'I don't know if I needed that at three in the afternoon,' he said ungratefully, his small blue eyes baleful, 'but I've been up since two this morning dealing with women, tears, minor miracles and this perishing rain.' He rubbed his broad face, and presented it scarlet and exasperated at Mr Campion's back. 'If there's one thing that makes me savage it's futility!' he added.

Mr Albert Campion, who had been staring idly out of the window watching the rain on the roofs, did not glance round. He was still and lean, a somewhat ineffectual-looking man to whom the Special Branch had turned often in the last twenty years. His very fair hair had bleached into whiteness and a few lines had appeared round the pale eyes which were still, as always, covered by large horn-rimmed spectacles, but otherwise he looked much as Kenny first remembered him . . . 'Friendly and a little simple . . . the old snake!'

'So there's futility in Barraclough Road too, is there?' Campion's light voice sounded polite rather than curious.

Kenny drew a sharp breath of annoyance.

'The Commissioner has 'phoned you? He suggested I should look you up. It's not a great matter . . . just one of those stupid little snags which has some perfectly obvious explanation. Once it's settled, the whole case is open-and-shut. As it is, we can't keep the man at the station indefinitely.'

Mr Campion picked up the early edition of the evening newspaper from his desk.

'This is all I know,' he said holding it out. 'Mr Oates didn't 'phone. There you are, in the Stop Press, *Rich Widow shot in Barraclough Road West. Nephew at police station helping investigation.* What's the difficulty? His help is not altogether wholehearted, perhaps?'

To his surprise an expression remarkably like regret flickered round Kenny's narrow lips.

'Ruddy young fool,' he said, and sat down abruptly. 'I tell you, Mr Campion, this thing is in the bag. It's just one of those ordinary, rather depressing little stories which most murder cases are. There's practically no mystery, no chase . . . nothing but a wretched little tragedy. As soon as you've spotted what I've missed, I shall charge this chap and he'll go before the magistrates and be committed for trial. His counsel will plead insanity and the jury won't have it. The Judge will sentence him, he'll appeal, their Lordships will dismiss it. The Home Secretary will

2

sign the warrant and one morning they'll take him out and they'll hang him.' He sighed. 'All for nothing,' he said. 'All for nothing at all. It'll probably be raining just like it is now,' he added inconsequentially.

Mr Campion's eyes grew puzzled. He knew Kenny for a conscientious officer, and, some said, a hard man. This philosophic strain was unlike him.

'Taken a fancy to him?' he inquired.

'Who? I certainly haven't.' The Inspector was grim. 'I've got no sympathy for youngsters who shoot up their relatives, however selfish the old bottoms may be. No, he's killed her and he must take what's coming to him, but it's hard on . . . well, on some people. Me, for one.' He took out a large old-fashioned notebook and folded it carefully in half. 'I stick to one of these,' he remarked virtuously. 'None of your backs of envelopes for me. My record is kept as neatly as when I was first on the beat, and it can be handed across the court whenever a know-all counsel asks to see it.' He paused. 'I sound like an advertisement, don't I? Well, Mr Campion, since I'm here, just give your mind to this, if you will. I don't suppose it'll present any difficulty to you.'

'One never knows,' murmured Mr Campion idiotically. 'Start with the victim.'

Kenny returned to his notebook.

'Mrs Mary Alice Cibber, aged about seventy or maybe a bit less. She had heart trouble which made her look frail, and, of course, I didn't see her until she was dead. She had a nice house in Barraclough Road, a good deal too big for her, left her by her husband who died ten years ago. Since then she's been alone except for a maid

3

who cleared off in the war and now for another old party who calls herself a companion. *She* looks older still, poor old girl, but you can see she's been kept well under' – he put his thumb down expressively – 'by Mrs C. who appears to have been a dictator in her small way. She was the sort of woman who lived for two chairs and a salad bowl.'

'I beg your pardon?'

'Antiques.' He was mildly contemptuous. 'The house is crammed with them, all three floors and the attic, everything kept as if it was brand-new. The old companion says she loved it more than anything on earth. Of course she hadn't much else *to* love, not a relation in the world except the nephew . . .'

'Whose future you see so clearly?'

'The man who shot her,' the Inspector agreed. 'He's a big nervy lad, name of Woodruff, the son of the old lady's brother. His mother, father, and two young sisters all got theirs in the blitz on Portsmouth. Whole family wiped out.'

'I see.' Campion began to catch some of Kenny's depression. 'Where was he when that happened?'

'In the Western Desert.' The DDI's protuberant eyes were dark with irritation. 'I told you this was just an ordinary miserable slice of life. It goes on the same way. This boy, Richard Woodruff . . . he's only twenty-eight now . . . did very well in the war. He was in the landings in Sicily and went through the fighting in Italy where he got the MC and was promoted major. Then he copped in for the breakthrough in France and just before the finish he became a casualty. A bridge blew

4

up with him on it . . . or something of the sort, my informant didn't know exactly . . . and he seems to have become what the boys call "bomb happy". It used to be "shellshock" in my day. As far as I can gather, he always had been quick-tempered, but this sent him over the edge. He sounds to me as if he wasn't sane for a while. That may help him in his defence, of course.'

'Yes.' Campion sounded depressed. 'Where's he been since then?'

'On a farm mostly. He was training to be an architect before the war but the motherly old Army knew what was best for him and when he came out of the hospital they bunged him down to Dorset. He's just got away. Some wartime buddy got him a job in an architect's office under the old pals' act and he was all set to take it up.' He paused and his narrow mouth, which was not entirely insensitive, twisted bitterly. 'Ought to have started Monday,' he said.

'Oh dear,' murmured Mr Campion inadequately. 'Why did he shoot his aunt? Pure bad temper?'

Kenny shook his head.

'He had a reason. I mean one can see why he was angry. He hadn't anywhere to live, you see. As you know, London is crowded, and rents are fantastic. He and his wife paying through the nose for a cupboard of a bed-sitting room off the Edgware Road.'

'His wife?' The lean man in the horn rims was interested. 'Where did she come from? You're keeping her very quiet.'

To Campion's surprise the Inspector did not speak at once. Instead he grunted, and there was regret, and surprise at it, in his little smile. 'I believe I would if I could,' he said sincerely. 'He found her on the farm. They've been married six weeks. I don't know if you've ever seen love, Mr Campion? It's very rare . . . the kind I mean.' He put out his hands deprecatingly. 'It seems to crop up . . . when it does . . . among the most unexpected people, and when you do see it, well, it's very impressive.' He succeeded in looking thoroughly ashamed of himself. 'I shouldn't call myself a sentimental man,' he said.

'No.' Campion was reassuring. 'You got his war history from her, I suppose?'

'I had to but we're confirming it. He's as shut as a watch . . . or a hand grenade. "Yes" and "No" and "I did not shoot her" . . . that's about all his contribution amounted to, and he's had a few hours of expert treatment. The girl is quite different. She's down there too. Won't leave. We put her in the waiting-room finally. She's not difficult . . . just sits there.'

'Does she know anything about it?'

'No.' Kenny was quite definite. 'She's nothing to look at,' he went on presently, as if he felt the point should be made. 'She's just an ordinary nice little country girl, a bit too thin and a bit too brown, natural hair and inexpert make-up, and yet with this . . . this blazing radiant steadfastness about her!' He checked himself. 'Well, she's fond of him,' he amended.

'Believes he's God,' Campion suggested.

Kenny shook his head. 'She doesn't care if he isn't,' he said sadly. 'Well, Mr Campion, some weeks ago these two approached Mrs Cibber about letting them have a room or two at the top of the house. That must have

6

been the girl's idea; she's just the type to have old-fashioned notions about blood being thicker than water. She made the boy write. The old lady ignored the question but asked them both to an evening meal last night. The invitation was sent a fortnight ago, so you can see there was no eager bless–you–my–children about it.'

'Any reason for the delay?'

'Only that she had to have notice if she were giving a party. The old companion explained that to me. There was the silver to get out and clean, and the best china to be washed, and so on. Oh, there was nothing simple and homely about that household!' He sounded personally affronted. 'When they got there, of course, there was a blazing row.'

'Hard words or flying crockery?'

Kenny hesitated. 'In a way, both,' he said slowly. 'It seems to have been a funny sort of flare-up. I had two accounts of it . . . one from the girl and one from the companion. I think they are both trying to be truthful but they both seem to have been completely foxed by it. They both agree that Mrs Cibber began it. She waited until there were three oranges and a hundredweight of priceless early Worcester dessert service on the table, and then let fly. Her theme seems to have been the impudence of Youth in casting its eyes on its inheritance before Age was in its grave, and so on and so on. She then made it quite clear that they hadn't a solitary hope of getting what they wanted, and conveyed that she did not care if they slept in the street so long as her precious furniture was safely housed. There's no doubt about it that she was very aggravating and unfair.'

7

'Unfair?'

'Ungenerous. After all, she knew the man quite well. He used to go and stay with her by himself when he was a little boy.' Kenny returned to his notes. 'Woodruff then lost his temper in his own way which, if the exhibition he gave in the early hours of this morning is typical, is impressive. He goes white instead of red, says practically nothing, but looks as if he's about to "incandesce" . . . if I make myself plain.'

'Entirely.' Mr Campion was deeply interested. This new and human Kenny was an experience. 'I take it he then fished out a gun and shot her?'

'Lord, no! If he had, he'd have a chance at least of Broadmoor. No. He just got up and asked her if she had any of his things, because if so he'd take them and not inconvenience her with them any longer. It appears that when he was in the hospital some of his gear had been sent to her, as his next of kin. She said yes, she had, and it was waiting for him in the boot cupboard. The old companion, Miss Smith, was sent trotting out to fetch it and came staggering in with an old officer's hold-all, burst at the sides and filthy. Mrs Cibber told her nephew to open it and see if she'd robbed him, and he did as he was told. Of course, one of the first things he saw among the ragged bush shirts and old photographs was a revolver and a clip of ammunition.' He paused and shook his head. 'Don't ask me how it got there. You know what hospitals were like in the war. Mrs Cibber went on taunting the man in her own peculiar way, and he stood there examining the gun and presently loading it, almost absently. You can see the scene?'

8

Campion could. The pleasant, perhaps slightly over-crowded room was vivid in his mind, and he saw the gentle light on the china and the proud, bitter face of the woman.

'After that,' said Kenny, 'the tale gets more peculiar, although both accounts agree. It was Mrs C. who laughed and said, "I suppose you think I ought to be shot?" Woodruff did not answer but he dropped the gun in his side pocket. Then he packed up the holdall and said, "Goodbye".' He hesitated. 'Both statements say that he then said something about *the sun having gone down*. I don't know what that meant, or if both women mistook him. Anyway, there's nothing to it. He had no explanation to offer. Says he doesn't remember saying it. However, after that he suddenly picked up one of his aunt's beloved china fruit bowls and simply dropped it on the floor. It fell on a rug, as it happened, and did not break, but old Mrs Cibber nearly passed out, the companion screamed, and the girl hurried him off home.'

'With the gun?'

'With the gun.' Kenny shrugged his heavy shoulders. 'As soon as the girl heard that Mrs Cibber had been shot, she jumped up with a tale that he had *not* taken it. She said she'd sneaked it out of his pocket and put it on the window sill. The lamest story you ever heard! She's game and she's ready to say absolutely anything, but she won't save him, poor kid. He was seen in the district at midnight.'

Mr Campion put a hand through his sleek hair. 'Ah. That rather tears it.'

'Oh, it does. There's no question that he did it. It

9

hardly arises. What happened was this. The young folk got back to their bed-sitting room about ten to nine. Neither of them will admit it, but it's obvious that Woodruff was in one of those boiling but sulky rages which made him unfit for human society. The girl left him alone . . . I should say she has a gift for handling him . . . and she says she went to bed while he sat up writing letters. Quite late, she can't or won't say when, he went out to the post. He won't say anything. We may or may not break him down, he's a queer chap. However, we have a witness who saw him somewhere about midnight at the Kilburn end of Barraclough Road. Woodruff stopped him and asked if the last eastbound 'bus had gone. Neither of them had a watch, but the witness is prepared to swear it was just after midnight . . . which is important because the shot was fired two minutes before twelve. We've got that time fixed.'

Mr Campion, who had been taking notes, looked up in mild astonishment.

'You got that witness very promptly,' he remarked. 'Why did he come forward?'

'He was a plainclothes man off duty,' said Kenny calmly. 'One of the local men who had been out to a reunion dinner. He wasn't tight but he had decided to walk home before his wife saw him. I don't know why he hadn't a watch' – Kenny frowned at this defect – 'anyway, he hadn't, or it wasn't going. But he was alert enough to notice Woodruff. He's a distinctive chap you know. Very tall and dark, and his manner was so nervy and excitable that the dick thought it worth reporting.'

Campion's teeth appeared in a brief smile.

'In fact, he recognised him at once as a man who looked as though he'd done a murder?'

'No.' The Inspector remained unruffled. 'No, he said he looked like a chap who had just got something off his mind and was pleased with himself.'

'I see. And meanwhile the shot was fired at two minutes to twelve.'

'That's certain.' Kenny brightened and became businesslike. 'The man next door heard it and looked at his watch. We've got his statement and the old lady's companion. Everyone else in the street is being questioned. But nothing has come in yet. It was a cold wet night and most people had their windows shut; besides, the room where the murder took place was heavily curtained. So far, these two are the only people who seem to have heard anything at all. The man next door woke up and nudged his wife who had slept through it. But then he may have dozed again, for the next thing he remembers is hearing screams for help. By the time he got to the window, the companion was out in the street in her dressing gown, wedged in between the lamp-post and the mail box, screeching her little grey head off. The rain was coming down in sheets.'

'When exactly was this?'

'Almost immediately after the shot, according to the companion. She had been in bed for some hours and had slept. Her room is on the second floor, at the back. Mrs Cibber had not come up with her but had settled down at her bureau in the drawing-room, as she often did in the evening. Mrs C. was still very upset by the scene at the meal, and did not want to talk. Miss Smith

11

says she woke up and thought she heard the front door open. She won't swear to this, and at any rate she thought nothing of it, for Mrs Cibber often slipped out to the mail box with letters before coming to bed. Exactly how long it was after she woke that she heard the shot she does not know, but it brought her scrambling out of bed. She agrees she might have been a minute or two finding her slippers and a wrapper, but she certainly came down right away. She says she found the street door open, letting in the rain, and the drawing-room door, which is next to it, wide open as well, and the lights in there full on.' He referred to his notes and began to read out loud. '"I smelled burning" – she means cordite – "and I glanced across the room to see poor Mrs Cibber on the floor with a dreadful hole in her forehead. I was too frightened to go near her, so I ran out of the house shouting 'Murder! Thieves!'"'

'That's nice and old-fashioned. Did she see anybody?'

'She says not, and I believe her. She was directly under the only lamp-post for fifty yards and it certainly was raining hard.'

Mr Campion appeared satisfied but unhappy. When he spoke his voice was very gentle.

'Do I understand that your case is that Woodruff came back, tapped on the front door, and was admitted by his aunt? After some conversation, which must have taken place in lowered tones since the companion upstairs did not hear it, he shot her and ran away, leaving all the doors open?'

'Substantially, yes. Although he may have shot her as soon as he saw her.'

'In that case she'd have been found dead in the hall.'

Kenny blinked. 'Yes, I suppose she would. Still they couldn't have talked much.'

'Why?'

The Inspector made a gesture of distaste. 'This is the bit which gets under my skin,' he said. 'They could hardly have spoken long . . . *because she'd forgiven him.* She had written to her solicitor . . . the finished letter was on her writing pad ready for the post. She'd written to say she was thinking of making the upper part of her house into a home for her nephew, and asked if there was a clause in her lease to prevent it. She also said she wanted the work done quickly, as she had taken a fancy to her new niece and hoped in time there might be children. It's pathetic, isn't it?' His eyes were wretched. 'That's what I meant by futility. She'd forgiven him, see? She wasn't a mean old harridan, she was just quick-tempered. I told you this isn't a mystery tale, this is ordinary sordid life.'

Mr Campion looked away.

'Tragic,' he said. 'Yes. A horrid thing. What shall I do?'

Kenny sighed. 'Find the gun.'

The lean man whistled.

'You'll certainly need that if you're to be sure of a conviction. How did you lose it?'

'He's ditched it somewhere. He didn't get rid of it in Barraclough Road because the houses come right down to the street, and our chaps were searching for it within half an hour. At the end of the road he caught the last 'bus, which ought to come along at midnight but was a bit late last night. I'm morally certain. These

13

drivers make up time on the straight stretch by the park; it's more than their jobs are worth, so you never get them to admit it. Anyhow, he didn't leave the gun on the 'bus, and it's not in the house where his room is. It's not in the old lady's house at 81 Barraclough Road because I've been over the house myself.' He peered at the taller man hopefully. 'Where would you hide a gun in this city at night, if you were all that way from the river? It's not so easy, is it? If it had been anywhere obvious it would have turned up by now.'

'He may have given it to someone.'

'And risked blackmail?' Kenny laughed. 'He's not as dumb as that. You'll have to see him. He says he never had it . . . but that's only natural. Yet where did he put it, Mr Campion? It's only a little point but, as you say, it's got to be solved.'

Campion grimaced.

'Anywhere, Kenny. Absolutely anywhere. In a drain . . .'

'They're narrow gratings in Barraclough Road.'

'In a sandbin or a static water tank . . .'

'There aren't any in that district.'

'He threw it down in the street and someone, who felt he'd rather like to have a gun, picked it up. Your area isn't peopled solely with the law-abiding, you know.'

Kenny became more serious. 'That's the real likelihood,' he admitted gloomily. 'But all the same, I don't believe he's the type to throw away a gun casually. He's too intelligent, too cautious. Do you know how this war has made some men cautious even when they're being the most reckless? He's one of those. He's hidden it. Where? Mr Oates said you'd know if anyone did.'

Campion ignored this blatant flattery. He stood staring absently out of the window for so long that the Inspector was tempted to nudge him, and when at last he spoke, his question did not sound promising.

'How often did he stay with his aunt when he was a child?'

'Quite a bit, I think, but there's no kid's hiding-place there that only he could have known, if that's what you're after.' Kenny could hardly conceal his disappointment. 'It's not that kind of house. Besides, he hadn't the time. He got back about twenty past twelve: a woman in the house confirms it . . . she met him on the stairs. He was certainly spark out when we got there at a quarter after four this morning. They were both sleeping like kids when I first saw them. She had one skinny brown arm around his neck. He just woke up in a rage, and she was more astounded than frightened. I swear . . .'

Mr Campion had ceased to listen.

'Without the gun the only real evidence you've got is the plainclothes man's story of meeting him,' he said. 'And even you admit that gallant officer was walking for his health after a party. Imagine a good defence lawyer enlarging on that point.'

'I have,' the Inspector agreed, drily. 'That's why I'm here. You must find the gun for us, sir. Can I fetch you a raincoat? Or,' he added, a faintly smug expression flickering over his broad face, 'will you just sit in your armchair and do it from there?'

To his annoyance his elegant host appeared to consider the question.

'No, perhaps I'd better come with you,' he said at last.

'We'll go to Barraclough Road first, if you don't mind. And if I might make a suggestion, I should send Woodruff and his wife back to their lodgings ... suitably escorted, of course. If the young man was going to crack, I think he would have done so by now, and the gun, wherever it is, can hardly be at the police station.'

Kenny considered. 'He may give himself away and lead us to it.' He agreed although without enthusiasm. 'I'll telephone. Then we'll go anywhere you say, but as I told you I've been over the Barraclough Road house myself and if there's anything there it's high time I retired.'

Mr Campion merely looked foolish, and the Inspector sighed and let him have his way.

He came back from the telephone smiling wryly.

'That's settled,' he announced. 'He's been behaving like a good soldier interrogated by the enemy, silly young fool ... after all, we're only trying to hang him! The girl has been asking for him to be fed, and reporters are crawling up the walls. Our boys won't be sorry to get rid of them for a bit. They'll be looked after. We shan't lose 'em. Now, if you've set your heart on the scene of the crime, Mr Campion, we'll go.'

In the taxi he advanced a little idea.

'I was thinking of that remark he is alleged to have made,' he said, not without shame. 'You don't think that it could have been "Your sun has gone down", and that we could construe it as a threat within the meaning of the act?'

Campion regarded him owlishly.

'We could, but I don't think we will. That's the most enlightening part of the whole story, don't you think?'

16

If Inspector Kenny agreed, he did not say so, and they drove to the top of Barraclough Road in silence. There Campion insisted on stopping at the first house next to the main thoroughfare. The building had traded on its proximity to the shopping centre and had been converted into a dispensing chemist's. Campion was inside for several minutes, leaving Kenny in the cab. When he came out he offered no explanation other than to observe fatuously that they had a 'nice time' and settled back without troubling to look out at the early Victorian stucco three-storey houses which lined the broad road.

A man on duty outside, and a handful of idlers gaping apathetically at the drawn blinds, distinguished 81 Barraclough Road. Kenny rang the bell and the door was opened after a pause by a flurried old lady with a duster in her hand.

'Oh, it's you, Inspector,' she said hastily. 'I'm afraid you've found me in a muddle. I've been trying to tidy up a little. *She* couldn't have borne the place left dirty after everyone had been trampling over it. Yet I don't mean to say that you weren't all very careful.'

She led them into a spotless dining-room which glowed with old mahogany and limpid silver, and the wan afternoon light showed them her reddened eyes and worn navy-blue house-dress. She was a timid-looking person, not quite so old as Kenny had suggested, with very neat grey hair and a skin which had never known cosmetics. Her expression was closed and secret with long submission, and her shoulder blades stuck out a little under the cloth of her dress. Her hands still trembled slightly from the shock of the evening before.

17

Kenny introduced Campion. 'We shan't be long, Miss Smith,' he said cheerfully. 'Just going to have another little look around. We shan't make a mess.'

Campion smiled at her reassuringly. 'It's difficult to get help these days?' he suggested pleasantly.

'Oh, it is,' she said earnestly. 'And Mrs Cibber wouldn't trust just anyone with her treasures. They are so very good.' Her eyes filled with tears. 'She was so fond of them.'

'I daresay she was. That's a beautiful piece, for instance.' Campion glanced with expert interest at the serpentine sideboard with its genuine handles and toilet cupboard.

'Beautiful,' echoed Miss Smith dutifully. 'And the chairs, you see?'

'I do.' He eyed the Trafalgar set with the cherry-leather seats. 'Is this where the quarrel took place?'

She nodded and trembled afresh. 'Yes. I . . . I shall never forget it, never.'

'Was Mrs Cibber often bad-tempered?'

The woman hesitated, and her firm small mouth moved without words.

'Was she?'

She shot a swift unhappy glance at him.

'She was quick,' she said. 'Yes, I think I ought to say she was quick. Now, would you like to see the rest of the house or . . . ?'

Campion glanced at his watch and compared with the Tompion bracket clock on the mantelshelf.

'I think we've just time,' he said, idiotically. 'Upstairs first, Inspector.'

The next thirty-five minutes reduced Kenny to a state of jitters rare to him. After watching Campion with breathless interest for the first five, it slowly dawned on him that the expert had forgotten the crime in his delight at discovering a treasure-trove. Even Miss Smith, who betrayed a certain proprietorial pride, flagged before Campion's insatiable interest. Once or twice she hinted that perhaps they ought to go down, but he would not hear of it. By the time they had exhausted the third floor and were on the steps to the attic, she became almost firm. There was really nothing there but some early Georgian children's toys, she said.

'But I must just see the toys. I've got a "thing" on toys, Kenny.' Campion sounded ecstatic. 'Just a minute . . .'

A vigorous tattoo on the front door interrupted him and Miss Smith, whose nerves were suffering, emitted a little squeak.

'Oh, dear. Somebody at the door. I must go down.'

'No, no.' Campion was uncharacteristically effusive. 'I'll see who it is and come back. I shan't be a moment.'

He flung himself downstairs with boyish enthusiasm, Miss Smith behind him, and Kenny, seeing escape at last, following as quickly as the narrow stairs would permit.

They reached the hall just in time to see him closing the door.

'Only the post,' he said, holding out a package. 'Your library book, Miss Smith.'

'Oh, yes.' She came forward, hand outstretched. 'I was expecting that.'

'I rather thought you were.' His voice was very soft and suddenly menacing. He held the cardboard box high

19

over his head with one hand, and with the other released the flap which closed it. The soft gleam of metal appeared in the light from the transom, and a service revolver crashed heavily to the parquet floor.

For a long minute there was utter silence. Even Kenny was too thunderstruck to swear.

Miss Smith appeared frozen in mid-air, her hands clawing at the box.

Then, most dreadfully, she began to scream . . .

A little over an hour later Kenny sat on a Trafalgar chair in a room which seemed to quiver and shudder with terrible sound. He was pale and tired-looking. His shirt was torn and there were three livid nail scratches down his face.

'God,' he said, breathing hard. 'God, can you beat that?'

Mr Campion sat on the priceless table and scratched his ear.

'It was a bit more than I bargained for,' he murmured. 'It didn't occur to me that she'd become violent. I'm afraid they may be having trouble in the van. Sorry, I ought to have thought of it.'

The CID man grunted. 'Seems to me you thought of plenty,' he muttered. 'It came as a shock to me . . . I don't mind admitting it since I can't very well help it. When did it come to you? From the start?'

'Oh, Lord, no.' Campion sounded apologetic. 'It was that remark of Woodruff's you quoted about the sun going down. That's what set me on the train of thought. Weren't you ever warned as a kid, Kenny, and by an aunt perhaps, never to let the sun go down on your wrath?'

'I've heard it, of course. What do you mean? It was a sort of saying between them?'

'I wondered if it was. They knew each other well when he was a child, and they were both quick-tempered people. It seemed to me that he was reminding her that the sun *had* gone down, and he showed her he could have smashed her precious bowl if he had liked. It would have broken, you know, if he hadn't taken care it shouldn't. I wondered if, like many quick-tempered people, they got sorry just as quickly. Didn't you think it odd, Kenny, that directly after the row they should *both* have settled down to write letters?'

The detective stared at him.

'She wrote to her solicitor,' he began slowly. 'And he . . . ? Good Lord! You think he wrote to her to say he was sorry?'

'Almost certainly, but we shall never find his letter. That's in the kitchen stove by now. He came back to deliver it, pushed it through the door and hurried off looking just as your plainclothes man said, as if he'd got something off his chest. Then he could sleep. The sun had not gone down on his wrath.' He slid off the table and stood up. 'The vital point is, of course, that *Mrs Cibber knew he would*. She sat up waiting for it.'

Kenny sucked in his breath.

'And Miss Smith knew?'

'Of course she knew. Mrs Cibber hadn't the kind of temperament one can keep a secret. Miss Smith knew from the moment that Mrs Cibber received the initial letter that the nephew would get his way in the end . . . *unless she could stop it somehow!* She was the one with the bee in her bonnet about the furniture. I realised that as soon as you said the whole house was kept like a bandbox. No woman with a weak heart can keep a three-storey house like a palace, or compel another to do it . . . unless the other wants to. Miss Smith was the one with the mania. Who was to get the house if the nephew died in the war? Mrs Cibber must have made some provision.'

Kenny rubbed his head with both hands. 'I knew!' he exploded. 'The lawyer's clerk told me this morning when I rang up to find out if Woodruff was the heir. I was so keen to confirm that point that I discounted the rest. If he died the companion was to have it for her lifetime.'

Campion looked relieved.

'I thought so. There you are, you see. She had to get rid of them both . . . Woodruff and his new wife. With a young and vigorous woman in the house there was a danger of the companion becoming . . . well, redundant . . . Don't you think?'

Kenny was fingering his notebook.

'You think she'd planned it for a fortnight?'

'She'd thought of it for a fortnight. She didn't see how to do it until the row occurred last night. When she found the gun on the window sill, where young Mrs Woodruff left it, and Mrs Cibber told her that the boy would come back, the plan was obvious.' He shivered. 'Do you realise that she must have been waiting, probably on the stairs, with the gun in her hand and the book box addressed to herself in the other, listening for Woodruff's letter to slide under the door? As soon as she heard it, she had to fly down and get it and open the door. Then she had to walk into the drawing-room, shoot the old lady as she turned to see who it was, and put the gun in the book box. The instant she was certain Mrs Cibber was dead, she then had to run out screaming to her place between the lamp-post and the mail box and . . . *post the package!*'

Kenny put down his pencil and looked up.

'Now here,' he said with honest admiration, 'there I hand it to you. How in the world did you get on to that?'

'You suggested it.'

'*I* did?' Kenny was pleased in spite of himself. 'When?'

'When you kept asking me where one could hide a gun in a London street with no wide gratings and no sandbins. There was only the mail box. I guessed she'd posted it herself . . . no one else would have been safe. Even the dead letter office eventually gives up its dead. That's why I was so keen to get her to the top of the house . . . as far away from the front door as possible.' He sighed. 'The book box was misguided genius. The gun was an old Luger, did you notice? Loot. That's why he never had to turn it in. It just fitted in the box. She must have had a thrill when she discovered that.'

Kenny shook his head wonderingly. 'Well, blow me down!' he said inelegantly. 'Funny that *I* put you on to it!'

Mr Campion was in bed that night when the tele-phone rang. It was Kenny again.

'I say, Mr Campion?'

'Yes?'

'Sorry to bother you at this time of night but there's something worrying me. You don't mind, do you?'

'Think nothing of it.'

'Well. Everything is all right. Smith has been certified by three doctors. The little girl is very happy comforting her boy, who seems to be upset about his aunt's death. The Commissioner is very pleased. But I can't get off to sleep. Mr Campion, *how did you know what time the afternoon post is delivered in Barraclough Road?*'

The lean man stifled a yawn.

'Because I went into the chemist's shop on the corner and asked,' he said. 'Elementary, my dear Kenny.'

Margery Allingham (1904–66) published her first novel in 1923. Albert Campion, her celebrated detective, was introduced five years later in The White Cottage Mystery, *and by the time of the formation of the CWA, Allingham had just published the book that many people regard as her masterpiece,* The Tiger in the Smoke. *She died leaving a Campion novel,* Cargo of Eagles, *unfinished; it was completed by her husband, the artist Philip Youngman Carter. Several of the Campion novels were successfully televised, with Peter Davison in the title role. She continues to be acknowledged as one of the most important British crime novelists of the twentieth century. A prolific writer of short stories, she contributed to the early CWA anthologies* Some Like Them Dead *and* Crime Writers' Choice.

ERIC AMBLER

The Blood Bargain

Ex-President Fuentes enjoys a peculiar distinction. More people would like to kill him now that he is in retirement than wanted to kill him when he was in power.

He is a puzzled and indignant man.

What he fails to understand is that, while men like General Perez may in time forgive you for robbing them, they will never forgive you for making them look foolish.

The *coup d'état* which overthrew Fuentes' Social Action Party government was well organised and relatively bloodless.

The leaders of the *coup* were mostly Army officers, but they had understandings with fellow-dissidents in the Air Force and Navy as well as the discreet blessing of the Church. A price for the collaboration of the Chief of Police had been agreed upon well in advance, and the lists of certain left-wing deputies, militant trade union officials, pro-government newspaper editors, Castro-trained subversives, and other undesirables whose prompt arrest would be advisable, had been compiled with his help. Similar arrangements had been made in the larger provincial towns. Although the conspirators were by no means all of the same political complexion, they had for once found themselves able to sink their differences in the pursuit of a common goal. Whatever might come afterwards, they were all agreed upon one thing; if the country were to be saved from corruption, Communist subversion, anarchy, bankruptcy, civil war, and, ultimately, foreign military intervention, President Fuentes had to go.

One evening in September he went.

The tactics employed by the Liberation Front conspirators followed the pattern which has become more or less traditional when a *coup* is backed by organised military forces and opposed, if it is opposed at all, only by civilian mobs and confused, lightly armed garrison units.

As darkness fell, the tanks of two armoured brigades together with trucks containing a parachute regiment, signals units, and a company of combat engineers rolled into the capital. Within little more than an hour, they had secured their major objectives. Meanwhile, the Air Force had taken over the international airport, grounded all planes, and established a headquarters in the customs and immigration building. An infantry division now began to move into the city and take up positions which would enable it to deal with the civil disturbances which were expected to develop as news of the *coup*, and of the mass arrests which were accompanying it, reached the densely populated slum areas with their high concentrations of Fuentes supporters.

A little after eight-thirty a squadron of tanks and a special task force of paratroopers reached the Presidential Palace. The Palace guard resisted for a quarter of an hour and suffered casualties of eight wounded. The order to surrender was given personally to the guard commander by President Fuentes 'in order to avoid further bloodshed'.

When this was reported to General Perez, the leader of the *coup*, he drove to the Palace. He was accompanied by five senior members of the Liberation Front council, including the Chief of Police, and no less than three representatives of the foreign press. The latter had been flushed out of the Jockey Club bar by an aide earlier in the evening and hastily briefed on the aims and ideals of the Liberation Front. General Perez wished to lose no time in establishing himself abroad as a magnanimous, reasonable, and responsible man, and his regime as worthy of prompt diplomatic recognition.

The newsmen's accounts of the interview between President Fuentes and General Perez, and of the now-notorious 'blood bargain' which emerged from it, were all in substantial agreement. At the time the bargain seemed to them just another of those civilised, oddly chivalrous agreements to live and let live which, by testifying to the continued presence of compassion and good sense even at moments of turmoil and destruction, have so often lightened the long, dark history of Latin American revolution. The reporters, all experienced men, can scarcely be blamed for misunderstanding it. They knew, as everyone else knew, that President Fuentes was a devious and deeply dishonest man. The only mistake they made was in assuming that the other parties to the bargain had made due allowance for that deviousness and dishonesty and knew exactly what they were doing. What the reporters had not realised was that these normally wary and hard-headed officers had become so intoxicated by the speed and extent of their initial success that by the time they reached the Presidential Palace they were no longer capable of thinking clearly.

President Fuentes received General Perez and the other Liberation Front leaders in the ornate Cabinet Room of the Palace to which he had been taken by the paratroopers who had arrested him. With him were the other male occupants of the Presidential air raid shelter at the time of his arrest. These included the Palace guard commander, the President's valet, the Palace majordomo, two footmen, and the man who looked after the Palace plumbing system, in addition to the Minister of Public Welfare, the Minister of Agrarian Education, the Minister of Justice, and the elderly Controller of the Presidential Secretariat. The Minister of Public Welfare had brought a bottle of brandy with him from the shelter and smiled glassily throughout the subsequent confrontation. Agrarian Education and Justice maintained expressions of bewilderment and indignation, but confined their oral protests to circumspect murmurs. The thinlipped young captain in charge of the paratroopers handled his machine pistol as if he would have been glad of an excuse to use it.

Only the President seemed at ease. There was even a touch of impatience in the shrug with which he rose to face General Perez and his party as they strode in from the anteroom; it was as if he had been interrupted by some importunate visitor during a game of bridge.

His calm was only partly assumed. He knew all about General Perez's sensitivity to foreign opinion, and he had immediately recognised the newsmen in the rear of the procession. They would not have been brought there if any immediate violence to his person had been contemplated.

The impatience he displayed was certainly genuine; it was impatience with himself. He had known for weeks that a *coup* was in preparation, and had taken the precaution a month earlier of sending his wife and children and his mistress out of the country. They were all now in Washington, and he had planned, using as a pretext his announced wish to address personally a meeting of the Organisation of American States, to join them there the following week. His private spies had reported that the *coup* would undoubtedly be timed to take advantage of his absence abroad. Since the *coup* by means of which he himself had come to power five years earlier had been timed in that way, he had been disposed to believe the report.

Now, he knew better. Whether or not his spies had deliberately deceived him did not matter at the moment. A mistake had been made which was, he knew, likely to cost him more than temporary inconvenience. Unless he could retrieve it immediately, by getting out of the country within the next few hours, that mistake would certainly cost him his liberty, and most probably his life, too.

He had risked death before, was familiar with the

physical and mental sensations that accompanied the experience, and with a small effort was able to ignore them. As General Perez came up to him, the President displayed no emotion of any kind. He merely nodded politely and waited for the General to speak.

For a moment the General seemed tongue-tied. He was sweating too. As this was the first time he had overthrown a government he was undoubtedly suffering from stage fright. He took refuge finally in military punctilio. With a click of the heels he came to attention and fixed his eyes on the President's left ear.

'We are here . . .' he began harshly, then cleared his throat and corrected himself. 'I and my fellow members of the Council of the Liberation Front are here to inform you that a state of national emergency now exists.'

The President nodded politely. 'I am glad to have that information, General. Since telephone communication has been cut off I have naturally been curious as to what was happening. These gentlemen' – he motioned to the paratroopers – 'seemed unwilling to enlighten me.'

The General ignored this and went on as if he were reading a proclamation. In fact, he was quoting from the press release which had already been handed to the newsmen. 'Directed by the Council and under its orders,' he said, 'the armed forces have assumed control of all functions of civil government in the state, and, as provided in the Constitution, formally demand your resignation.'

The President looked astounded. 'You have the effrontery to claim constitutional justification for this mutiny?'

For the first time since he had entered the room the General relaxed slightly. 'We have a precedent, sir. Nobody should know that better than you. You yourself set it when you legalised your own seizure of power from your predecessor. Need I remind you of the wording of the amendment? "If for any reason, including the inability to fulfil the duties of his office by reason of ill-health, mental or physical, or absence, an elected president is unable to exercise the authority vested in him under the constitution, a committee representative of the nation and those responsible to it for the maintenance of law and order may request his resignation and be entitled . . ."'

For several seconds the President had been waving his hands for silence. Now he broke in angrily. 'Yes, yes, I know all about that. But my predecessor was absent. I am not. Neither am I ill, physically or mentally. There are no legal grounds on which you are entitled to ask for my resignation.'

'No legal grounds, sir?' General Perez could smile now. He pointed to the paratroopers. 'Are you able to exercise the authority of a president? *Are* you? If you think so, try.'

The President pretended to think over the challenge. The interview was so far going more or less as he had expected; but the next moves would be the critical ones for him. He walked over to a window and back in order to give himself time to collect himself.

Everyone there was watching him. The tension in the room was mounting. He could feel it. It was odd, he thought. Here he was, a prisoner, wholly at their mercy; and yet they were waiting for him to come to a decision, to make a choice where no choice existed. It was absurd. All they wanted from him was relief from a small and quite irrational sense of guilt. They had the Church's blessing; now the poor fools yearned for the blessing of the law, too. Very well. They should have it. But it would be expensive.

He turned and faced General Perez again.

'A resignation exacted from me under duress would have no force in law,' he said.

The General glanced at the Chief of Police. 'You are a lawyer, Raymundo. Who represents the law here?'

'The Council of the Liberation Front, General.'

Perez looked at the President again. 'You see, sir, there are no technical difficulties. We even have the necessary document already prepared.'

His aide held up a black leather portfolio.

The President hesitated, looking from one face to another as if hoping against hope that he might find a friendly one. Finally he shrugged. 'I will read the document,' he said coldly and walked towards the cabinet table. As he did so he seemed to become aware again of his fellow prisoners in the room. He stopped suddenly.

'Must my humiliation be witnessed by my colleagues and my servants as well as the foreign press?' he demanded bitterly.

General Perez motioned to the paratrooper captain. 'Take those men into another room. Leave guards outside the doors of this one.'

The President waited until the group from the air raid shelter had been herded out, then sat down at the table. The General's aide opened the portfolio, took out a legal document laced with green ribbon and placed it in front of the President.

He made a show of studying the document very carefully. In fact, he was indifferent to its contents. His intention was simply to let the tension mount a little further and to allow the other men there to feel that they were on the point of getting what they wanted.

For three minutes there was dead silence in the room. It was broken only by the sound of distant machine-gun fire. It seemed to be coming from the south side of the city. The President heard a slight stir from the group of men behind him and one of them cleared his throat nervously. There was another burst of firing. The President took no notice of it. He read the document through a third time then put it down and sat back in his chair.

The aide offered him a pen with which to sign. The President ignored it and turned his head so that he could see General Perez.

'You spoke of a resignation, General,' he said. 'You did not mention that it was to be a confession also.'

'Hardly a confession, sir,' the General replied drily. 'We would not expect you voluntarily to incriminate yourself. The admission is only of incompetence. That is not yet a criminal offence in a head of state.'

The President smiled faintly. 'And if I were to sign this paper, what kind of personal treatment might I expect to receive afterwards? A prison cell perhaps, with a carefully staged treason trial to follow? Or merely a bullet in the head and an unmarked grave?'

The General reddened. 'We are here to correct abuses of power, sir, not to imitate them. When you have signed you will be conducted to your former home in Alazan

33

province. You will be expected to remain there for the present and the Governor of the province will be instructed to see that you do so. Apart from that restriction you will be free to do as you please. Your family will naturally be permitted to join you.'

'You mention the house in Alazan province. What about my other personal property?'

'You will be permitted to retain everything you owned when you took office.'

'I see.' The President stood up and moved away from the table. 'I will think about it. I will let you have my decision tomorrow,' he added casually.

The silence that followed this announcement did not last long, but one of the newsmen reported later that it was one of the loudest he had ever heard. Another remembered that during it he suddenly became conscious of the presence and smell of a large bowl of tropical flowers on a side table by the anteroom door.

The President had walked towards the windows again. General Perez took two steps towards him, then stopped.

'You must decide at once! You must sign now!' he snapped.

The President turned on him. 'Why? Why now?'

It was the Chief of Police who answered him. 'Son of a whore, because we tell you to!' he shouted.

Suddenly they were all shouting at him. One officer was so enraged that he drew his pistol. The General had difficulty in restoring order.

The President took no notice of them. He kept his eyes on General Perez, but it was really the newsmen he was addressing now. As the din subsided he raised his voice.

'I asked a question, General. Why now? Why the haste? It is a reasonable question. If, as you say, you already control the country, what have you to fear from me? Or is it, perhaps, that your control is not in fact as complete and effective as you would have us believe?'

The General had to quell another angry outburst from his colleagues before he could answer, but he preserved his own temper admirably. His reply was calm and deliberate.

'I will tell you exactly what we control so that you may judge for yourself,' he said. 'To begin with, all provincial army garrisons, air force establishments, and police posts have declared for the Liberation Front, as have five out of eight of the provincial governors. The three objectors – I am sure you will have guessed who they are – have been rendered harmless and replaced by military governors. None of this can come as a great surprise to you, I imagine. You never had much support outside the capital and the mining areas.'

The President nodded. 'Stupidity can sometimes be charted geographically,' he remarked.

'Now as to the capital. We control the airfields, both military and civil, the naval base, all communications including telephone and radio and television broadcast facilities, the power stations, all fuel-oil storage facilities, all main traffic arteries, all government offices and city police posts together with the offices and printing presses of *El Correo* and *La Gaceta*.' He glanced at his watch. 'In connection with the broadcast facilities, I may mention that while the television station is temporarily off the air the radio station will shortly begin broadcasting an announcement of the establishment of the New Liberation Front regime, which I recorded two days ago. As I told you before, everything is now under our control.'

The President smiled and glanced significantly at the newsmen. 'Are the *sumideri* under control, General?'

Sumideri, meaning sinks or drains, was the popular slang term used to describe the slum areas on the south side of the capital.

The General hesitated only an instant. 'The southern area is effectively contained,' he replied stiffly. 'The first infantry division reinforced by the third tank brigade has that responsibility.'

'I see.' The President looked again at the newsmen. 'So the civil war may be expected to begin at any moment.'

With a quick motion of his hands the General silenced the chorus of objections from his colleagues. 'We are fully prepared to deal firmly with any mob violence which may occur,' he said. 'Of that you may be sure.'

'Yes,' said the President bitterly, 'perhaps civil war is not the phrase to use for the planned massacre of unarmed civilians.' He swung around suddenly to face the newsmen and his voice hardened. 'You have been witnesses to this farce, gentlemen. I ask you to remember it well and let the civilised world know of it. These men come to ask for my resignation as head of state. That is all they want! Why? Because outside in the streets of the city their tanks and guns are waiting to begin the slaughter of the thousands of men and women who will protest their loyalty to me. And the way to bring them out for the slaughter is to fling my resignation like so much filth in their faces!'

General Perez could stand it no longer. 'That is a lie!' he shouted.

The President turned on him savagely. 'Do you think they will *not* come out? Why else are they "contained" as you call it? Why else? Because they are my people and because they will listen only to me.'

A glow of triumph suffused General Perez's angry face. 'Then their blood will be on *your* hands!' he roared. He stabbed a forefinger at the newsmen. 'You heard what he said, gentlemen. *They do what he tells them!* It is his responsibility, then, not ours, if they oppose us. *He* will be the murderer of women and children! Let him deny it.'

This time the President made no reply. He just stood there looking about him in bewilderment, like a boxer who has staggered to his feet after a count of ten and can't quite realise that the fight is over. At last he walked slowly back to the cabinet table, sat down heavily and buried his head in his hands.

Nobody else moved. When the President raised his head and looked at them again his eyes were haggard. He spoke very quietly.

'You are right,' he said; 'they are my people and they will do as I tell them. It is my responsibility. I accept it. There must be no senseless bloodshed. I think it is my duty to tell them not to protest.'

For a moment they all stared at him incredulously. The Chief of Police started to say something, then stopped as he caught General Perez's eye. If the man were serious this was too good an opportunity to miss.

General Perez went over and addressed the President.

'I cannot believe that even you would speak lightly on such a matter, but I must ask if you seriously mean what you say.'

The President nodded absently. 'I will need about an hour to draft my statement. There is a direct line to the radio station here in the Palace and the necessary equipment. The station can record me on tape.' He managed a rueful smile. 'In the circumstances, I imagine that you would prefer a recording to a live broadcast.'

'Yes.' But the General was still reluctant to believe in his triumph. 'How can you be sure that they will obey you?' he asked.

The President thought before he answered. 'There will be some, of course, who will be too distressed, too angry perhaps, to do as I ask,' he said. 'But if the officers commanding troops are ordered to use restraint, casualties can be kept to a minimum.' He glanced at the Chief of Police. 'There should be moderation, too, in respect of arrests. But the majority will listen to me, I think.' He paused. 'The important thing is that they must believe that I am speaking as a free man, and not out of fear because there is a pistol at my head.'

'I myself can give them that assurance,' said the General. The fact that he could make such an ingenuous suggestion was an indication of his mental confusion at that point.

The President raised his eyebrows. 'With all respect, General, I don't think we could expect them at this time to believe you of all people. I also think that the news that I am to be kept under what amounts to house arrest in Alazan province will not help to convince them either.'

'Then what do you propose? You can scarcely remain here in the capital.'

'Naturally not.' The President sat back in his chair. He had assumed a statesmanlike air now. 'It is quite clear,' he said, 'that we must achieve an orderly and responsible transfer of power. I shall, of course, resign in order to make way for the Liberation Front. However, in your place, I must say that I would regard my continued presence anywhere in this country as undesirable. These people to whom I am to appeal tonight will only respond with restraint because of their loyalty to me. That loyalty will continue as long as they are able to give expression to it. You would do better really to get rid of me. As soon as I have spoken to my people you should get me out of the country as quickly as you can.'

'Exile?' It was the Chief of Police who spoke up now. 'But if we exile you that looks no better than house arrest in Alazan. Worse, possibly.'

'Exactly.' The President nodded approvingly. 'The solution I suggest is that I am permitted to announce to my people that I will continue to serve them, the nation, and the Liberation Front, but in a different capacity and abroad. Our embassy in Nicaragua is without an ambassador at present. That would be a suitable appointment. I suggest that after I have recorded my broadcast I leave the country immediately in order to take up my post.'

The council discussion that ensued lacked the vehemence of the earlier exchanges. The strain of the past twenty-four hours was beginning to tell on General Perez and his colleagues; they were getting tired; and the sounds of firing from the south side were becoming more insistent. Time was running out. It was one of the newsmen who drew their attention to the fact.

'General,' he said to Perez, 'has it occurred to you that if the President doesn't talk to these people of his pretty soon they're all going to be out on the streets anyway?'

The President recognised the urgency, too, but refused to be hurried. As he pointed out, there were matters of protocol to be dealt with before he could make his appeal to the people. For one thing, his resignation would have to be redrafted. Since, he argued, he was now to be appointed his country's ambassador to Nicaragua, references in the present draft to his incompetence would obviously have to be deleted. And there were other clauses which might be interpreted as reflections on his personal integrity.

In the end, the President wrote his own act of resignation. It was a simple document but composed with great care. His radio speech, on the other hand, he scribbled out on a cabinet desk pad while technicians, hastily summoned by jeep from the central radio building, were setting up a recording circuit in the anteroom.

Meanwhile, telephone communication had been restored to the Palace, and the Controller of the Presidential Secretariat had been released from arrest and put to work in his office.

His first task had been to contact the Nicaraguan Ambassador, give him a discreetly censored account of the current situation and request him to ascertain immediately, in accordance with Article 8 of the Pan-American

Convention, if his government would be prepared to accept ex-President Fuentes as *persona grata* in the capacity of ambassador to their country. The Nicaraguan Ambassador had undertaken to telephone personally to the Minister of Foreign Relations in Managua and report back. His unofficial opinion was that there would be no opposition to the proposed appointment.

With the help of the air force council member present the Controller next spoke to the officer in charge at the International Airport. He learned that of the two civil airliners grounded earlier that evening, one had been southbound to Caracas, the other, a Colombian Avianca jet, had been northbound to Mexico City. Fortunately a Vice-Consul from the Colombian Consulate-General was already at the airport, having been summoned there by the Avianca captain to protest the grounding. The Controller spoke with the Vice-Consul who said that Avianca would be willing to carry ex-President Fuentes as a passenger to Mexico City if the Mexican Government would permit him to land. A call to the Mexican Embassy explaining that ex-President Fuentes would be in transit through Mexican territory on his way to his post as an accredited diplomatic representative to the Republic of Nicaragua secured the necessary permission.

The President already had a diplomatic passport which needed only minor amendments to fit it for its new role. All that was needed now to facilitate his departure was confirmation from the Nicaraguan Ambassador that he would be accorded diplomatic status in Managua. Within an hour, the Nicaraguan

Government, acting promptly in the belief that they were helping both parties to the arrangement, had replied favourably.

The escape route was open.

President Fuentes made two tape-recordings of the appeal to his supporters, one for the radio, the second for use by a loudspeaker van in the streets of the *sumideri*. Then he signed his resignation and was driven to the airport. General Perez provided an escort of armoured cars.

The plane, with ex-President Fuentes on board, took off a little after midnight. Five hours later it landed in Mexico City.

News of the Liberation Front *coup* and of the President's voluntary resignation and ambassadorial appointment had been carried by all the international wire services, and there were reporters waiting for him. There was also, despite the early hour, a protocol official from the Department of External Relations to meet him. Fuentes made a brief statement to the reporters, confirming the fact of his resignation. On the subject of his appointment as ambassador to Nicaragua he was vague. He then drove to a hotel in the city. On the way there he asked the protocol official if it would be convenient for him to call upon the Minister of External Affairs later that day.

The official was mildly surprised. As Ambassador Fuentes was merely passing through Mexico, a brief note of thanks to the Minister would normally be the only courtesy expected of him. On the other hand, the circumstances of Fuentes' sudden translation from President to

Ambassador were unusual and it was possible that the Minister might be glad of the opportunity of hearing what Fuentes himself had to say on the subject. He promised that he would consult the Minister's personal assistant at the earliest possible moment.

The Minister received Ambassador Fuentes at five o'clock that afternoon.

The two men had met before, at conferences of the Organisation of American States and on the occasion of a state visit to Mexico paid by Fuentes soon after he became President. It was a tribute to the Minister's natural courtesy as well as his self-discipline that Fuentes believed that the Minister liked him. In fact the Minister viewed him with dislike and disapproval and had not been in the least surprised or distressed by the news of the Liberation Front *coup*. However, he had been amused by Fuentes' ability to emerge from the situation not only alive and free but also invested with diplomatic immunity; and it modified his distaste for the man. He was, one had to admit, an engaging scoundrel.

After the preliminary politeness had been disposed of the Minister enquired courteously whether he could be of any service to the Ambassador during his stay in Mexico.

Fuentes inclined his head: 'That is most kind of you, Mr Minister,' he said graciously. 'Yes, there is one thing.'

'You only have to ask.'

'Thank you.' Ambassador Fuentes straightened up a little in his chair. 'I wish,' he said, 'to make formal application to be considered here as a refugee, and formally

43

to request political asylum in the United States of Mexico.'

The Minister stared for a moment, then smiled.

'Surely you must be joking, Mr Ambassador.'

'Not in the least.'

The Minister was puzzled, and because he was puzzled he put into words the first obvious objection that came into his head.

'But in the United States of Mexico, even though you are not accredited to the Federal Government, you already, by virtue of the Pan-American Convention, enjoy diplomatic status and privileges here,' he said.

It was a statement which he was later to regret.

Ambassador Fuentes never took up his post in Nicaragua.

One of the first official acts of General Perez's Council of the Liberation Front was to set up a committee, headed by the Professor of Political Economy at Bolivar University, to report on the financial state of the Republic.

It took the committee only a few days to discover that during the past three years ex-President Fuentes had authorised printings of five-hundred-peseta bank-notes to a total value of one hundred million dollars and that twenty of those hundred millions could not be accounted for.

The Governor of the National Bank was immediately arrested. He was an old man who had spent most of his life in the National Archives gathering material for a scholarly study of colonial Spanish land grants. He had been appointed to the bank by Fuentes. He knew nothing about banking. He had merely carried out the orders of the Minister of Finance.

Fuentes had been his own Minister of Finance.

Interviewed on the subject by the press in Mexico City, ex-President Fuentes stated that the committee's revelations had shocked, horrified, and amazed him. He also said that he had no idea where the missing twenty millions might be. Regrettably, he was unable quite to refrain from smiling as he said it.

Ex-President Fuentes' retirement has not been peaceful.

During the five years he held office as President there was only one serious attempt on his life. Since he resigned the Presidency, ceased to concern himself with politics, and went to live abroad, no less than three such attempts have been made. There will doubtless be others. Meanwhile, he has had to fight off two lots of extradition proceedings and a number of civil actions directed against his European bank accounts.

He is wealthy, of course, and can afford to pay for the protection, both physical and legal, that he needs; but he is by no means resigned to the situation. As he is fond of pointing out, other men in his position have accumulated larger fortunes. Moreover, his regime was never unacceptably oppressive. He was no Trujillo, no Batista, no Porfirio Diaz. Why then should he be hounded and harassed as if he were?

Ex-President Fuentes remains a puzzled and indignant man.

Eric Ambler (1909–98) was a pioneer of the realistic novel of espionage. His first novel, The Dark Frontier, published in 1936, anticipated nuclear weapons. Ambler remains best known for The Mask of Dimitrios, which has earned classic status and was filmed with Peter Lorre and Sydney Greenstreet. His ventures into more conventional crime fiction include The Light of Day, while his last novel, The Care of Time (1981), is concerned with the menace of chemical weapons in the hands of a Middle Eastern despot. A long-time member of the CWA, Ambler received many awards, including the CWA Cartier Diamond Dagger in 1986.

ROBERT BARNARD

Everybody's Girl

When the sound came of mail pushed through the letter box and plopping on to the front doormat, Hannah Lowton saw a gleam of hope come into her husband's eye. He pushed aside his plate.

'At least it's come before I go to work,' he said.

Hannah was already in the hall, and he heard her pick up the post and slit open an envelope.

'It's from her, from Ruth,' she said, coming back into the dining room and extracting a letter from the envelope. Peter looked at her hopefully. He could not fail to see her mouth drop. 'Oh dear. She doesn't seem any happier . . . She seems more confused than ever . . . "Dearest Mum and Dad. I'm sorry I sounded so depressed and scatty in my last. I do try to get more settled, do want to make a go of it . . ." Then she blames herself that she can't settle down.'

'Typical Ruthie. Protects everyone except herself.'

'Says she can't fit in because she won't go along with the crowd. The history course doesn't help. The Dark Ages – I ask you!'

'I think it's only dark because there's not much known about it.'

'She says her only friend is this boy called George, the one she's mentioned before: "He's a friend because he's lonely and mixed-up like me."'

'Poor, poor Ruthie!'

'Oh dear – then she says, "I don't see the point in a life that's going nowhere."'

'Right. That's it.' Peter Lowton pushed his chair back from the table and stood up. 'That's the second time she's said something like that. I'm going to Leeds to talk to her.'

'Oh Peter, is that wise? Shouldn't she sort it out for herself?'

'It's six weeks since she started there. If she feels there's no point in her life, something's gone terribly wrong.'

'Do you want me to come, Peter?'

'No – you stay here in case she rings. And tell the office I won't be in.' The look on his face was wild with anxiety. The next thing she heard was his pulling on a coat and banging the front door.

Across the road at number 18, Sheila McCartney saw Peter dash out to his car. She registered the panic in his face and body movements.

'God, Peter looks desperate,' she said. It was the first time she had spoken to her husband in ten days. He merely grunted. 'He's reversing the car into the drive. He's not going into work. He's going towards Leeds. It must be something to do with Ruth. They've been getting worrying letters from her.'

Neville McCartney muttered: 'You got too involved with that girl.'

'*I* got too involved with her?' Their eyes met, it seemed for the first time in months. '*I* did?'

'She was never more than a sweet girl across the road to me.'

'Well? *Well?*'

'You were in love with her.'

'Oh, and you weren't? Well, at least I admit it. At least I know myself. All right, I loved her. *Love* her. Why these past tenses?'

'Because she's gone to university. Gone out of your life.'

'Our lives. Maybe she has, maybe not. It doesn't alter the fact that I love her.' Her voice raised itself to a shout. 'Do you think I'm ashamed of it? I need some love. God knows I need some love.'

When she had washed up and heard her husband leave the house she went next door to her father, now over seventy and increasingly immobile.

'Everything all right, Dad?'

He turned a troubled gaze in her direction.

'Shouldn't I be asking you that?'

'Oh, did you hear?' She made a gesture of dismissal. 'Just the usual.'

'Couldn't you both make an effort? He's not a bad man, Sheila.'

'I never said he was. He's a nothing man.'

'It wasn't about Ruthie, was it, Sheila?' He saw at once in her face that it was. 'Oh, I am sorry. The pair of you like that, quarrelling over a sweet young girl. It's disgusting.'

'It's not disgusting, Dad. She's just a good friend to me.'

'I should hope so. But what about Neville? A man of forty-five.'

'Can't we forget about Neville? I do all the time. Now what do you want at the shops, Dad?'

Ruthie's bedsit in Kirkstall, three miles out of Leeds, was in Cannock Road, and Peter and Hannah had seen it when they brought her from Barnsley in September. He turned the car upwards from Kirkstall Abbey and found the right road without difficulty. Ruth's was in the middle of a set of named bells, a first-floor room, but three rings produced no response. Peter had been conscious of a shape moving around in the bay-windowed room to his right, and he pressed one of the lower bells on spec.

'Yes?'

The name, apparently, was Kit Wakeham. He was a big young man in tracksuit bottoms and T-shirt, and he clearly felt himself in control. Peter had to repress a sense of being menaced.

'I'm trying to make contact with my daughter, Ruth Lowton. There's no answer when I ring.'

'I'd say she was out, wouldn't you?'

'Yes. I'm sorry to trouble you, but we had a letter this morning that worried us. She sounded at the end of her tether.'

'News to me if she is.'

'When did you last see her?'

'Two or three days ago. And I think she was supposed

to be going out with a friend here last night. Beyond that—'

'You see, we're afraid she might commit suicide.'

The young man looked at him.

'Frankly, I think you're barking. Look, if you want to talk to someone who's close to her, try George Carlson, three doors up.'

'Oh yes, she mentioned someone called—'

But he was speaking to a closed door.

On his way to work, Neville McCartney stopped at the newsagent's for a *Guardian* and a packet of cigarettes. He frowned when he saw Isobel Franklin at the counter.

'Something the matter, Mr McCartney?'

'Oh, nothing . . . Well, you were her history teacher. It seems the Lowtons are very worried about Ruth not settling. We think he's gone to Leeds today.'

'Oh, really? Surely he should have left her to sort things out for herself. She's a *very* bright girl. No reason why she shouldn't settle down, left alone.'

'Perhaps you pushed her too hard.'

'I didn't push her at all. I was very conscious she was more intelligent than me. Perhaps you involved her too much in your domestic affairs.'

'I didn't involve her at all. *She* came to *me*. She wanted to make peace between us. She was so sweet, so under-standing.'

'A teenager can hardly understand a twenty-year marriage that's gone wrong.'

'She tried so hard to. She didn't realise that by being there, by being so sweet—'

51

But Neville thought better of it, and walked abruptly out of the shop. Mrs Franklin walked slowly toward the Bygrove Comprehensive School where she taught, thinking of how often Ruth Lowton had shown how much quicker and brighter she was than the teacher who had been forced back into teaching when her soldier husband died and she was left with a family to support. Of course Ruthie didn't know she was doing it, but she made her teacher feel so inadequate, so dull, so middle-of-the-road. Every lesson with Ruth had made Isobel feel she was on trial.

The bedsitter was shabby and sad, but the saddest thing about it was its total lack of character. George Carlson did not apologise for it. He was too worried by the arrival of Ruth's father.

'I was beginning to wonder,' he said. 'I hadn't seen her, and normally I'd . . . I was *worried*.'

'When did you last see her?'

'It was Tuesday morning. We were at a lecture on King Alfred.'

'How was she?'

'Well, much as usual . . . She wasn't happy with the course.'

'I know. She told us you were her only real friend here.'

'Oh, I don't know about . . . She said she might be going out on Thursday, that's last night. Clubbing, I suppose. She didn't ask me along because she knows that's not my kind of place.'

'Not hers either, from what she said. Where is your kind of place? Where do you talk together?'

'Oh, anywhere. The lecture room, the Brotherton Library, in the queue at the bank, down at the Abbey.'

'Kirkstall Abbey?'

'Yes, it's one of her favourite places. We go there quite often. It's only five minutes away. It really gives me a lift, talking to Ruth. She's so . . . understanding.'

'You're not happy here either, she says.'

'I don't know about *either* . . . Ruth seemed . . . It's a wonderful university of course, but I don't fit in. I thought it would be different from school, but . . .'

Peter felt that if he was not careful he would have to sit there for hours listening to Carlson's problems, as poor Ruthie so obviously had done, so he interrupted: 'Kirkstall Abbey – you said it was one of Ruthie's favourite places.'

'Oh it is. So peaceful. It puts things into perspective, she always says.'

'Do you think we could walk there? Just in case?'

On the way down George got back on to Ruth – himself and Ruth.

'Ruth is so good with people. She'll do anything for anyone, not just me. She'll go clubbing with the people from her house, even though from what you said she couldn't have enjoyed it. I know she hates some of the things going on there. I think she feels they need someone honest to be there and warn them, stop them going on drugs or sex binges.'

'Ruth is always there for people who need her.'

'She and I walk around Kirkstall on a fine day, and she'll tell me a little about herself, but mostly she listens to me, and I tell her about school, how out of things I always felt there, and how my parents are always bullying me and pushing me to stand up for myself. One time, when we'd been walking for nearly two hours, she had to go and get an essay done, and she said, "Doesn't time fly when you're having fun?" and I thought she might have been making fun of me, but I just looked in her eyes and I knew she wasn't.'

They had passed the Abbey Museum and its car park and had reached the Abbey Road. Suddenly Peter became aware that further up, on the way to Horsforth, three police cars were parked. For a second he was stunned. Then he heard the siren of another police car approaching. Ignoring the crossing he weaved his way through the heavy traffic and ran through the Abbey grounds in the direction of the police activity.

The body had lain underwater, visible but trapped, just under the weeds and dead leaves up beyond the Abbey grounds and edging Kirkstall rugby pitch. A strong current had released it, and it came down a hundred yards, to be trapped again by vegetation just beside a little bridge where many people and their dogs passed. It was wearing a skirt of dark blues, purples and clarets – Laura Ashley colours – and a charcoal-grey top. It had been quite warm until the frosts came on Thursday night, so perhaps she had gone in before that happened.

Charlie Peace looked down at the fragile body and the blonde hair and shuddered. The corpse was suddenly his daughter's, anyone's daughter's.

'What are you thinking?' said Superintendent Oddie, coming up.

'Thinking maybe she went in before the weather turned cold.'

'Haven't you noticed how little clothing young people wear these days, even when it's freezing? They seem to have some sort of internal heating.'

'Eh oop,' said Charlie, feigning broad Yorkshire. 'Who's this then?'

From the direction of the Abbey two men were running towards them, the older man easily outstripping the younger. When they got near, the uniformed policeman tried to bar their way, but the older man turned to Oddie: 'Please. You've got to let me through. Is it a girl? My daughter is missing, and she loved this place.'

Oddie looked at Charlie Peace, then taking the man firmly by the arm he led him through the cordon of policemen. The body was just being eased on to dry land. The face was uppermost. When he saw it the man fell on his knees and sobbed his heart out. Oddie left him for a minute, then raised him and led him back to the little group.

'It's what we feared, my wife and I. We had a letter this morning. It sounded as if she was thinking of suicide.'

But Oddie and Charlie Peace had seen the back of the body's head, and the wound at the crown that did not look like suicide to them.

Half an hour later the pair were driving up the hill towards 13 Cannock Road and Ruth Lowton's bedsit. Oddie had talked to her father. Through his tears Peter had told them how Ruth had somehow failed to fit in at the university of her choice, had been increasingly unhappy, and had sounded suicidal in the letter he and his wife had received that morning. He said that Ruth was someone who always felt deeply for people in trouble, and he thought she was saddened and upset by many of the aspects of Leeds student life she saw around her.

Charlie had talked to George Carlson, who had told him – also with sobs – much the same as he had told her father earlier. Charlie had a strong impression of a loner, an outsider, an unhappy young man who entirely lacked the capacity to change the conditions of his life. If anyone was a potential victim, it was Carlson, Charlie thought.

Both men were beginning to get the faint outline of a picture of the dead girl: the first stage in getting a picture of her killer. Ten minutes later they were in armchairs in the airy front room of Kit Wakeham.

'I'm sorry I swore at you,' he was saying. 'It's been one of those days. Her father was here earlier. I should never have taken a ground-floor room. But this is awful . . . horrible.'

'Was she a popular girl?' Charlie asked. Kit shrugged.

'It was early days. She'd only been here a few weeks. She went around with some of the gang in these houses. Half of the places on this street are student residences. She went clubbing, to films, things at the student union. She mixed in all right, so far as I could see . . . I'm third year, and I've done all that. I didn't have a lot to do with her.'

'When did you last see her?'

'Couple of days ago, maybe three. I didn't notice.

She wasn't interested in me, probably because I *didn't* notice.'

'You didn't like her, did you?' Oddie asked.

'Like I said, I didn't notice . . . She spent a lot of time with that miserable specimen George Carlson up the road. On the surface it was very good of her . . . too good, I thought. It didn't ring true, not to her other self, the clubbing, good-time girl. I felt she used people, or led them on, tried to bring out their worst side, their unhappiest side . . . I dunno . . . Ignore me. I'd make a rotten psychiatrist.'

But would he? After two hours of interviewing friends and acquaintances in the Kirkstall area and the history department, Oddie and Charlie were far from sure. Ruth seemed to be a girl who presented a different face to different people, took on a new identity whenever it suited her. What was not clear was *why* it suited her, what she was trying to do. It certainly went beyond just trying to fit in, chameleon-like, to any environment she happened to be in. Sometimes it did seem as if she was trying to bring out the worst in the people around her, or to encourage behaviour likely to lead them into disaster and unhappiness.

Her movements began to be clearer after a time.

'She was supposed to be coming out with us on Thursday, yesterday,' said Edwina Faye, the other girl on the first floor of number 13. 'It was all arranged. We were going together – into town around nine, then on to the Jurassic Club when things began to liven up there. Only she wasn't around here all evening, and finally I went on my own.'

'When did you last see her?'

'I heard her singing in the bathroom that morning.'

'You're sure it was her?'

'I know her voice, and I know what she sings.'

'What sort of girl was she, to your way of thinking?'

'Liked having a good time. Up for anything.' Edwina thought for a moment. 'But sly with it. She never let herself get out of hand, but she didn't mind at all watching while other people went over the edge. Got a kick out of that, I sometimes thought. And as far as I know she hadn't slept with anyone all the time she'd been here. I mean, that's six weeks. It just wasn't natural, not first time away from home.'

One of the men in the house had had a brief talk with her in the kitchen on Wednesday. She had been very full of herself because she'd written what she called 'a great work of fiction'. It was in the form of a letter, which she put down briefly on one of the surfaces of the kitchen, but the man had not tried to see the addressee. Charlie concluded that students were too wrapped up in their own selves to have any natural curiosity about others.

Talking it over, Charlie and Oddie felt they were beginning to get a picture, but were still a long way from finding out anything about Ruth that could suggest a reason for anyone wanting to kill her.

'I could imagine George Carlson committing suicide if he found out she'd been having him on to have a laugh at his expense,' said Charlie. 'But not committing murder – no way. She would have had to have been playing games with a really strong character, someone with deep feelings that she'd trodden on. Kit Wakeham might fit the bill, but I believed him when he said he didn't care for her.'

'A letter suggests someone back home, and having it with her in the kitchen suggests it was posted that day. Posts are unpredictable, but on balance the letter to her parents would have been posted on Thursday, to get there today. So who was it she posted that one to on Wednesday?'

'Strong feelings suggest long-matured ones,' said Charlie.

'Middle-aged people,' said Oddie. 'That surely means Barnsley.'

'Someone there who she had driven mad over the years,' agreed Charlie, as Oddie started the car.

When they got to the suburb of Barnsley where Ruth had lived they found the street without difficulty. They stood outside her house for a moment or two, but registered there was no sign of life within. Peter, her father, had been driven home some time ago, and they were reluctant to pressure him for a second time so soon after the devastating discovery. Standing indecisive in the street, and looking at the neighbouring houses, they saw a middle-aged woman at a window, watching them. A moment later she appeared in her front door, and they went over. Crying had made rivulets down her make-up, and her lipstick had been smudged around the edges. She looked a mess.

'Will you come in?' she said, as Oddie showed her his ID. 'I guessed you were policemen. Hannah rang me and told me of Ruthie's death, and I've been telling those who were close to her. Hannah's grief-stricken, of course, and so am I. She meant so much to me, to all of us.'

'Are you a relative?' Charlie asked.

'No, just a friend. Such a *good* friend – I mean she was to me, more than I to her. She was so understanding, such a wonderful support.'

'Support in what?' Oddie asked.

'Oh, you know, personal troubles. My husband is a pig. Tell me something new, I hear you say. Let's not go into it. The point is that Ruthie was always interested, always listened, really helped, even when she was hardly more than a girl.'

'You know she'd told her parents she was unhappy in Leeds?'

'Yes. Hannah just told me that. I can't understand it. She had so many friends here. Everyone at school, in the neighbourhood, loved her.'

'Your husband too?'

'Well . . . yes, she was nice to him. Nicer than he deserved. She was to my father too. He's chairbound, with nothing much to do all day. She did little bits of shopping for him, but mostly just talked. He thought the world of her.'

Oddie nodded.

'Can you think of any reason why Ruth should be unhappy at Leeds University, if she was?'

'Oh, she was. She made that quite clear in letters home. I think she felt she had been pressured to go there by her history teacher. You know how teachers live alternative lives through their pupils. In fact Mrs Franklin wanted her to try for Oxbridge, but Ruth wasn't willing to go so far from home. People who are pressured like that – not that Ruth put it like that, or felt anything other than grateful – often develop a sense of resentment, don't they? Almost *want* things to go badly. She'd have been so much better off staying at home and going to Sheffield or the nearest poly-that-was.'

'I suppose what you say makes sense,' said Oddie cautiously. 'Maybe we should have a word with Mrs Franklin.'

So it was that the last talk of the day took place two streets away from Ruth Lowton's home, in a post-war semi which periodically erupted with the sounds made by teenagers coming in or going out, and the incursion of loud music suddenly hushed as they remembered Charlie's stern injunction to keep the noise down.

'I'm glad you've come, but I'm afraid you'll find me a sadly muddled witness,' said Isobel Franklin, serving them instant coffee. 'I've been thinking about Ruth all day, and of course talking about her at school, and I've been forced to look at her and wonder about my assessment of her.'

'In what ways?' asked Oddie.

'In every way. My headmaster talked to me this afternoon, and he said: "I think she robbed you of confidence in yourself." And that I know was true, though I always believed it was the reverse of what she intended.' She paused, and took a draught of her coffee. 'My husband was a regular army officer, killed on winter exercises in north Norway. I went back into teaching on the basis of a teaching certificate, and a general interest in history.

I found myself teaching it further and further up the school because they couldn't get anyone properly qualified. I was always perfectly confident about facing a class. What I had doubts about was whether I was knowledgeable enough, sophisticated enough in my approach to teach at O and A levels.'

'And Ruth Lowton?'

'She once said to me: "I think you're wonderful, being able to teach history so well without a degree." There were lots of other remarks to similar "encouraging" effect.'

'And you never saw through her?'

'No. I don't think anyone she targeted did. Something Neville McCartney said to me in the newsagent's this morning suggested that he was wondering whether Ruth's "sweet" and "understanding" attempts to bring peace to his marriage weren't really sexual teasing designed to make matters worse. And the headmaster reminded me this afternoon of a boy who left school, didn't find work, and sank further and further into apathy, staying in bed all day, losing all his friends. Ruth visited him, over and over, trying to get him to snap out of it and make an effort, she said. But his mother asked her to stop coming, and privately she said she thought she was driving him to suicide.'

'What happened to him?' Charlie asked.

'He met a girl, got a job, everything turned out OK. Typical teenage phase. But . . . it seems like there's a pattern.'

Yes, it seems like there's a pattern, Charlie and Oddie said to themselves.

The next morning they did not set out from Leeds

until after ten, wanting the day to have settled down before they arrived in Barnsley. They went first to Fred Mortimer, Sheila McCartney's old and chairbound father, then to the local PO sorting office to see if they could get on to the scent of Ruth Lowton's Wednesday letter. They didn't feel they should hurry to report progress to Ruth's parents, and it was nearly lunchtime when they rang the doorbell of number 15. Hannah Lowton's eyes were red, and she was near to tears when she explained that they couldn't talk to her husband.

'I had such a night with him,' she said. 'She was the apple of his eye. The doctor's just been and given him a sedative.'

'We do understand,' said Oddie. 'I wonder if we could see the letter from your daughter, the one that made him go to Leeds yesterday.'

'Of course,' she said, and fetched the cream pages from the sideboard.

It was what they had expected: her unhappiness, her inability to settle, her doubts about the activities of her fellow-students, her feelings of desperation at the point-lessness of her life in Leeds. It ended with love to her 'dear old stepmum' and the assurance that they had both 'done all you can for me'.

'You're her stepmother then?' asked Charlie.

'Her mother died of breast cancer when she was one. I married Peter when she was three. To everybody I am her mother.'

Except to Ruthie apparently, thought Charlie. He felt that that 'step' could have been left out.

'Have you got the envelope?' asked Oddie.

'The envelope? I don't think so. I've probably thrown it out.'

'Never mind. The postmark wouldn't have proved anything.'

'What do you mean?'

'You see, Mr Mortimer opposite says he saw you come out of this house on Thursday, soon after the postman had been, with a letter in your hand, in a cream envelope. You got into your car and drove away.'

'I expect he got the day wrong. You would, being there all the time.'

'I don't think so. Because on Friday morning your husband's car was parked in the road and your car was in the garage. That all depended on who was home first, didn't it? And on Friday you stayed home in case there was a call from Ruth. Your husband told me that.'

'I expect Mr Mortimer mistook something I was holding for a letter. My husband can tell you it arrived on Friday.'

'He heard you tearing open a letter, and saw you come in with this one. That doesn't prove it arrived yesterday. It may be that you wanted him to think it arrived yesterday.'

Hannah Lowton looked from one face to the other, from the middle-aged white man to the young black one, both faces filled with professional certainty: they knew. They thought they knew. But how could they really know?

It had started so long ago, when Ruthie was about seven and, like so many children, learning the art of playing off one parent against the other. She soon realised that, whatever she wanted, her father would eventually give her, however strong the opposition from her stepmother. As soon as these contests began to be a struggle for Peter Lowton's heart, Hannah gave in. Constant victories of that sort would be bad for Ruthie, bad for all three of them.

But as the child grew older it became clear that victories she must have, that emotional dominance was a sort of drug to her. Time after time she would work her way into people's lives, let them attach themselves – and all their hopes, fears and fantasies – to her, and then bring disaster, chaos, disruption to their lives. Hannah only once tried to bring her understanding of what Ruth was doing into the open.

'I'm just trying to do my little bit to make the world a better place,' Ruth had said, looking at her with a smirk on her face. The smirk seemed to Hannah to say: 'Your turn is coming.'

The tone of disillusion and discontent had begun to enter her letters almost as soon as she had moved to Leeds. 'She doesn't lose much time,' Hannah said despairingly to herself. If she had questioned the truth of the letters, Peter would have called her heartless, jealous of his love for his – and only his – daughter. She knew Ruth was playing with them, driving her father to desperation, and getting from it the same pleasure she had got from fostering despair among her neighbours and schoolfellows in Barnsley. When the letter came on Thursday, her first thought was gladness that Peter had gone to work: the suggestion of suicide was new, and something had to be done before he returned home.

She left the car at the Woodhouse Lane multi-storey and walked up to the University. It was easy to find out where the history lectures were, and she lingered and mixed in with the students when they came out, leaving Ruth a little to the front. She could see the girl was happy, carefree, and already knew most of her year. She waved, smiled and made plans.

'We're out tonight at the Jurassic,' she shouted to someone. 'If I don't see you there, see you at the Majestic on Saturday.'

To another person in the crowd she shouted that he should make sure he had plenty of the white stuff. Ruth, Hannah had no doubt, was in her element at Leeds, and was busy spreading chaos and desperation.

Nothing could be done until classes and library work were over. She drove down to Cannock Road, had lunch in a nearby pub, then waited. At one point in the long wait she got out of the car, went to the boot, removed the monkey-wrench, then put it in her capacious string bag. It was said at the trial that this was for self-protection. It was not believed.

When Ruth arrived back in Cannock Road Hannah got out of the car and met her as she was alighting from a bus. Her expression was one of satisfaction rather than surprise. When Hannah asked if they could talk, Ruth said: 'Let's go down to Kirkstall Abbey. I talk to a lot of people there. It's such a peaceful, spiritual place.'

And she had smirked. Hannah had kept her anger bottled up until they were in the Abbey grounds, then it burst out.

'You are just playing with your father. Driving him

mad with pain and worry because that's what you do best. I've seen you with your friends here. You're perfectly happy!'

'Haven't you heard of the clown with the broken heart, step-mama? I smile even though their dreadful deeds and habits break my heart. Dad knows what a caring person I am.' The voice oozed with sneer.

'He's deceived by your disgusting games with people. What has he done to deserve this? He's always given you what you demanded.'

'Yes, he has, hasn't he? In spite of you. But I think he was always pleasing himself, don't you? He wasn't thinking whether I ought to have those things: he was thinking of the pleasure he would get in letting me have them. We're all selfish at heart, aren't we?'

'I don't know of a less selfish person than your dad.'

'Have it your own way.' Ruth shrugged. 'I suppose you'd know. He only married you to provide a mother for me. Pity you never did.'

They were under the weeping willows, near-leafless now, by the rugby pitch. Hannah's hand had been on the wrench for some time. As Ruth came out with those last words she smirked again and turned towards the flowing river. Hannah gripped the wrench, took it from the bag, and with all her strength bashed it into Ruth's skull. As her stepdaughter fell into the water Hannah put the wrench away and composedly walked back to the car.

Hannah looked at the two men opposite. Professional men, men whose business was crime. It would be so easy to tell them what they already knew, to confess.

But to do that would be to hand Ruth her last victory, to give her on a plate the ruin of her own and Peter's fragile marriage. She couldn't do it. She had to fight back.

She stood up.

'Could we continue this at the police station?' she asked. 'I need to have a lawyer to advise me, don't I? Do you think you could ask Mrs McCartney opposite to come and sit with Peter till he wakes. He'll be lonely and upset, and I may be gone a long time.'

And she started with them out to the police car.

Robert Barnard *was born in 1936 and brought up near Colchester in Essex. After Balliol, he worked for the Fabian Society, then went to teach in an Australian university in 1961 (which later formed the backdrop of his first crime novel,* Death of an Old Goat*). He and his wife Louise went to Norway in 1966 where he taught English at the universities of Bergen and Tromsø, and began writing crime fiction. He returned to England in 1983, becoming a full-time writer. He has now written over forty mysteries, as well as books on Agatha Christie, Dickens and Emily Brontë, and a Short History of English Literature.* He is the recipient of the 2003 CWA Cartier Diamond Dagger.*

LESLIE CHARTERIS

The Mystery of the Child's Toy

George Kestry slanted his two hundred pounds of brawn and bone back in his chair, stuck his thumbs in the armholes of his waistcoat, and spoke past a cigar that jutted out of the corner of his mouth as squarely and truculently as a cannon out of an old-time battleship.

'That's all there was to it,' he stated. 'And that's the way it always is. You get an idea – just a little one. You spread a net out among the stool-pigeons. You catch a man. And then you grill him till he comes clean. That's how a real detective does his job; and to heck with Sherlock Holmes.'

Andy Herrick, slim and almost frail-looking opposite the Homicide Squad's toughest case-breaker, grinned amiably and beckoned the waiter for his bill. The orchestra yawned and went into another dance number. It was three o'clock in the morning, and a fair proportion of the crowd of assorted millionaires, racketeers, sight-seers, and show-girls who packed New York's most expensive restaurant had some work to think of before the next midnight.

'Maybe you're right,' said Andy, mildly.

'I know I'm right!' roared Kestry; and then, while Andy slid greenbacks on to a plate, he chuckled. 'I'm not bein' personal, kid – you know that. If you can make a living writing that detective-story stuff I'm glad about it. I wish I could do it. But when it comes to real crimes – well, it just makes me mad.' He stood up and grabbed Andy's shoulder. 'C'mon, kid – I gotta go home.'

He steered their way round the tables and up the stairs to the hotel lobby, with his stubby fingers locked round Andy's arm and his iron features set in a contented grin. It was not the first time they had had the same argument over the supper table, nor by any means the first time that George Kestry had settled it in a similar manner to his own satisfaction. He had a voice that matched his mighty build, and a belligerent crash of his massive fist on the table to go with it.

A self-made man from the soles of his shoes, self-architectured, self-educated, who had fought every inch of his own way up from a Brooklyn slum, he took an innocent and almost ingenuous delight in getting the better of anyone out of the class which he ungrudgingly ranked as 'gentlemen' – even by no sounder logic than a loud voice and a thumping fist that made the knives and forks dance and quiver. And at the same time, between those arguments, he treated Andy with a naïve respect which at times was almost comic in an unconsciously elephantine way, like a docile giant gambolling deferentially with a child. To call Andy by his first name, go about with him, clap him on the shoulder, dine with him, be introduced to his friends as an equal, gave the big, hard-boiled detective a sense of his own conquest of environment which he himself would have been the last to admit.

'Come down to Headquarters next time I'm working on a case, sir,' Kestry said in the lobby, with an abrupt return to that naïve respect which would have been humorous if it had been less completely unselfconscious. 'You'll see for yourself how we really break 'em up.'

'I'd like to,' said Andy; and if there was the trace of a smile in his eyes when he said it, it was without malice. He liked the big detective sincerely, enjoyed his company like a great, healthy, blustering breeze, despaired of ever carrying a point against that thunderous, dogmatic voice, and was cheerfully contented to provoke and listen to its outbursts.

Andy settled his soft hat on his straight, fair hair and glanced round the lobby with the vague aimlessness which ordinarily precedes a parting at that hour. A little group of three men had discharged themselves from a nearby elevator, and were moving boisterously and a trifle unsteadily towards the main entrance. Two of them were hatted and overcoated – a tallish man with a thin line of moustache and a tubby, red-faced man with rimless spectacles. The third member of the party, who appeared to be the host, was a flabby, flat-footed man of about fifty-five, with a round, bald head and a rather bulbous nose that would have persuaded any observant onlooker to expect that he would have drunk more than the others, which, in fact, he obviously had. All of them had the dishevelled and rather tragically ridiculous air of

Captains of Industry who have gone off duty for the evening.

'That's Lewis Enstone – the guy with the nose,' said Kestry, who knew everyone. 'Wall Street man. Might have been one of the biggest financiers in the country if he could have kept off the bottle.'

'And the other two?' asked Andy, incuriously.

'Just a coupla smaller men in the same game. Gamblers. Abe Costello – that's the tall one – and Jules Hammel. If we put all the crooks in that precinct into our portrait gallery, Police Headquarters'd have to take over another annexe.'

Kestry chewed his cigar over to the other side of his mouth, where it stood out at the same pugnacious angle as before; but for his surroundings, he would probably have spat expressively. 'I'd rather be seen with an honest racketeer than one of those snakes, any day.'

The detective was only one of millions who had lost money in the recent collapse of an artificial boom, and his sentiments were characteristically vehement. Andy Herrick murmured some sympathetic commonplace and watched the trio of celebrators without interest.

'You do understan', boys, don't you?' Enstone was articulating pathetically, with his arms spread across the shoulders of his guests in an affectionate manner which contributed helpfully towards his support. 'It's jus' business. I'm not hard-hearted. I'm kind to my wife an' children an' everything, God bless 'em. An' any time I can do anything for either of you – why, you jus' lemme know.'

'That's real white of you, Lew,' said Hammel, with the blurry-eyed solemnity of his condition.

'Let's have lunch together Tuesday,' suggested Costello. 'Maybe we might be able to talk about something that'd interest you.'

'OK,' said Enstone, dimly. 'Lush on Tooshday.'

'An' don't forget the kids,' said Hammel, confidentially.

Enstone giggled.

'I shouldn't forget that!' In obscurely elaborate pantomime, he closed his fist, with his forefinger extended and his thumb cocked vertically upwards, and aimed the forefinger waveringly between Hammel's eyes. 'Shtick 'em up!' he commanded gravely, and at once relapsed into further merriment, in which his guests joined somewhat hysterically.

The group separated at the entrance amid much hand-shaking and back-slapping and laughter; and Lewis Enstone wended his way back with cautious and preoccupied steps towards the elevators. Kestry took a fresh bite on his cigar and squared his jaw disgustedly.

'Is he staying here?' asked Andy.

'Lives here,' said Kestry, shortly. 'Got a terrace apartment that costs forty thousand dollars a year. There's plenty of suckers to help him pay for it.' The detective ruminated sourly. 'If I told you some of the tricks those guys get up to you'd call me a liar. Why, I remember one time—'

He launched into a lengthy anecdote which had all the decorative vitality of personal bitterness in the telling. Andy Herrick, listening with the half of one well-trained ear that would prick up into instant attention if the story

73

took any twist that might provide the germ of a plot, but would remain intently passive if it did not, lighted a cigarette and gazed abstractedly into space.

'. . . So the word came down for me to lay off, and I laid off. It was OK with me,' concluded Kestry rancorously; and Andy took the last inhalation from his cigarette and dropped the stub into an ashtray.

'Thanks for the tip, George,' he said lightly. 'I gather that when I really murder somebody you'd like me to make it a Wall Street financier.'

George Kestry snorted, and hitched his coat round.

'I gotta be off now. Come in an' see me again soon.'

They walked towards the street doors. On their left they passed the information desk; and beside the desk had been standing two bored and sleepy bell-boys. Andy had observed them and their sleepiness as casually as he had observed the colour of the carpet, but all at once he realised that their sleepiness had vanished. He had a sudden queer sense of suppressed excitement; and then one of the boys said something loud enough to be overheard which stopped Kestry in his tracks and turned him round abruptly.

'What's that?' demanded Kestry.

'It's Mr Enstone, sir. He just shot himself.'

Kestry scowled. To the newspapers it would be a surprise and a front-page sensation; to him it was a surprise and a potential menace to his night's sleep if he butted into any responsibility. Then he shrugged.

'I'd better give it a look-over. D'you say he shot himself?'

'Yes, sir. His valet just 'phoned down.'

Kestry flashed his badge, and there was a scurry to lead him towards the elevators. He strode bulkily and impersonally ahead, and Andy followed him into the nearest car. One of the bell-boys supplied a floor number, and Kestry pushed his hands into his pockets and glowered in mountainous aloofness at the latticed inner gate of the elevator. Andy, the intruder, studiously avoided his eye, and had a pleasant shock when the detective addressed him almost genially.

'Say, Andy, didn't I tell you those guys were nutty as well as crooked? Did Enstone look as if he'd anything to shoot himself about, except the head that was waitin' for him when he woke up?'

It was as if the decease of any financier, however caused, was a benison upon the earth, in the face of which Kestry could not be anything but good-humoured. That was the impression he gave of his private feelings; but the rest of him was impenetrable stolidity and authoritativeness. He dismissed the escort of bell-boys and strode on to the door of the millionaire's suite. It was closed and silent. He hammered on it commandingly, and after a moment it opened six inches and disclosed a pale, agitated face. Kestry showed his badge again, and the door opened wider, enlarging the agitated face into the unmistakable full-length portrait of an assistant hotel manager. Andy followed the detective in, endeavouring to look equally official.

'This will be a terrible scandal, captain,' said the assistant manager.

Kestry glared at him over an aggressive cigar.

'Were you here when it happened?'

'No. I was downstairs – in my office—'

Kestry collected the information, and thrust past him. On the right, another door opened off the large lobby, and through it could be seen another elderly man whose equally pale face and air of suppressed agitation bore a certain general similarity and also a self-contained superiority to the first. Even without his sober black coat and striped trousers, grey side-whiskers, and passive hands, he would have stamped himself as something more cosmic than the assistant manager of an hotel – the assistant manager of a man.

'Who are you?' demanded Kestry.

'I am Fowler, sir. Mr Enstone's valet.'

'Were you here?'

'Yes, sir.'

'Where is Mr Enstone?'

'In the bedroom, sir.'

They moved back across the lobby, with the assistant manager in the lead. Kestry stopped. 'Will you be in your office if I want you?' he asked with great politeness; and the assistant manager seemed to disappear from the scene even before the door of the suite closed behind him.

Lewis Enstone was dead. He lay on his back beside the bed, with his head half-rolled over to one side, in such a way that both the entrance and the exit of the bullet which had killed him could be seen. It had been fired squarely into his right eye, leaving the ugly trail that only a heavy-calibre bullet fired at close range can leave . . . The gun lay under the fingers of his right hand.

'Thumb on the trigger,' Kestry noted aloud.

He sat on the bed, pulling on a pair of gloves, inscrutable and unemotional. Andy Herrick observed the room. An ordinary, very tidy bedroom, barren of anything unusual except the subdued costliness of furnishing and accessories. Two French windows opening on to the terrace, both shut and fastened. On a table in one corner, the only sign of disorder – the remains of a carelessly opened parcel. Brown paper, ends of string, a plain cardboard box – empty. The millionaire had gone no farther towards undressing than loosening his tie and unbuttoning his collar.

'What happened?' asked Kestry.

'Mr Enstone had had friends to dinner, sir,' explained Fowler. 'A Mr Costello—'

'I know that. What happened when he came back from seeing them off?'

'He was going straight to bed, sir.'

'Was this door open?'

'At first, sir. I asked Mr Enstone about the morning, and he asked me to call him at nine. Then he closed the door, and I went back to the sitting-room.'

'Did you leave that door open?'

'Yes, sir. I was doing a little clearing up. Then I heard the shot, sir.'

'Do you know any reason why Mr Enstone should have shot himself?'

'No, sir.'

Kestry jerked his head towards a door on the other side of the room.

'What does that communicate with?'

'Another bedroom, sir. Mrs Enstone's maid sleeps there with the children.'

'Where are they?'

'They have been in Bermuda, sir. We are expecting them home tomorrow.'

'What was in that parcel, Fowler?' ventured Andy.

The valet glanced at the table.

'I don't know, sir. I believe it must have been left by one of Mr Enstone's guests. I noticed it on the dining table when I brought in their coats, and Mr Enstone came back for it on his return and took it into the bedroom with him.'

'You didn't hear anything said about it?'

'No, sir.'

Kestry looked up at Andy, derisively.

'Why don't you get out your magnifying glass and go over the cigar ash?' he inquired.

Andy smiled apologetically, and, being nearest the door, went out to open it, as a second knocking disturbed the silence. For half an hour he stood about inconspicuously in the background, while the room and the body were photographed from different angles, fingerprints developed and photographed, and the police surgeon made his preliminary examination. All the formalities were familiar to him, and after a while he drifted into the sitting-room. The hallmarks of a convivial dinner were all there – cigar butts in the coffee cups, stains of spilt wine on the cloth, crumbs and ash everywhere – but those things did not interest him.

He was not quite sure what would have interested him; but he wandered rather vacantly round the room, gazing introspectively at the prints of character which a long tenancy inevitably leaves even on anything so characterless as a hotel apartment. There were pictures on the walls and on the side tables, mostly enlarged snapshots revealing Lewis Enstone in relaxation in the bosom of his family.

On one of the side tables he found a curious object. It was a small wooden plate on which half-a-dozen wooden fowls stood in a circle. Their necks were pivoted at the base, and underneath the plate were six short strings joined to the necks and knotted together some distance farther down, where they were all attached at the same point to a wooden ball. It was these strings, and the weight of the ball at their lower end, which kept the birds' heads raised; and Andy discovered that when he moved the plate so that the ball swung round in a circle underneath and slackened and tightened each string in turn, the fowls mounted on the plate pecked vigorously in rotation at an invisible and apparently inexhaustible supply of corn, in an ingenious mechanical display of gluttony.

He was still playing thoughtfully with the toy when the howl of Kestry's gargantuan laughter brought him back to earth with a jar, and he realised that the photographers and fingerprint men had gone.

'So that's how the great detective works!' Kestry jeered.

'I think it's rather clever,' said Andy seriously. He put the toy down, and blinked at Fowler. 'Does it belong to one of the children?'

'He brought it home with him this evening, sir, to give to Miss Annabel tomorrow,' said the valet. 'Mr

Enstone was always picking up things like that. He was a very devoted father, sir.'

Kestry grunted.

'C'mon, kid. I'm goin' home.'

Andy nodded pacifically, and accompanied him to the elevator. On the way down he asked: 'Did you find any clue?'

Kestry's teeth clamped on a fresh cigar.

'The guy committed suicide,' he said, addressing an obvious half-wit. 'He shot himself. What sort of clues d'you want?'

'Why did he commit suicide?' asked Andy, almost childishly.

'How do I know? I told you those guys were nutty. Probably he dropped ten million while he was picking up one, and he only wanted to talk about the one. Come down to my office in the morning and I'll tell you.'

Andy Herrick went home and slept fitfully. Lewis Enstone had shot himself; Kestry said so, and without any wild stretches of imagination it seemed an obvious fact. The windows had been closed and fastened. The valet had had the door and the lobby under surveillance from the sitting-room; there remained the communicating door of the second bedroom . . . or Fowler himself . . . Why not suicide, anyway?

But Andy could run through his mind every word and gesture and expression of the leave-taking, which he himself had witnessed in the hotel lobby, and none of it carried even a hint of suicide. The only oddity about it had been the queer, inexplicable piece of pantomime – the fist clenched, with the forefinger extended and the thumb cocked up, in crude symbolism of a gun. The abstruse joke which had dissolved Enstone into a fit of inanely delighted giggling, with the hearty approval of his guests.

It was like the opening of one of Andy's own stories, a set of intriguing circumstances of which he, himself, would have to devise an explanation and a solution towards the fourth or fifth instalment; and the psychological problem absorbed him. It muddled itself up with a litter of brown paper and a cardboard box, a wooden plate of pecking chickens, photographs ... and the tangle kaleidoscoped through his dreams in a thousand different convolutions until morning.

At half-past twelve he found himself walking slowly down the long corridor to Kestry's office. The detective was chewing his cigar over a sheaf of typewritten reports, and he was in one of his short tempers.

'What do you want?' he snapped.

Andy unbuttoned his coat and opened a packet of cigarettes.

'Have you found out why Enstone committed suicide?'

'I haven't found out nothing,' said Kestry, with ungrammatical emphasis. 'His broker says it's true he cleaned up the market – sold Associated Stone Mills down to six-and-a-half and covered yesterday. Maybe he was working something else through another broker. We'll find out.'

Kestry buried himself again in his papers. Andy might have been off the earth.

'Have you seen Costello or Hammel?' Andy asked, unabashed.

'I've sent for them. They're due here about now.'

In a few minutes Costello and Hammel were announced. Kestry 'phoned for a stenographer, and applied a match to his cigar in grim detachment while the two witnesses seated themselves. He opened the brief examination in his own time.

'Mr Abe Costello?'

The tall man with the thin black moustache nodded. 'Yes.'

'How long have you known Enstone?'

'About eight or nine years.'

'Ever in partnership?'

'No. We were just friends.'

'Ever quarrel?'

'No.'

'Have you any idea why he should have shot himself?'

'None at all, captain. It was a great shock. He had been making more money than most of us. When we were with him – last night – he was in very high spirits. He'd made a lot on the market, and his family was on the way home – he was always happy when he was looking forward to seeing them again.'

'Did you hold any Associated Stone Mills?'

'No.'

'You know we can investigate that?'

Costello smiled slightly.

'I don't know why you should take that attitude, but my affairs are open to any examination.'

'Been making money yourself lately?'

'No. As a matter of fact, I've lost a bit,' said Costello, frankly.

'What are you in?'

'I'm controlling International Cotton.'

Kestry paused to reach for matches and Costello fore-stalled him with a lighter. Andy Herrick suddenly found his eyes riveted on the device – it was of an uncommon shape, and seemed to ignite the fuel by means of an electric spark, for when Costello pressed the button there was a preliminary crackle quite distinguishable from the usual grate of a flint.

Almost without realising his own temerity, Andy said: 'That's something new, isn't it?'

Costello turned the lighter over and answered, 'I don't think you'll see one in a shop. It's an invention of my own – I made it myself.'

'I wish I could do things like that,' said Andy, wistfully. 'I suppose you must have had a technical training.'

Costello hesitated for a second. Then:

'I started in an electrical engineering workshop when I was a boy,' he explained briefly, and turned back to Kestry's desk.

After a long pause Kestry turned to the tubby man with glasses.

'Mr Jules Hammel?'

'Yes.'

'You in partnership with Mr Costello?'

'A working partnership – yes.'

'Were you on the same terms with Enstone?'

'About the same – yes.'

'What were you talking about at dinner last night?'

'It was about a merger. I'm in International Cotton, too. One of Mr Enstone's concerns was Cosmopolitan

Textiles. His shares are standing high and ours are not doing too well, and we thought if we could induce him to sign a merger it would help us.'

'What did Enstone think about that?'

Hammel spread his hands.

'He didn't think there was enough in it for him. We had certain things to offer, but he decided they weren't sufficient.'

'Wasn't there some bad feeling about it?'

'Why no. If all the businessmen who have refused to combine with one another at different times became enemies, there would be nobody speaking to anybody on Wall Street today.'

'Do you know why Enstone might have shot himself?'

'No.'

Andy Herrick cleared his throat.

'What was your first important job, Mr Hammel?' he queried.

Hammel turned his eyes without moving his head.

'I was sales psychologist in a department store in Minneapolis.'

Kestry closed the interview curtly, shook hands perfunctorily with the two men, and dismissed the stenographer. Then he glared at Andy like a cannibal.

'Why don't you join the force yourself?' he inquired heavily. 'The Police Academy's just across the street – I'll send you over with a letter.'

Andy took the sally like an armoured car taking a snowball.

'You big sap!' he retorted startlingly. 'Do you look as if the Police Academy could teach anyone to solve a murder?'

Kestry gulped. 'What murder are you talking about?' he demanded. 'Enstone shot himself.'

'Yes, Enstone shot himself,' said Andy. 'But he was murdered just the same. They made him shoot himself.'

'What d'you mean – blackmail?'

'No.'

Andy pushed a hand through his hair again. He had thought of things like that. He knew that Enstone had shot himself, because no one else could have done it. Except Fowler, the valet – but that was the man whom Kestry would have suspected if he had suspected anyone, and it was too obvious, too hopelessly amateurish. No man in his senses could have planned a murder with himself as the most obvious suspect. Blackmail, then? But the Lewis Enstone he had seen in the hotel lobby had never looked like a man bidding farewell to blackmailers. And no one else could have blackmailed him. There had been no letters, no telephone calls – Andy took that for granted; if there had been, Fowler must have mentioned them. How could he have been blackmailed?

'No, no, no,' said Andy. 'It wasn't that. They just made him do it.'

'They just said: "Lew, why don't you take yourself for a ride?" and he thought it was a swell idea – is that it?' Kestry gibed.

'It was something like that,' Andy said soberly. 'You see, Enstone would do almost anything to amuse his children.'

Kestry's mouth opened, but no sounds came from it. His expression implied that a whole volcano of devastating sarcasm was boiling on the tip of his tongue.

85

'Costello and Hammel had to do something,' said Andy. 'International Cottons have been very bad for a long time. On the other hand, Enstone's interest – Cosmopolitan Textiles – was good. Costello and Hammel could have pulled out in two ways: either by a merger, or else by having Enstone commit suicide, so that Cosmopolitans would tumble down in the scare, and they could buy them in. If you look at the papers this afternoon you'll see that all Enstone's securities have dropped through the bottom – no one in his position can commit suicide without starting a panic. Costello and Hammel went to dinner to try for the merger, but if Enstone turned it down they were ready for the other thing.'

'So what?' rapped Kestry; but for the first time there seemed to be a tremor in the foundations of his disbelief.

'They made only one big mistake. They didn't arrange for Enstone to leave a letter.'

'People have shot themselves without leaving letters.'

'I know. But not often. That's what started me thinking.'

'Well?'

Andy rumpled his hair into more profound disorder, and said: 'You see, George, I write those detective stories: and writing detective stories is just a kind of jigsaw puzzle. For the author, I mean. You take a lot of mysterious events and a lot of mysterious characters, and somehow you have to tie them all together. And while the story's going on you have to be thinking all the time, "Now, what would A do? – and what would B do? – and what would C do?" You have to be a practical psychologist – just like a sales psychologist in a department store in Minneapolis.'

Kestry's cigar came out of his mouth, but for some reason which was beyond his conscious comprehension he said nothing. And Andy Herrick went on, in the same disjointed and rather apologetic way:

'Sales psychology is just a study of human weaknesses. And that's a funny thing, you know. I remember the manager of one of the biggest novelty manufacturers in the world telling me once that the soundest test of any idea for a new toy was whether it would appeal to a middle-aged businessman. It's true, of course. If the mighty, earth-shaking businessmen weren't like that they could never have helped to create an economic system in which the fate of nations, all the hunger and happiness and achievement of the world, was locked up in a few bars of yellow gold.'

Andy raised his eyes suddenly – they were unexpectedly bright and in some queer fashion sightless, as if his mind was separated from every physical awareness of its surroundings. 'Lewis Enstone was just that kind of man,' he said.

'You still thinking of that toy you were playing with?' asked Kestry, restlessly.

'That – and other things we heard. And the photographs. Did you notice them?'

'No.'

'One of them was Enstone playing with a clockwork train. In another of them he was under a rug, being a bear. In another he was working a big model merry-go-round. Most of the pictures were like that. The children came into them, of course, but you could see that Enstone was having the swellest time.'

Kestry, who had been fidgeting with a pencil, shrugged and sent it clattering across the desk.

'You still gotta show me a murder,' he stated.

'I have to find it myself,' said Andy, gently. 'You see, it was a kind of professional problem – the old jigsaw puzzle with a missing piece. Enstone was happily married, happy with his family, too happy to give any grounds for blackmail, no more crooked than any other Wall Street gambler, nothing on his conscience, rich and getting richer – how were they to make him commit suicide? If I'd been writing a story with him in it, how could I have made him commit suicide?'

'You'd of told him he had some fatal illness,' said Kestry, 'and he'd have fallen for it.'

Andy shook his head.

'No. If I'd been a doctor – perhaps. But if Costello or Hammel had told him, he'd have wanted confirmation. And did he look like a man who'd just been told he might have got a fatal illness?'

'It's your murder,' said Kestry. 'You go ahead an' break it.'

'There were lots of pieces missing at first,' said Andy. 'I only had Enstone's character and weaknesses. And then it came out – Hammel was a psychologist. That was good, because I'm a psychologist myself, and his mind would work something like mine. And then Costello could invent mechanical gadgets and make them himself. He shouldn't have brought out that lighter, George – it

88

gave me another of the missing pieces. And then there was the cardboard box – on Enstone's table, with the brown paper. You know, Fowler said he thought either Costello or Hammel left it. Have you got it here?'

'It's somewhere in the building.'

'Could we have it up?'

Kestry looked at him and burst out laughing. Then, with the gesture of a hangman reaching for a noose, he took hold of the telephone.

'You can have the gun, too, if you like,' he said.

'Yes, please,' said Andy, hurriedly. 'I wanted the gun.'

Kestry gave the order; and they sat and looked at each other in silence till the relics arrived. Kestry's silence explained in fifty different ways that Andy would be refused no facility for nailing down his own coffin in a manner that he would never be allowed to forget; but Andy was only squatting on the edge of his chair and ruffling his hair like a schoolboy. When they were alone again, Andy went to the desk, picked up the gun, and put it in the box. It fitted very well.

'That's what happened, George. They gave him the gun in the box.'

'And he shot himself without knowing what he was doing,' said Kestry.

'That's just it,' said Andy. 'He didn't know what he was doing.'

'Well, for the love of a piebald mule!' said Kestry.

'But I've got an idea,' said Andy, jumping up excitedly. 'Come out and lunch with me. I know a new place.'

Kestry gathered up a handful of cigars from a drawer,

thrust them into his pocket, crushed his hat on his head, and they went out to a taxi.

Kestry roared noisily on the ride. Andy sat on the edge of the seat, as he had sat on the edge of the chair in Kestry's office, and twiddled the brim of his hat awkwardly. Presently the taxi stopped in a turning off Park Avenue, and Andy looked out of the window at the numbers of the houses and hopped out. He led the way into an apartment building and into an elevator, saying something to the elevator boy which Kestry did not catch.

'What is this?' Kestry asked, as they shot upwards. 'A new speakeasy?'

'It's a new place,' said Andy, hazily.

The elevator stopped, and they got out. They went along the corridor, and Andy rang the bell of one of the doors. It was opened by a liveried Japanese.

'Police Department,' said Andy, brazenly, and squeezed past him.

He found his way into the sitting-room before anyone could stop him. Kestry, reviving from the momentary paralysis of the shock, followed him; then came the Japanese manservant.

'I'm sorry, sir – Mr Costello is out.'

Kestry's bulk obscured Japan. All the joviality had smudged itself off the detective's face, giving place to blank amazement and fury.

'What the deuce is this joke?' he demanded.

'It isn't a joke, George,' said Andy. 'I just wanted to see if I could find something – you know what we were talking about—'

His eyes were darting about the room, and then they lighted on a big, cheap kneehole desk whose well-worn shabbiness looked strangely out of keeping with the other furniture. On it was the litter of coils and wire and drilled ebonite of a radio set in course of construction. Andy ran over to the desk and began pulling open the drawers. Tools of all kinds, various gauges of wire and screws, odd wheels and sleeves and bolts and scraps of sheet iron and brass – all the junk which accumulates around an amateur mechanic's workshop. Then he came to a drawer that was locked. Without hesitation he grabbed up a large screwdriver, rammed it in about the lock, and splintered the drawer open, with a skilful wrench and an unexpected effort of strength.

Kestry let out a shout and started across the room. Andy's hand dived into the drawer, came out with a nickel-plated revolver. It was exactly the same as the one with which Lewis Enstone had shot himself. Andy turned the muzzle of the gun close up to his right eye, with his thumb on the trigger, exactly as Enstone must have held it. Kestry lurched forward and knocked the weapon spinning, with a sweep of his arm; then he grabbed Andy by his coat lapels and lifted him off his feet.

'If you pull any more of that stuff you're gonna have to get busted on the jaw.'

Andy looked up at him and smiled.

'But, George, that was the gun Enstone thought he was playing with!'

The Japanese servant was under a table with the telephone. Kestry let go of Andy and yanked him out, displaying his badge.

'I'm from Police Headquarters, all right,' he growled. 'When I want you to telephone I'll tell you.'

He swung back to Andy. 'Now – what's this you're getting at?'

'The gun, George. Enstone's toy.'

Andy went and picked it up again. He put it to his eye and pulled the trigger – pulled it, released it, pulled it again, keeping up the rhythmic movement. Something inside the gun whirred smoothly, as if wheels were whizzing round under the working of the lever. Then he pointed the gun straight into Kestry's face and did the same thing. Kestry stared frozenly down the barrel and saw the black hole leap into a circle of light. He was looking at a flickering cinematographic film of a boy shooting a masked burglar. It was tiny, puerile in subject, but perfect. It lasted about ten seconds, and then the barrel went dark again.

'Costello's present for Enstone's little boy,' said Andy, quietly. 'He invented it and made it himself, of course – he always had a talent that way. Haven't you seen those electric flashlights that work without a battery? You keep squeezing a lever, and it turns a miniature dynamo. Costello made a very small one, and fitted it into the hollow casing of a gun. Then he geared a tiny strip of film in with it. It was a good new toy, George, and he must have been proud of it. They took it along to Enstone's; and when he'd turned down their merger and there was nothing else for them to do, they let him play with it just enough to tickle his palate, at just the right hour of the evening. Then they took it away from him and put it back in its box and gave it to him. They

92

had a real gun in another box ready to make the switch.'

Kestry stood like a rock, clamping his cigar. Then he said: 'How did they know he wouldn't shoot his son, Andy?'

'That was Hammel. He knew that Enstone wasn't capable of keeping his hands off a toy like that; and just to make certain, he reminded Enstone of it the last thing before they left. He was a practical psychologist.'

Andy Herrick ran his fingers through his hair and fished a cigarette out of his pocket. 'I got all that out of a stool-pigeon, George,' he announced modestly.

Kestry swallowed painfully, and picked up the telephone.

Leslie Charteris (1907–93) *published his first novel,* X Esquire, *in 1927. The following year, his third book,* Meet the Tiger, *introduced Simon Templar, otherwise known as 'The Saint'. Templar is essentially a modern Robin Hood and his exploits in a lengthy series of novels achieved international popularity long before the successful 1960s television series starring Roger Moore. Charteris was awarded the CWA Cartier Diamond Dagger in 1992.*

JOHN CREASEY

The Chief Witness

1

The child lay listening to the raised, angry voices. He was a little frightened, because he had never heard his mother and father quarrel so. Quarrel, yes; but nothing like this. Nor had he known such silence or such awkward handling from his mother while he had been washed and put to bed.

He was six; a babyish rather than a boyish six.

He could hear them in the next room, now his father, shouting, next his mother, shouting back. Once she screamed out words he understood, but most of the time there was harsh shrillness, or the rough, hard tones of his father.

He had not known that they could make such noise, for they were always so gentle.

The child lay fighting sleep, and fearful, longing for a gleam of light to break the darkness, or for a sound at the door to herald their coming, but there was no relief for him that way.

There was relief of a kind.

The voices stilled, and the child almost held his breath, not wanting to hear the ugly sounds again. He did not. He heard the sharp slam of a door – then, his mother crying.

Crying.

Soon sleep came over the child in great, soothing waves which he could not resist. The darkness lost its terror, the longing for the door to open faded away into oblivion.

2

Usually, the child woke first in this household, and waking was gentle and welcome. This morning was no different. There was spring's early morning light, bright yet not glaring, for the morning sun did not shine into this room. But there was the garden, the lawn he could play on, the red metal swing, the wide flower bed along one side, the vegetable garden at the far end, rows of green soldiers in dark, freshly turned soil.

From his bed, which was near the window, he stared pensively at the heads of several daffodils which he had plucked off yesterday. He frowned, then turned his attention to the small gilt clock on the mantelpiece. When the hands pointed to half-past six, he was allowed to get up and play quietly; at seven, if neither his mother nor his father had been in to see him, he could go and wake them.

The position of the clock's hands puzzled him. He could not tell the time, except when it was between half-past six and seven – which it ought to be by now.

Disappointed, he reached for a much-thumbed book,

and began to look at the familiar pictures of animals, and to puzzle and stumble over the unfamiliar words. In a cooing voice he read to himself in this way, until abruptly he looked at the clock again.

The hands were in exactly the same position. Obviously this was wrong. He studied them earnestly, then raised his head with a new, cheering thought. A smile brightened his eyes and softened his mouth and he said:

'It's stopped.'

He got out of bed and went to the window, his jersey-type pyjamas rucked up about one leg and exposing part of his little round belly. He pressed his nose against the window and for a few minutes his attention was distracted by starlings, sparrows and thrushes. One starling pecked at a worm cast, quite absorbing to the boy, until his attention was distracted by a fly which buzzed against the inside of the window. He slapped at it with his pink hand, and every time it flew off, he gave the happy chuckle of the carefree.

Suddenly, he pivoted round and looked at the clock. Birds, fly and joy forgotten, he pattered swiftly to the door. He opened it cautiously and softly on to the small living-room.

All the familiar things were there.

He looked at the clock on the wall, and was astonished, for the hands told him at least that it was past seven. Eagerly, happily, he crossed to his parents' room, and opened the door.

Silence greeted him.

His mother lay on her back in bed, with her eyes closed. The bedclothes were drawn high beneath her chin, and her arms were underneath the clothes. There were other unusual features about the room, which he saw with a child's eye, but did not think about.

His father was not by his mother's side.

He went to the bed, and called: 'Mummy.' His mother did not stir. He called her again and again and when she took no notice, he touched her face, her cold, cold face, not wondering why it was so cold.

'Mummy.'

'Mummy, Mummy, Mummy.'

Soon, he gave up.

3

For Chief Inspector Roger West of New Scotland Yard, it was a normal morning. There was too much to do; like the rest of the Criminal Investigation Department's staff, he was used to that, and dealt with each report, each query and each memo with complete detachment. He was between cases, having just prepared a serious one for the Director of Public Prosecutions. Whenever he took his mind off the documents on his desk, he wondered what he would have to tackle next.

'Mr Cortland would like a word with you, sir.'

This would be the job. With a nod to the messenger, Roger went at once, to Superintendent Cortland's office.

'Looks pretty well cut and dried,' said the massive, dark-haired, aging Cortland, sixty to Roger's forty. 'Woman found strangled, out at Putney. When a milkman called, a child opened the door and said he couldn't wake his mother. The milkman went to find out why. The child is with a neighbour now. The family's name is Pirro, an Italian name, and here's the address — 29 Greyling Crescent. It's the end house or bungalow, fairly new — but you'll soon know all about it. Better go to Division first; they'll fix anything you want. Let me know if you need help from me.'

'Thanks,' said Roger, and went out, brisk and alert. He collected his case from his office, and hurried down to his car.

It was then a little after eleven o'clock.

An hour later he approached the bungalow in Greyling Crescent, with misgivings which always came whenever a case involved a child. Most policemen feel the same but, partly because his own sons were still young, he was acutely sensitive. He had learned a little more about the Pirro child from Divisional officers, who were only too glad to hand the inquiry over to a Yard man. It was apparent that everyone saw this as a clear-cut job; husband-and-wife quarrel, murder, flight. From the Divisional Headquarters Roger had telephoned Cortland, asking him to put out a call for Pirro — an accountant with a small firm of general merchants — who might, of course, be at his daily job in a city office.

The bungalow was dull; four walls, square windows which looked as if they had been sawn out of reddish brown bricks, brown tiles and brown paint. It had been dumped down on a piece of wasteland, and the nearest neighbouring houses were fifty years old, tall, grey and drab.

But the front garden transformed the bungalow.

In the centre a small lawn was trim and neat as a

billiard table. About this were beds of flowers, each a segment of a circle, alternating clustered daffodils, wall-flowers, bushy and bright as azaleas, and polyanthus so large and full of bloom that Roger had to look twice to make sure what they were.

Two police cars, two uniformed policemen and about twenty neighbours were near the front door. Roger nodded and half-smiled at the policemen as he went in, and was received inside by Moss, of the Division, an old friend and an elderly, cautious detective, with whom he exchanged warm greetings.

'Our surgeon called the pathologist. He's in the bedroom now – hardly been there five minutes.'

'I'll wait.'

'Do you good!' grinned Moss. 'P'raps you'd like to fill in the time by finding Pirro for us!'

'Sure you want him?' asked Roger.

'Oh, we want him.'

'Seen in the act of murder, was he?'

'Damned nearly.'

'Who by?'

'A neighbour,' Moss said. 'The son's with her now. For once we've got a woman who doesn't get into a flap because we're around.' Moss was leading the way to an open door, beyond which men were moving and shadows appearing to the accompaniment of quiet sounds. 'She was taking her dog for a walk last night, nine-ish, and heard Pirro and his wife at it. Says she's never heard a row like it.'

'I'll have a word with her later,' Roger said. 'How about the boy?'

Moss shrugged, drawing attention to his thick, broad shoulders.

'Doesn't realise what's happened, of course, and thinks his mother's still asleep. Poor sort of a future for him, I gather. No known relatives. Pirro's an Italian by birth, the neighbours know nothing about his background. The dead woman once mentioned that she lost her parents years ago, and was an only child.'

'Found any documents?' Roger asked.

'A few. Not much to write home about,' Moss said. 'Ordinary enough couple, I'd say. Hire purchase agreements for the furniture, monthly payments made regularly. Birth certificates for the mother and child, naturalisation papers for Pirro, death certificates for Mrs Pirro's parents; the dead woman was born Margent. Evelyn Ethel Margent. Age twenty-seven.' Moss pointed. 'There's a family photograph over there, taken this year, I'd say. The kid looks about the same.'

The photograph was a studio one, in sepia, and the parents and child were all a little set; posed too stiffly. The woman was pleasant to look at, the man had a dark handsomeness; she looked as English as he looked south European.

The child, unexpectedly, was nothing like either. He had a plain, round face, with a much bigger head, proportionately, than either man or woman, big, startled eyes, and very thin arms.

'Did you say you'd seen the child's birth certificate?' Roger asked.

'Yes.'

'All normal?'

'Take a look and see.'

There it was: father, Anthony Pirro, mother Evelyn Ethel, maiden name Margent, date—

'What's the date on the marriage certificate?' Roger asked, and Moss handed the certificate to him. 'Thanks. February 7th, 1950, and the child was born October 1st, 1950.'

'Must have got married for love anyway,' Moss said. 'They couldn't have known for sure the kid was on the way when they got spliced.'

'No. Let's have a look round,' Roger said, and still kept out of the bedroom.

He went into each small room and the kitchen, and everywhere was spick-and-span, except for the morning's dust. For a small suburban house, the furniture was good and in excellent taste. Here was a home that was loved, where happiness should live.

The door of the bedroom was opened and the pathologist – who turned out to be Dr Sturgeon, another old friend – beckoned to Roger.

Death had not spoiled Mrs Pirro's pleasant face, except for the dark, browny bruises at her throat.

Photographers and a fingerprint man were finishing.

'Well, Handsome!' Sturgeon's smile was placatory. 'You'll want to know too much too soon. Better wait until I've done the PM.'

'All right, Dick! When did she die?'

Sturgeon pursed and puckered his full lips.

'Some time between eight o'clock last night and midnight.'

'Playing safe, aren't you?' Roger commented drily, and

studied the woman's pale, untroubled face. He was hard-ened to the sight of death, in the young as well as the old, yet Evelyn Pirro stirred him to deep pity. Add the bright gaiety of life to her features, and one would see a kind of beauty.

'Any other injuries?' Roger asked.

'None that I've noticed yet.'

'General condition?'

'Excellent.'

'Any sign of another child?'

'No. You're a rum 'un,' Sturgeon added, thoughtfully. 'What put that into your head?'

'Go and have a look at the family photograph in the next room and also have a look round,' Roger advised. 'That might give you some ideas. Then you'd better take her away.'

'Photographs finished?' he asked the youthful, red-faced photographer who had been standing by.

'Yes, sir.'

'Good. Fingerprints any good?' Roger asked a tall and sallow man who had a little dank, grey hair.

'Three sets.' The man nodded at the bed. 'Hers, another set, probably a man's, and the child's.'

'Anything else?'

'No, sir.'

'Forced entry, or anything like that?'

'I checked the windows and doors,' Moss answered.

'Thanks,' said Roger.

'What I want to know is, why did it happen?' Moss said, suddenly. 'Look at the house, and the way it's kept. What makes a man come home and kill his wife and run out on his kid?'

'You couldn't be more right. We want the motive as badly as we want Pirro,' Roger agreed, almost sententiously.

The morning sun caught his face and hair as he stood by the window looking out on to the back garden. There the lawn was less trim than that at the front, obviously because the child had been allowed to play on it. There were bare dirt patches beneath a metal swing, which showed bright red in the bright light. Roger studied all this, and considered the evidence of what he had seen and heard, only vaguely aware that Moss, Sturgeon and the others had taken time to study him. He looked strikingly handsome, with his fair, wavy hair, and features set and grim just now, as if something of this tragedy touched him personally.

Then he caught sight of a movement in a garden beyond a patch of wasteland; brightness, a flash of scarlet, and soon a woman, calling:

'Tony! . . . Tony!'

But she was too late, for a child in a red jersey had started to climb a wooden fence, the stakes of which were several inches apart, nimble and sure-footed. The woman hurried after him, tall, pleasant-faced, anxious.

'Tony, don't fall!'

'I won't fall,' the boy said clearly, as Roger opened the French windows and stepped outside.

At sight of Roger, the child stopped. The sun touched him on one side, and made his fair hair look silky and bright. His fair, round face was puzzled. One long leg was this side of the fence, and he held on to the top firmly with both small hands.

The neighbour caught up with him.

'Who is that man?' he demanded firmly. 'Is it a doctor?'

'Tony, please . . .'

'Is it a doctor come to wake Mummy up?'

So they had not yet told the child the truth!

Roger felt quite sure that they should soon. It was false kindness not to, and it would probably shock and surprise soft-hearted people to find how calmly the child would take the news. Six was a strangely impersonal age, when such hurts could be absorbed without outward sign of injury.

'I'll call you when the doctor comes,' the woman promised.

She was nice. Fifty-ish, with dark hair turning grey, a full figure, a navy blue dress. Her hand was firm on the child's thin shoulder, and he turned away from Roger and climbed down.

'I'm sorry, but I'm not a doctor,' Roger said, and won a grave scrutiny.

Then Moss called out quietly from the French windows.

'I'll have to go,' Roger went on gravely. 'Goodbye for now.'

'Goodbye, sir!' the child said, and Roger turned away thoughtfully, and went to Moss.

'What's on?'

'We've just had a flash from the Yard, a message from Keeling and Keeling – Pirro's office. He hasn't turned up this morning.'

'Right!' said Roger. 'I'll come and talk to the Yard.'

He moved swiftly, suddenly decisive, and the sight of the

stretcher being pushed into the ambulance did not make him pause. He slid into his own car, noticing that the crowd had swollen to forty or fifty. Windows were open at the drab houses, women stood at their front doors. Roger flicked on his radio, and when the Yard Information Room answered he asked for Mr Cortland.

A small car swung into the crescent and stopped abruptly, and two men got out: newspapermen, one with a camera. Roger watched them as he waited.

'What are you after, West?' Cortland demanded.

'I'd like the whole works here,' Roger said promptly. 'Enough men to question all the neighbours, and to try to find out exactly what time Pirro left home last night. Quick inquiry at his office, too, to find out if he's been nervy lately. Check on any boyfriends his wife might have had just before they married, and whether any old flame has come on the scene again lately. How about it?'

'Take what men you need, but release 'em as soon as you can.' Cortland was almost curt.

'Thanks,' said Roger.

Soon it was all on the move. Detectives from the Yard and the Division swarmed the crescent, neighbour after neighbour was questioned, statement after statement was made and written down.

Roger himself went to see the neighbour who was looking after the boy, and heard her story first-hand; it was simple enough and exactly what Moss had already told him. The woman, a Mrs Frost, was calm and obviously capable; frank, too.

'I'll gladly look after the boy for a few days, but I

don't know what's likely to happen after that,' she said. 'Mrs Pirro had often told me she had no relations.'

'And her husband?'

'She knew of none, anyhow.'

'Did they often quarrel, Mrs Frost?' Roger asked without warning.

'I've never known a more contented couple, and I've seldom heard a wry word,' she said. 'It was almost too good to be true. They both doted on Tony, too.'

'Has anything unusual happened recently?'

Mrs Frost, the nice woman, hesitated as if she didn't quite know how to answer; but Roger did not need to prompt her.

'Not really, except one thing, and I feel beastly even mentioning it, but she had a visitor yesterday morning. Tony was at school, of course. I saw a man drive up in a small car, and go in, and—' Mrs Frost paused, but set confusion quickly aside. 'I dare say you'll think I'm being catty, but I was surprised. It was a young man, and he was there for at least two hours. He left just before Mrs Pirro went to fetch Tony from school.'

She had never seen the caller before and hadn't noticed much about him, except that he was tall and fair. There was no way even of guessing whether the visitor had anything to do with what had happened.

Roger left her, without seeing the child, had a word with Moss, and then went to Keeling and Keeling's offices, in Fenchurch Street, in the City. It was the third floor of an old, dark building with an open-sided lift and an elderly one-armed attendant.

Pirro had not come back.

107

Pirro had been quite normal all of yesterday, his short, stoutish employer asserted. An exemplary worker. A happy man. No interests outside his home. In receipt of a good salary. Special friends? No, no confidants here, either. Kept himself to himself. By all means question the staff, if it would help.

There were thirteen members of the staff. Two men seemed to have known Pirro rather better than the others, and the picture of the man became clearer in Roger's mind. Pirro brought sandwiches to lunch every day, went straight home every night, was passionately devoted to his wife, doted on the child.

It was impossible to believe that he had killed his wife, they said. *Impossible.*

Did anyone know where his wife had worked before her marriage?

Of course; at an office on the floor below – Spencer's.

Roger went there, to find a benign-looking, round-headed elderly man who made a living out of selling insurance; obviously a good living, too. Did he remember Evelyn Margent? A *charming* girl, and most capable. Surely no *trouble*? So devoted to her Italian young man! Other boyfriends? We-*ell* – was there anything wrong in a boyfriend or two before marriage? Surely it was customary, even wise? What girl knew her mind while she was in her teens?

'Mr Spencer, do you know if Mrs Pirro had an affair just before her marriage?' Roger was now almost curt, for benignity could be too bland. This man's round head and round face worried him, too; by now Sturgeon would know why.

'As a matter of fact, Chief Inspector, yes, she did. But I insist that it was perfectly normal, and certainly no harm came of it.'

'With whom, please?'

Spencer became haughty. 'With my son, Chief Inspector.'

'Thank you,' Roger said. 'Have you a photograph of your son here, Mr Spencer?'

'I really cannot see the purpose of such an inquiry. My son—'

Spencer didn't finish, but lost a little of his blandness, opened a drawer in an old-fashioned desk, and took out several photographs: of a woman and a boy, the woman and a youth, the woman and a young man perhaps in his early thirties.

'There is my wife and son, Chief Inspector, at various ages. Take your choice.'

Roger studied the photographs impassively. He did not speak for some time, although he already knew exactly what he wanted to ask next. Spencer's son, over the years, was fair-haired and round-faced; and in the photograph of him as a child, he was remarkably like little Tony Pirro.

'Thank you, Mr Spencer,' Roger said at last. 'Will you be good enough to tell me where your son is?'

'He should be here at any time,' Spencer said, and his own round face was red with an embarrassment, perhaps distress, that he couldn't hide. 'He is my partner in business. Why do you want to see him, Chief Inspector?'

'I would like to know whether he has seen Mrs Pirro recently.'

Spencer was now a harassed, resigned man.

'I can tell you that,' he said. 'Yes, Chief Inspector, he has. It is a long story, an unhappy story. By dismal chance he saw Mrs Pirro and her son only a few days ago. He – he told me about it. He was in great distress, very great distress. The likeness—'

'Likeness?'

'You are a man of the world, Chief Inspector, and there is no point in beating about the bush. My son and Mrs Pirro were once on terms of intimacy – her marriage to Pirro was a great shock. A *great* shock! He did not dream that her child was *his* child, but he told me that once he saw them together, it was beyond all doubt. Naturally, he wanted to see his son. He was quite prepared to do so without disturbing Mrs Pirro's domestic life, but it was more than flesh and blood could stand not to see – his own child! All last evening he talked to me about it. My advice was that he should try to put everything out of his mind, but I doubt if he ever will. It's a great tragedy, there is positively no other word for it.'

'Has he seen Mrs Pirro since the chance encounter?'

'Oh, yes! He went there yesterday morning. He – but here is Charles, he can speak for himself.'

Charles Spencer came in, and the likeness between him and Mrs Pirro's son put the identity of the father beyond any reasonable doubt.

4

'Dead,' echoed Charles Spencer, just two minutes later. 'Evelyn *dead*?' He looked from Roger to his father, and back again, as if unbelieving. 'But *how*?'

'That's what I'm trying to establish, Mr Spencer,' Roger said.

'It's fantastic! I can't believe it. She – she didn't give me the slightest indication.' The round face was red in this man's own kind of dismay.

'Indication of what, Mr Spencer?'

'That she would do away with herself! She – she agreed that as I knew about the boy I couldn't be expected to lose sight of him. It's dreadful. It—'

'Mrs Pirro was murdered, Mr Spencer.'

'Oh, my God,' breathed Charles Spencer. 'Oh, my God.' Then, as if the words were wrung from him: 'She said he'd kill her if he ever found out.'

Roger went into Cortland's office about six o'clock that evening.

'Still no sign of Pirro,' he said abruptly. 'Will you give the okay to put that call for him all over the country?'

'Can do. What's worrying you?'

'I'd rather he didn't kill himself before we get him,' Roger said, brusquely.

Cortland gave the order on the telephone.

'Now, what've you got so far?'

A summary of the investigation took twenty minutes in the telling. Cortland listened attentively, and made little comment, beyond:

'Well, it's all adding up. You've found two neighbours who saw Spencer go there yesterday morning, three who heard last night's quarrel, two who saw Pirro leave just after nine-fifteen. Any doubt about that time?'

'No. It was just after a television programme. The

neighbours, husband and wife, took their dog for an airing.'

'Seems straightforward enough,' Cortland said. 'We've had a few false reports that Pirro's been seen, but that's all. Seldom went anywhere else, as you know; just a home bird!' Cortland handed over some papers. 'We've got his history.'

Roger scanned the papers.

Pirro's parents had settled in England a little before the war; when they had died, he had been sixteen, and had already spent most of his life in England. There were details about people he and his parents had known, much to show that Pirro had always been regarded as wholly trustworthy. During the war, he had worked with the Civil Defence.

'None of the people who knew him then seem to have kept in touch,' said Cortland. 'But you know pretty well all there is about him since he got married, don't you?'

'Yes,' admitted Roger. 'We've got an even-tempered, home-loving man, no outside interests, nice wife, apparently thoroughly happy, who comes home one night and is heard shouting and raving, for the first time ever. That morning, the wife's old lover had appeared, and we now know he was the child's father. So—'

'If Mrs Pirro decided to tell her husband the truth, that could explain what happened,' Cortland interrupted. 'Enough to drive a man of Pirro's kind off his rocker, too, and it's easy to go too far. We'll soon pick him up, and he'll—'

'I hope we don't pick his body out of a river,'

Roger said gruffly. 'I'm trying to think where a man in his position would go in such a crisis. Home wrecked and life wrecked. Where—' He broke off, and snapped his fingers. 'I wonder where they spent their honeymoon.'

'Margate, probably,' Cortland commented drily.

'Mrs Frost would know,' said Roger. 'I'll have the Division ask her.' He saw Cortland's grin at his impatience, but that didn't worry him. All he wanted was an answer, and one soon came: the Pirros had honeymooned in Bournemouth.

It was almost an anti-climax when Pirro was picked up on the cliffs at Bournemouth late that evening.

'All alive, too,' Cortland jeered.

'That could be a good thing,' Roger said. 'Does he know why he's been picked up?'

'No.'

'When did he go, has he said?'

'Last night's mail train – 10.42 from Waterloo. He went to Putney Station, was seen hanging about for twenty minutes or so, caught a train to Waterloo for the 10.42 to Bournemouth, with a few minutes to spare.'

'I'll go down and get him,' said Roger.

5

Pirro was smaller than Roger had expected, but even better-looking than in his photograph, a short, compact man with jet black hair, and fine, light blue eyes which made him quite striking. His lips were set and taut and his hands were clenched as he jumped up from a chair when Roger and a Bournemouth detective entered the room where he was guarded by a uniformed policeman; but he didn't speak.

'Good evening, Mr Pirro,' Roger greeted mildly. 'I am Chief Inspector West of New Scotland Yard, and I would like you to answer a few questions.'

'Is it not time you answered questions?' Pirro demanded, with restrained anger. 'Why am I kept here? Why am I treated as a criminal? I demand an answer.'

His English had a slight trace of an accent, and was a little too precisely uttered; that was all.

There was only one way; to use shock tactics. Roger used them, roughly, abruptly:

'Anthony Pirro, it is my duty to arrest you in connection with the murder of your wife, Mrs Evelyn Ethel Pirro, at about ten o'clock last night, and I must inform you that anything you say will be written down and may be used in evidence.'

Pirro started violently; then his expression and his whole body seemed to go slack, and suddenly a new expression came into his eyes. Did he will that expression? Had he carefully and cunningly prepared for this moment of crisis?

His next reaction took both Roger and the Bournemouth men by surprise. He leapt forward as if to attack, snatched at Roger's hands and gripped his wrists tightly.

'You are lying. She is not dead,' he said fiercely. 'You are lying.'

His body quivered, his white teeth clenched, his fingers dug into Roger's wrists.

'You know very well she is dead,' Roger said coldly, nodding the Bournemouth man to stand back.

'No!' cried Pirro, as if real horror touched him now. 'No, she is not dead, she cannot be. I pushed her away from me, that is all. I felt that I hated her, but *dead*—'

It was an hour before he could talk rationally, and much that he said was obviously true. His wife had told him the truth about the child, and in the rage and hurt of the revelation, Pirro had wished both her and himself dead, had raved and cursed her, had struck her and stormed out of their home. But—

'I did not kill her,' he said in a hushed voice. 'When I came here I knew she remained everything to me. I could not live without her . . .

'I *cannot* live without her,' he went on abruptly. 'It is not possible.' Then calmness took possession of him, as if he knew that further denials were useless, and did not really matter.

'The child?' Roger asked.

'He is not mine,' said Pirro. 'I have no wife and I have no son.'

6

'Well, you've got everything you can expect,' Cortland said, next afternoon, at the Yard. 'Motive, opportunity, and an admission that he struck her. He could have had a brainstorm and not remember choking the life out of her. Don't tell me you're not satisfied.'

'I'm still not happy about it,' Roger said. 'Pirro closed up completely when he realised his wife was dead, and behaved as if nothing mattered after that. He hasn't said a word since. We've checked that he caught the 10.42 from Waterloo to Bournemouth. He seems to have retraced the steps he and his wife took on their honeymoon. They loved each other so much for so long that I feel I must find out exactly what happened to cause all this.'

'If he won't talk, who will?' Cortland demanded.

'The child might,' Roger said slowly. 'I wanted to avoid it, but I'm going to question him.'

Little Tony Pirro looked up into Roger's face, his own grey eyes grave and earnest. He stood by the chair in the living-room of the bungalow, and Roger sat back, a cigarette in his hand, aware that Mrs Frost was anxious and disapproving in the kitchen, with the door ajar. Tony had said: 'Good morning, sir,' with well-learned politeness, and waited until Roger said:

'Do you know who I am, Tony?'

'Yes, sir. You are a policeman.'

'That's right. Do you know why I'm here?'

'Aunt May said you were going to ask me some questions.'

'That's right, too. They're important questions.'

'I know. They're about my mummy being ill.'

'Ill?'

'Yes, she's very ill, you know. The doctor said she was going to die,' announced Tony, with no inflection in his voice, 'but it won't hurt her.'

Damn good doctor!

'It won't hurt at all,' Roger assured the child. 'Did you see her last night?'

116

'No; I was living here, with Mrs Frost.'

'When was the last time you saw her?'

'Oh, lots of times.'

'Can you remember the very last time?'

'Yes, of course.'

'When was it, Tony?'

'Not last night, but the night before that.'

'Where were you?' asked Roger, almost awkwardly.

'In my bedroom.'

Roger's eyes widened as if in surprise.

'Have you a whole bedroom all to yourself?'

'Oh, yes.' Tony's eyes lit up, and he turned and pointed. 'It's over there.'

'I'd like to see it,' Roger said, and got up. 'Will you show me?'

'Oh, yes,' said Tony eagerly. 'It's a big room, and Daddy papered the walls specially for my birthday.'

He went, hurrying, to open the door on to the small room, with the Robin Hood *motifs* on the walls, the bed, the toys, the books. He stood proudly, waiting for Roger's look of surprised approval, and also waiting on his words.

'Well!' Roger breathed. 'This is wonderful! Robin *Hood*, too. Look at him! I hope he won't shoot you with his bow and arrow.'

'Oh, he won't; he's only a picture,' Tony announced, as a statement, not reproof.

'Oh, of course,' Roger said, and continued to look round for several minutes, before asking: 'Did Mummy come in to say good night, the night before last?'

'Yes.'

'Like she always does.'

117

'Yes.'

'Was she ill then?'

'No,' said Tony, thoughtfully. 'She wasn't ill, but she wasn't happy like she usually is.'

'Oh, what a pity! How do you know?'

'She was crying.'

'Did she cry very much?'

'No, only a little bit; she didn't want me to see.'

'Did she cry very often?' Roger persisted.

'Well, only sometimes.'

'When did she usually cry, Tony?'

'When Daddy was ill,' Tony said, very simply. 'It was Christmas, and Daddy had to see the doctor.'

'Did she ever cry when Daddy was well?'

'Oh, no, *never.*'

'That's good. When she cried the night before last, was Daddy here?'

'No; Daddy wasn't home then.'

'Did you hear him come home?'

'Oh, yes, I always recognise his footsteps, and Mummy does, too.'

'Did he come to you and say good night?'

'Yes.'

'Was he crying?'

'Oh, Daddy doesn't cry,' Tony said with proud emphasis. 'He's a man.'

'Of course, how silly of me! Was he happy that night?'

'He was happy with me,' Tony declared.

'The same as usual?'

'Just the same.'

'Was he happy with Mummy?'

'Well, he was at first,' Tony said quietly, and then went on without any prompting: 'Then he shouted at Mummy, ever so loud. It woke me up, and I listened for ever such a long time. Daddy shouted and shouted, and Mummy cried, and then *she* shouted back at him. I didn't like it, so I put my head right under the bedclothes.'

'That was a good idea. When you took it out again, were they still shouting?'

'Well, yes, they were.'

'Both of them?'

'Well, no,' said Tony, after a pause. 'Only Daddy was.'

'Did you hear Mummy at all?'

'She was crying again.'

'Was she crying very much?'

'Well, quite a lot, really.'

'How long did Daddy shout at her?'

'Not long, then. He went out.'

'How do you know?'

'Well, I heard him bang the door, and walk along the street. He was going ever so fast.'

'Was he by himself?'

'Oh, yes.'

'Didn't Mummy go with him?'

'She just cried and cried,' Tony said, quite dispassionately. 'And then she went all quiet. I thought she'd gone to sleep; I didn't know she was ill.'

'Tony,' said Roger, very softly, 'I want you to think very carefully about this. Did your mummy cry after your daddy banged the door?'

'Oh, yes, like I told you.'

'Did she cry a lot?'

'Ever such a lot.'

'Did she come and see you then?'

'No; she didn't.'

'What did happen?'

'I just went to sleep,' Tony said, with the same complete detachment, 'and when I went to see Mummy in the morning, she wouldn't wake up.'

'I see,' said Roger, and he had to fight to keep from showing his excitement to this child. 'Thank you very much for answering my questions so nicely. I'm going away now, but I'll see you again soon.'

In the next room, he asked the sergeant who had been there with a notebook: 'Get all that?'

'Every word, sir.'

'Fine!' enthused Roger. 'The child says that his mother cried after Pirro left! If that's true, she was alive when he went out. I'd believe that Pirro would kill his wife in a rage, but not that he'd go out, cool down, and come back and kill her in cold blood.'

The Yard and the Division put every man they could spare on to the inquiry. Results weren't long in coming.

Charles Spencer had left his father's Chelsea House at half-past nine on the night of the murder, giving him ample time to get to the Putney bungalow in time to kill Mrs Pirro. His car had been noticed in a main road near the bungalow. He had been seen walking towards Greyling Crescent. No one had actually seen him enter the bungalow, but he had been seen driving off in the car an hour later.

By middle afternoon of that third day, Roger saw him at the Fenchurch Street office, the man so like his young son, protesting his innocence mildly at first, then indignant, then angry, eventually frightened, his round face reddening, his big, strong hands clenching and unclenching.

'Mr Spencer, I want to know why you went to see Mrs Pirro that night, and what happened while you were there,' Roger insisted coldly.

'Supposing I did see her for a few minutes; that's no crime! I went to see that she was okay. She was perfectly well when I left her. Her brute of a husband had run out on her, she was terrified in case he'd come back and do her some harm. And he came back and strangled her, he—'

'No, he didn't,' Roger said flatly. 'He walked to Putney Station, waited twenty minutes for a train to Waterloo, then caught the mail train to Bournemouth, the ten forty-two. He couldn't possibly have had time to go back to the bungalow. Mr Spencer, why did you kill Mrs Pirro?'

'Damn good thing you decided to tackle the child again,' Cortland said, on the following day. 'How about motive? Made any sense of it yet?'

'It's showing up clearly,' Roger told him. 'Spencer always hated Pirro for taking his mistress away from him. When he discovered the child, all the old resentment boiled up. I doubt if we'll ever know whether he meant to kill Mrs Pirro; he might have gone there to try to get back to the old relationship, and hurt Pirro that way. Whatever the motive, we've got him tight.'

'Only bad thing left is that kid's future,' Cortland said gruffly.

'Pirro's going to see him tonight,' Roger said, thought-fully. 'A man of his kind of heart-searching honesty can't throw six years away so easily. You get fond of a child in six weeks, never mind six years. I'm really hopeful, anyhow.'

'Fine,' Cortland said, more heartily. 'Now, there's a job out at Peckham—'

John Creasey (1908–73) *famously accumulated 743 rejection slips before publishing his first novel in 1932. After that there was no stopping him and, maintaining an extraordinary rate of productivity up to his death, he published over 500 novels as well as many short stories. A man of astonishing energy, he not only conceived and set up the CWA, but also found time to establish his own mystery magazine and even a political party. His many series characters include the Scotland Yard Detective George Gideon, and John Mannering, alias 'The Baron', both of whose exploits were turned into television series.*

LIONEL DAVIDSON

Indian Rope Trick

The Spey is one of the greatest of the great Scottish east coast rivers. Its rate of flow is the fastest of any major river in the United Kingdom. Below Grantown it begins to swell into a big river flowing mostly through a dramatic and precipitous valley where it rushes and boils between a mixture of boulders and sandbanks.

Bang on, thought Waring. That was exactly what it was doing. He could hear it. He was sitting and reading about it. He was doing this in a comfortable chair, in a comfortable lounge, some hundreds of yards from where the boiling and rushing was going on. Even at this distance the tumult of the mighty river was like an engine in the air. It excited him. He sensed great salmon beating up it, in darkness, in snow. *And doing it right now.* Right now Waring wanted to go out in the dark and see them.

However, he didn't. It was months since his operation but he still tired easily. He took a sip of whisky instead; an extra big sip.

'Darling,' his wife said warningly.

'Don't fuss.'

'Your heart will race.'

'Nag.' But he laid whisky and book aside. 'They do it to one,' he told Nigel.

'They want to hang on to one,' Nigel said.

Nigel looked sleepy; contentedly sleepy. Nigel had fished the Blackrock today and got three fine springers; now sacked and ready for smoking in Aberdeen. Waring had fished the smaller pool and had got nothing. His turn for the Blackrock tomorrow!

Again the sound of the river excited him and again he wanted to go out in the dark to it.

'What I wouldn't mind having a dab at in the morning,' he said to Estelle, 'is the Indian rope trick. If you feel up to it.'

'If *you're* up to it, and the river's up to it.'

'It's what I'd like,' he said.

'Brucie won't,' Nigel said.

'Bugger Brucie.'

'Brucie rules.' Brucie was the gillie.

'Not on our beat.'

Nigel's beat, actually. A beautiful little beat, two rods, syndicate water. By chance Nigel had managed to buy into it years before. The firm had held the syndicate covered against legal costs arising from accidents. When the scion of a tobacco family had managed to drown himself in the Blackrock Nigel had handled the matter and had been in a position to jump the queue and buy the scion's water; for the first two weeks of April. They had been coming up every year since.

'If the snow keeps up,' Estelle said, 'won't it do something to the water? Then there'll be no tricks of any kind.'

'Not this snow,' Waring said. 'It's settling.' But he didn't mind what it did. Snow-melt, peat-stain. He looked forward to using some big gaudy flies in it. A Thunder-and-Lightning, a flashy great Childers. Above all he looked forward to the Indian rope trick.

He felt very happy.

He felt happy just looking forward. Months ago there had been nothing to look forward to. Yet he hadn't minded. In this incredible year he had learned an incredible thing. Dying, he found that though he enjoyed what he had, he didn't mind seeing it all go. It was easy to die; everybody did it; a common affair. But now he had his life back he liked it. He appreciated it more. He appreciated his wife Estelle, and her great qualities. With this year's huge bills and the unlikelihood of his working much longer, his appreciation had rocketed. Estelle's main great quality was her thirty thousand a year.

He had never really lied about it. She knew he didn't love her in the way that she wished to be loved. But she loved *him*. That was the main thing. And he had denied her nothing, while able. He had early discovered another curious truth. Sexually unattractive women were very big on sex. Dame Nature seemed to make them so: some fine adjustment perhaps in the handicapping before the great race for renewal. Whatever the reason, Estelle was certainly a tigress at it. She enjoyed it awfully.

Pondering this, he looked round the big hotel room and wondered if anyone could guess at the jumbo appetites in his smallish plain wife. The room was full of bores all yawning away at their own potty wives, so he looked away again in case one of them should come and talk to him.

He looked at Nigel and caught him having the most enormous yawn himself. All of Nigel was yawning, from the tips of his outstretched fingers right down to his feet. One of these feet, Waring noticed, was close to Estelle's. He had an impression that moments before it had been touching; also that Nigel's tremendous stretching of himself had less to do with actual weariness than with a kind of limbering-up.

OK, Waring thought. Situation under control. Much less OK would have been a situation not under control, one that he didn't even know about. This one he knew all about.

He had an idea that Estelle had actually wanted to tell him: to explain that it didn't *matter*; that it was just something she had to do; that he was the one she loved and cherished. And he would have been glad if she had said this because he knew she always spoke truthfully.

However, she hadn't said it, and in the tricky situation he couldn't help her to say it. In any case, though she might think it true now, he knew it wouldn't go on being true.

He knew a tremendous amount lately. Since his brush with death he seemed to know practically everything. He felt special knowledge of the imperatives of life, of the programmes laid down for all the living.

Lying in hospital, his life slipping away, he had watched all the people coming and going; coming and going so seriously about their business. He had watched as if from the wrong end of a telescope, and he thought what a silly game! He had enjoyed the game while playing it but he saw that it had no meaning. With his life restored, the joy of the game had returned. What had brought back meaning to the game? He didn't know. Yet mysteriously it was back. Its imperative was back – the same imperative that brought the salmon back, every year, to this river.

The great fish came battling in from the sea, from thousands of miles away, to find just this estuary, just this river, and struggle up it (through rapids, through waterfalls), to spawn where they themselves had been spawned. They couldn't help it, couldn't stop it, had to do it.

As with Estelle: who also had to do what she was doing. Perhaps she thought it just a passing affair, and perhaps it would have been. Except that on this trip, he had seen most plainly, she was growing fond of Nigel. And Nigel was evidently meeting her needs in bed. There was not much doing with *him* in the bed line lately; nothing at all, of course, during his illness, and very little since. He knew each night, after his sleeping draught, that she slipped out to Nigel's room, and he didn't grudge her. But he saw what would come of it.

Estelle was not a woman to go chasing after men. But Nigel didn't need chasing. He was there, and an old friend; and one who had been showing signs lately of wanting to settle down himself. Yes, he could see it all coming. She had a *need* for sex, and a dislike of deception. She would want to regularise her life, and slowly a dissatisfaction with him would grow. She loved him now; he didn't doubt it. As Nigel had said, she certainly wanted to hang on to him. She didn't know herself the blind force, the life imperative, that would at first weaken and then destroy the tie between them. But Waring knew. He knew such a lot now.

He was honest with himself and knew that if he had to choose between Estelle and her thirty thousand he would go for the thirty thousand; even if it meant the sad demise of Estelle. But he did not have this choice. Estelle's money was life money. No Estelle, no money.

He thought the best formula would be for Nigel to go and get a wife for himself, preferably one who also had thirty thousand of her own. But he knew Nigel was indolent and probably wouldn't. So he had lately revised the formula to a more abbreviated and manageable one.

Nigel would simply have to go.

Estelle had been picking up her knitting, and they were now walking through the lounge, offering cheerful goodnights to those remaining.

Outside he could hear the muffled thudding of the river. It was going like an engine: rushing, boiling. His heart raced, but he didn't mind. Indian rope trick tomorrow!

It was still dark after breakfast, and still a few minutes early, but Brucie was already waiting. He was waiting in the vestibule; standing like a tree in it, smoking his pipe. He had the carrier's note for the Aberdeen salmon-smokers.

'Morning, Brucie,' Nigel said, taking the note with pleasure. 'How's the water?'

'High,' Brucie said.

'Fishable?'

'A touch colour.'

'Is it cold?' Estelle said, shivering.

'Healthy,' Brucie said, and took his pipe out.

Estelle tightened the leather belt round her fur coat and pulled her hat over her ears. She knew Brucie meant germs would not survive such healthy conditions.

Brucie had removed his pipe to stare curiously at the coil of rope Waring was carrying. For a moment Waring almost explained. Then he remembered and thought Bugger Brucie, and led the way himself out to the car.

Brucie had de-snowed the car, but with all their breaths and his pipe going it misted up at once. Nigel turned everything on, engine, headlamps, wipers, blower, and in a mild uproar and fuggy discomfort they circled the wide gravel and went slowly out into the village.

The indigo light was paling into a kind of gunmetal. Snow lay everywhere and a few flakes still drifted in the air. Behind them other headlamps swung out of the hotel and turned away.

Nigel kept slowly on, through the village, and out of it, and up, and up, to the hut.

They parked a couple of hundred yards from the hut, and walked up to it through the undergrowth. The chimney was already smoking in the hut. Brucie didn't live in the place but left various bits of gear more or less permanently outside. He left them quite untended, knowing no hand dare touch them. His own ham-like hands were known in the vicinity. For the same reason he never bothered locking the hut. He just went right at it now and pushed the door in without a word. He was offended at Waring for not explaining the rope.

An oil-lamp was burning in the hut and the kettle was singing on the side of the wood stove. By old routine Estelle made the tea while Brucie assembled the tackle and the two men got into their wading gear.

The chest waders, of a rubberised fabric, were stiff and unwieldy, iron cold to the touch. Waring took his shoes off and stepped into his and drew them up to his chest and slipped the braces over his shoulders. Then he sat down and pulled on his heavy woollen stockings and his nailed boots. He felt tired. He sat and drank his tea and watched Brucie continuing to assemble the tackle.

Brucie laid the two fly rods and the two spinning rods on the floor and went out and looked at the water. Then he came back and described it and asked what flies they wanted to use. He did this without expression (and without any mention of spinners, which he abjured); and when they had made their suggestions he told them what to use.

Waring barely listened to him. He had caught him looking at the rope again. He wondered if there was a rule against it. There were rules for practically everything. The bugger might well produce a rule or run off and phone somebody for one. He did not think there could be one; but he didn't know so he kept quiet. He thought he'd first get the rope in the water and then outface Brucie if problems arose. The position for Brucie to be in was of one obeying orders and not giving rulings or tendering opinions. It was important that

130

Brucie should immediately do as he was told when Waring told him the important thing he had to do. He didn't think that Brucie's pride in its present state of offence would allow him to ask about the rope.

Brucie didn't ask about the rope, and he continued being offended. When they left the hut he picked up Nigel's tackle and went straight down with him to the small pool, leaving Waring to carry his own.

Waring didn't mind. With Estelle he collected the gear and they started the long walk down to the Blackrock.

Outside the hut everything was very beautiful. The snowbank was beautiful, and the trees, and the jagged broken valley of the river. The river was immensely beautiful. The air was now totally full of the sound of it, its force and vibration so shattering that Waring laughed out loud. He saw Estelle smiling herself, though her face was pinched with cold.

'You'll warm up!' he called in her ear.

'I'm warm. Let me carry the rope.'

'You're carrying enough.' He had the rope round his neck.

'You're not really going in with it today?'

'I'll see,' he said.

The water was so high he didn't know if he'd get in at all. It was reddish brown, and going fast. But when they reached the bank he saw it was possible. Five or six feet of beach were still exposed. The fingers of shingle were exposed. The fingers ran out to the stream, and he knew the ground on both sides, and it was not deep. Even where it deepened, it wasn't dangerous. It was a question of keeping his footing.

He shook out the rope and slipped the bight over his head.

'Henry, it's dangerous,' Estelle said.

'Don't fuss.'

'The water's much too fast.'

'You'll guide me out.' He tightened the rope under his shoulders. 'I'll wave to you. I'll blow my little whistle.' He dangled the whistle at her from its lanyard, having to shout now, unable to stop laughing. He saw she was laughing herself; lips puckered in alarm but laughing. It was the water. It was the astounding flood of water, endlessly rounding the Blackrock; spume-flecked, magnificent, spray smacking the air. A world of water, and in the water the salmon, wild things in from the sea.

'I'll try the fly,' he said.

Brucie had already put on a fly, a big sunk one.

'Don't, Henry.'

'Just a cast or two.'

'Henry, I'm asking you.'

'And don't pull. You don't have to pull,' he said. 'It's only to guide me back.' But she couldn't hear him now. He was walking cumbrously out along the spit, rod in his left hand and gaff in the right. He used the gaff as a wading stick and came cautiously down off the spit, and took a step, and a few more, and right away knew it was dangerous. The river bed had changed. The water was quite suddenly over his knees, his waist. Even despite the evidence of his eyes he was shocked by the force of it.

He struggled to keep his balance, leaning hard on the gaff. The rod was almost torn from his hand, the long whippy length of it wrenching and thrumming in the water. He managed to lift it and edge farther out, feeling for level footing. He was confused and deafened by the uproar, by the dizzying race of foam. He didn't know how far he'd gone, and daren't turn to see. A backward glance would unbalance him, would have the water up over the top of his chest waders, filling them, sinking him. It had happened to the tobacco man.

He found rock, a solid boulder, and wedged his feet there, leaning against the current. The breath was almost battered out of him. He knew he had to turn and go. He had to do it immediately. His heart was thumping, head spinning with vertigo from the racing water. He closed his eyes against it, planning the moves. But just as he opened them again a salmon leaped. It leaped clean out of the spray, not ten yards from him. 'Oh, my God,' he said. It was big as a big dog, thirty or forty pounds at least. In the air the salmon looked at him. Its cold eye watched him all the way through its long arc until it re-entered the river.

Waring saw where it entered and knew why it had leapt. It had leapt the long ridge of rock that formed one wall of the pool. The salmon was now in the pool. Dozens of other salmon would be there with it, resting before the next onslaught up river.

'Jesus,' he said, and knew he would have to try. He would have just one try. His vertigo had gone suddenly, and he had got the feel of the current. He thought if he was careful he could stand unaided. He tried it and he could. He released the fly from its ring, stripping off line from the reel. He stripped four or five yards off, and raised the big rod double-handed, and got it swishing

133

there and back till he had ten, then fifteen yards in the air, and he shot it. He shot it across and down and saw the heavy line snaking out through the spray and the few see-sawing snowflakes, and felt it belly at once as the current took it. He rolled the rod in the air, mending the line on the water, and it came round very fast. He couldn't see the end of the line but he saw the angle change sharply at his rod tip and knew he was over the pool, and that his fly was in it, bobbing down among the salmon. He willed one of them to come and get it and began drawing in line to keep the fly moving. He held a finger on the line to keep contact with the fly. If a salmon took, it would turn away, and as it turned the fly would check in its jaw; and his finger would feel it.

He stood deep in the current, feeling the adrenalin flowing in him. He was barely aware of the battering pressure now. He brought the line in slowly, brought all of it in, and no salmon took, and he thought *once more: just once.* The salmon were there – dozens, scores of them were there! But he knew it was madness, that at any moment vertigo could seize him again. Also there was the rope trick to be attempted, the *Indian* rope trick; and attempted now before Brucie appeared.

The moment he stopped fishing the vertigo hit him again. He stood stock still in the water, steadying himself with the gaff, and closed his eyes and slowly turned, and didn't open them till he thought he was facing the beach. He wasn't quite facing it but he saw it there, thirty or forty feet away, and Estelle hopping on it, gesticulating at him. Her face was pink with cold and she was shouting. He couldn't hear her but he waved back, and almost at once tension came on the rope, and he realised she was pulling him in. He didn't want this. He didn't want it! He saw that every gesture counted, and motioned her to stop, but she couldn't understand. He pointed at the black rock, the huge hump that lay at the far side of the beach, and after a moment she nodded, and he began wading there.

All the river was coming at him now and he leaned into it, prodding with the gaff in front. He prodded carefully, finding the holes where boulders had been, where he could drown so easily now. He knew he was sweating heavily. He had to get beyond the black rock, but he made right for it and once there almost kissed it. He hung on to the gaff and hugged the rock tightly. There was just a narrow ledge under him now, and below it the pool, very deep, very dangerous.

He shuffled his way round the ledge, holding the rock with both arms, and found the beach at the other side, smaller than the one he had left; but still exposed.

He came down off the ledge exhausted but still with no time to rest. He laid his rod on the shingle and slipped the bight of rope over his head. He had marked a projection of rock yesterday, and he found it and attached the rope and tightened up. Then he let the slack of the rope go in the water and saw the current take it. He watched a moment and bent and felt it. The rope was thrumming in the water, but far away at the other end he could still feel Estelle, as he had felt the fly. Indian rope trick. A man went up a rope, and the rope stayed up. Was the man still at the end of the rope? Estelle knew he was at the end of this one. He looked at his watch and started counting.

And now he could rest. And he sat on the beach. At the far side of it was another outcrop of rock, quite small, and beyond that sloping shingle. From there it was just uphill and over the top to the position where Nigel would be fishing below; immediately below at the right time. It wasn't the right time yet.

By ten o'clock Nigel would be there, having worked down from the head of the pool. And once there, Nigel would have to remain there: for a good half hour. It was the only way the river could be fished at that point: too deep to wade. It had to be fished up, across and down, all from the same small point. There was no more than a yard of leeway at either side; and wherever Nigel stood in it, Waring could get him. He had already loosened the boulder. The thing must weigh a couple of hundredweight. It was firmly wedged but movable. Waring had already moved it, and he knew he could topple it without great effort. All understandable. Loosened by rain and snow. Not the gillie's fault. Not the angler's. Hazard of the sport.

It had taken him several minutes yesterday to get there and back from that point to this one. Now he gave it nine, to allow for contingencies.

The nine minutes ticked away, and he got moving. He fixed himself to the rope, picked up his rod and shuffled round the rock again. Estelle was watching most anxiously, and waved at once. He didn't wave back. Brucie hadn't appeared yet, but he might at any moment. He didn't want Brucie to see him coming from the rock.

He put distance between it. He struggled out to midstream. He stayed a full calculated minute watching the water before turning away. Then he waved. Then she pulled.

She pulled too hard. She'd have him over! He hung back on the rope, steadying himself. But the thing was a help. He was desperately tired now, heart thumping, and with double vision into the bargain. He knew he'd never make it if he had to watch the beach and the racing water in between. Guided by the rope he could concentrate on his feet, and in a few minutes was stumbling out.

Brucie was coming down the slope.

'Darling, that was *lunacy*!' Estelle cried.

Waring couldn't speak.

'I thought I'd literally have a *seizure*!'

She was babbling on but he barely heard her; still trying to catch his breath and remove the rope as Brucie arrived.

The giant stared at him open-mouthed. 'You planning to catch a whale?' he said.

Waring didn't answer. Estelle would babble in explanation soon enough. And there were things in store for Brucie yet.

Estelle almost immediately was babbling. 'I told him not to go in, that the water was too fast. The rope's supposed to guide him back. He can't get a fly out far enough since his illness. But he goes so far!'

'Why so?' Brucie said. 'The fly fishes from here.'

'The fly won't fish.'

'It fishes *parfectly*. Mr Clintock fishes the fly.'

'I want the spinner,' Waring said.

'The spinner?' The spinner was guaranteed to unhinge Brucie. 'Why the spinner? It's fly water. They want fly.'

'Take the spinning rod,' Waring said, 'and go to the next pool. I'll join you shortly.'

'They will take fly, Mr Waring,' Brucie said desperately. 'You must give them a chance, sir. You must have patience.'

The 'Mr Waring, sir' was an advance. And there was no nonsense about the rope: nothing about it frightening fish. There couldn't be a rule about it.

'Don't waste time, Brucie,' Waring said, pressing on. 'Take the spinning rod. Take all the tackle. Don't forget the gaff.'

He made Brucie come and get the gaff. Brucie bit hard on his pipe but he came and got it and stumped off, deranged.

'Henry, it was so dangerous,' Estelle said.

'You did well,' he told her.

'And you were so miserable to Brucie.'

'Brucie *will* do well.'

'I'll have to make it up to him somehow.'

'Easily done.' There was always a reliable way of making it up to Brucie. The flask was in her shoulder bag now.

'Only you don't have to pull so hard,' Waring said. 'The rope does all the work, and it only upsets you.'

'It's nothing to do with the rope.'

'It's everything to do with the rope,' Waring said.

It was a good ten-minute slog to the pool, and Brucie wasn't there when they arrived. The tackle was there, but Brucie himself had gone up to sulk in the hut. From the hut he could view all the beat.

And that was the next thing, Waring thought. Brucie had to be removed from his view of the beat. It was the reason for putting him through his paces today. D-Day would be the day after tomorrow, when Nigel would once more be in position. That was also D for Departure day, for they'd be checking out after lunch. It would give him only the morning to do it. Not that he needed all morning. He needed nine minutes; and Brucie's instant obedience in the nine minutes.

He fished the spinner for an hour without success, then it began snowing hard. It was still early for elevenses but they went to the hut, and found Nigel there before them. He and Brucie were weighing a ten-pounder.

'Caught on the fly,' said Brucie heavily.

Estelle sweetened the brute with her flask, and soon had him telling of other great malts he had known so that the atmosphere became quite affable.

Waring distanced himself from all the affability.

No toadying, he told himself. Brucie had to be kept in his place. There was a job ahead for Brucie.

The snow kept on till lunch, and afterwards turned to driving sleet; which meant no more fishing for the day. They did the tweed factory instead. They usually did the tweed factory on every visit. This time Waring was distracted half out of his mind.

He stayed that way all through dinner. The wind driving the sleet had risen. He could hear it slamming away outside. He wondered what it would do to tomorrow's fishing; if there would *be* any fishing. On all the beats there were good stations and not so good ones; it accounted for the strict rotation of rods. If the river was not fishable, the rotation was simply held up. But he couldn't have it held up. He had to have the small pool tomorrow so that Nigel would get it the day after: D-Day.

Later on, in the lounge, the wind began fairly howling. It drowned the sound of the river, and he saw the keener anglers about the room anxiously tapping the barometer.

He kept his nerve, drank his whisky, read his book.

The kind of deep whirling water that often lies beyond these banks is the most likely place for a fisherman, encumbered with heavy equipment, to be sucked down and drowned. This is where he must keep his head. Unless help is close to hand and immediately available . . .

He read the passage again, and then once more, almost faint with longing. The vision it depicted of Nigel on D-Day was so perfect it was almost a prophecy. The deep whirling water was *just* beyond the bank. Nigel would not be keeping his head, not after a boulder had fallen on it. The only help close to hand would be Waring's, which would in no way be available.

Nigel had begun yawning again and Estelle was folding her knitting. Waring finished his whisky and rose.

Let tomorrow be fishable, he thought. Let it be!

He was slow in turning out in the morning so that Estelle went down before him. This gave him an opportunity to be sick in the bathroom. The snow was going horizontally outside. His legs were so weak he thought he'd faint.

He pulled himself together, however, went down, had his porridge, had a kipper, had two cups of coffee.

'I don't know about you,' Nigel said, peering out of the window. 'But it does not look top o' the morning, does it?'

'See what Brucie says.'

'Oh, Brucie,' Estelle said. Brucie had not yet found any conditions unfishable; which was Waring's remaining hope, and the only thing keeping his kipper down. He didn't know for certain but he seemed to recall a rule that stated that the whole rotation of a beat must proceed if any particular member chose to fish his part of it. He thought he was going to be that member. Brucie must have his say, though.

Brucie was waiting in the vestibule, pipe going.

'Well, Brucie,' Nigel said. 'How is it?'

'Fresh,' Brucie said. Beyond the glass panels of the vestibule something very like a tempest seemed to be in progress.

'Is it fishable?' Waring said.

Brucie took his pipe out and paused, causing Waring's heart almost to stop. 'It's no' *un*fishable,' Brucie said. 'It's no *parfect*,' he amplified. 'There's a breeze.'

The breeze just at that moment very nearly took the door off.

'Will it be so bad down at the small pool?'

'*No-o*,' Brucie said cautiously. 'You have the high bank there. The small pool would be – fishable.'

'I'll fish it,' Waring said.

He said it quickly. Much too quickly. They all stared at him and Nigel burst out laughing. 'You old weasel,' he said. 'You stoat. You fox. You cunning old swine. You want the Blackrock tomorrow, don't you?'

'Well, I – I'm game to try today,' Waring said, toes curling in his shoes.

Nigel's laughter roared on, and even Brucie's broken teeth bared in a grin. 'Silly old sausage,' Nigel said, prodding him affectionately. 'Of course have it tomorrow. I've had the most marvellous bag. Be my guest, Henry.'

'I'm quite prepared to fish today,' Waring said stiffly.

'Oh, Henry,' Estelle said.

'Give it away, old boy! Take your chance on the Blackrock tomorrow if it's OK.'

'Tomorrow will be parfect,' Brucie said.

'Will it?' Waring said.

'Not a doubt. And there's elsewhere today.'

'Where?'

'The distillery,' Brucie said.

'Oh,' Estelle said.

'The Glentorran. If there's a whole *day*.' He'd been trying to sell them the Glentorran for years now; it was forty miles off, too far for an afternoon jaunt.

'Well, it's very big of you, Nigel,' Waring said.

'Nonsense. I've had splendid value this trip.'

So he had, Waring thought, taking one thing with another. 'OK, then. Fine.'

'Wonderful! Lead on, MacBruce.'

Waring quietly glowed in the car; but retained his caution. There were details to be sewn up yet. His mind roamed over the familiar ones. Fingerprints on boulders. Could there be? But if so, why not? He'd been there many times. *Footprints in snow.* Yes. He'd have to work on that; work backwards, obliterating them. And on shingle, the upward path? But who would look? Foul play not suspected. A boulder had gone over, weakened by weather. Unless he dropped something in his excitement: a knife, fishing scissors, any of a dozen bits of paraphernalia he'd have with him. Even his fishing hat. But he'd be using the hat, to brush the snow. That one already worked out. Remove *flies* from hat. Flies so easily droppable. Memorise a check list. Above all, keep calm. He wouldn't even look after the boulder, to see what happened. There couldn't be any doubt, after all. And no one else would be looking. Brucie wouldn't. *That* was the vital element: still the one that needed working on. But before they reached the distillery he'd worked that one out, too.

The Glentorran was a small family pot-still whose raw product was in high demand for premium blends. Rarely, bottles of the mature single malt appeared in the haunts of butlers at the highest of Highland Flings. More rarely still, a sacred bottle of Partners' Reserve became available every millennium or so, for royalty and above. None of the Reserve was below forty years old, its padlocked oak casks under religious scrutiny by the Excise authorities. However there was a mysterious evaporation known as ullage . . . Brucie was still holding forth on this mystery as they entered the ramshackle gates.

Brucie had friends at the Glentorran and they were soon having tiny samples as they made the rounds. At Waring's behest Brucie discreetly enquired into ullage, and before they left a lorry driver was asking him as a special favour to deliver a small wee food parcel to an old auntie of his, now very infirm; and fifteen pounds of Waring's money had changed hands.

Waring took charge of the food parcel himself as they returned after lunch. There was barely half a pint in it, and it had not ulled from the oldest of the casks; but its antiquity still seemed to have Brucie in a trance.

'Should we no' just *try* a drop?' he asked.

'Tomorrow. At elevenses,' Waring said. 'As a final celebration. If I've caught anything to celebrate.'

He thought he would be needing a drop by then. He thought they all would; except one, of course.

And that sewed Brucie up. D-Day ahead.

D-Day dawned dim, but afterwards turned absolutely marvellous: the perfection prophesied by Brucie. The wind had dropped, the snow was hard, the sky was blue and a sun of exceptional cheeriness shone in it. Waring suspected all this. There was too much general goodness about. He saw he would need more and not less determination in such blithe conditions, and concentrated grimly on his check list.

Brucie met them with a face so unnaturally ravaged by smiles as to be almost unrecognisable. 'Mr and Mrs Waring, Mr Clintock! Did I deliver the right weather?'

'You did, Brucie, you did,' Nigel said genially.

'A fine bonny fish for you today, Mr Waring!'

'I hope so,' Waring said.

'For sure, for sure. Have we got everything? Your wee bit rope,' he said, nodding with great good humour at Waring's coil. 'Everything *else*?' His eyes were roaming.

Estelle patted her bag. 'All here, Brucie.'

'Ah, we'll have a grand morning!'

He got them in the car, and out of it, and bustled about the hut with such pleasing deference that it wasn't till he was striding ahead of them with the tackle to the Blackrock that Waring noticed Estelle was without her bag.

'He'll drive me round the bend this morning,' she said, vexed. 'It must be in the car. We can get it later.'

'He won't forget. His mind is wonderfully concentrated today.'

He kept his own mind that way.

'Brucie,' he said as they were on the river bank, 'a word in your ear. I want to catch something today.'

'You will, you will, Mr Waring. Make no doubt!'

'I'll try the fly, but I'd like to give the spinner a go, too.'

'Where's the harm in it?' said Brucie tolerantly.

'And I'll cover as much water as possible. So keep an eye on me, and when I give the word just run every bit of tackle I'm not using down to the next pool.'

'Good as done,' Brucie said. 'I'll be up yonder, watching the pair of you, you and Mr Clintock both.'

'I'll give you a wave. I'll blow the whistle. Just come right down and get the stuff and I'll follow you round.'

'Rely on me.'

'And if I'm lucky — a *special* celebration, remember.'

'Say no more, Mr Waring,' said Brucie, chuckling. 'If you're all set I'll just take a wee look at Mr Clintock, get him off right.'

'But watch out for me, mind.'

'I will, sir. Be of good heart.'

Waring's heart wasn't good. It was bumping unevenly. He couldn't believe he'd be doing it within the hour; in less than *half* an hour. It was gone half past nine now. Nigel would be in position in thirty minutes. It was happening too fast. And in conditions he hadn't expected. He'd imagined a harsh scene of wind and snow, himself doggedly going about the task, almost a part of the natural violence, a part he might later confuse, even forget. In this smiling day none of it seemed real.

He slipped the bight of rope over his head.

'Henry, do be careful. It's still very fast.'

'I'll be all right.'

'Don't go so far.'

He didn't answer her. He tightened the rope, took his fly rod and gaff and went out along the spit. He entered the water carefully, knowing about it now, using the gaff cannily. The force of it still almost knocked him sideways, but he braced himself and proceeded. Keep careful check of the time. He'd get in position and try a few casts. He'd have to do that.

He found the position, the boulder he'd found before, and steadied himself at it again. Everything seemed absurdly unreal; the uproar, the tumultuous water, his own physical danger in it, apart from the coming dangers. But he did not feel danger. Unreal, all of it. He thought perhaps he had to feel like this, that he'd subconsciously prepared himself for it. Some part of him was going on working. He was stripping off line. He was swishing the big rod there and back. He had his line out fishing. And it was part of the unreality that almost at once he was into a fish. He felt it, with his finger; felt it without any

146

question. The unseen salmon took the fly, turned, checked. He let it go, didn't strike, felt the fly run free again. The powerful beast would take upwards of twenty minutes to play, to tire out, and then would have to be beached. He didn't have twenty minutes.

He looked at his watch and saw that he had fifteen: it was twenty to ten. Before ten to, he would turn and give Brucie the signal in his hut. At five to, he would check that Brucie was down on the beach and going off with the tackle: going off in the other direction. He could start moving then.

He cast half a dozen times more, all from the same position. He knew Brucie, if watching, wouldn't approve. You had to move steadily down the beat. He wasn't moving from where he was, not till necessary.

Before ten to, he halted and closed his eyes in the torrent and went over the check list. Then he opened them and checked the whistle. He did it balancing awkwardly, with the hand holding the gaff, and right away the whistle came off its lanyard. First damned thing. *After use, lose whistle.* He didn't want to lose it elsewhere. It unsettled him suddenly and a touch of vertigo came on. He closed his eyes again and put it out of mind; and with eyes still closed stripped off some line. He had to be seen to be in action. He opened his eyes and cast, and again as if in a dream was immediately into a fish.

He knew then it was going to be all right. There was an inevitable feeling about it. It was the feeling he'd had in hospital: something that seemed totally incredible was in fact happening.

He let the fish go, and checked with his watch, and got

the whistle in his teeth, and turned and blew. He waved at the same time, and saw a tiny answering movement outside the hut, and with the strangest feeling knew that it was now on. It was on! He got the line out a couple of times more, not even watching it, and turned, and saw Brucie was picking up the tackle and walking away.

He was walking the wrong way.

He was walking towards Nigel.

Waring blinked, and shook his head to clear it, and looked again. Brucie was still walking the wrong way.

He blew the whistle. He blew as hard as he could, and waved, and saw Brucie turn and motion to him. But he still kept walking in the same direction and didn't look back any more.

Something had gone terribly wrong; Waring knew it. He blew and kept blowing, but Brucie didn't turn and he saw that he couldn't hear him.

Brucie heard quite well, and clucked to himself. The wee man could surely wait a few minutes. The missis had just this minute told him she'd left her bag with the Reserve in the car and would he take it in preparation to the hut. For sure he would! He'd have a quick wee glance to see how Clintock was doing below at the same time – tips due from both of them – and get the Reserve and pop it in the hut and from there run directly with the tackle down to the other pool. He had the tackle with him now. In a question of something like the Reserve did a few minutes here and there matter? The wee man was keeping on with his whistle, tooting away. It seemed more discreet just to keep on and no' look back. So Brucie didn't.

Waring spat the whistle out and started for the bank. There were still minutes in hand and he could still turn him around. He waved wildly at Estelle, and she responded at once. He felt the tension come on the rope.

It came too hard. She was pulling like mad. He signalled her not to pull so hard, but she kept on, and he clutched tightly on the rope, leaning back on it. He had to clutch so tightly, the rod slipped from his hand, and he let it go. He had the line still out, and it caught in some way about his ears, and then his neck. With the same sense of unreality he suddenly realised that he was into another fish. Or rather, the fish was into him. The fish had the fly. He did not have the rod.

At just about the moment that he realised this, Waring realised something else. Estelle had let go of the rope.

He was leaning heavily against its pull, and then there was no pull, and he was on his back, in the torrent.

He felt the icy water pouring into the top of his waders, and tried to stand, and couldn't. He was water-logged. He was also in some way going backwards, at speed. He was no longer in control. Something else was in control. For fleeting moments he got his arms out and waved. He saw Estelle was waving back, and mouthing something. He couldn't hear her, but he saw she was smiling.

In a series of simultaneous impressions he registered a number of things. He registered a grating feeling under his back. He registered that Nigel was wrong and Estelle didn't want to hang on to him, for she had let him go. She had let all the rope go. He realised that the grating under his back was caused by the ridge of rock that formed the wall of the pool and that the salmon had just taken him into the pool. And he realised finally – with a kind of rage that he had not experienced when seeing it all go before – what it was that Estelle was mouthing as she continued to smile so. It was only one word, but she kept on mouthing it. And her hand kept waving goodbye too.

Lionel Davidson has published a mere seven crime novels (and only two crime short stories, one of which is 'Indian Rope Trick'), yet so formidable are his gifts that three of his books – The Night of Wenceslas, A Long Way to Shiloh and The Chelsea Murders – have won the CWA Gold Dagger. Davidson has written in a variety of sub-genres; hence the freshness of his work. His most recent novel is Kolymsky Heights. He was awarded the CWA Cartier Diamond Dagger in 2001.

LINDSEY DAVIS

Something Spooky on Geophys

Luckily, they uncovered the grave on Day One.

They would only be given five days to finish; their more famous competitors usually had three, but *The Trowel 'Tecs* were beginners and were working up their act. At Mordaunt Castle they were confident of creating good TV, because it had been known since the sixteenth century that there were 'anciente ruines' in the grounds. Sir Mawdesley Mordaunt – the Elizabethan poet, statesman and home owner – had written to Sir Philip Sidney that the stones on which he once stubbed his toe while crossing the paddock might date 'fromme ye tyme of ye grate Julius Caesar'. So *The Trowel 'Tecs* were hoping to discover a previously unknown Roman road. They would settle for that, though their greater objective was to demonstrate that Mordaunt Castle had been continuously occupied since at least the first century of the Common Era (the TV diggers were very post-modern in their terminology) and that it stood on the site of a Roman fort. They always announced objectives of this type, though they were added to the programme last, once it was known whether the team had found anything.

Had the young, sunburned archaeologists looked up while they worked, they *might* have observed above them, peering over the battlements, the distant heads of three curious bystanders. Watching was a quiet group of ghosts. While less real, they were much more realistic than *The Trowel 'Tecs*. Sir Mawdesley Mordaunt was particularly intense, since it was his four-hundred-year-old theory being tested in the trench below and he really did not want to find that he had misled that famed lover of learning, Sir Philip Sidney.

Sir Mawdesley was flanked by his eternal companions, Major Penitence Rackstraw of the New Model Army, who had died in a castle dungeon during the Civil War, and the White Lady, a daft girl who submitted to anorexia when it was called dying of love. Normally the Black Dog gambolled around annoying them, but he was down below, sniffing among the archaeologists, his medieval nose wildly excited by the whiffs of historic rubbish pits that clung to their boots. Ed, the TV director, scratched his groin; however, that was a frequent occurrence and not caused by the Dog.

The Trowel 'Tecs was a new programme from the Bandwagon Channel. Deliberately set up as part of Bandwagon's youth-flavoured culture strand, it was supposed to be a 'more accessible' rival to its more famous (and perfectly accessible) competitor. A focal group had suggested that the blatant rip-off needed a celebrity presenter, two eccentric archaeologists with vivid accents, and a very attractive, extremely intelligent woman in shorts. *The Trowel 'Tecs* could hire only one senior archaeologist, though Rick 'Plummy' Duff was good value: he spoke of postholes in a warm burr like the molten jam in a microwaved Pop Tart. For glamour, they managed to get the excellent Xenobia Smith, who yearned to be on rescue digs in Mesopotamia, but her mum wouldn't let her go to a war zone. After hiring a couple of cameramen and a snack wagon, the producers had had their hearts set on a TV cook for presenter, but could only afford a reject from *Pets in Peril*. That Darren, the one the goat once bit. He knew nothing about archaeology. No problem: his job was to run about fast and breathlessly read the autocue. He still had post-traumatic stress after the goat incident; they had promised there would be no animals here, but Darren had a funny feeling that someone was winding him up. For once he was right. He was being licked by the ecto-plasmic tongue of the Black Dog. It sniffed his trousers intimately. Darren had a funny turn.

Sir Mawdesley huffed in his ruff as the castle's owner appeared, lurking with sleazy intent near the girl caterers as they handed out feta sandwiches to the volunteer archaeologists. Known to the ghosts as the Current Incompetent, he was taking a keen interest in the TV programme, especially where it involved young women in cotton vests. Sir Hardwicke Hall was a dastardly knight of industry who had bought the castle (along with his knighthood) during the decline of stately houses after the war. He had squeezed a great deal of ticket money from the public, but now toyed with reselling to a developer who would turn it into a business conference centre.

More recently he had been in email consultation with Ainslie Mordaunt, the once-hippie granddaughter of the last family occupant, now a dotcom millionairess, who wanted to reacquire her heritage. Sir Hardwicke thought she was a boy, which was just as well. His appalling past behaviour included the time he chased a nice young woman from English Heritage all around the Buttery, causing her to go back to the office in tears and – when the Department refused to support her claim of sexual harassment – to ask for a move to Pensions.

To the TV people, nervous property owners were a regular menace. When Sir Hardwicke started hovering, they prepared to keep him out of the way among the potwashers. However, his anxiety caused murmurs of a different kind among the ghosts on the battlements. They had despised most recent owners of the castle, though the Current Incompetent had incurred more contempt than the rest. His modernisation was particularly crass and as a punishment they had subjected him to an array of chills, smells, and bad resonances. Worse, they knew he had something to hide.

They could do nothing about it. Interfering in the future was against the rules.

Xenobia Smith was ecstatic. Trench One contained a skeleton. *The Trowel 'Tecs* would now have to wait for statutory confirmation that it was old enough to count as archaeology not foul play. The police had been called and the coroner informed. The delays to their filming were outweighed by the fact that having police in attendance would draw the press, while bones always made for good ratings. They were happy. The ghosts could wait too. They had time on their hands perpetually. And *they* could see something even more interesting. A Roman was sitting on the edge of the trench.

He was a clean-shaven, short-haired dark man in coarse woollen underpants and one-toed knitted socks, looking bleary. Coping with daylight again was making him panic. It was obvious he felt a bit bendy as he looked down in puzzlement at his own skeleton, which lay half curled at his feet. He reacted very slowly. He had been there a long time.

Without consultation – for they had been together for centuries and could read each other's minds – the ghosts stepped off the parapet. Sir Mawdesley and the Major disappeared, then rematerialised neatly at ground level. Deprived of sex while living, the White Lady had become hopelessly keen on it since, so she wafted slowly all the way down, just so she could experience the thrill of her draperies moulding themselves to her meagre body. Well, disembody.

Together the ghosts approached the new arrival. He saw them. As a fellow ghost he was bound to. Spirits would be constantly bumping into each other – and passing awkwardly through one another – were not this the norm; there is traffic control in the afterlife. Courteously they stood nearby, allowing him to react in his own time.

'Don't sit there!' snapped a passing archaeologist. More perceptive than his colleagues, he had spotted the Roman. 'Never sit on the edge of a trench; haven't you been taught anything?' In a kinder voice he went on, 'You could crumble the edge, get loose spoil all over the cleaned area. Besides, on a telly set you look untidy.'

Uncomprehending, the Roman struggled to rise; his phantom buttocks sank deeper into the turf, passing down through broken willow-pattern dishes, past an interesting bellarmine jar, and almost as far as the crude grey rim of a basic Bronze Age cooking pot. At once Sir Mawdesley stepped forward and warned him to think himself into motion like a bubble rising in a millstream. The metaphysics were lost on the Roman, but he responded better to some brisk advice from Major Rackstraw. This Roman must have had some military training. It was hard to tell, now he was wearing only underpants, but when ordered to stand to and present his musket, he straightened up. Simpering, the White Lady offered him a hand, but as he gave his mind to wondering what a musket was he climbed out by himself.

Major Rackstraw removed his lobster-tailed helmet so he looked less threatening. 'They dig a puny breast-work, these antiquarians,' he commented.

'A crude *fossa*,' the Roman agreed, gazing back at Trench One, deciding that it would not stop a wave of barbarian spearmen attacking the . . . *what?* He craned up at the castle, with its enormous towers, crenellated roofs and haphazard Gothic additions; it seemed a mad, overcomplicated fantasy to one who had been used to the economic lines of Roman forts.

'*Salve!*' Sir Mawdesley showed off his fluent Latin until the Roman (a Briton who barely spoke it) felt certain this was some prick from the officer class. The military man in his breastplate and pot had seemed reassuring, but the nymph with the soulful eyes looked as dangerous to health as an amphora of cheap fish pickle that had stood in a back alley too long in a hot summer.

'Will you tell us what happened to you?' asked the White Lady, with what would have been breathless excitement, had ghosts possessed breath. 'We know that *something* happened, or you would not be here now.'

'Death,' stated the Roman, a literalist. He cleared his throat, suddenly unsure of his own voice, which he had not heard for two thousand years.

'Aye, you now hear the buzzing of a thousand souls above Lethe's brine,' Sir Mawdesley sympathised, making a polite allusion to the classical Underworld. It was a curiosity that the Elizabethan was steeped in Virgil's *Aeneid*, yet the Roman, a provincial farmer, had never read it. However, he had once met a man who had been in a villa where they had a mosaic of Dido and Aeneas, the Queen of Carthage rather pot-bellied with bad hair and her lover looking like a shifty nincompoop.

'Something untoward occurred,' prompted the Major.

The Roman kept silent, not wanting to own up to a stupid quarrel in a tavern over who had to pay the mules' hay bill. Thinking back to it, he started to look warm, though of course he and his immediate environment remained eerily cold. He made up his mind. He wanted the truth known. He wanted public recognition, and if possible an outcry, over his murder.

'Ah, it was murder!' sighed Major Rackstraw, though the Roman had not spoken. 'Well, be of good cheer.

157

Here is the Provost Marshal who will put all to rights for ye!'

The police had arrived.

'Necessary procedure,' oozed Plummy Duff at the Current Incompetent, with the intention of reassuring him about the police presence. Sir Hardwicke Hall, who had once goosed Mrs Thatcher at a Tory fundraiser, had a reputation for knowing no fear. The one long-quashed anxiety he harboured, as the ghosts recognised, was well hidden. 'Bones that we find are usually from animals, but they have to be checked. Pretty damn obvious when there's a whole spine and the skull grinning up at you, though—' A frisson of glee ran around the ghosts as they crowded Sir Hardwicke Hall, watching him react. After years of enduring five-hour board meetings, he managed not to. 'We stop while the cops deliberate,' Plummy went on. 'What happens next depends on context. In close relation to a known ancient site, you can fairly quickly say that you have a historic burial.'

'Then they leave you alone?' Sir Hardwicke demanded narrowly.

'Actually, they often hang around,' Plummy disappointed him. 'Unless they are having a blitz on car-thieves locally, they like to stay and watch us.'

The White Lady nudged Sir Hardwicke's ribs, her sharp elbow passing through his flesh; as she prodded him intimately in the organs, she gave him an unexpected urge to vomit. She had a strong feminist interest in seeing him brought down.

'And does this count yet as a "known ancient site"?' he asked Plummy.

'Well, we may have a bit of road. But there is no building stone, not even robbed-out. This could be a ritual burial of a type we don't understand yet. But it looks as if our John Doe – or our *Junius Delta* –' Plummy Duff quipped heavily – 'was a ritual burial of a type we understand all too well – I mean, the poor shmuck was mugged and then dumped in a ditch.'

Sir Hardwicke Hall wandered over to Trench One. A couple of constables were chatting to some volunteer diggers, mainly about television. Meanwhile the coroner's officer was bending forwards over the trench, inspecting the skeleton from above as she looked for trauma marks on the bones. It was too tempting. The Current Incompetent responded automatically; seeing a well-formed female rump in comfy-fit slacks, he fondled it.

The coroner's officer straightened up. She was a retired police officer, now working from the local station, a job she had won because of her experience, unflappability and tact. These qualities were needed for dealing with suspects and the bereaved, of course, but her selection board had hoped they would assist in enduring the brusque manners and ego of the coroner, a solicitor of the usual single-minded sort.

She gave Sir Hardwicke Hall a look. She was ten years older than he had thought, she taught aerobics in her spare time, and she looked ready to arrest him for assault. Taken aback, he apologised. It was unacceptable

159

for ghosts to snigger, so the bystanders settled on peals of laughter in an off-stage operatic manner.

'What do you think, ma'am?' quavered Sir Hardwicke, not sounding much like a magnate.

'Oh, we won't cause bother.' The coroner's officer jumped nimbly into the trench. Applying a latex glove, she appeared to stick two fingers down the skeleton's throat, a startling manoeuvre from which she withdrew holding a corroded coin between the fingers. 'If this is from the Roman era, he's all yours,' she told Plummy Duff. 'A copper for Charon – to pay the boatman at the Styx, yes?' In her spare time from being a spare-time aerobics teacher, she had taken an Open University course in Classical Studies.

The Roman was encouraged. Placing the coin beneath his tongue was the one kindness his killers had done him. Anyone should now work out that he had met a misadventure: that he was not simply a victim of a heart attack on the road or of hypothermia, and that he lay outside any proper cemetery, with sinister implications. *The Trowel 'Tecs* were too busy perfecting a close-up of the coin.

'Will we have to wait for a pathologist?' called Xenobia Smith.

The coroner's officer shook her head, as she whistled up the constables and went off to make her report. 'Don't wait – but he's coming anyway. He'll say he's keen on archaeology—'

Xenobia laughed. It was not unkind. 'But the bugger is just hankering to be on TV?'

'What is this TV?' enquired the Roman. The White

Lady, who loved to play at being flickery lines on the castle caretaker's portable set, explained.

Filming eventually continued, with the experts expertly discussing the skeleton. They were missing the point. The Roman was strangled. That had left no evidence. A knife had been stuck in him. It had failed to graze a rib. All his possessions except his underwear had been stolen. The archaeologists omitted to spot rust marks left by the abandoned weapon or the preserved weave of the vanished pants and socks fabric. He had been poisoned. They had no funding to send the stomach contents to a lab and analyse its contents. With nothing to explain this death, *The Trowel 'Tecs* called it a routine burial and lost interest.

Frustrated, the Roman wanted to call in an expert. He knew the one he wanted too. He had been listening to the volunteers discussing their favourite fiction, particularly 'an ace Roman' called Didius Falco.

'Nay, 'tis an impossibility,' Sir Mawdesley protested. 'If this popinjay, this Falco, digs you up and solves your death for your contemporaries, then you will not be here now to be exposed by the antiquarians.' It was all one to the Roman, who only wanted justice for his battered corpse, but Sir Mawdesley Mordaunt had a vested interest. If there should be no skeleton to excite interest, he feared the programme would never be made. He was proud of his epistolary skills and wanted to hear experts on the Bandwagon Channel discussing his letter to Sir Philip Sidney. Like everyone else, the still-aspiring poet longed to be on TV.

The Roman's dilemma depressed him, but the ghosts of Mordaunt Castle were exercised by another matter. It was an issue of conscience, although custom dictated they should take no action, leaving all to fate. They decided to give fate a shove.

The Trowel 'Tecs had to devise a scene where an ancient art or craft was reconstructed. Petrina, the researcher, who came fresh from her History of Art degree and really wanted a job in Florence where her boyfriend lived, was struggling. 'Something with Roman food?' she offered, tossing her thin blonde hair and gazing at the muscular cameraman as he strutted about with his dead-weight equipment supported on one shoulder. He was keen to dress up in segmented armour and show off his knees and other attributes. 'Stuffed doormice?' Petrina tried gamely.

'Bloody hell, no.' Ed, the director, could see problems. 'Drop the scoff. We don't carry insurance, if anyone gets listeria.'

'Risk it! We could improvise a link into Roman medicine—'

'Over my dead body.' Ed's favourite archaeological joke. 'Didn't the Romans come to Britain because of the pre-Crufts hunting dogs?'

'I know a woman who supplies puppies for adverts.' Petrina was on the right wavelength. 'Mind you, you have to ban them from the Portaloos or they ruin the lav paper.'

'No budget, darling. Find us a freebie. As for training, that bloody Darren can use his *Pets in Peril* skills.'

The ghosts knew this could be their only chance.

They put their heads together (being careful not to clash, lest their auras should tangle); good at logistics, the Major took charge. He whistled up the Black Dog, who was enjoying himself digging holes all over Trench Two. 'You will have to materialise.'

'I want to go in my basket,' whined the Dog unhelpfully.

'Don't give us lip, slave!' commanded the Roman. 'Jump to it!' The Black Dog sulkily decided being trained might be a good game.

'Oh what a pooch!' shrieked Ed, as the Dog turned into visible form, slavering as was his habit. 'What a great historic-looking breed!' The Dog's audition was brief; it was enough that no master came forward demanding a fee for using him. The unpleasant peasant who once owned him would have been furious.

Soon *The Trowel 'Tecs* had geared up Darren to reconstruct training Roman dogs. '*Sede! Vene!* Ow, droppit! *Male cane!*'

Filming proceeded, with its usual pauses and apparent chaos. A band of part-time Celts and some freelance legionaries arrived and helped Darren. The Black Dog enjoyed the attention, but he remembered his role. Like the other ghosts, he knew where the bodies were buried. One body, anyway.

The Black Dog fetched a twig, which a reenactor was calling a centurion's vine stick, then he peed on Ed the producer's trousers and ran off.

Darren, the presenter, followed, with orders to retrieve the Dog for socialisation. It scrabbled into the walled garden, leapt up on a hot bed and started furiously digging. Darren, who happened to be carrying a geophysical survey instrument, turned it on for fun. 'What have you found, boy? . . .'

Things moved quickly after that. Everyone agreed it was uncanny. That Darren just picked up a machine, and on his first try they discovered something spooky on geophys.

To be precise, the first find unearthed was a lump of brownish material. The coroner's officer identified it: 'A nineteen seventies handbag clasp.'

'How can you be sure?' asked the Current Incompetent.

'I had one when I was a Mod,' she snapped. 'Trust me, it's plastic!' By then the archaeologists had exposed human remains which made her send for a SOCO team. 'I wonder who she is?' mused the coroner's officer aloud, before enquiring of Sir Hardwicke Hall, with what passed for a teasing grin, 'You ever been married, sir?'

She knew that he had. She loathed him so much she had looked him up in *Who's Who*. Who Was Who, it should have been, in the case of Madeleine Hall, m. 1976, no death or divorce specified, though now curiously absent from Mordaunt Castle. People reckoned her money had bought Hall's knighthood. A wife, pondered the coroner's officer, who may have worked out what a bastard she had married and fatally tackled him . . .

How lucky that the pathologist arrived. He set about his grim evaluation of the scene. Satisfied, the ghosts watched.

One was preoccupied. The Roman was trying to interest someone in his own case. 'So it's the usual mess,' complained this apparition wearily. He had good looks, a sharp wit and expert talents. 'You are offering me a job where it is impossible to say what happened, and no chance of being paid?'

'You might get on television,' promised the Roman Briton, pretending he had influence.

'The name's Falco,' replied his companion with alacrity. 'Suddenly I am available.' He took out a stylus and a shadowy note tablet. '*So! Did you have any enemies, and when were you last seen alive? . . .*'

Lindsey Davis published her first crime novel in 1989. The Silver Pigs introduced Marcus Didius Falco, a gumshoe with a difference who walks down the mean streets of Imperial Rome in AD 70. In 1995, she was awarded the CWA Dagger in the Library, given to the crime author whose work is judged to give most pleasure to library readers, and in 1999 she became the first winner of the CWA Ellis Peters Historical Dagger. She chaired the CWA in 2002–3.

COLIN DEXTER

The Double Crossing

I trust this statement will clarify the situation in which I find myself. It was with some reluctance that I signed the original transcript and think my own version of the relevant facts may perhaps be clearer. DC Watson was very patient and polite when I came into Reading Police Station, but I'm afraid I cannot see him as a serious contender for the Booker Prize. All I am trying to do is to clarify the complex sequence of events which it has been my unhappy lot to experience.

My wife Kathryn and myself (we have no children) had decided to spend a week in northern France. It would have been ungrateful not to invite Kathryn's mother, Mary, to join us. She had been living with us for the past seven years; and although Kathryn and I knew how good it would be to have a holiday on our own, we never seriously considered such an arrangement. Mary was in her mid seventies – her health progressively going downhill, with her memory sadly degenerating. In any case, she deserved a break just as much as we did. She had been wonderfully kind to us, especially after the death of her husband when she'd sold her Georgian property in Cheltenham and given us £45,000 – money with which we were able to take out a mortgage on our present house at 53, Christie Drive, Cholsey. (You will remember the most illustrious gravestone in our village churchyard?)

The only hiccup in the plan was that Mary insisted, absolutely, that she must fund the whole holiday herself – otherwise she would remain at home and try to look after things while we were away. It was a bit of emotional blackmail, yes; but it was a generous offer and we finally agreed to it. Yet in reality it wasn't *all* that generous. I had recently bought a spanking new three-berth caravan which we parked at the bottom of the drive. Any B&B or hotel bills would therefore be nil. And apart from the three sites into which I'd already booked (car-plus-caravan) the only heftyish expense was the fare for the ferry-crossing: £430 return – irrespective of the number of passengers. But, yes, we did hope to indulge ourselves with cheeses and wines and some of the local specialities. We could hardly wait.

Our local travel agency arranged the holiday, and we were booked for an 8 a.m. crossing – it seems an eternity but it is only two days ago! I followed the advice given quite meticulously: to allow about two and a half hours for the drive down to Dover; to be at the dockside one hour before the scheduled departure time; and to give ourselves an extra hour, just in case. I decided therefore that we should set off at 3 a.m.; and after checking everything for the umpteenth time, we left Cholsey at 3 a.m. precisely.

With traffic virtually non-existant, we had ample time to take a break for coffee and croissants at a deserted service station. And at Dover we found ourselves drawn up in third place in the ferry queue – wide awake and happily anticipating the holiday. The sky was light now, with the sea calm, and prospects appearing well-nigh perfect.

At 7.05 a.m. the Tannoy informed waiting vehicles that boarding was imminent and that documents should be ready for customs and passport clearance. Seated beside me, Kathryn turned to her mother. 'Give me your passport then, Mum.'

After a minute or so I heard a groan of semi-panic behind me; and after a couple of minutes, a high squeak of semi-hysteria:

'Oh, no! I must have . . . It must still be . . . Oh, *no!*' Despair. Tears. Repeated self-incrimination.

Kathryn and I climbed the metallic stairs to the upper deck, where we ordered two Full-Monty breakfasts in the restaurant. As the Met Office had forecast, the crossing was smooth; and we arrived ten minutes early in Calais, where we passed through Customs and Immigration without the slightest difficulty. Things had turned out far better than anticipated.

I should (I now realise) have pulled up at some lay-by on our journey south to St Nicholas-sur-Somme, where I had pre-booked a space for two nights. But I am not too confident a driver on the continent and I was anxious to reach our destination. Just over an hour later, I needed no more than an occasional *oui* and *non* before a spotty-faced youth pointed the way towards our plot on the caravan site. When I pulled up the hand-brake on the parched little area that would temporarily be our home, my shoulder muscles finally managed to relax. And as Kathryn unfastened her safety-belt I found myself smiling ruefully as she leaned across and kissed me, before opening her passenger door and walking down the side of the Rover to the caravan. When she came back to the car her cheeks were a ghastly white as she spoke the words so slowly:

'She's dead, John! Mum's *dead*.'

Inside the caravan there was a low wooden box, about eight feet long, affixed to the off-side panel, on which three persons could sit reasonably comfortably; and inside this box was ample space for us to store duvets, blankets, pillows, etc. It was here that Mary had reluctantly agreed to conceal herself before our embarkation at Dover. Such reluctance, I believe, had little to do with the dishonesty of her concealment – only with the thought of lying there for the key crossing-time. Yet perhaps this was not quite such an ordeal as it might appear. The lightweight wooden lid would be lying alongside her, to be pulled across and over only in the extremely unlikely event of some shipping official checking for illegal stowaways. 'Still like a coffin, though,' I remember poor Mary saying.

We must have been mad, I agree. Yet we had one slim consolation. When I entered the caravan, it seemed clear to me that she could not have died from suffocation. The lid still lay alongside her, and the expression on her face was free from any trace of pain or panic. We could only hope and pray that she had died comparatively peacefully from – well, from something like a stroke.

What could we do? What should we do? What *did* we do?

After anchoring the seperated caravan, Kathryn and I walked twice around the perimeter of the site, desperately debating the situation and finally agreeing on the most cowardly course of all. We returned to the car and drove off, minus caravan, for the Coq d'Or, some ten kilometres distant, a restaurant I had already earmarked as the best in the immediate locality. But we could peck only occasionally at the veal as our thoughts continued to circle round and round in our heads – although in truth we drank considerably more claret than was wise.

As we drove back, we found we had agreed (at last!) on the course of action we should have taken many hours previously: to report *everything* to the nearest French authorities. We just wanted to tell the truth; to face the music; to accept whatever we had to accept; above all, to be able to arrange, sometime, somewhere, a decent burial service for Mary. Hitherto, perhaps the biggest barrier to such a course had been the wretched language problem. But we were past that now.

It was dark when we were checked in, wordlessly, by the same spotty-faced youth now sporting a pair of bulky earphones. But the site was well lit, and we had no trouble finding our plot, No. 36, just beneath a high beech-hedge.

But there was no caravan in No. 36.

No caravan-cum-corpse in No. 36.

Plot No. 36 was completely deserted.

★   ★   ★

Luckily a few places (for cars only) were still available on the dawn-ferry at Calais – where I explained as best I could that my holiday plans had been curtailed because of a family bereavement.

'But you 'ad a caravan, monsieur?'

I nodded. 'Left it with my friends – mes amis – vous comprenez?'

We were allowed to proceed without further ado.

I drove the Rover up the ramp and soon we were crossing the Channel the other way, the waves now considerably choppier than they'd been the day before. Kathryn said she appreciated the irony – if little else.

Once back home, I rang you immediately, and spent over two hours with DC Watson. I was invited to read through my statement and to initial any changes that I wished made. There were so many changes though that I suggested it might help if I submitted my own version. Watson assured me that he personally would take no offence at such a procedure.

You are reading that version now.

John Graham.

As requested, I attach a sheaf of relevant documents – tickets, bills, receipts, etc.

When Detective Chief Superintendent Stratton first read through the statement, he'd known that the situation would be far from easy to handle. The corpse was in a foreign country; was not even (officially) registered dead; was still nowhere to be found; and might well have been sprinkled with concentrated curry powder in order to confuse any intelligent sniffer-dog – before being fed into some Gallic timber-shredder. And why for heaven's sake should *he* need to be involved? What were those bloody gendarmes doing?

Yet now, after a leisurely second reading, he found himself pushing his bi-focals a little further down his nose, and then – yes! – even smiling slightly. It was at least well-written stuff, certainly of higher literary quality than he'd come to expect from his own underlings. No spelling mistakes in the whole caboodle . . .

He reached for one of his telephones and rang the newly appointed Detective Inspector, summoning him into the sanctum sanctorum – pronto.

Stratton held up the stapled pages of the Revised Version: 'You've already, er . . . ?'

'Yessir.'

'Writes well, eh?'

The DI nodded. 'Only those two spelling mistakes as far as I could see.'

'Mm.' Stratton seemed momentarily unsure of himself. 'Just remind me . . .'

'Well, he can't spell "separated" and he can't spell "non—" '

'Mm. Yes. Those are the only two mistakes I'd, er . . .'

'It's just my old boss. He was a real stickler about—'

'What do you make of all this?'

'Needle in the proverbial, as far as I can see. Unless those Frenchies come up with—'

'Think they will?'

'Well, they know the reg. of the caravan but—'

'Ever tried to dump a caravan yourself?'

'No, sir. But like I was saying, as far as I can—'

The DCS interrupted him irritably: 'That's the third time in a minute you've told me how far you can bloody well see! But shall I tell you something? I'm beginning to wonder if you can see all that far at all. So just *listen* a minute, will you, Lewis?'

Stratton was soon in full swing!

'Mum-in-law in her mid-seventies, OK?'

'Yessir.'

'Memory going downhill sharpish?'

'Yessir.'

'Selling her posh Cheltenham place at the top of the housing-market –'

'Yessir.'

'– then insisting on paying for a joint holiday?'

Lewis nodded.

'So? Do you reckon there's just a possibility she's got a few spare spondulicks somewhere that some people might want to get their greedy paws on?'

'Well, I—'

'What are the three main motives for murder? Come on!'

'Well—'

'For Christ's sake stop saying "well"!'

'Sorry, sir.'

'Well?'

'Well, jealousy, sex, money – that's what my old boss used to say.'

'Agreed, Lewis. But there's only *one* of that immortal trio that's running right through all this bullshit.' The DCS flicked the statement with a podgy right forefinger. 'Tell me! Why do you think this splendid fellow of ours, Mr Gray—'

'Graham, sir.'

'– left Cholsey at – what was it? – 2.30 a.m.'

'3 a.m., I think, sir.'

'The small hours – the *dark* hours – that's all I'm saying.'

'Yessir.'

'So why— Augh! Forget it! You're new, Lewis, and no one's going to blame you for that. But we've all got to start learning somewhere. So? So what do you do? One, you try to find out how much Mrs Whatsername's got stashed away somewhere. Two, you'll find out as confidentially as you can whether the old gal's last will and testament isn't exactly disappointing reading as far as her only daughter is concerned. Third, you get in touch with—'

But Lewis was bemused: 'You don't mean, sir – you're not saying—?'

'That's exactly what I *do* mean – that's exactly what I *am* saying – and that's exactly what *you're* thinking, Lewis. We've got a *murder* on our hands. Listen!'

Lewis, a comparatively simple soul, was aware of his own inexperience. So he sat back quietly and listened.

'We're never going to find the old gal in France. Know why? Because she never left England in the first place. Just think a minute. Who saw her leaving Cholsey, eh? Nobody. Who saw her on the ferry-crossing?

175

Nobody. Who caught a single glimpse of her once she was over the channel? Nobody.'

Unconvinced but not wholly unimpressed, Lewis sat back meekly as Stratton completed his tutorial.

'Just one further piece of advice, my son. Before you start taking up the floorboards and digging up the flower-beds at 35 Christie Drive—'

'53, sir.'

Stratton let it go at that.

As he walked back to his open-plan office, mentally list-ing his priorities, Lewis realised that the DCS was a clever enough cop, one who had just put a wholly differ-ent perspective on events, but one who could never hold a candle to his old boss.

Sergeant Kate Lucan looked up from her computer screen when he came in. She'd been in the force long enough to make some shrewd assessment of any new-comer. All right, the latest DI was unlikely to become the brightest star in the firmament; but he was pleasant and honest and, well, clever *enough*. As she watched him though, she witnessed a colleague who was not exactly over the moon or over Mars. And very soon afterwards she sensed that he was pretty amateurishly learning next to nothing about whether some recently deceased old lady had bequeathed a healthy bank-balance to an only daughter – or, instead, perhaps become a posthumous patron of the Donkey Sanctuary.

Forty-eight hours later the message came through from the French police: the missing person had been found, lying serenely dead in an elongated box inside a caravan, a dozen kilometres from St Nicholas-sur-Somme. Identification was firmly established by the passport found in the caravan: somehow it seemed to have slipped through the lining of a very expensive, albeit rather ancient, cashmere overcoat.

Having received the e-mail herself, it was Sergeant Kate Lucan who personally communicated its import to the DI, the latter reading it through with more than a hint of amusement and gratification.

'Exactly what I told him,' he mumbled to himself.

'Good news . . . er, Lewis? You did say it would be all right if I called you—'

'Course it is – only if I can call you Kate, though.'

'Course you can.'

'No problem then.'

'No. It's just that – well, a lot of people still think your Christian name is your *surname* – like, you know, that TV Sergeant in *Inspector Morse*.'

Early that same evening, in the station's entrance-lobby, one of the telephonists smiled a farewell to her (now) favourite policeman:

'Goo' night, sir.'

'Goo' night, luv.'

And he smiled back at her.

After all, it hadn't been a bad day at all for Detective Inspector Lewis David Robinson.

With acknowledgement to David Robinson, one of my former pupils.

Colin Dexter graduated from Cambridge University in 1953 and has lived in Oxford since 1966. *His first novel,* Last Bus to Woodstock, *was published in 1975 and introduced a detective pairing, Inspector Morse and Sergeant Lewis, which was to become the stuff of legend.* The Wench is Dead *and* The Way Through the Woods *won the CWA Gold Dagger for the best crime novel of the year in 1989 and 1992 respectively, while* Service of All the Dead *and* The Dead of Jericho *both earned CWA Silver Daggers. Dexter was awarded the CWA Cartier Diamond Dagger in 1997. The Inspector Morse novels were televised with immense success starring the late John Thaw as Morse and Kevin Whately as Lewis.*

DICK FRANCIS

The Gift

When the breakfast-time Astrojet from La Guardia was still twenty minutes short of Louisville, Fred Collyer took out a block of printed forms and began to write his expenses.

Cab fare to airport, fifteen dollars.

No matter that a neighbour, working out on Long Island, had given him a free ride door to door: a little imagination in the expense department earned him half as much again (untaxed as the *Manhattan Star* paid him for the facts he came up with every week in his Monday racing column).

Refreshments on Journey, he wrote. *Five dollars.*

Entertaining for the purpose of obtaining information, six dollars fifty.

To justify that little lot he ordered a second double bourbon from the air hostess and lifted it in a silent good luck gesture to a man sleeping across the aisle, the owner of a third-rate filly that had bucked her shins two weeks ago.

Another Kentucky Derby. His mind flickered like a

scratched print of an old movie over the days ahead. The same old slog out to the barns in the mornings, the same endless raking-over of past form, searching for a hint of the future. The same inconclusive work-outs on the track, the same slanderous rumours, same gossip, same stupid jocks, same stupid trainers, shooting their goddam stupid mouths off.

The bright, burning enthusiasm which had carved out his syndicated by-line was long gone. The lift of the spirit to the big occasion, the flair for sensing a story where no one else did, the sharp instinct which sorted truth from camouflage, all these he had had. All had left him. In their place lay plains of boredom and perpetual cynical tiredness. Instead of exclusives he nowadays gave his paper rehashes of other turfwriters' ideas, and a couple of times recently he had failed to do even that.

He was forty-six.

He drank.

Back in his functional New York office the Sports Editor of the *Manhattan Star* pursed his lips over Fred Collyer's account of the Everglades at Hialeah and wondered if he had been wise to send him down as usual to the Derby.

That guy, he thought regretfully, was all washed up. Too bad. Too bad he couldn't stay off the liquor. No one could drink and write, not at one and the same time. Write first, drink after; sure. Drink to excess, to stupor, maybe. But *after*.

He thought that before long he would have to let Fred go, that probably he should have started looking around for a replacement that day months back when

Fred first turned up in the office too fuddled to hit the right keys on his typewriter. But that bum had had everything, he thought. A true journalist's nose for a story, and a gift for putting it across so vividly that the words jumped right off the page and kicked you in the brain.

Nowadays all that was left was a reputation and an echo: the technique still marched shakily on, but the personality behind it was drowning.

The Sports Editor shook his head over the Hialeah clipping and laid it aside. Twice in the past six weeks Fred had been incapable of writing a story at all. Each time when he had not phoned through they had fudged up a column in the office and stuck the Collyer name on it, but two missed deadlines were one more than forgivable. Three, and it would be all over. The management were grumbling louder than ever over the inflated expense accounts, and if they found out that in return they had twice received only sodden silence, no amount of for-old-times-sake would save him.

I did warn him, thought the Sports Editor uneasily. I told him to be sure to turn in a good one this time. A sizzler, like he used to. I told him to make this Derby one of his greats.

Fred Collyer checked into the motel room the newspaper had reserved for him and sank three quick mid-morning stiffeners from the bottle he had brought along in his briefcase. He shoved the Sports Editor's warning to the back of his mind because he was still sure that drunk or sober he could outwrite any other commentator in the business, given a story that was worth the trouble. There just weren't any good stories around any more.

He took a taxi out to Churchill Downs. (*Cab fare, four dollars fifty*, he wrote on the way; and paid the driver two seventy-five.)

With three days to go to the Derby the racecourse looked clean, fresh, and expectant. Bright red tulips in tidy columns pointed their petals uniformly to the blue sky, and patches of green grass glowed like shampooed rugs. Without noticing them Fred Collyer took the elevator to the roof and trudged up the last windy steps to the huge glass-fronted press room which ran along the top of the stands. Inside, a few men sat at the rows of typewriters knocking out the next day's news, and a few more stood outside on the balcony actually watching the first race, but most were engaged on the day's serious business, which was chat.

Fred Collyer bought himself a can of beer at the simple bar and carried it over to his named place, exchanging Hi-yahs with the faces he saw on the circuit from Saratoga to Hollywood Park. Living on the move in hotels, and altogether rootless since Sylvie got fed up with his absence and his drinking and took the kids back to Mom in Nebraska, he looked upon racecourse press rooms as his only real home. He felt relaxed there, assured of respect. He was unaware that the admiration he had once inspired was slowly fading into tolerant pity.

He sat easily in his chair reading one of the day's duplicated news releases.

'Trainer Harbourne Cressie reports no heat in Pincer

Movement's near fore after breezing four furlongs on the track this morning.'

'No truth in rumour that Salad Bowl was running a temperature last evening, insists veterinarian John Brewer on behalf of owner Mrs L. (Loretta) Hicks.'

Marvellous, he thought sarcastically. Negative news was no news, Derby runners included.

He stayed up in the press room all afternoon, drinking beer, discussing this, that and nothing with writers, photographers, publicists and radio newsmen, keeping an inattentive eye on the racing on the closed-circuit television, and occasionally going out on to the balcony to look down on the anthill crowd far beneath. There was no need to struggle around down there as he used to, he thought. No need to try to see people, to interview them privately. Everything and everyone of interest came up to the press room sometime, ladling out info in spoonfed dollops.

At the end of the day he accepted a ride back to town in a colleague's Hertz car (*cab fare, four dollars fifty*) and in the evening, having laid substantial bourbon foundations in his own room before setting out, he attended the annual dinner of the Turfwriters' Association. The throng in the big reception room was pleased enough to see him, and he moved among the assortment of pressmen, trainers, jockeys, breeders, owners, and wives and girlfriends like a fish in his own home pond. Automatically before dinner he put away four doubles on the rocks, and through the food and the lengthy speeches afterwards kept up a steady intake. At half after eleven, when he tried to leave the table, he couldn't control his legs.

It surprised him. Sitting down, he had not been aware of being drunk. His tongue still worked as well as most around him, and to himself his thoughts seemed perfectly well organised. But his legs buckled as he put his weight on them, and he returned to his seat with a thump. It was considerably later, when the huge room had almost emptied as the guests went home, that he managed to summon enough strength to stand up.

'Guess I took a skinful,' he murmured, smiling to himself in self-excuse.

Holding on to the backs of chairs and at intervals leaning against the wall, he weaved his way to the door. From there he blundered out into the passage and forward to the lobby, and from there, looking as if he were climbing imaginary steps, out into the night through the swinging glass doors.

The cool May evening air made things much worse. The earth seemed literally to be turning beneath his feet. He listed sideways into a half circle and instead of moving forwards towards the parked cars and waiting taxis, staggered head-on into the dark brick front of the wall flanking the entrance. The impact hurt him and confused him further. He put both his hands flat on the rough surface in front of him and laid his face on it, and couldn't work out where he was.

Marius Tollman and Piper Boles had not seen Fred Collyer leave ahead of them. They strolled together along the same route making the ordinary social phrases and gestures of people who had just come together by chance at the end of an evening, and gave no impression at all that they had been eyeing each other meaningfully across the room for hours, and thinking almost exclusively about the conversation which lay ahead.

In a country with legalised bookmaking Marius Tollman might have grown up a respectable law-abiding citizen. As it was, his natural aptitude and only talent had led him into a lifetime of quick footwork which would have done credit to Muhammad Ali. Through the simple expedient of standing bets for the future racing authorities while they were still young enough to be foolish, he remained unpersecuted by them once they reached status and power; and the one sort of winner old crafty Marius could spot better even than horses was the colt heading for the boardroom.

The two men went through the glass doors and stopped just outside with the light from the lobby shining full upon them. Marius never drew people into corners, believing it looked too suspicious.

'Did you get the boys to go along, then?' he asked, standing on his heels with his hands in his pockets and his paunch oozing over his belt.

Piper Boles slowly lit a cigarette, glanced around casually at the star-dotted sky, and sucked comforting smoke into his lungs.

'Yeah,' he said.

'So who's elected?'

'Amberezzio.'

'No,' Marius protested. 'He's not good enough.'

Piper Boles drew deep on his cigarette. He was hungry. One eleven pounds to make tomorrow, and only a five-ounce steak in his belly. He resented fat people,

185

particularly rich fat people. He was putting away his own small store of fat in real estate and growth bonds, but at thirty-eight the physical struggle was near to defeating him. He couldn't face many more years of starvation, finding it worse as his body aged. A sense of urgency had lately led him to consider ways of making a quick ten thousand that once he would have sneered at.

He said, 'He's straight. It'll have to be him.'

Marius thought it over, not liking it, but finally nodded. 'All right, then. Amberezzio.'

Piper Boles nodded, and prepared to move away. It didn't do for a jockey to be seen too long with Marius Tollman, not if he wanted to go on riding second string for the prestigious Somerset Farms, which he most assuredly did.

Marius saw the impulse and said smoothly, 'Did you give any thoughts to a diversion on Crinkle Cut?'

Piper Boles hesitated.

'It'll cost you,' he said.

'Sure,' Marius agreed easily. 'How about another thousand, on top?'

'Used bills. Half before.'

'Sure.'

Piper Boles shrugged off his conscience, tossed out the last of his integrity.

'OK,' he said, and sauntered away to his car as if all his nerves weren't stretched and screaming.

Fred Collyer had heard every word, and he knew, without having to look, that one of the voices was Marius

Tollman's. Impossible for anyone long in the racing game not to recognise that wheezy Boston accent. He understood that Marius had been fixing up a swindle and also that a good little swindle would fill his column nicely. He thought fuzzily that it was necessary to know who Marius had been talking to, and that as the voices had been behind him he had better turn round and find out.

Time however was disjointed for him, and when he pushed himself off the wall and made an effort to focus in the right direction, both men had gone.

'Bastards,' he said aloud to the empty night, and another late homegoer, leaving the hotel, took him compassionately by the elbow and led him to a taxi. He made it safely back to his own room before he passed out.

Since leaving La Guardia that morning he had drunk six beers, four brandies, one double Scotch (by mistake), and nearly three fifths of bourbon.

He woke at eleven the next morning, and couldn't believe it. He stared at the bedside clock.

Eleven.

He had missed the barns and the whole morning merry-go-round on the track. A shiver chilled him at that first realisation, but there was worse to come. When he tried to sit up the room whirled and his head thumped like a pile driver. When he stripped back the sheet he found he had been sleeping in bed fully clothed with his shoes on. When he tried to remember how he had returned the previous evening, he could not do so.

He tottered into the bathroom. His face looked back at him like a nightmare in the mirror, wrinkled and red-eyed, ten years older overnight. Hungover he had been any number of times, but this felt like no ordinary morning-after. A sense of irretrievable disaster hovered somewhere behind the acute physical misery of his head and stomach, but it was not until he had taken off his coat and shirt and pants, and scraped off his shoes, and lain down again weakly on the crumpled bed, that he discovered its nature.

Then he realised with a jolt that not only had he no recollection of the journey back to his motel, he could recall practically nothing of the entire evening. Snatches of conversation from the first hour came back to him, and he remembered sitting at table between a cross old writer from the *Baltimore Star* and an earnest woman breeder from Lexington, neither of whom he liked; but an uninterrupted blank started from halfway through the fried chicken.

He had heard of alcoholic blackouts, but supposed they only happened to alcoholics; and he, Fred Collyer, was not one of those. Of course, he would concede that he did drink a little. Well, a lot, then. But he could stop any time he liked. Naturally he could.

He lay on the bed and sweated, facing the stark thought that one blackout might lead to another, until blackouts gave way to pink panthers climbing the walls. The Sports Editor's warning came back with a bang, and for the first time, uncomfortably remembering the twice he had missed his column, he felt a shade of anxiety about his job. Within five minutes he had reassured himself that they would never fire Fred Collyer, but all the same he would for the paper's sake lay off the drink until after he had written his piece on the Derby. This resolve gave him a glowing feeling of selfless virtue, which at least helped him through the shivering fits and pulsating headaches of an extremely wretched day.

Out at Churchill Downs three other men were just as worried. Piper Boles kicked his horse forward into the starting stalls and worried about what George Highbury, the Somerset Farms' trainer, had said when he went to scale at two pounds overweight. George Highbury thought himself superior to all jocks and spoke to them curtly, win or lose.

'Don't give me that crap,' he said to Boles' excuses. 'You went to the Turfwriters' dinner last night, what do you expect?'

Piper Boles looked bleakly back over his hungry evening with its single martini and said he'd had a session in the sweat box that morning.

Highbury scowled. 'You keep your fat ass away from the table tonight and tomorrow if you want to make Crinkle Cut in the Derby.'

Piper Boles badly needed to ride Crinkle Cut in the Derby. He nodded meekly to Highbury with downcast eyes, and swung unhappily into the saddle.

Instead of bracing him, the threat of losing the ride on Crinkle Cut took the edge off his concentration, so that he came out of the stalls slowly, streaked the first quarter too fast to reach third place, swung wide at the bend and lost his stride straightening out. He finished sixth. He was a totally experienced jockey of above-average ability. It was not one of his days.

On the grandstand Marius Tollman put down his raceglasses shaking his head and clicking his tongue. If Piper Boles couldn't ride a better race than that when he was supposed to be trying to win, what sort of a goddam hash would he make of losing on Crinkle Cut?

Marius thought about the ten thousand he was staking on Saturday's little caper. He had not yet decided whether to tip off certain guys in organised crime, in which case they would cover the stake at no risk to himself, or to gamble on the bigger profit of going it alone. He lowered his wheezy bulk on to his seat and worried about the ease with which a fixed race could unfix itself.

Blisters Schultz worried about the state of his trade, which was suffering a severe recession.

Blisters Schultz picked pockets for a living, and was fed up with credit cards. In the old days, when he'd learned the skill at his grandfather's knee, men carried their billfolds in their rear pants pockets, neatly outlined for all the world to see. Nowadays all these smash and grab muggers had ruined the market: few people carried more than a handful of dollars around with them, and those that did tended to divide it into two portions, with the heavy dough hidden away beneath zips.

Fifty-three years Blisters had survived: forty-five of them by stealing. Several shortish sessions behind bars had been regarded as bad luck, but not as a good reason for not nicking the first wallet he saw when he got out. He had tried to go straight once, but he hadn't liked it: couldn't face the regular hours and the awful feeling of working. After six weeks he had left his well-paid job and gone back thankfully to insecurity. He felt happier stealing two dollars than earning ten.

For the best haul at racemeets you either had to spot the big wads before they were gambled away, or follow a big winner away from the pay-out window. In either case, it meant hanging around the pari-mutuel with your eyes open. The trouble was, too many racecourse cops had cottoned to this modus op, and were apt to stand around looking at people who were just standing there looking.

Blisters had had a bad week. The most promisingly fat wallet had proved, after half an hour's careful stalking, to contain little money but a lot in pornography. Blisters, having a weak sex drive, was disgusted on both counts.

For his first two days' labour he had only twenty-three dollars to show, and five of these he had found on a stairway. His meagre room in Louisville was costing him eight a night, and with transport and eating to take into account, he reckoned he'd have to clear three hundred to make the trip worthwhile.

Always an optimist, he brightened at the thought of Derby Day. The pickings would certainly be easier once the real crowd arrived.

Fred Collyer's private Prohibition lasted intact through Friday. Feeling better when he woke, he cabbed out to Churchill Downs at seven-thirty, writing his expenses on the way. They included many mythical items for the previous day, on the basis that it was better for the office not to know he had been paralytic on Wednesday night. He upped the inflated total a few more dollars: after all, bourbon was expensive, and he would be off the wagon by Sunday.

The initial shock of the blackout had worn off, because during his day in bed he had remembered bits and pieces which he was certain were later in time than the fried chicken. The journey from dinner to bed was still a blank, but the blank had stopped frightening him. At times he felt there was something vital about it he ought to remember, but he persuaded himself that if it had been really important, he wouldn't have forgotten.

Out by the barns the groups of pressmen had already formed round the trainers of the most fancied Derby runners. Fred Collyer sauntered to the outskirts of Harbourne Cressie, and his colleagues made room for him with no reference to his previous day's absence. It reassured him: whatever he had done on Wednesday night, it couldn't have been scandalous.

The notebooks were out. Harbourne Cressie, long practised and fond of publicity, paused between every sentence to give time for all to be written down.

'Pincer Movement ate well last evening and is calm and cool this a.m. On the book we should hold Salad Bowl, unless the track is sloppy by Saturday.'

Smiles all round. The sky blue, the forecast fair.

Fred Collyer listened without attention. He'd heard it all before. They'd all heard it all before. And who the hell cared?

In a rival group two barns away the trainer of Salad Bowl was saying his colt had the beating of Pincer

Movement on the Hialeah form, and could run on any going, sloppy or not.

George Highbury attracted fewer newsmen, as he hadn't much to say about Crinkle Cut. The three-year-old had been beaten by both Pincer Movement and Salad Bowl on separate occasions, and was not expected to reverse things.

On Friday afternoon Fred Collyer spent his time up in the press room and manfully refused a couple of free beers. (*Entertaining various owners at track, twenty-two dollars.*)

Piper Boles rode a hard finish in the sixth race, lost by a short head, and almost passed out from hunger-induced weakness in the jocks' room afterwards. George Highbury, unaware of this, merely noted sourly that Boles had made the weight, and confirmed that he would ride Crinkle Cut on the morrow.

Various friends of Piper Boles, supporting him towards a daybed, asked anxiously in his ear whether tomorrow's scheme was still on. Piper Boles nodded. 'Sure,' he said faintly. 'All the way.'

Marius Tollman was relieved to see Boles riding better, but decided anyway to hedge his bet by letting the syndicate in on the action.

Blisters Schultz lifted two billfolds, containing respectively fourteen and twenty-two dollars. He lost ten of them backing a certainty in the last race.

Pincer Movement, Salad Bowl, and Crinkle Cut, guarded by uniformed men with guns at their waists, looked over the stable doors and with small quivers in their tuned-up muscles watched other horses go out to the track. All three could have chosen to go. All three knew well enough what the trumpet was sounding for, on the other side.

Saturday morning, fine and clear.

Crowds in their thousands converged on Churchill Downs. Eager, expectant, chattering, dressed in bright colours and buying mint juleps in takeaway souvenir glasses, they poured through the gates and over the in-field, reading the latest sports columns on Pincer Movement versus Salad Bowl, and dreaming of picking outsiders that came up at fifty to one.

Blisters Schultz had scraped together just enough to pay his motel bill, but self-esteem depended on better luck with the hoists. His small, lined face with its busy eyes wore a look near to desperation, and the long preda-tory fingers clenched and unclenched convulsively in his pockets.

Piper Boles, with one-twenty-six to do on Crinkle Cut, allowed himself an egg for breakfast and decided to buy property bonds with the five hundred in used notes which had been delivered by hand the previous evening, and with the gains (both legal and illegal) he should add to them that day. If he cleaned up safely that afternoon, he thought, there was no obvious reason why he shouldn't set up the same scheme again, even after he had retired from riding. He hardly noticed the shift in his mind from reluctant dishonesty to habitual fraud.

Marius Tollman spent the morning telephoning to various acquaintances, offering profit. His offers were accepted. Marius Tollman felt a load lift from his spirits and with a spring in his step took his two-sixty pounds down town a few blocks, where a careful gentleman counted out ten thousand dollars in untraceable notes. Marius Tollman gave him a receipt, properly signed. Business was business.

Fred Collyer wanted a drink. One, he thought, wouldn't hurt. It would pep him up a bit, put him on his toes. One little drink in the morning would certainly not stop him writing a punchy piece that evening. *The Star* couldn't possibly frown on just *one* drink before he went to the races, especially not as he had managed to keep clear of the bar the previous evening by going to bed at nine. His abstinence had involved a great effort of will: it would be right to reward such virtue with just one drink.

He had however finished on Wednesday night the bottle he had brought with him to Louisville. He fished out his wallet to check how much he had in it: fifty-three dollars, plenty after expenses to cover a fresh bottle for later as well as a quick one in the bar before he left.

He went downstairs. In the lobby however his colleague Clay Petrovitch again offered a free ride in his Hertz car to Churchill Downs, so he decided he could postpone his one drink for half an hour. He gave himself little mental pats on the back all the way to the racecourse.

Blisters Schultz, circulating among the clusters of people at the rear of the grandstand, saw Marius Tollman going by in the sunshine, leaning backwards to support the weight in front and wheezing audibly in the growing heat.

195

Blisters Schultz licked his lips. He knew the fat man by sight: knew that somewhere around that gross body might be stacked enough lolly to see him through the summer. Marius Tollman would never come to the Derby with empty pockets.

Two thoughts made Blisters hesitate as he slid like an eel in the fat man's wake. The first was that Tollman was too old a hand to let himself be robbed. The second, that he was known to have friends in organised places, and if Tollman was carrying organisation money Blisters wasn't going to burn his fingers by stealing it, which was how he got his nickname in the first place.

Regretfully Blisters peeled off from the quarry, and returned to the throng in the comforting shadows under the grandstand.

At twelve seventeen he infiltrated a close-packed bunch of people waiting for an elevator.

At twelve eighteen he stole Fred Collyer's wallet.

Marius Tollman carried his money in cunning under-arm pockets which he clamped to his sides in a crowd, for fear of pickpockets. When the time was due he would visit as many different selling windows as possible, inconspicuously distributing the stake. He would give Piper Boles almost half of the tickets (along with the second five hundred dollars in used notes), and keep the other half for himself.

A nice tidy little killing, he thought complacently. And no reason why he shouldn't set it up some time again.

He bought a mint julep and smiled kindly at a girl showing more bosom than bashfulness.

The sun stoked up the day. The preliminary contests rolled over one by one with waves of cheering, each hard-ridden finish merely a sideshow attending on the big one, the Derby, the roses, the climax, the ninth race.

In the jocks' room Piper Boles had changed into the silks for Crinkle Cut and began to sweat. The nearer he came to the race the more he wished it was an ordinary Derby day like any other. He steadied his nerves by reading the *Financial Times*.

Fred Collyer discovered the loss of his wallet upstairs in the press room when he tried to pay for a beer. He cursed, searched all his pockets, turned the press room upside down, got the keys of the Hertz car from Clay Petrovitch, and trailed all the way back to the car park. After a fruitless search there he strode furiously back to the grandstands, violently throttling in his mind the lousy stinking son of a bitch who had stolen his money. He guessed it had been an old hand, an old man, even. The new vicious lot relied on muscle, not skill.

His practical problems were not too great. He needed little cash. Clay Petrovitch was taking him back to town, the motel bill was going direct to the *Manhattan Star*, and his plane ticket was safely lying on the chest of drawers in his bedroom. He could borrow twenty bucks or so, maybe, from Clay or others in the press room, to cover essentials.

Going up in the elevator he thought that the loss of his money was like a sign from heaven; no money, no drink.

Blisters Schultz kept Fred Collyer sober the whole afternoon.

★ ★ ★

Pincer Movement, Salad Bowl, and Crinkle Cut were led from their barns, into the tunnel under the cars and crowds, and out again on to the track in front of the grandstands. They walked loosely, casually, used to the limelight but knowing from experience that this was only a foretaste. The first sight of the day's prices galvanised the crowds towards the pari-mutuel window like shoals of multicoloured fish.

Piper Boles walked out with the other jockeys towards the wire-meshed enclosure where horses, trainers and owners stood in a group in each stall. He had begun to suffer from a feeling of detachment and unreality: he could not believe that he, a basically honest jockey, was about to make a hash of the Kentucky Derby.

George Highbury repeated for about the fortieth time the tactics they had agreed on. Piper Boles nodded seriously, as if he had every intention of carrying them out. He actually heard scarcely a word; and he was deaf also to the massed bands and the singing when the Derby runners were led out to the track. 'My Old Kentucky Home' swelled the emotions of a multitude and brought out a flutter of eye-wiping handkerchiefs, but in Piper Boles they raised not a blink.

Through the parade, the canter down, the circling round, and even into the starting stalls, the detachment persisted. Only then, with the tension showing plain on the faces of the other riders, did he click back to realisation. His heart-rate nearly doubled and energy flooded into his brain.

Now, he thought. It is now, in the next half-minute,

that I earn myself one thousand dollars; and after that, the rest.

He pulled down his goggles and gathered his reins and his whip. He had Pincer Movement on his right and Salad Bowl on his left, and when the stalls sprang open he went out between them in a rush, tipping his weight instantly forward over the withers and standing in the stirrups with his head almost as far forward as Crinkle Cut's.

All along past the stands the first time he concentrated on staying in the centre of the main bunch, as unnoticeable as possible, and round the top bend he was still there, sitting quiet and doing nothing very much. But down the backstretch, lying about tenth in a field of twenty-six, he earned his thousand.

No one except Piper Boles ever knew what really happened; only he knew that he'd shortened his left rein with a sharp turn of his wrist and squeezed Crinkle Cut's ribs with his right foot. The fast-galloping horse obeyed these directions, veered abruptly left, and crashed into the horse beside him.

The horse beside him was still Salad Bowl. Under the impact Salad Bowl cannoned into the horse on his own left, rocked back, stumbled, lost his footing entirely, and fell. The two horses on his tail fell over him.

Piper Boles didn't look back. The swerve and collision had lost him several places which Crinkle Cut at the best of times would have been unable to make up. He rode the rest of the race strictly according to instructions, finishing flat out in twelfth place.

Of the one hundred and forty thousand spectators at

Churchill Downs, only a handful had had a clear view of the disaster on the far side of the track. The buildings in the in-field, and the milling crowds filling all its furthest areas, had hidden the crash from nearly all standing at ground level and from most on the grandstands. Only the press, high up, had seen. They sent out urgent fact-finders and buzzed like a stirred-up beehive.

Fred Collyer, out on the balcony, watched the photographers running to immortalise Pincer Movement and reflected sourly that none of them would have taken close-up pictures of the second favourite, Salad Bowl, down on the dirt. He watched the horseshoe of dark red roses being draped over the winner and the triumphal presentation of the trophies, and then went inside for the re-run of the race on television. They showed the Salad Bowl incident forwards, backwards and sideways, and then jerked it through slowly in a series of stills.

'See that,' said Clay Petrovitch, pointing at the screen over Fred Collyer's shoulder. 'It was Crinkle Cut caused it. You can see him crash into Salad Bowl . . . there! . . . Crinkle Cut, that's the joker in the pack.'

Fred Collyer strolled over to his place, sat down, and stared at his typewriter. Crinkle Cut. He knew something about Crinkle Cut. He thought intensely for five minutes, but he couldn't remember what he knew.

Details and quotes came up to the press room. All fallen jocks shaken but unhurt, all horses ditto; stewards in a tizzy, making instant enquiries and re-running the patrol-camera film over and over. Suspension for Piper Boles considered unlikely, as blind eye usually turned to rough riding in the Derby. Piper Boles had gone on record as saying 'Crinkle Cut just suddenly swerved. I didn't expect it, and couldn't prevent him bumping Salad Bowl.' Large numbers of people believed him.

Fred Collyer thought he might as well get a few pars down on paper: it would bring the first drink nearer, and boy how he needed that drink. With an ear open for fresher information he tapped out a blow-by-blow I-was-there account of an incident he had hardly seen. When he began to read it through, he saw that the first words he had written were 'The diversion on Crinkle Cut stole the post-race scene . . .'

Diversion on Crinkle Cut? He hadn't meant to write that . . . or not exactly. He frowned. And there were other words in his mind, just as stupid. He put his hands back on the keys and tapped them out.

'It'll cost you . . . a thousand in used notes . . . half before.'

He stared at what he had written. He had made it up, he must have. Or dreamt it. One or the other.

A dream. That was it. He remembered. He had had a dream about two men planning a fixed race, and one of them had been Marius Tollman, wheezing away about a diversion on Crinkle Cut.

Fred Collyer relaxed and smiled at the thought, and the next minute knew quite suddenly that it hadn't been a dream at all. He had heard Marius Tollman and Piper Boles planning a diversion on Crinkle Cut, and he had forgotten because he'd been drunk. Well, he reassured himself uneasily, no harm done, he had remembered now, hadn't he?

No he hadn't. If Crinkle Cut was a diversion, what

was he a diversion *from*? Perhaps if he waited a bit, he would find he knew that too.

Blisters Schultz spent Fred Collyer's money on two hot dogs, one mint julep, and five losing bets. On the winning side, he had harvested three more billfolds and a woman's purse: total haul, ninety-four bucks. Gloomily he decided to call it a day and not come back next year.

Marius Tollman lumbered busily from window to window of the pari-mutuel and the stewards asked to see the jockeys involved in the Salad Bowl pile-up.

The crowds, hot, tired, and frayed at the edges, began to leave in the yellowing sunshine. The bands marched away. The stalls which sold souvenirs packed up their wares. Pincer Movement had his picture taken for the thousandth time and the runners for the tenth, last, and least interesting race of the day walked over from the barns.

Piper Boles was waiting outside the stewards' room for a summons inside, but Marius Tollman used the highest-class messengers, and the package he entrusted was safely delivered. Piper Boles nodded, slipped it into his pocket, and gave the stewards a performance worthy of Hollywood.

Fred Collyer put his head in his hands, trying to remember. A drink, he thought, might help. Diversion. Crinkle Cut. Amberezzio.

He sat up sharply. *Amberezzio*. And what the hell did that mean? *It has to be Amberezzio*.

'Clay,' he said, leaning back over his chair. 'Do you know of a horse called Amberezzio?'

Clay Petrovitch shook his bald head. 'Never heard of it.'

Fred Collyer called to several others through the hubbub, 'Know of a horse called Amberezzio?' And finally he got an answer. 'Amberezzio isn't a horse, he's an apprentice.'

'*It has to be Amberezzio. He's straight.*'

Fred Collyer knocked his chair over as he stood up. They had already called one minute to post time on the last race.

'Lend me twenty bucks, there's a pal,' he said to Clay.

Clay, knowing about the lost wallet, amiably agreed and slowly began to bring out his money.

'Hurry, for Chrissake,' Fred Collyer said urgently.

'OK, OK.' He handed over the twenty dollars and turned back to his own typewriter.

Fred Collyer grabbed his racecard and pushed through the post-Derby chatter to the pari-mutuel window further along the press room. He flipped the pages . . . Tenth race, Homeward Bound, claiming race, eight runners . . . His eye skimmed down the list, and found what he sought.

Phillip Amberezzio, riding a horse Fred Collyer had never heard of.

'Twenty on the nose, number six,' he said quickly, and received his ticket seconds before the window shut. Trembling slightly, he pushed back through the crowd, and out on to the balcony. He was the only pressman watching the race.

Those jocks did it beautifully, he thought in admiration. Artistic. You wouldn't have known if you hadn't known. They bunched him in and shepherded him along, and then at the perfect moment gave him a suddenly clear opening. Amberezzio won by half a length, with all the others waving their whips as if beating the last inch out of their mounts.

Fred Collyer laughed. That poor little so-and-so probably thought he was a hell of a fellow, bringing home a complete outsider with all the big boys baying at his heels.

He went back inside the press room and found everyone's attention directed towards Harbourne Cressie, who had brought with him the owner and jockey of Pincer Movement. Fred Collyer dutifully took down enough quotes to cover the subject, but his mind was on the other story, the big one, the gift.

It would need careful handling, he thought. It would need the very best he could do, as he would have to be careful not to make direct accusations while leaving it perfectly clear that an investigation was necessary. His old instincts partially re-awoke. He was even excited. He would write his piece in the quiet and privacy of his own room in the motel. Couldn't do it here on the racecourse, with every turfwriter in the world looking over his shoulder.

Down in the jockeys' changing room Piper Boles quietly distributed the pari-mutuel tickets which Marius Tollman had delivered: five hundred dollars' worth to each of the seven 'unsuccessful' riders in the tenth race, and one thousand dollars' worth to himself. Each jockey subsequently asked a wife or girlfriend to collect the winnings and several of these would have made easy prey for Blisters Schultz, had he not already started home.

Marius Tollman's money had shortened the odds on Amberezzio, but he was still returned at twelve to one. Marius Tollman wheezed and puffed from pay-out window to pay-out window, collecting his winnings bit by bit. He hadn't room for all the cash in the under-arm pockets and finally stowed some casually in more accessible spots. Too bad about Blisters Schultz.

Fred Collyer collected a fistful of winnings and repaid the twenty to Clay Petrovitch.

'If you had a hot tip, you might have passed it on,' grumbled Petrovitch, thinking of all the expenses old Fred would undoubtedly claim for his free rides to the racecourse.

'It wasn't a tip, just a hunch.' He couldn't tell Clay what the hunch was, as he wrote for a rival paper. 'I'll buy you a drink on the way home.'

'I should damn well think so.'

Fred Collyer immediately regretted his offer, which had been instinctive. He remembered that he had not intended to drink until after he had written. Still, perhaps one . . . And he did need a drink very badly. It seemed a century since his last, on Wednesday night.

They left together, walking out with the remains of the crowd. The racecourse looked battered and bedraggled at the end of the day: the scarlet petals of the tulips lay on the ground, leaving rows of naked pistils stick-ing forlornly up, and the bright rugs of grass were dusty grey and covered with litter. Fred Collyer thought only of the dough in his pocket and the story in his head, and both of them gave him a nice warm glow.

A drink to celebrate, he thought. Buy Clay a thank-you

drink, and maybe perhaps just one more to celebrate. It wasn't often, after all, that things fell his way so miraculously.

They stopped for the drink. The first double swept through Fred Collyer's veins like fire through a parched forest. The second made him feel great.

'Time to go,' he said to Clay. 'I've got my piece to write.'

'Just one more,' Clay said. 'This one's on me.'

'Better not.' He felt virtuous.

'Oh come on,' Clay said, and ordered. With the faintest of misgivings Fred Collyer sank his third: but couldn't he still outwrite every racing man in the business? Of course he could.

They left after the third. Fred Collyer bought a fifth of bourbon for later, when he had finished his story. Back in his own room he took just the merest swig from it before he sat down to write.

The words wouldn't come. He screwed up six attempts and poured some bourbon into a tooth glass.

Marius Tollman, Crinkle Cut, Piper Boles, Amberezzio . . . It wasn't all that simple.

He took a drink. He didn't seem to be able to help it.

The Sports Editor would give him a raise for a story like this, or at least there would be no more quibbling about expenses.

He took a drink.

Piper Boles had earned himself a thousand bucks for crashing into Salad Bowl. Now how the hell did you write that without being sued for libel?

He took a drink.

The jockeys in the tenth race had conspired together to let the only straight one among them win. How in hell could you say that?

He took a drink.

The stewards and the press had had all their attention channelled towards the crash in the Derby and had virtually ignored the tenth race. The stewards wouldn't thank him for pointing it out.

He took another drink. And another. And more.

His deadline for telephoning his story to the office was ten o'clock the following morning. When that hour struck he was asleep and snoring, fully dressed, on his bed. The empty bourbon bottle lay on the floor beside him, and his winnings, which he had tried to count, lay scattered over his chest.

Dick Francis was a successful jockey before turning to crime in 1962. That year saw the publication of his thriller Dead Cert, which derived much strength from its convincing background in the racing world. Francis, who had previously published his autobiography and established himself as a sports writer, was encouraged by the reception his novel received and embarked on a new career in fiction. By the time of his recent retirement, he had become one of the world's most popular thriller writers. He chaired the CWA in 1973–4 and won the CWA Gold Dagger in 1979, being awarded the CWA Cartier Diamond Dagger a decade later.

ANTONIA FRASER

The Twist

Something about the way the woman twisted her rings, took one off, swapped it round with another, transferred rings from finger to finger, hand to hand, surveyed the result and then began the nervous twisting all over again, reminded me of Margaret. But these rings, so far as I could see, were not the gleaming diamond clusters, glinting ruby half-hoops, heavy sapphire globules with which Margaret had been wont to play. These were plain white rings, ivory rings at best, but more likely plastic, gold rings which were so clearly not made of precious metal that they reminded one disagreeably of curtain rings.

The woman opposite me in the carriage continued to twist her rings. In that nervously repeated gesture was all the resemblance: for one thing this woman looked far older than Margaret must be now, last seen in all her pampered glory of fur and silk. However Margaret had aged – and she must of course have aged to some degree over the intervening years – she would have managed to age gracefully. And she could never have aged *downhill* as it were. I knew exactly the kind of old – or rather middle-aged – woman Margaret would have become; you see them sometimes at parties, fragile, elegant and protected, still candles for all the male moths while the younger beauties sulk at their unexpected neglect. This woman, in a blackish overcoat and dirty boots, was near to a tramp: what was more, there were bruises on her face.

Then I looked again, at the woman still twisting her shoddy rings. I looked again and saw that the woman was Margaret. Margaret, my ex-wife.

I will not deny that I experienced one short, savage pang of sheer pleasure. After that pity and pity alone overwhelmed me. Had Margaret remained as svelte and beautiful as she had been under my besotted care, I should certainly have felt very differently, experiencing neither the pleasure nor the pity. I might have felt a brief stab of pain for the past on first sighting her; after that I would have tried to escape from the encounter. Certainly I should have tried to escape if she had been accompanied by Jason.

Jason: her second husband and my ex-partner, as I suppose I must call him. But I have never seen either of them following the divorce, I took care of that, and perhaps they did too; so to me he is still in my thoughts Jason, her lover and my partner. Just as she is still, somewhere in my thoughts, still Margaret, my Margaret and my wife. It was that thought which provoked the pity, that and her total physical degradation.

The bruises – who? Surely Jason was not responsible. I had accused my partner – ex-partner – of many things in my mind over the last twenty years, but violence or even a tendency towards violence was not amongst them. As for poverty, our business affairs were no longer linked as they had been, but even I knew enough to realise that Jason must remain an extremely rich man. Besides, this Margaret at whom I was gazing with pity was not only poor but had evidently been poor for some years. No sudden fall from wealth would account for the haggard, battered face, the cast-off clothing.

At that moment, Margaret looked up. Her eyes, her once beautiful eyes, met mine. To my horror, I found that my own filled with tears. But Margaret herself gazed back without expression, merely continuing that twisting, that eternal twisting of the rings.

'Meg,' I said.

The woman, Margaret, said nothing in reply; her gaze was in fact quite vacant as though she had not recognised me. Of course I had not recognised *her* at first. But then I, I am well preserved. Everyone says so. I have taken care of myself (having no one to take care of me). Or perhaps it would be more realistic to admit that I have always looked much as I do now, which is staid, middle-aged, and respectable. 'Darling, you look like a man of sixty already,' had been one of Margaret's favourite jibes. 'Why can't you go to a better tailor?' After a bit, I realised that this meant: why can't you go to Jason's tailor? And I stopped my pathetic, earnest attempts to please her sartorially. I think that cruel moment was when I knew that Margaret was going to leave me.

I stood up and crossed the carriage. I touched the woman on the shoulder.

'Margaret,' I said. 'It's me, Andrew.'

Margaret looked up at me; her fingers at the rings were suddenly still. Then I saw the white stick lying beside her, previously hidden by her black coat.

'Andrew?' she said rather doubtfully. 'I thought I recognised your voice just now. But sometimes one hears voices. You know how it is.' Then with more energy she added, 'You *don't* know how it is.'

'Meg,' I said tenderly, finding all the familiar protective yearning come back to me.

'Oh, Andrew,' she cried suddenly, feeling up towards my arm and anchoring her hand upon it. 'Andrew, help me.' It was a voice of pleading and need that she had never used in all the years of our marriage, the teasing, critical Margaret gone for ever. 'Please will you help me? You don't know what happened to me—'

There and then in the carriage, I kissed her, stopped her speaking with my gentle kiss. There would be time for her to tell me these things. I held her bruised face in mine, marking how old she looked, the skin lined, the hair listless, and touched the hands adorned with their cheap rings, which had brought her back to me.

Her hands! The state of her hands alone chilled me when I thought of my Margaret's soft white hands and pearly nails, hands which belonged as much to her manicurist (as I once lightly told her) as they did to me. I do not know what I would have done then. Taken her home, bathed her, kissed her again many times, always gently, to show that I could overlook the loss of her beauty, cared for her—

But at that point I found myself waking from this dream, this delicious dream (for it was certainly no

212

nightmare). And I felt the warm hand of my wife Margaret, lying beside me on the pillow between us in our bed. I could feel the nobbles and sharpness of her rings, the many rings which she never took off, even at night. I would like to have wrenched off those rings from her fingers, before I killed her, twisting her own silk scarf round her neck, twisting it many times as she herself was wont to twist her jewellery. I would like her to have lain dead there with curtain rings and cheap plastic on her beautiful fingers.

But there was no time. So I killed her as she lay, still in her jewels, I killed her for her treachery and her adultery and her mockery and her twisting, twisting fingers which even in death would not give up their sparkling secrets. Margaret, now my dead wife.

Antonia Fraser is a highly regarded historian who won the CWA Gold Dagger for the best non-fiction crime book of the year in 1996. She has, however, established a distinct reputation as an author of crime fiction, notably as creator of Jemima Shore. Jemima is a television journalist with a taste for sleuthing and her cases include Quiet as a Nun, A Splash of Red *and* Cool Repentance. *In addition to her novels, Lady Antonia Fraser has published two collections of short crime fiction:* Jemima Shore's First Case *and* Jemima Shore at the Sunny Grave.

MICHAEL GILBERT

Judith

Two hundred years ago Belling was an island. A hundred years later, with the draining of the fens, it had turned into a prosperous farming community. Fifty years after that, as its nearest neighbour, Woodhall Cross, developed into an industrial complex, it became something between a large village and a small town. It had always had a church and a school. When the census showed that the number of its inhabitants had topped two thousand its upward progress was crowned by the award of its own police station.

Through all these changes and developments it had remained, as PC Hennessy often told the vicar, a village at heart. 'And thank the Lord,' he would add, 'a quiet village. A little noisy, perhaps, at the Annual Feast, but no one minds a bit of horseplay once a year.'

A Monday in early December was to change all that.

Mrs Franklund lived in one of the three cottages in Binders Lane, on the northern fringe of the village. She had lost her husband shortly after the birth of her only child, Ellen. Ellie was a fair-haired mite, eleven years old, but looking much younger. She had attended the village school since she was six and had now been promised a place at Woodhall Grammar School. To take it up she had to pass a fairly stiff entrance exam. To make sure that she did so Miss Hooker, headmistress of the village school, had offered to give her an hour's extra tuition on Mondays and Thursdays. This would take place after the younger children had left the school, at half-past three.

Mrs Franklund was grateful, but one thing worried her. As the year ran on towards Christmas, by half-past four dusk was going to be setting in. True, the distance between the school and her house was not much more than a quarter of a mile; up East Street, along the flank of Abbacy Copse, turn right at the top into Binders Lane and there you were. But alone! And in the dusk, with a mist coming up as it did so often from the fenland which encircled the village to the north. Ellie was the whole of her mother's life. Unthinkable to take chances with her.

In spite of a rheumatic hip which made walking difficult Mrs Franklund would willingly have hobbled down to the school and brought Ellie home herself. Happily, an alternative had presented itself. Miss Hooker had extended her offer of extra tuition to Martin Amherst, eldest son of the vicar. He was a stalwart boy of twelve. For a small addition to his weekly pocket money he had agreed to escort Ellen to her front door.

On this particular evening he carried out three-quarters of his duty. The lane along the left side of Abbacy Copse curved slightly, but by standing on the verge of the roadway he could see Ellie almost up to the corner. When she was perhaps twenty yards from it

216

he turned and ran. He was late for a most important date with Tim Pollard, who had acquired a video-taper which he proposed to use on the BBC programme which started at 4.30. It was now 4.35.

When Ellie was not home by twenty to five her mother comforted herself by remembering that, more than once, Miss Hooker had kept her back to finish a piece of work. But never for more than a quarter of an hour. By five o'clock that wisp of comfort had faded. She telephoned the school, but got no answer. There was just one more possibility. Might Ellie have gone back with Martin to the rectory? It had happened once before. She tried the rectory, but got no reply there either. The rector and his wife were out and Martin had gone straight to Tim Pollard's house.

Not knowing what to do, she did what most people in Belling seemed to do when in distress. She hobbled along to the cottage on her left where she found Judith Lyte in the kitchen, playing Animal Snap with her two younger children, Sarah and Jenny. Tea was waiting for the return of the older two, Becky and Mark. They were at Woodhall Grammar and had not yet got home.

As soon as she understood what the distraught Mrs Franklund was trying to tell her, Judith rang the police station.

PC Hennessy was a great admirer of Mrs Lyte. She was not only chairman of the Parish Council and one of the acknowledged leaders of the community, but was something else – something difficult to describe. He listened carefully to what she had to say, switched his telephone to 'answer', shouted to his wife to mind the front desk and set out into the thickening mist.

When he reached Binders Lane he found that Mrs Lyte had telephoned the post office, as the quickest way of spreading the news, and a small search party was already on hand. The news had even penetrated the Pollard house and a white-faced Martin had told them where he had seen Ellie last. He said, over and over again, 'At the corner. She'd almost turned the corner,' as though speaking the words somehow exculpated him.

Abbacy Copse was clearly the first place to search. It produced no sign of Ellie. On the other side of the copse and filling the space between it and the end of Binders Lane was an odd patch of waste land known as the Rectory Piece. It was part of the old glebe and the rector's predecessor had allowed half a dozen structures to be put up on it, the rents of which helped out his slender stipend. Two of them were solid, breeze-block affairs, one used by Newton, the clearance contractor, to park his heavy machinery; the other by the rector himself for the storage of church furniture and oddments. The other four were smaller and were built of tarred timber. Since they were all securely padlocked they were, for the moment, ignored.

With the arrival of the bus bringing back children from the Grammar School and cars with men returning from their work, the search party grew and set out on what seemed to be a hopeless search of the fen. It was quite dark now and the mist was thicker than ever. After an hour had produced only frustration and falls into the dykes which criss-crossed the fields, the rector, in consultation with Ted Willows, called a halt. Ted was an expert on fen weather. 'Like as not,' he said, 'we'll have a breeze by early morning. And the moon will be up.'

The searchers retired for repairs and refreshment to the Bull, which was the unofficial centre of Belling. By one o'clock Ted had been proved a true prophet and it was under a cold moon, three hours later, that the bedraggled body of Ellen Franklund was lifted from a dyke, four hundred yards north of the village. Her dress had been pulled off and then knotted round her neck. Her face was a mass of blood and bruises.

Hennessy then did what he should have done many hours earlier. He sent for help.

It arrived at half-past six in two cars. The first one contained Detective Inspector Waite and the County Pathologist. The second, Detective Sergeant Copsey and the Coroner's Officer. Waite was a smallish man, with the eyes and teeth of a fox terrier. He said, 'I want all the men in the village – and when I say men I include boys of twelve or more—' As he said this he looked at Copsey, who nodded. He had just concluded a case in which three boys had raped a schoolgirl. 'Get them together in whatever's the most convenient place.'

'The church,' said Judith and the rector nodded. 'We could get five hundred in there, standing.'

Very few people in the village had gone to bed and whilst the few men who had were being roused, Waite and the pathologist examined the child's body and paid a visit to Abbacy Copse.

At seven o'clock the Inspector climbed on to the step beside the pulpit and addressed the crowd which filled the aisles and transepts and had spread into the choir and sanctuary. He said, 'Yesterday evening, at twenty-five minutes to five, somebody took Ellen Franklund into the wood up there—' He gestured over his shoulder and heard the murmur, 'Abbacy Copse.' 'Is that what you call it? Well, that's where he took her. She may even have gone willingly. We think she probably knew the man.' Heads turned and people started to look at each other as the significance of this sank in. 'When he had her safely in the wood, I expect he terrified her by telling her what he'd do if she made a sound. Then he ripped off her dress, pushed her down on to the ground and got on top of her. When he had had whatever satisfaction he could get from her small body he got up, seized her by the ankles and swung her head, two or three times, against the trunk of a tree.'

When he stopped speaking the silence was absolute. It was a silence of shock and held breath. Then he said, 'We *know* that this is what happened. We have seen the blood and flesh on the tree and there are shreds of bark on the child's forehead. Now you know as much as we know. The rest will have to come from you. I and my sergeant will be questioning you. More than once perhaps. We shall go on until we have the truth.' He added, in a more conversational tone, 'I know that many of you work outside the village. Before you leave, give your names and a note of your destinations to my sergeant.'

Probably only Judith Lyte really understood what the Inspector was doing. That he had painted the picture of Ellen's death in the coldest and most brutal words possible, in order to secure the co-operation of everyone who heard him. It had to be the whole-hearted sort of co-operation that would hold steady during the days – maybe the weeks – of questioning that were to come.

Most of the Inspector's attention on the first day centred on the six buildings on Rectory Piece. He did not suspect that they had played an immediate part in the crime. He had another reason which, for the moment, he kept to himself. The huts were subjected to minute examination. The team, which now included a forensic scientist, started at the south-east corner with the one used by Mr Greenslade as a bicycle repair shop. North of that was the hut of Mr Pollard, a photo-maniac. It housed an elaborate enlarger and other expensive photographic apparatus. The one above that was empty. Beyond that, the hut used by Mr Coleman, an estate agent with a hobby of making mechanical toys. Next to it were the two more elaborate structures: the depot where George Newton kept his heavy machinery and the rector's private store, where Sergeant Copsey spent a baffling hour inspecting presentation vases, broken monuments and three versions of the Christmas crib.

Binders Lane had to be acquitted. The three cottages in it belonged to Mrs Franklund, Judith Lyte and old Mrs Ambrose, who was deaf and bedridden. The far end of the lane was more promising. Fronting the road up which Ellen had walked to her death were the back gardens of four houses. The Inspector had good reasons for concentrating on them. He argued that a man coming from any of the houses behind them would have to pass many windows before reaching the copse, while a man coming from one of them had only to slip quietly down his own back garden and cross the road.

Further investigation had narrowed the possibilities.

The house owners, starting from the north end, were Mr Marcus, Mr Harris, the Misses Farrant and Mr Vosper. Mr Marcus had been in bed with pleurisy, with either his wife or his daughter Angela in attendance. Mr Harris worked in Woodhall Cross and was vouched for by his secretary and others. Mr Vosper had been at home all afternoon, allegedly writing letters. No one had seen him until he joined in the search.

At the end of seven days of exhaustive and exhausting work the Inspector reported his conclusions to the Chief Constable. He said, 'Having the advantage of knowing when and where this crime was committed, we've been able to acquit the great majority of the village, either by their own testimony or the testimony of their friends and neighbours. They were not my prime suspects. I was merely, as you might say, clearing the undergrowth. Nor was I looking for outsiders. There are only two bridges over the Skirm Dyke and a stranger would have been noticed at once. So I was able to concentrate on this proposition. That the crime must have been committed by someone who knew exactly what Ellen's programme was. Someone who had watched her walking back and had calculated that if her escort took his eyes off her he would have a chance. Therefore it must either be someone with a sound reason for hanging around Binders Lane – which means one of the owners of the huts in it – or someone whose house overlooks it.'

The Chief Constable nodded his agreement.

'Taking the house owners first, we've been able to eliminate three of them.' He explained the steps he had taken.

The Chief Constable said, 'So Vosper seems the most likely.'

'He heads my list. Then there are the hut owners. George Newton and the rector have got rock-solid alibis. But I can't eliminate any of the other three. Pollard, Greenslade and Coleman. They're all self-employed and being their own bosses they can slip out of their offices as soon as their day's work's over and get on with what really interests them – model cars or the like. In fact, Greenslade and Coleman admit that's just what they did. Pollard says he spent some time out in the fen looking for a hide for his bird photography.'

'Pollard?' said the Chief Constable thoughtfully. 'Wasn't it his son who lured young Martin away from his job as escort?'

'He's number two on my list.'

'Vosper, Pollard, Greenslade, Coleman. It's not a long list, but it's still three too many.'

'I agree,' said the Inspector. 'And that's where we come to the real difficulty. If there'd been one suspect, we could have justified asking for a warrant, gone through his house and his clothing and maybe picked up the clues we wanted. No chance of that now. Vosper, Greenslade and Coleman are bachelors. Pollard's a widower. Like most of the houses in the village they have wood-burning stoves. By now they could have destroyed every atom of the clothing they were wearing that evening.'

'So you're stuck?'

'For the moment, yes.'

'You realise that if he gets away with it he'll probably do it again.'

'Next time,' said the Inspector, 'they may call us in at once. Before they've trampled over every helpful mark on the ground.'

Constable Hennessy, who was in the Inspector's confidence, was able to report the gist of this to the only person in the village he felt able to confide in. Judith Lyte listened in silence. Then she said, 'If the professionals are giving up, the amateurs must take a hand.'

That evening she mustered her private army. It consisted of her four children: Rebecca, fifteen; Mark, thirteen; Sarah, eleven, and Jennifer, nine. They showed no open surprise at what she said to them, although her idea was startling.

So far the search had proceeded along the upper level, the level inhabited by responsible adults, all willing to help, most of them speaking the truth. Now Judith had resolved to explore the lower level, the underworld where children lived and moved.

From studying her own family and their wide circle of friends she had concluded that the eyes and ears of children formed an astonishing information service which would tell you all you wanted to know, if you were patient, and if you could read its code.

It was not an easy code. Children had their private customs and taboos. They lied consistently and successfully. They talked sense and nonsense mixed. This was the network she was asking her children to tune into.

She said, 'I'm convinced that some child knows something. Maybe they don't appreciate the significance of it. Maybe they're frightened to speak. I'm particularly interested in the girls. Girls talk to each other.'

'Non-stop,' said Mark.

'Boys are just as bad,' said Rebecca.

They both attended Woodhall Grammar School. The two younger ones were still at the village primary school. Thus she had spies in both camps and found, at the conferences which took place each evening, that she was being presented slowly with a conspectus of both schools: the loyalties and treacheries, the feuds and alliances, the double-cross and the treble-cross. A pattern as intricate as in any medieval Italian city.

'Look for abnormalities,' she said. 'Time's running out. We must do this before the end of term.'

It was on the fifth evening, among a host of other trivialities, that Mark said, 'If you want abnormalities, here's one for you. Billy Sherwood came to school today with a lovely black eye – a real shiner.'

'Nothing unusual about that,' said little Jennifer virtuously. 'Boys are always fighting.'

'What was unusual about it was that it was his older brother, Roger, who hit him. Normally they're pretty good friends. This time Roger lost his temper because Billy was teasing him about losing his girlfriend.'

'Girlfriend?' said Judith. 'For goodness' sake, isn't he a bit young for that sort of thing?'

The look on her family's faces showed Judith that she had committed the serious crime of being square.

'Most of the boys have girlfriends,' said Mark. 'What really upset him was that his steady had dropped him *for another girl*. She'd stolen her from her regular pash.'

To re-establish her position Judith said, 'You don't have to explain about pashes. After all, I was six years at boarding school.'

'I think it's a bit more organised now than it was in your day,' said Rebecca kindly. 'All older girls are supposed to have one or two young adorers. They're called strings.'

'I suppose you've got half a dozen,' said Mark. 'Did you know that she was the most popular girl in the school?'

'Pipe down,' said his mother. 'I want to understand this. Let's have it again, with names.'

'Well, there was this girl Lucilla. She had two regular strings. Angela and Vicky. Vicky's a bit of a smasher herself, so she thought the time had come to stop being a string and pick up a couple of adorers. And the first one she collected was Patricia who had been Roger's steady. OK?'

'Say it all again slowly,' said Judith. And when he had done this, 'So Lucilla's left with only one string, Angela. Bad luck, no doubt, but—'

'It was worse than that, because Angela suddenly went right off her, too. In fact, she seemed to go right off everything.'

'Meaning what?'

'Went broody. Seemed frightened to open her mouth.'

'Has she got a surname?'

'Her name's Marcus.'

'The girl who was looking after her father with pleurisy?'

'That's the one. She was allowed two afternoons off a week so that her mother could get out and do the shopping.'

Judith felt like an angler who has fished long and

patiently and sees the float disappear and feels the line grow taut. Too soon to be sure what it would lead to, but the catch was there. No doubt of it.

She said, 'You've got just the one job now, Becky. Sack all your existing adorers and fasten Angela Marcus to you with hoops of steel.'

'I'm not sure—'

'If you're as popular as Mark says, I'm sure you'll be able to do it. I suppose there's an accepted technique—'

'What you do is, you smile at her during morning prayers. If she doesn't look away, you get hold of her afterwards and ask her what her favourite hymn is – they've all got favourite hymns – and you go off to Miss Norton, who plays the piano, and ask if you can have it next morning. She's a decent sort and usually says "yes".'

'And then?'

'When the hymn's being sung you smile again. If she smiles back, she's hooked.'

'Can you do it?'

Rebecca giggled. 'It'll be a bit of a rush job.'

Two days later she reported that the first step had been taken.

'The hymn she chose did it. "Lead, kindly light, amid the encircling gloom." Now I'm the light and she's the gloom. And then some! Yesterday behind the pavilion she told me her life story.'

'But she didn't tell you what had upset her.'

'No. But I'm sure she's going to. She's longing to tell someone.'

That was on the Wednesday. On the Friday when Becky came home her mother saw that her face was white and that she looked as if she had been sick, or was going to be. She took her into the kitchen and bolted the door. Then she said, 'Let's have it, love.'

'It was horrible. If I'd had any idea what it was going to be, I couldn't have gone on with it. Before she'd tell me, she made me swear not to tell anyone. Then she agreed I could tell you, if you swore the same thing.'

Her mother thought about this for some time whilst the other children, realising that something serious had happened, stopped trying to break down the kitchen door. Then she said, 'Very well. You have my word.'

'That evening, you know — when it happened — she'd left her father's bedroom to fetch something from the kitchen at the back of the house. She saw Ellie coming up the road and she saw Mr Coleman step out, say something to her, and lead her by the hand, back into the wood.'

'And said nothing about it to anyone.'

'She couldn't. Her father works for Mr Coleman *and* owes him money. If the police tried to get the story out of her, she'd deny it. I'm sure of that.'

'All right,' said her mother. 'Now you can forget all about it.'

'But what are you going to do?'

'I'm going to think about it.'

For three weeks she did nothing, except think. And her thoughts were confused and uncomfortable.

If she passed on Angela's story to the police, they would question her, and she would deny it. Would probably say that she'd made it all up. If she kept quiet, Coleman would have got away with his filthy crime.

More, when a suitable interval had elapsed, as the desire built up, and the secret itch became intolerable, he would try again. Who would be the next little Ellie?

As an estate agent he had every excuse for touring the countryside in his car, finding empty houses he could use. In the end a child would be dragged into one of them. On this occasion he would have more time to enjoy himself. Thinking about all of this she came to a conclusion.

Traditionally her two eldest went for the last week of the Christmas holidays to stay with her elder sister and sample the mild dissipations of the country town. On the night after they left, with the two younger ones safely in their beds, she was able to make the first move.

She went out just after midnight. On her way to Coleman's workshop hut she had only two cottages to pass and no observation to fear from either. Mrs Franklund's was empty – the vicar's wife had taken her under her wing and she slept at the rectory. Old Mrs Ambrose's was as tightly shut as the eyes and ears of its occupant. The moon escaped the clouds from time to time and glinted on the trowel she held in her hand.

The door and tiny barred window of Coleman's hut were both in the front wall. The rear wall had no openings in it and weeds and undergrowth were encroaching on its base. She used her gloved hand to pull them away and scooped out the earth underneath. Six inches down she struck the concrete base of the hut.

After half an hour of careful work she had formed a sharp-sided trench, running the length of the wall. This she covered by allowing the weeds and undergrowth to fall back over it.

There was one other thing to do before she left. She went round to the front of the hut to examine the door. Its fastening was a metal flange that fitted over a staple and was held there by a padlock. She had brought with her a wooden peg and this she whittled down with a knife until she estimated it would fit snugly into the staple when the padlock was removed.

After that she went back to bed.

She had studied Coleman's movements. He left his office as late as six o'clock if he was busy, as early as four o'clock if things were slack, and usually made his way straight up to the hut. As a bachelor he had little else to occupy him in the evenings. He was never away before eight and sometimes stayed there until ten o'clock. She would see his light go on and hear the clatter of his metal cutter.

Now she had to wait on the weather.

On the third night the wind got up, gusting from the south-west. She packed her shopping bag and set off to destroy Mr Coleman.

First she re-fastened the metal flange, driving her wooden peg firmly into the staple. Then she arranged six paraffin-based fire lighters end to end along the trench she had dug and put a match to them. When she was sure they were well alight she started back towards her house. Already she could hear the crackling as the flames, driven by the wind, caught hold of the tarred wood of the wall. She saw the door shaking as though someone was trying, desperately, to open it.

The fire was building up now. Standing ten yards away she could feel the heat of it on her cheeks. At one moment she thought she saw hands clinging to the bars of the little window.

By that time the flames had reached the roof.

Hennessy said, 'When the fire people could get into what was left of the hut they said they could smell paraffin. According to Greenslade, Coleman had a paraffin stove and kept a small reserve of the stuff. He'd once borrowed some from him for his own stove.'

'And you think,' said Inspector Waite, 'that he may have upset the stove and panicked when he couldn't get the door open. Why couldn't he?'

'I can only think the latch may have jammed. There was nothing left of the door to go by, but they did find the padlock inside the hut.'

'And that's your idea of what happened?'

Hennessy took some time thinking out his answer to this. Then he said, 'I can tell you one thing. It's not what the village think.'

'And what do they think?'

'You must bear in mind, sir, that this is rather a primitive place. They think that what happened proves beyond question that Coleman was the murderer and that he's been punished for his crime.'

'Punished by whom?'

'In their eyes, it was fire from heaven that destroyed him.'

'And is that unanimous?'

'I'd say so, yes.'

Hennessy was nearly right, but not quite.

The vicar had been the first on the scene of the fire.

Although it was clearly too late to do anything effective he had rushed down to Judith Lyte's house to use her telephone. He had met Judith coming out of her front door. The fire was now so strong that its flames lit up her face.

He said, 'If poor Coleman was trapped inside, I'm afraid it's too late to save him.'

'Much too late,' said Judith.

It was not only the tone of her voice. It was the look on her face that troubled him. Calm, composed, triumphant. He had seen that look before. But where?

It was three years later that he found it, in the Louvre, in the painting by Raphael, of Judith leaving the tent of the tyrant Holofernes, carrying his head in a bag. She had that same look of remorseless triumph on her face.

Michael Gilbert was one of the first fellow-writers whom John Creasey approached when proposing to establish the CWA. Born in 1912, Gilbert has edited CWA anthologies and was awarded the CWA Cartier Diamond Dagger in 1994. A solicitor whose clients included Raymond Chandler, he made splendid use of his knowledge of the law in The Queen Against Karl Mullen *and that classic detective novel* Smallbone Deceased. *Death in Captivity, set in a prisoner-of-war camp, was filmed by Don Chaffey as* Danger Within. *The range of Gilbert's work is extremely wide and includes thrillers, spy novels, plays for stage, radio and television and non-fiction books, including studies of Dr Crippen and the Tichborne Claimant as well as anthologies of legal anecdotes and essays about crime fiction.*

CYRIL HARE

Name of Smith

On the death of Sir Charles Blenkinsop, some-time Judge of the High Court of Justice, the benchers of his Inn, as was only proper, arranged a memorial service for him. It was not so well attended as such functions usually are, for Sir Charles, in spite of his acknowledged competence as a lawyer, had never been popular. Moreover, there had been certain rumours concerning his private life of a type particularly detrimental to judges. Some of his colleagues had breathed a sigh of relief when Sir Charles, a few years before, had earned his pension and quitted the Bench without open scandal.

Francis Pettigrew, still 'of counsel' but now in country retirement, was at the service. His friend MacWilliam, the Chief Constable of Markshire, had thought it his duty to attend, since the deceased had been a Markhampton man; and Pettigrew accompanied him, more on the chance of meeting old Temple acquaintances than as a tribute to Blenkinsop's memory. He was disappointed to see so sparse a congregation and was correspondingly pleased on leaving the church to find himself behind the familiar, square-built figure of his old friend Challoner, a well-known City solicitor.

He overtook Challoner at the door, introduced him to MacWilliam, and was standing with them in the porch when his eye was caught by a shabby man of about forty who smiled at him in a friendly but slightly embarrassed fashion and walked hastily away.

'Friend of yours?' asked Challoner, as they strolled down Fleet Street.

'Apparently,' said Pettigrew. 'He certainly seemed to know me, and I have an idea I've seen him before, but where, I haven't the remotest notion.'

'Name of Smith.'

'The name is certainly familiar.'

'Charles Smith. Does a certain amount of reporting in the Courts. I dare say he was covering the service.'

'Charles Smith,' said Pettigrew meditatively. 'Charles—!' He stopped dead on the pavement. It may have been mere coincidence that it was at the door of a saloon bar. He took the solicitor by the arm and gently impelled him inside, leaving MacWilliam to follow. 'Of course I know the chap. I defended him once – on a charge of murder.'

'Really?' said Challoner with polite interest. 'I don't read the Old Bailey reports.'

'This wasn't at the Bailey. It was at Markhampton Assizes, six or seven years ago. And, what is more, old Blenkinsop, whose demise we have just been mourning, tried him. That would be before your time, MacWilliam.'

'As a matter of fact—' said the Chief Constable. But Pettigrew's attention was devoted to ordering drinks, and he did not bother to complete the sentence.

'Odd running into Smith like that,' Pettigrew went on a few minutes later. 'I may forget faces, and cases too, as often as not, but that was a case I shall remember all my life. Cheers!'

'Your health, Pettigrew! Was it a difficult task to – ah – "get him off" is the phrase, is it not?'

Pettigrew smiled grimly. 'Very. Too difficult for me, at all events,' he said. 'On that evidence and before a local jury he never had an earthly. The case was as dead as mutton.'

'That being so, I don't quite see why Smith isn't—'

'Isn't also as dead as mutton? Therein lies a mystery which will always puzzle me. Charles Smith escaped hanging solely and entirely through the positively goat-like conduct of Blenkinsop.'

'As a matter of fact,' said MacWilliam again, and this time he was allowed to go on. 'As a matter of fact, I had occasion to read the summing-up in that case quite recently. It was remarkable.'

'Remarkable? The Court of Criminal Appeal used stronger adjectives than that. I've never heard such a performance in my life. And from Blenkinsop, of all people! Now that we've done our duty by him in church we can speak the truth about him and we all know that by and large Charlie Blenkinsop was a pretty nasty piece of work, but, hang it all, the man was a lawyer. If anybody on the Bench knew his stuff, I should have said he did. But in this case the old boy went completely hay-wire. When I tell you that he actually directed the jury, as a matter of law . . .'

To detail all the iniquities of the summing-up took

Pettigrew a full five minutes of blistering technicalities.

'Of course the thing was a push-over on appeal,' he concluded. 'The conviction was quashed with more rudery than I have ever heard applied to a Judge of Assize. That case should go down in history as Blenkinsop's biggest boner. But what will always puzzle me is – why on earth did he do it?'

'Had he – er – lunched very well on that day?' Challoner ventured.

'Not a bit of it. He was as sober as – as a judge, if you follow me.'

'I have my own theory about the matter,' MacWilliam put in. 'I think the explanation is that all the parties involved – including the judge – were Markhampton people. You'll remember, Mr Pettigrew, that your client came from what was locally considered pretty poor stock. His mother, Mary Smith – she's still alive, by the way – was no better than she should be, and nobody ever knew who his father was. The girl he was accused of killing, on the other hand, belonged to one of the most respectable families in the town. Her father was a pillar of the strictest sect we have – and when Markhampton people are moral they take their morality seriously. Smith had got her into trouble, and she was desperate to be made an honest woman of – which didn't suit Smith's book at all, as he had engaged himself to a much wealthier woman. His defence was that she had committed suicide rather than face her family with the news of her downfall.'

'Precisely,' said Pettigrew. 'Not the line of defence to commend itself to a jury of townspeople inflamed with

236

piety and rectitude, even if the medical evidence hadn't killed it stone dead.'

'Very true. Local feeling was strong against Smith. And my point is, that in this matter the judge was a local man.'

'He left the town quite young, did he not?'

'He did, sir, and according to my information he left it under a cloud. Young Blenkinsop had not been one of the respectables. My belief is that he took this opportunity to put himself right with the town, by taking the part of respectability, and ramming home every point against the young sinner. Only, of course, he overdid it.'

'It's an idea, certainly,' said Pettigrew. 'There must have been some explanation for Blenkinsop's extraordinary lapse. But why should you know so much about the case? I should have thought there was enough current crime in Markshire to occupy you without digging up the past.'

'The past has a habit of digging itself up,' said MacWilliam. 'The Smith case came alive again last week. That is why I turned up the records.'

'Then you've been wasting your time. They can't try Smith again, you know.'

'Unfortunately for Smith, they cannot. He was innocent.'

'*What?*'

'The girl's father died a few days ago. He left a full confession. He killed her himself to punish her for her sins. He quoted a number of texts to justify his action. He was a religious maniac – poor fellow.'

Nobody said anything for an appreciable time after

that, and then Challoner remarked quietly, 'I think this round is on me.' When the drinks had been brought, he asked MacWilliam abruptly, 'What is Mary Smith's address?'

'Whose?'

'Mary Smith's – Charles Smith's mother.'

'Why, she lives where she always has lived – Lower River Lane. Why do you—?'

'Number Nine?'

'That's right. How did you know?'

Challoner pursed his lips.

'I was the late Sir Charles Blenkinsop's solicitor,' he said. 'By his will, he left a substantial sum of money in trust for this lady during her life. You can draw your own conclusions.'

Pettigrew whistled.

'There is one obvious conclusion to draw,' he said. 'But beyond it, I see another. The judge was Charles Smith's father.'

'It certainly seems probable.'

'But this is outrageous!' cried MacWilliam. 'He tries his own son for murder and does his damnedest to send him to the gallows. What sort of a father do you call that?'

'I should describe him as somewhat unnatural, I admit. But there are the facts.'

'The old devil!'

It was at this point that Pettigrew burst out laughing. MacWilliam looked at him in disapproving surprise.

'I don't see what there is funny about it,' he said severely.

'Don't you?' spluttered Pettigrew. 'I bet Blenkinsop does, if he can see anything now. He always had a low sense of humour. I've just seen the point of that famous summing-up of his. It explains everything. He made a muck of it *on purpose*! He knew that Smith hadn't a chance with the jury, so he did the next best thing, by giving him a cast-iron case on appeal. Unnatural father, my foot! He was a damned affectionate one, who was prepared to spoil his reputation and pervert justice to save his son's neck. I never thought the old ruffian had so much humanity in him.'

He raised his tankard.

'Here's to you, Charlie Blenkinsop, wherever you are,' he said. 'When you misdirected a jury you knew what you were about – which is more than I can say of some of your learned brothers!'

'It is satisfactory to think,' MacWilliam added, 'that the misdirection prevented a grave miscarriage of justice.'

'That, my dear Chief Constable,' said Pettigrew loftily, 'is a mere side issue. Your irrelevancy will cost you another round of drinks.'

Cyril Hare was the pseudonym which A. A. Gordon-Clark (1900–58) employed when writing crime fiction. Hare was a barrister who became a county court judge, and much of his work combines a credible legal setting with plot developments deriving from subtleties of the law. Hare's principal series characters were Inspector Mallett and a fellow barrister, Francis Pettigrew. Both Mallett and Pettigrew appeared in Tragedy At Law *(1942), an unorthodox murder mystery which most critics regard as Hare's masterpiece. Far from prolific, he nevertheless contributed stories to three CWA anthologies:* Planned Departures, Some Like Them Dead *and* Choice of Weapons. *His friend and fellow-lawyer Michael Gilbert edited a posthumous volume of Hare's short stories.*

REGINALD HILL

The Game of Dog

It was Charley Fields the landlord of the Punchbowl who started it.

Like his great namesake, Charley didn't much care for dogs or children. In fact, being a Yorkshire publican down to his tap-roots, Charley didn't much care for anything except brass, Geoff Boycott, and his own way.

But if the price of getting the brass out of his customers' pockets into his till was admitting their little companions into his pub, he bit the bullet and said that as long as they didn't yap, fight, defecate or smell too high, they were welcome in the rather draughty and uncomfortable rear bar.

That was the children. The dogs were allowed in the cosy front snug under the same very reasonable conditions.

One misty October evening, Charley peered through the snug hatch to make sure no one was sitting there with an empty glass and he saw a scene to warm a canophilist's cockles.

In one corner, a terrier sat with its bright eyes fixed

on the face of its owner, who appeared to be dozing. Stretched out across the hearth in front of the glowing fire lay an aged bloodhound, looking as if it were carved out of bronze till the crinkling of cellophane brought its great head up to receive its tribute of barbecued beef flavour crisps. Beneath the window-nook table a Border collie and a miniature poodle were sharing an ashtray-ful of beer while above them their owners enjoyed one of those measured Yorkshire conversations that make Pinteresque dialogue sound like a Gilbert and Sullivan patter song. At the table by the door, a small mongrel by dint of crawling round in ever-decreasing circles was contriving to bind the leg of its blissfully unaware owner to the leg of his chair.

This last was Detective Chief Inspector Peter Pascoe, the newest member of this canine club. The mongrel was Tig and belonged to his young daughter. As the nights drew in, he didn't care to have her wandering the streets even with such a fiercely defensive compan-ion, so he'd taken over the evening walk, whose turn-ing point was the Punchbowl. Observing the bloodhound drooping in behind its owner one damp night, he'd followed suit and over the past couple of weeks had become almost a regular, though he never stayed long enough to exchange more than a polite good evening with the others nor to identify them beyond their dogs.

'Bugger me!' said Charley Field after drinking in the scene for a few moments. 'You lot and your bloody dogs. You'd think you'd given birth to 'em! I bet if there were a fire and you'd only got time to rescue one human being or your dog, you lot would have to think twice!'

'Nay, Charley,' said the poodle. 'If it were thee, I'd not have to think once!'

Before Charley could respond to this sally he was summoned to the bar, leaving the poodle to enjoy the approving chuckles of his fellow drinkers.

As they died away the Border collie suddenly said, 'Hitler.'

'Eh?'

'I'd rescue Floss here afore I'd rescue Hitler, no question.'

The others considered. There was no dissent.

'Joe Stalin,' said the poodle.

'The Yorkshire Ripper,' said the bloodhound.

Both went through on the nod.

The collie looked towards the terrier, who still seemed to be dozing, then turned his gaze on Pascoe. He thought of explaining to them that as a policeman he was duty bound to regard all human life as sacred. Then he thought of trying to explain this to his daughter when he returned home with an incinerated Tig. Then he thought, lighten up, Pascoe. It's only pub talk!

'Maggie Thatcher?' he said tentatively.

This gave them pause.

'Nay,' said the bloodhound. 'She had her bad side, agreed, but she did some good things too. I don't think we can let her burn.'

'I bloody could. Aye, and throw coals on the fire if I could find any to throw,' growled the poodle. 'She closed my pit and threw me and most of my mates on the slag heap, the cow.'

The bloodhound looked ready to join issue, but the

collie said, 'Nay, we need to agree one hundred per cent on something like this.'

And the terrier defused the situation entirely by suddenly sitting up straight, opening his eyes, and saying, 'My mother-in-law!'

Over the next few weeks the game took shape, without formal rules but with rules that its participants instinctively understood, and their choice of candidates for the fire gave Pascoe more information about his fellow players than he was likely to get from general enquiry. In a Yorkshire pub a man's private life is a man's private life. You can ask a direct question, but only if you can take a direct answer. Pascoe on one occasion, finding himself alone with the bloodhound, had enquired casually what the man did for a living.

'I'm by way of being an expert,' replied the bloodhound.

'Oh yes. An expert in what?'

'An expert in minding my own bloody business.'

Which was reasonable enough, he decided, and had the up side of meaning he didn't have to tell them he was a policeman.

The one topic on which they all spoke freely was their dogs, and Pascoe, by listening and by observation, was soon familiar with all their little ways. Fred, the ancient bloodhound, had three times been pronounced dead by the vet and three times given him the lie. He loved barbecue beef crisps and howled in derision if offered any other flavour. Floss, the collie, was a rescue dog, having been kicked off a farm when the farmer realised she was frightened of sheep. She was in love with Puff the poodle, who shared her beer but showed no sign of wanting to share anything else, which was why his non-PC owner had changed his name from Percy. Tommy, the terrier, was a genius. He could die for England, stand on his hind legs and offer left or right paw as requested. His pièce de résistance, when given the command *Light!*, was to go to the fireplace, extract one of the wooden spills from a container standing on the grate, insert it in the flame and bring it back to light its master's cigarette. Tig always watched this performance with a sort of sneering yawn. The human race, apart from Rosie Pascoe whom he adored, was there to serve dogs, not the other way round. He didn't want any dog's nose up his behind that had already been up a human's.

The one thing the dogs had in common was that their owners could all find someone, indeed several some-ones, whom they asserted they would put beneath their pets on a rescue priority list, and the game soon became a regular part of their evening encounter, its rules estab-lished by intuitive agreement rather than formal debate.

It was always initiated by someone saying, 'Hitler!' Thereafter the others spoke as the spirit moved them. Approval of a nomination was signified by an aye or a nod, and if unanimous, the game moved on. In the event of objection, the proposer was given a fair hearing, after which objectors either stated their case or admitted them-selves persuaded. Unless the vote was unanimous the nominee was declared saved. And the game was usually closed by the terrier declaring, 'My mother-in-law!' though it was possible for someone else to close it by calling out, '*His* mother-in-law!'

Pascoe, after his initial failure with Mrs Thatcher, restricted himself to historical characters. Nero was given a universal thumbs-down and he successfully argued the case for leaving Richard the Third to the flames, but when he ventured closer to living memory and suggested Field Marshal Haig, who commanded the British Forces in the First World War, he met surprising resistance and failed to carry the field. On the other hand it was only his unyielding opposition which pulled the fingers of the Hand of God, Diego Maradona, out of the fire.

When he explained the game to his wife, Ellie, she wrinkled her nose in distaste and said, '*Men!*' 'Hang about,' he protested. 'It's only a bit of fun. Anyway, you tell me, you've got the choice between saving Tig and saving George Bush, who do you grab?' 'That's what I mean,' she said. 'This stuff's too serious to make a game out of.' To which he replied, '*Women!*'

One December evening when the frost was so sharp that even Tig's normal indifference to sub-zero temperatures was sorely tested, the pair of them burst into the snug like a pair of Arctic explorers discovering a Little Chef at the Pole.

They got as close as they could to the roaring fire without standing on the bloodhound and gave themselves over to the delicious agony of defrosting. It wasn't till the process was sufficiently advanced to make him admit the wisdom of stepping back a foot or so that Pascoe became aware that the atmosphere in the room, though physically warm, was distinctly depressed. His greeting had been answered by a series of noncommittal grunts, and even the dogs looked subdued.

He went to the hatch and attracted Charley Field's attention.

'I'll have a Scotch tonight, Charley,' he said. Then, lowering his voice, he asked, 'What's up with this lot? I've seen livelier wakes.'

'You're not so far wrong,' said Charley. 'You've not heard about Lenny then?'

So used was he to thinking about the others only in terms of their dogs, it took Pascoe a moment to work out that Lenny was Tommy the terrier's owner, who was absent tonight.

'No. What?'

'There was a fire at his house last night.'

'Oh God. Is he all right?'

'He's fine.'

'And Tommy?'

'He's fine too.'

Pascoe thought for a second and didn't like where his thoughts were taking him.

'Was anyone hurt?' he asked.

'Aye,' said Charley Field. 'His mother-in-law. Burnt to a cinder.'

The following morning Detective Superintendent Andy Dalziel sat listening to Peter Pascoe with growing disbelief.

When he'd finished, the Fat Man said, 'I had a dream the other night. Wieldy came to see me to say he were getting married to Prince Charles and it was going to be a white wedding and he wanted my advice on whether he should sell the photo rights to *Hello!* or *OK*.'

'And which did you go for?'

'I went downstairs for a stiff drink. But thinking about it, I reckon my dream made more sense than what you've just told me.'

He looked at the local paper spread out on his desk. Its headline was THE HERO OF HARTSOP AVENUE over a photo of a man with a terrier in his arms and a blanket round his shoulders being comforted by a fireman outside a smouldering house. The legend below read: *Mr Leonard Gold (38) returned from a meeting at the Liberal Club to find his house in Hartsop Avenue ablaze. Knowing that his mother-in-law, Mrs Brunnhilde Smith (62), was still in the building, despite all efforts to stop him, he rushed inside in an attempt to rescue her. Unhappily his courageous act was in vain, the fire was too far advanced for him to reach the upstairs room from which Mrs Smith's body was later recovered, and it was only the arrival of the fire brigade that enabled Mr Gold himself to make his escape.*

'Let me get this straight,' said Dalziel. 'This guy's a hero, nearly gets burned to death trying to rescue his ma-in-law, ends up in hospital being treated for second-degree burns, and because of some daft game some dog fanciers play in a pub, you want to investigate him for choosing to get his dog out and leaving the old girl to fry? Have I got the gist?'

'That's about it,' said Pascoe.

'And have you got any evidence to support this, apart from this dog game you play?'

'No,' said Pascoe. 'But I haven't looked into it yet. I only heard about the fire last night and I wanted to run it past you first.'

'I think you need to run a lot bloody faster,' said Dalziel. 'Preferably out of my sight. Have you got nowt better to do, like for instance your job? Best keep your hobbies for your own time.'

'In actual fact,' said Pascoe prissily, 'this is my own time. I've got the day off, remember? But in any case, I always thought the investigation of suspicious death was a large part of my job.'

'Suspicious? Has anyone from the fire department been in touch with us to say there's something dodgy about the fire? Or anyone from the path lab to say they've got worries about the way the old girl died?'

'No. But it's not that kind of suspicion.'

'So what kind of suspicion is it, Pete? I mean, even supposing what you say is true, where's the sodding crime?'

'I'm sure there's got to be something,' said Pascoe. 'I'll ring up the CPS and talk to a lawyer, shall I?'

'If you must,' sighed Dalziel. 'And while you're at it, ask 'em which they'd go for, *Hello!* or *OK.*'

It wasn't often that the CPS and Andy Dalziel were in accord but this seemed to be one of those occasions.

The lawyer he spoke to was a young woman called, appropriately, Portia Silk, who had what might have been in other circumstances an infectious laugh, which he heard as she quoted at him, 'Thou shalt not kill but need'st not strive / Officiously to keep alive.'

'But surely if you let someone die when you could have saved them . . .' he protested, whereupon she interrupted with, 'Only if you have a professional relationship

249

as in doctor/patient, or a duty of care as in teacher/pupil. But if you're walking along the canal bank and you see someone struggling in the water, it may be regarded by some people as reprehensible of you not to dive in and try to save them, but it's not a criminal act. Even if it were, in the circumstances you cite, proving deliberate choice of dog over woman would be very difficult.'

Pascoe had not survived and prospered under the despotic rule of Andy Dalziel by being easily deterred from a chosen path, and after his disappointing talk with Ms Silk, he immediately dialled the fire station and had a chat with Keith Little, the officer who'd been given the job of looking at the Hartsop Avenue blaze.

'No, nothing suspicious else we'd have been on to you. Fire started downstairs in the living room. Dead woman was a chain-smoker by all accounts. From the look of things, it started in an old sofa, fag end down between the cushions, which pre-dated the fire retardant regulations, and eventually you'd get a nice little blaze going which once it burnt through to the stuffing would really explode. After that, well, it's an old house, wooden floors, wooden beams, even wood panelling on some of the walls. Some of them old places are bonfires just waiting for someone to toss a match on to them. Why are you asking, by the way? You got a sniff of something iffy?'

'No,' replied Pascoe honestly. 'Just curiosity. It was in my neck of the woods and I know Mr Gold slightly. You've spoken to him?'

'Yeah. He's still in hospital. Hero they're calling him. Right idiot in my book. Two of our lads had to go in there to get him out. Found him crouched down in the shower room, half unconscious from smoke inhalation. Could have cost them their lives too if things had gone wrong.'

'Did they get the dog out as well? The one he's holding in the *Evening News* picture.'

'No. I gather it were waiting for him when our boys brought him out. They remarked what a fuss it made of him. The paramedics had to let it in the ambulance with him. If you want to be loved, get a dog, eh?'

'Wasn't there a window in the shower room?'

'Aye, but far too small for a grown man.'

'Where did they find the dead woman?'

'Her room was right above the sitting room. Seems her favourite hobby was lying on her bed with a bottle of vodka and listening to music full blast. She'd not have heard anything. In fact it's likely, if she'd drunk enough, she'd have died in her sleep afore the fire erupted through the floorboards. Let's hope so. No way our lads could get to her. They did well to get our sodding hero out.'

When a further call to the pathology lab confirmed that Mrs Smith had indeed been asphyxiated by smoke inhalation before the flames got to work on her, it seemed to Pascoe he'd reached the end of the road. Ellie hadn't been all that pleased when he'd announced that morning that despite having the day off there was something he had to check out at work, so now he made his exit before the Fat Man found him something to do.

Hartsop Avenue was a mile and a half the far side of the Punchbowl from where Pascoe lived, and there was no reason for him to go anywhere near it on his way home. Nevertheless, somehow or other he found himself parked outside the burnt-out shell of the Gold house thirty minutes later.

He got out of his car and stood looking at the wrecked building. Two women walked by him, carrying shopping bags. As they passed, one said to the other in a deliberately loud voice, 'I think it's disgusting the way some people make an entertainment out of other folk's disasters.'

She then turned into the gateway of the house next door while her companion went on her way.

Pascoe hurried towards the neighbour, pulling his warrant card out of his pocket.

'Excuse me,' he called.

She turned an unfriendly face towards him, but when she saw the card her manner became conciliatory.

'I'm sorry what I said just now,' she apologised. 'I thought you were just one of them sightseers. We had a lot of them yesterday, just walking or driving by to take a look. Ghouls, I call them.'

'I agree,' said Pascoe. 'But it's human nature, I'm afraid. You know the Golds well, do you?'

'Oh yes. Greta, that's Mrs Gold, is staying with us till they get something sorted out. Poor woman, she's devastated.'

'I gather she was away when it happened.'

'Down in London, visiting an old school friend and doing some Christmas shopping. *She* wanted to go too, but I think Greta's friend made it quite clear the invitation was for Greta only.'

She Pascoe took to refer to Brunnhilde Smith.

'So you get on well with the Golds then?'

'Oh yes. Lovely couple. Very quiet. At least they were till *she* came to live with them. But I shan't speak ill of the dead.'

Pascoe's long experience recognised this as the precursor of ill-speaking in the same way as a wassailer in a Danish mead-hall knew that *Hwaet!* signalled the start of *Beowulf*.

Two minutes later he was seated in Mrs Woolley's kitchen drinking tea and listening to an account of Lenny Gold's mother-in-law which put her on a par with Grendel's mother.

Mrs Woolley was a friend and confidante of Greta Gold and had got the family background from her. It seemed her mother, Brunnhilde Hotter, a native of Hanover, had married a British soldier in the sixties and on his demob they'd settled in London, where Greta was born. She'd married Lenny Gold in 1985 and they made the error of setting up home only ten minutes' drive from Greta's family home in Kilburn. By 1990, Lenny had had enough. Despite being a Londoner born and bred, he started looking for a job as far away from the capital as he could get, which in the event turned out to be mid-Yorkshire.

'Everything was fine,' said Mrs Woolley. 'She came visiting occasionally, but you can put up with a short visit, can't you? So long as you can see an end. And Mr Smith never liked to be away from home too long. Then five years ago he died. Naturally Greta made her mother come and stay with her for a while to help her come to terms with things. Couple of weeks, she thought.

Month at the most. Well, the way Greta put it, there was never a time when they actually asked her to live with them permanently, but somehow it just happened. Hilda – that's what she was known as; Brunnhilde's too much of a mouthful – Hilda had a bad leg. Circulatory problem she said. Fat problem I said. Human limbs weren't made for that kind of load-bearing. She was a big woman, must have cost a fortune to feed. I've seen her sitting where you are now, Mr Pascoe, and watched her eat the whole of one of my Victoria sponges, four slices and it was gone. Plus I had to get my husband to strengthen the chair she sat on, she left it so wobbly.'

As well as her dietary excesses, there were plenty of other strikes against the Widow Smith, according to Mrs Woolley. She was a chain-smoker, she dominated conversations, she often said things in German to her daughter which were clearly comments on others present too rude to be spoken in English, she liked to lie on her bed and play her favourite records very loud ('Wagner, it was,' said Mrs Woolley. 'I know because George, that's my husband, he likes that kind of stuff, but he listens through his headphones, knowing I can't put up with all that screeching and howling'), and she complained bitterly to any who couldn't avoid listening that it was a tragedy her Greta had married such a useless idle man as Lenny ('One time she said to me,' said Mrs Woolley, 'she said, "Don't you think that's a Jew name, Lenny Gold? All right, they got married in a church but I have seen him coming out of the shower and his thing was like a skinned rabbit." I told her live and let live, she should be ashamed saying such things but she just laughed

254

and tapped her nose'). Above all she hated Tommy, saying the dog was unhygienic, and she was allergic, and it ought to be put down ('Such a nice little dog,' concluded Mrs Woolley. 'And so clever. I bet if it was one of those things like wolves they had at Colditz, she'd have been a bit fonder of it!').

With the woman's permission Pascoe wandered out into the garden and looked up at the burnt-out shell next door. The garage was on this side, its sloping roof joining the main house wall just below a small square window which was closed, though its glass was cracked, presumably by the heat of the fire.

'Right mess, isn't it?' said a cheerful voice.

He turned to see a round bald man who introduced himself as George Woolley.

'That window,' said Pascoe. 'Is that the shower room where they found Lenny?'

Woolley confirmed that it was.

'Like a door it was to that dog,' he went on. 'Lenny used to leave it open for Tommy so he could get out to do his business when he was shut in the house by himself. A bloody marvel, that dog. Many's the time I've seen him hop out, run down the garage roof, jump down on to the rain barrel there, do the job, then head back in the same way.'

'But the window's closed,' said Pascoe. 'Presumably Lenny didn't bother to open it last night because he wasn't leaving Tommy shut in the house by himself. Mrs Smith was there.'

'*Her*,' said Woolley with the same intonation as his wife. 'She'd not have bothered to let him out even if she'd noticed he wanted to go. In fact she'd rather he messed up in the house so that she'd have something else to complain about.'

'You don't seem to have liked her much,' said Pascoe.

'Sorry, I know she's dead, but I'm not going to lie. She was a pain and I doubt if even Greta will mind very much that she's gone, not once she gets over the first shock. No, if Lenny had been killed trying to save her, that would have been the real tragedy. I couldn't believe it when he set off into the house.'

'You were there?' said Pascoe.

'Oh yes. I'd been at the Liberal Club with him. Not that we're Liberals. Who is, these days? But it's a good pint and not too pricey.'

'But he didn't take Tommy?'

'No. No dogs in the club, that's the rule.' He grinned and added, 'And no women either, except on Ladies' Night. Oh yes, it's a grand place.'

'It sounds it. So where did he leave Tommy? He can't have been in the house, can he?'

'I suppose not. He's got a kennel in the garden, sometimes he stays out there when the weather's fine.'

'I see. And you came back together from the club . . .' prompted Pascoe.

'That's right. In my car. We turned into the Avenue and I said, hello! What's going off? We could see one or two people standing around and it's usually dead quiet. Then Lenny said, oh my God, it's my house! Well, the ground floor was already well alight. I knew that Hilda must still be in there, there was a light on in her bedroom and you could hear her hi-fi system belting out Wagner. Lenny jumped out of the car, I've never seen him so agitated. He didn't seem to know what to do with himself. I asked someone if they'd rung the brigade and they said yes. Lenny ran up the side of the house, I presume to see if he could get in the back, then he appeared at the front again. I got hold of him and said, it's no use, Lenny, we can't do anything, the fire brigade will be here any minute. But he broke loose and before I could do anything he was up the path and going in the front door. I went after him, but the heat was too much for me. I could hear the sirens in the distance and knew that help wouldn't be long, but I really did fear the worst. And what made it worse was Tommy came running round the side of the house, barking and agitated, like he knew Lenny was in there. I've never been so relieved in my life as I was when the firemen brought him out, and I thought Tommy was going to have a fit, he was so happy. He's at the hospital too, you know. Against all the rules, but there was no separating the two of them.'

'Yes, they really worship each other, don't they?'

'That's right. Hey, does that mean you know Lenny and Tommy?'

'Yes. In fact I meet them sometimes when I'm out with my dog.'

'That explains it,' said Woolley, smiling. 'I was wondering what a cop was doing looking around after the fire. So it's just personal interest, is it?'

'Oh yes. I live quite close and I thought, knowing Lenny, that I'd take a look,' said Pascoe, feeling rather guilty as he uttered the lie.

'Understandable,' said Woolley. 'You're not thinking of visiting him in hospital by any chance, are you?'

'I suppose I might, some time,' said Pascoe vaguely.

'It's just that I'd told my wife I'd take her in at lunchtime and we'd bring Greta home and make sure she got a bite of lunch. That's why I'm back here now, but to tell the truth it hasn't gone down too well at work, there's a meeting I should be at in half an hour's time, and there's no way I'd be able to make it . . . but if you were going to the hospital to see Lenny . . .'

Why not? thought Pascoe. His morning was knackered anyway, and his suspicions, which had been looking more and more stupid over the past half-hour, had left him feeling very guilty.

He said, 'Yes, I could do that.'

'Great! You're a star! I'll just tell my good lady.'

As they went back into the house, Woolley suddenly laughed and said, 'I know I shouldn't but I had to smile when I thought about it later . . .'

'What?'

'Do you know your Wagner, Mr Pascoe?'

'A bit.'

'Well, when we got out of the car and saw the house burning, the music blasting out of the upstairs window was *Götterdämmerung*. It was that bit right at the end when they've lit Siegfried's funeral pyre. Brunnhilde gets on her horse and sends him plunging into the heart of the flames. Ironic, eh?'

'Always good for a laugh, old Wagner,' said Peter Pascoe.

★   ★   ★

At the hospital, they found Lenny Gold fast asleep in a small private room. His wife was with him and so was Tommy, who greeted Pascoe like an old friend.

Greta Gold, a slender, pale-faced woman with more of the Rhine maiden about her than the Valkyrie, said, 'They let me bring him but I have to take him away with me. He doesn't mind. I think he understands he can come back.'

'I'm sure he does,' said Pascoe. 'He's a very clever dog. I know how fond Lenny is of him.'

'Yes, he is,' said Greta, smiling at the terrier. 'Sometimes I'd tell him I thought he loved the dog more than me.'

'Nonsense,' said Mrs Woolley. 'Lenny adores you.'

'I know he does. I was only joking. But Tommy means such a lot to him. Sometimes, if we were out for a long time, he would even ring home, just so Tommy could hear his voice on the answer machine and be reassured. I'm so glad we didn't lose him too, that would have been too much to bear . . .'

Her eyes filled with tears. Mrs Woolley put her arm round her shoulder and led her aside.

Pascoe stood awkwardly by the bed, looking down at the sleeping figure. Lenny's hands were encased in plastic bags to protect the dressings and his face and head had been scorched too. All this suffered in his brave attempt to save a woman he had every cause to hate, thought Pascoe, his guilt returning with interest.

Mrs Woolley said, 'I'm just taking Greta down to the waiting room for a cup of tea, Mr Pascoe. We won't be long.'

'Yes. That will be fine.'

The two women left. Tommy showed signs of wanting to accompany them but Pascoe called, 'Tommy, come. Down. Stay.'

The dog trotted back, lay down under the bed, and looked up at him, eyes bright, ears pricked, waiting for the next command.

Pascoe thought of Tig's likely reaction to such an instruction. He might obey in the end but it would involve a lot of thought and a great deal of yawning. Much as he loved the little mongrel, it must be nice to have a pet who didn't regard you as inferior, to whom your every word was like the voice of God . . .

God, which is dog backwards . . . The Game of Dog . . . the Game of God . . .

Into his mind came an image of Tommy lying in his basket in front of the fire in the Golds' parlour. The phone rings. After a while the answer machine switches on. The voice of God says, 'Tommy.' His ears prick. He sits up. The voice of God says, 'Light!' He goes to the fireplace, picks up a spill of wood left there, sticks it through the bars of the guard, and when it catches, he takes it to . . . where? To, say, the sofa, where a cigarette has been left stuck between two cushions. He lights the cigarette, drops the spill, gets back into his basket. And the cigarette burns, and the spill burns, and the cushion . . . Perhaps a small section of the cushion had had something rubbed into it, one of those cleaning solutions, for instance, which the instructions warn are highly inflammable . . .

The fire starts. The dog becomes aware of it. After a while he realises this is something it would be a good

260

idea to distance himself from. He wanders up the stairs to his usual exit, the shower room window.

But it is closed.

Brunnhilde, either because she thinks there's a draught, or out of sheer malice and in the hope that Lenny will be confronted by a dog mess on his return, has closed it. As the smoke drifts up the stairs, Tommy starts barking. But his warning cries are drowned by *The Twilight of the Gods* at full belt, and Brunnhilde on her bed is too deep into her vodka bottle and too immersed in Wagner's Germanic flames to be aware of this puny Anglo-Saxon fire building up beneath her.

Lenny comes home. He expects to be greeted by Tommy. When the dog doesn't appear, he rushes down the side of the house and sees that the shower room window has been closed.

And now in panic he returns to the front. The fire roars, the heat is intense. But Tommy is in there. He breaks free from his friend's grasp and rushes into the flames. He knows where Tommy will be. He opens the window, urges the dog out.

And then because he fears, probably foolishly, that the dog's love may match his own, he pulls the window shut again in case Tommy tries to get back in to be by his side. And he sinks to the floor and prepares to die.

A story of great ingenuity . . .

A story of great villainy . . .

A story of great courage . . .

A story of such absurdity that Pascoe shuddered at the thought of Andy Dalziel even suspecting that his right-hand man had let it pollute his mind.

Such ludicrous fantasies belonged, if anywhere, to the world of fairy tales, of escapist movies, of childish parlour games.

Like the Game of Dog.

He mouthed a silent *sorry* at the poor burnt hero who lay before him.

Lenny's eyes opened.

He looked up, focused, and recognition dawned.

He tried to say something.

Tommy, aware his master was conscious, put his front paws on the bed and raised his head to the level of the pillow, his tail wagging furiously.

Lenny reached out one of his bagged hands, touched the terrier's head and winced.

Then he looked at Pascoe and smiled and winked, and tried to speak again.

'What?' said Pascoe, stooping closer.

'Hitler!' said Lenny.

Reginald Hill *is the author of over forty books, including the internationally acclaimed novels about the mid-Yorkshire policemen Andy Dalziel and Peter Pascoe. The series has been successfully adapted for BBC television with Warren Clarke and Colin Buchanan in the lead roles. Hill's other series character is the Luton private eye Joe Sixsmith, and earlier in his career he wrote under several pseudonyms, most notably that of Patrick Ruell. His many awards include the CWA Cartier Diamond Dagger in 1995 and the CWA Gold Dagger in 1990 for* Bones and Silence.

H.R.F. KEATING

The Hound of the Hanging Gardens

Inspector Ghote sat, thoughts whirling through his head, as his car hurried him along streets mercifully almost free of traffic at this dawn hour. Oh, Bombay, he said to himself, always and always so full of nonsense rumours and gossips. And in full twentieth century also. Look at that Tulsi Pipe Road business of the miracle baby I was investigating at the time of Christmas not so long ago. One child born to that girl they were calling as a virgin mother. Riots expected with Christian community celebrating and boasting. Then whole thing fizzling to nothing when I was finding out who real father was. And now this only. One double life-size dog they are saying and repeating is stalking-palking by night through the locked-up Hanging Gardens when that nice oasis ought to be resting in peace on top of the reservoirs supplying water to the steamy city below. Nonsense only. Nonsense, nonsense, nonsense.

But now . . . Now a death there. In the Hanging Gardens. A death in the night. First-class Number One mystery. Wife of Mr Adik Desmukh, mill-owner they are calling as Polyester King, found dead somewhere inside. And, if First Information Report is hundred per cent correct, covered head to foot in slobber from a dog. But no dog must be inside there. And no lady also. What was Mrs Desmukh doing in the Gardens at night to be attacked and killed by a dog who is all the time not existing? Cannot be existing. No dog can be as huge as they are saying and stating in bazaar gup everywhere. Size of a pony, size of a lion.

His driver brought the car to a halt, in proper screaming fashion, at the tall locked gates of the Gardens. The Pathan gatekeeper, standing waiting outside, proudly drew himself up.

'Inspector sahib, I was finding body. It was myself who was finding. Reporting also. I am knowing my duty. Officer from nearmost police thana is standing over body.'

'Very well, very well. So show me where is said body. Ek dum.'

Hastily the Pathan unlocked the gates, saw the car through, locked them again and led Ghote away into the placid mist-wreathed Gardens.

And then, as they passed by the walled-off area devoted in daylight hours to gentlemen, usually somewhat fat, who wished to indulge in exercising, a dark figure came to light through the swirls of cold, clinging mist. With a thump of dismay, Ghote saw who it was who had been sent from the nearest police station to take charge until, since a person of influence was involved, an officer from Crime Branch headquarters arrived. It was Sub-Inspector Hasteen, a fellow he had had dealings with before. Big, brave, a worthy long-serving officer, he could nevertheless be trusted to get hold of the wrong end of each and every stick there was to be found.

But good-hearted, and so, if my patience is holding out, to be treated with kids' gloves.

Hasteen sprang to attention as they approached.

'Sir,' he boomed out, 'you must be examining clue of dog-slobber before same is being melted off by rays of sun. Sir, body is covered in slobber from one bhoot dog of lion-size.'

'SI,' Ghote said, more sharply than he had intended, 'there are no bhoot dogs. Dogs are not having ghosts.'

'No, sir. No, if you are saying. Sir, except, if I am knowing one thing about myself, it is I am a no-nonsense. But, sir, what I was seeing I was not able to believe eyes in my head itself. Sir, look.'

So, to please the fellow, however plain it was even from a distance that the richly embroidered sari of the woman lying dead there on the wet-glistening grass was indeed spotted and splashed with what appeared to be gobbets fallen from the jaws of a dog, a living dog, Ghote knelt and took a closer look, noting there were, as well as the dog's dribblings, one or two muddy pawprints. After a decent interval he pushed himself up.

'SI,' he said, patience lost as soon as it was tried, 'what you have done is to fail to note the one clue of any use to be found on the body.'

'Sir?'

'Yes, man. Did you not at all notice that from every inch of the lady's sari a peculiar odour is still emanating?'

'Sir? But, sir, I was smelling only odour of dog, of dog of lion-size.'

'And you were not at all aware of this other odour, strong though it is? Very well, I do not expect you to have recognised its exact nature, though it is reminding me very much of something. Of something . . . But, SI, the odour is unmistakably there. If you had not been intent on finding traces of one lion-dog bhoot you would have been able to pay better attention.'

Ghote, realising he had perhaps rebuked bluff old Hasteen more fiercely than he might have done, turned back to the waiting gatekeeper.

'Tell me,' he said, 'you were able to state when you were telephoning police thana that the body you found was that of Mrs Adik Desmukh. How was that? Were you already knowing the lady?'

'No, Inspector sahib. No. I was spotting beside her the handbag you are seeing there now, and I was looking inside same. Her name is on the cards she was carrying.'

A fact, Ghote registered, that an officer with less talent for getting things wrong than Sub-Inspector Hasteen might well have gathered from the Pathan earlier. If it had occurred to him to question the fellow. However, better to rescue the bag from further fingerprint contamination now than to leave it lying there. Fingerprints might produce a clue leading to the solving of the mystery. Unlike pawprints. Certainly not the pawprints of a bhoot dog.

He picked up the bag – it was in elegant gleaming crocodile skin – by the edge of its thin strap, determined not to add his own prints to the Pathan's. Its gold clasp was still undone, and by tilting it to one side he was able to inspect the contents. They were few enough, an embroidered handkerchief, two or three crumpled banknotes, a little shiny blue plastic inhaler and the clip of cards that the Pathan had looked at and left his prints on.

Then, before he could point out to Hasteen his error in failing to question the gatekeeper, a blast of noisy sound came from out of the mist.

'A lion-dog bhoot. A lion-dog bhoot. And you were daring to say there is no such thing.'

Hastily replacing the crocodile-skin bag exactly where it had lain before, Ghote turned to see who it was who had shouted out so contemptuously.

And, as he had half-expected, the man he saw emerging from the surrounding mistiness was wearing the skimpy loin-cloth and the head-cloth of a sadhu. But this holy man was no ordinary sadhu such as might be seen, begging bowl in hand, making his way calling and beseeching along any of Bombay's streets. No, he was a particularly notorious sadhu, or unholy pretence of a sadhu, going by the name, self-given, of Sensation Sadhu.

Whenever an event of even the least inexplicable nature was reported anywhere in the whole teeming city the half-mad fellow was bound to turn up. And promptly puff it into a tremendous sensation.

And now Ghote made a mistake.

'Sensation Sadhu,' he challenged him, 'how the hell did you get inside here?'

'Oh, Inspector, Inspector, are you still claiming and pretending that extraordinary powers do not exist? Have you never heard of translocation? Do you truly not believe that a full graduate, BA, plus MA, who has also spent years meditating naked amid the Himalayan snows, cannot reach this spot except by some bus?'

'I am believing,' Ghote replied drily, 'there must be ways of getting into the Gardens howeversomuch gate is locked.'

He had witnessed in his time events explicable only as being by translocation. But he was not going to give a charlatan like Sensation Sadhu any such credit.

'So you are claiming also,' the mad fellow replied, 'that the lady here in the Hanging Gardens struck down by death was not the victim of a bhoot hound?'

'I am a police officer. I deal in facts. And one fact before me is that you—'

But now yet another shape appeared through the rapidly dispersing mist. Again it was that of someone Ghote knew well, one Miss Pinky Dinkarrao, writer of the much-read gossip column, 'Pinky Thinking'. She was – he had been involved with her when he had succeeded in unmasking a highly notorious cat-burglar – a person for whom he had a certain reluctant liking, although he knew well that in pursuit of a story she would stick at nothing. If she got hold now of the possible link between the wife of influential Mr Adik Desmukh and the dog said to be haunting the Gardens, she would make of it a story that would bring the whole of Crime Branch into ridicule. And who would be blamed?

Myself, he recorded dismally.

And immediately he knew that the worst had come to the worst.

'A bhoot hound,' Pinky said with palpable glee. 'The

268

Hound of the Hanging Gardens. What a first-class headline.'

Yes, she had seen it. Heaped ridicule was about to descend on all the officers of Crime Branch from the Additional Commissioner downwards. The pick of detectives in the whole of the Bombay Police were about to be shown as attempting to solve a murder committed by a dog. No, worse, a bhoot hound. And the only way to avert such a fate would be to solve the case before the 'Pinky Thinking' column got into the hands of the pavement vendors.

But how? How?

'Madam,' he said to Pinky, in desperation. 'Madam, I am forbidding you to put into your column any mention of this death.'

'Of the death of the wife of Mr Adik Desmukh, very much wanting not any longer to be married to a woman whose dowry he has long ago spent and who is so crippled by asthma she is unable even to sit at his table when he is entertaining? Inspector, have you forgotten who I am?'

Yes, as always right up to date with her facts, Ghote thought. She is knowing everything about the sort of people she is writing about. What was it I was noticing inside Mrs Desmukh's handbag just only two minutes past? An inhaler. And Miss Pinky is knowing about such a small thing as that.

So how am I to get the better of her? Facts at her fingers at every moment of the day.

'Madam,' he repeated – it was all he could think of to do – 'Madam, once more I am forbidding mention of this case. Police orders.'

Pinky laughed.

She was proud of her tinkling laugh, Ghote remembered.

'Oh, Inspector, when into my column I will be able to put Mr Adik Desmukh, who has for all the week given those fellows on the finance pages so much of breath-holding copy? Inspector, you are so wrong. It is not the police who give orders to the press. No, no. It is altogether the other way round.'

Ghote felt rage boil up. And boil over.

'Sub-Inspector Hasteen,' he snapped. 'Take this lady out of the Gardens where she has no business to be before opening hour. And − and − and you can take that sham of a sadhu out also.'

At least Hasteen was big and burly enough to succeed in the task. And soon Ghote found that he was at last there, no longer harassed by unauthorised intruders, with the body of Mrs Adik Desmukh, mysteriously dead in the supposedly protected Hanging Gardens. But not, he said to himself, killed by any bhoot dog.

But how had she come to die? And, again he asked himself, what had she been doing in the Hanging Gardens in the middle of the night? All right, no difficulty, or not much difficulty, in seeing how she had got in. There must be gaps in the surrounding fences. How else has Sensation Sadhu got in? Or had he been here all night? Easy enough to imagine him hiding behind some bush when the closing hour came. So was he . . . ? No, absurd. Why would that fool want to murder someone as distant from him as the wife of the Polyester King? And why, come to think of it, was that crorepati, that millionaire, featuring in the finance pages just now? And, damn it, what was it about that odour I was noticing coming from Mrs Desmukh's sari that almost, almost said something to me?

Think. Think.

But what to think about? Which of all the mysteries surrounding this business is the one that I should be first of all trying and attempting to unravel?

He was not to get so much as another minute even to decide on his priorities. Not far off there came the sound of a car engine. It seemed, in fact, to be inside the Hanging Gardens themselves. And then, with the last shreds of the mist fast being dispelled by the now risen sun, he saw that there was indeed a car inside. And it was coming directly towards him. A big car, imported from foreign. A driver in uniform at the wheel.

Who? Why? What?

The car came to a halt, a discreet halt. Its nearside door opened. A man stepped out. A man in a suit of fine cloth. With good shoes on his feet, polished and shining. With a big, round, masterful face. With a notable paunch pushing out the suit's waistcoat.

And he knew who this final intruder must be. Mr Adik Desmukh, husband of the woman here dead at his feet. The Polyester King himself.

'So she is there?' Adik Desmukh banged out at once. 'Inspector, I am trying and trying to come. But every damn thing is delaying me. My car, best from UK, is breaking down. Breaking down. And I am left to sit and sit while the wife of my heart is reported dead from attack by the Hound of the Hanging Gardens.'

'Well, sir,' Ghote said, stepping forward, 'I am able to state that Mrs Desmukh was not killed by any hound whatsoever. Sir, no bhoot dog is existing. There is no sign of dog fangs upon the body, I am able to assure. It is true your wife may have been somewhat of attacked, or perhaps just only jumped at, by some canine creature. There were, when I was examining, some signs of something that may have come from the mouth of a dog and one or two paw marks also. But, sir, you must be well knowing a friendly dog will put such marks on clothes.'

Mr Desmukh seemed not to have listened.

'Killed by that dog,' he stated. 'The huge dog they have been saying has been seen at night in the Gardens. Killed even without so much as one mark on her.'

Ghote wondered how to contradict a man of such influence. It was not something to be done lightly. Instead, at last, he tried another approach.

'Sir, I am wondering why – why it was – sir, how did it come about that your wife was here in the Gardens by night?'

'Air.'

'Sir, air?'

'Yes, yes, you fool. Don't you know my wife was an asthmatic? Have you made no inquiries whatsoever? Don't you know that someone suffering from an asthma attack needs air? Fresh air? Mrs Desmukh often came into the Gardens in the evening if she felt an attack was coming on.'

'But, sir, why here? Into these Gardens? And, sir, how was she getting in when gates are shut?'

'Inspector, do you not even know where my wife and I live? Our Malabar Hill house is almost inside the Gardens, and naturally when I knew my wife could get the cool air she needed here in the Gardens I had a little private gate made.'

Ghote thought for a brief instant about the very different lives of the very rich.

Then, slowly, Adik Desmukh approached the body lying there on the cold grass.

But Ghote, watching the Polyester King's slow, reverent approach, heard now another vehicle coming through the Gardens. The Medical Examiner, he thought at once. It must be the Medical Examiner in person. When one of the very rich dies in seemingly inexplicable circumstances, things, of course, are done differently than when one of the poor dies, however mysteriously.

He gave a little cough and told Mr Desmukh who the new arrival was. The Polyester King glanced at the jeep drawing up behind his own enormous car. Then, picking up his wife's handbag, he walked away to a nearby bench and slumped down, as if the arrival of the Medical Examiner had somehow fully brought home to him the reality of her death. Ghote saw – it was fully daylight now – that tears were actually rolling down those wide cheeks.

The Medical Examiner took a considerable time making his preliminary, on-the-spot investigation. Ghote did not dare interrupt with questions, though there were many he wanted to ask. What exactly was the cause of the death? What was the true nature of the sticky jelly-like splotches on the dead woman's sari? Were they no more than the saliva that a friendly dog, jumping up, might have deposited there? Or were they something else? Was there anything, after all, that might indicate the presence of a spectral hound? And . . . and had the Medical Examiner also noticed the odour that appeared to be coming from the dead woman's sari? And, if he had, what did he think it was?

At last the great man rose from his knees.

'Sir, what it was?'

'An asthma attack, Inspector. A serious asthma attack. You were not thinking it was the result of some supernatural agency?'

He gave a brutal little laugh.

'No, sir, no. But . . .'

'No, Inspector. An attack of asthma. A pure and simple attack of asthma. There are all the signs. Or – or – well, there will, of course, be a full post-mortem. Yes. Yes, of course, a post-mortem.'

Ghote wondered then whether his own never-expressed doubts could be reflected in the great man's mind. But it was plain that if in any degree they were, he was certainly not going to allow them to be spoken aloud.

'Very well,' he said decisively now, 'I will have an ambulance sent to take the corpus to J.J. Hospital.'

'Yes, sir. I will see that all is in order. Are you wishing also, sir, to be telling Mr Adik Desmukh – he is sitting just there – what were your conclusions?'

For a moment the great man hesitated, as if he did not altogether wish to tell the bereaved husband what had caused his wife's death.

But why should he not? Ghote wondered.

But then, with an abrupt straightening of his shoulders, the Medical Examiner went over to where Mr Desmukh was sitting tightly clutching the crocodile-skin handbag, last link with his wife of long years.

And Ghote thought, with a heaving lurch of dismay, *But what if he will not let go of same? What if he will not let go of an object that may have to be put in as evidence?*

Then he too straightened his shoulders, even more decisively than the Medical Examiner had.

'Sir,' he said to the Polyester King. 'Excuse me, sir. Sir, I must – sir, I am regretting to say, it is necessary for me to take your wife's – your late wife's – handbag. Sir, evidence. It may be necessary . . .'

'Take, take,' the Polyester King snapped out. And he thrust the bag towards Ghote.

Ghote seized it and strode quickly away, only coming to a halt when he was on the far side of the waiting corpus. Then, struck by new doubts, he twisted open the catch of the bag which Mr Desmukh must have snapped closed and anxiously ran over in his mind the contents, thinking that if the Polyester King had in a moment of sentimentality taken some small memento from it, then that was bound, somehow, to be something that would be required when the inquest was held.

But, even as he clicked the bag's catch open and peered inside – when Mr Desmukh has clutched it so hard one more fingerprint will not at all matter – a thought came to him. A suddenly overwhelming thought, trivial though it might seem.

That odour. The odour that had been strong in his

nostrils when he had knelt, to end once and for all that idiot Hasteen's notion that it had been a spectral hound that had killed Mrs Desmukh, and examined her body. That odour which he had not been able to account for at the time, the odour he knew he had somewhere once smelt. That characteristic smell that had lurked at the edge of his consciousness ever since he had knelt beside the body.

It was Choclox.

His mind flew back over the years. That out-of-station case I was dragooned into investigating. In that frozen-in-time hill resort of Ooty, down in the south. The murderer I was nabbing, a left-over fellow from the days of the British Raj, had the habit of feeding his dog with treats called Choclox, little biscuits that had an over-powering smell of crude chocolate, a dog's delight.

Yes. Yes, yes, yes. That was what I was smelling on late Mrs Desmukh's very-very fine sari. But why was it there? When I was looking into her handbag when the Pathan had mentioned it there were none of those high-smelling biscuits there. So she was not at all in habit of feeding any dogs with Choclox. But then how did her sari come to be smelling of them?

And the answer . . . Yes, it must be. It must. Someone had impregnated the garment with Choclox. But why? Yes, again, answer is plain. To make a dog in the Hanging Gardens go rushing up to the lady and be smelling and sniffing at her sari. That is, to make it look as if she had been attacked by . . . by the Hound of the Hanging Gardens.

But if the idea had been to make all that seem so,

then surely there ought to have been some dog teeth marks. And there were not.

So ... so was Mrs Desmukh murdered in some other way?

And then the full story arrived in Ghote's mind as if it had been planted there intact.

What had he seen in the crocodile-skin handbag just a few seconds ago? Had looked at without for a moment taking in something different about it? The blue plastic inhaler. But – he did not need now to open the bag again – that little object had not been of the same bright unblemished blue he had seen when he had looked in the bag after the Pathan had said he had found Mrs Desmukh's name in it. No, now it was blackened with the dried sweat of frequent use. As, of course, since Mrs Desmukh was a confirmed asthmatic, it must be.

So her old inhaler had been substituted for a new one. And it must have been that one she had fumbled for in her handbag after a large dog, almost certainly put into the Gardens for the purpose, had come bouncing up to her attracted by the strong odour of Choclox. Yes, an inhaler, filled with some poison, had been slipped into her bag before she went out into the dark of the Gardens for some fresh air. No wonder the Medical Examiner had felt a twinge of doubt about the cause of death.

Yes, if there had been anything diabolic in the Gardens in the night, it had not been a spectral hound. No, it had been a diabolic plan to commit a murder and get away with it. And who, above all, might want to be rid of a wife whose dowry had long ago been despoiled

277

and who was not even fit to be an ornament at his table? Mr Adik Desmukh, the Polyester King, in trouble on the financial pages.

And he is the influential man, Ghote thought, his insides suddenly dissolving in dismay, that I have now got to arrest.

Nevertheless, he squared his shoulders and marched forward.

H.R.F. Keating was awarded the CWA Gold Dagger in 1964 for The Perfect Murder, *which introduced Inspector Ghote of Bombay. The Ghote series made Keating's name, but he has written many other crime novels, including* The Murder of the Maharajah *(1980), which has a neatly concealed link to the Ghote books, and historical mysteries written under the name of Evelyn Hervey. Keating won the CWA Cartier Diamond Dagger in 1996. Like his friend Julian Symons, Keating spent a year as Chairman of the CWA and has established a distinct reputation for his criticism of crime fiction, most notably as an editor of* Whodunit? *and author of* The Bedside Companion to Crime.

PETER LOVESEY

The Man Who Jumped for England

I laughed when I was told. I took it for a party joke. There was nothing athletic about him. People put on weight when they get older and they shrink a bit, but not a lot. Willy Plumridge was five-two in his shoes and the shape of a barrel. His waistline matched his height. If Sally, my hostess, had told me Willy sang at Covent Garden or swam the Channel, I'd have taken her word for it. *Jumped for England?* I couldn't see it.

'High jump?' I asked Sally with mock seriousness.

She shrugged and spread her hands. She didn't follow me at all.

'They're really big men,' I said. 'You must have watched them. If you're seven feet tall, there are two sports open to you — high-jumping and basketball.'

'Maybe it was the long jump.'

'Then you're dealing in speed as well as size. They're sprinters with long legs. Look at the length of his. And don't mention triple jumping or the pole vault.'

'Why don't you ask him which it was?'

'I can't do that.'

'Why?'

'He'd think I was taking the piss.'

'Well,' she said, 'all the time I've known him – and that's ten years at least – people have been telling me he once jumped for England.'

'In the Olympics?'

'I wouldn't know.'

'Bungee-jumping, I could believe.'

'Is that an international sport?'

'Oh, come on!'

Sally said, 'Why don't I introduce you? Then maybe he'll tell you himself.'

So I met Willy Plumridge, shook the hand of the man who jumped for England. I can't say his grip impressed me. It was like handling chipolatas. He was friendly, though, and willing to talk. I didn't ask him straight out. I came at it obliquely.

'Have we met before? I seem to know your face.'

'Don't know yours, sport,' he said, 'and my memory is good.'

'Could be from way back, like school, or college.'

'I doubt it, unless you were in Melbourne.'

'Melbourne, Australia?' My hopes soared. If he was an Aussie, I'd nailed the lie already.

'Yep. That's where I did my schooling. My dad worked for an Australian bank. The family moved there when I was nine years old.'

'You're English?'

'Through and through.'

Not to be daunted, I tried another tack. 'They like their sport in Australia.'

'And how,' he said.

'It's all right if you're athletic, but it wouldn't do for me,' I said. 'I was always last in the school cross-country.'

'If you were anything like me,' Willy said, 'you stopped halfway round for a smoke. Speaking of which, do you have one on you? I left my pack in the car.'

I produced one for him.

'You're a pal.'

'If I am,' I said, 'I'm honoured.'

That first dialogue ended there because someone else needed to be introduced and we were separated. Willy waved goodbye with the fag between his fingers.

'Any clues?' Sally asked me.

'Nothing much. He grew up in Australia, but he's English all right.'

She laughed. 'That's half of it, then. Next time, ask about the jumping.'

Willy Plumridge and his jumping interrupted my sleep that night. I woke after about an hour and couldn't get him out of my mind. There had to be some sport that suited a stunted, barrel-like physique. I thought of ski-jumping, an event the English have never excelled at. Years ago there was all that fuss about Eddie the Eagle, that likeable character who tried the jump in Calgary and scored less than half the points of any other competitor. A man of Willy's stature would surely have attracted some attention if he'd put on skis. The thought of Willy in skintight Lycra wasn't nice. It was another hour before I got any sleep.

I knew I wouldn't relax until I'd got the answer. I

281

called Sally next morning. 'Is it possible he did winter sports?'

'Who?'

'Willy Plumridge.'

'Are you still on about him? Why don't you look him up if you're so bothered about this?'

'Hey, that's an idea.'

I went to the reference library and started on the sports section, checking the names of international athletes. No Willy Plumridge. I looked at winter sports. Nothing. I tried the internet without result.

'He's a fraud. He's got to be,' I told Sally when I phoned her that night. 'I've checked every source.'

She said, 'I thought you were going to look him up.'

'I did, in the library.'

'You great dummy. I meant look him up in person. He's always in the Nag's Head lunchtimes.'

'That figures,' I said with sarcasm. 'The international athlete, knocking them back in the Nag's Head every lunchtime.'

But I still turned up at the bar next day. Sally was right. Willy Plumridge was perched on a bar stool. I suppose it made him feel taller.

'Hi, Willy,' I said with as much good humour as I could raise. 'We met at Sally's party.'

'Sure,' he said, 'and I bummed a fag off you. Have one of mine.'

'What are you drinking, then?'

The stool next to him was vacant. I stood him a vodka and tonic.

'Do you work locally?' I asked.

'Work?' he said with a wide grin. 'I chucked that in a long while ago.'

He was under forty. Of course, professional sportsmen make their money early in life, but they usually go into coaching later, or management. He'd made a packet if he could spend the rest of his life on a bar stool.

I had an inspiration. I pictured him slimmed down and dressed in silks and a jockey cap. 'Let me guess,' I said. 'You were at the top of your profession. Private jet to get you around the country. Cheltenham, Newbury, Aintree.'

He laughed.

'Am I right?' I said. 'Champion of the jumps?'

'Sorry to disappoint,' he said. 'You couldn't be more wrong. I wouldn't go near a horse.'

Another theory went down the pan.

'Wouldn't put money on one either,' he said. 'I invest in certainties. That's how I got to retire.'

'I wish I knew your secret,' I said, meaning so much more than he knew.

'It's simple,' he said. 'I got it from my dad. Did I tell you he was in banking? He knew the way it works. He told me how to make my fortune, and I did. From time to time I top it up, and that's enough to keep me comfortable.'

Believe it or not, I'd become so obsessed with his jumping that I wasn't interested in how he'd made his fortune through banking. Maybe that was why he persisted with me. I was a challenge.

'If you were to ask me how I did it, I couldn't tell you straight off,' he said. 'It wasn't dodgy. It was perfectly legit, well, almost. I'm an honest man, Michael. Thanks for the drink, but I have to be going. Next time it's on me.'

I ran into Sally a couple of days later. She asked if I was any the wiser. I told her I was losing patience with Willy Plumridge. I didn't believe he'd jumped for England. Ever.

'But are you getting to know him?' she asked.

'A bit. He strikes me as a bullshitter. He was on about making a fortune out of banks. No one does that without a sawn-off shotgun.'

'He's not kidding,' she said. 'He's fabulously rich. Drives a Porsche and updates it every year. If he offers to let you in on his secret, let me know.'

'Sally, the only thing I want to know—'

'Ask him, then.'

One more possibility came to me during another disturbed night. I broached it next lunchtime in the pub. 'You must have done plenty of flying in your life, Willy.'

'Enough.'

'I was wondering if you ever went in for parachuting.'

'Me? No way. What makes you think that?'

'Someone told me you were a very good jumper.'

'*That?*' he said with a laugh. 'That wasn't parachuting.'

'They said you jumped for England.'

'And it's true.' He took a sip of his drink.

I waited for more and it didn't come.

'What do you do to earn a crust, Mike?' he said.

'I'm a freelance illustrator. Kids' books, mostly.'

'Satisfying work – but not too well-paid, I reckon.'

'That's about right.'

'Suppose there was a way to set yourself up with a good amount of cash. Would you take it?'

'Depends,' I said. 'It would have to be honest.'

'I like you,' he said, 'so I'll tell you how I made my first million. You've heard about Swiss bank accounts?'

'Where people salt away money with no questions asked?'

'That's the myth. Actually a lot of questions are asked. It's no simple matter to open a Swiss bank account with a suitcase full of banknotes. The gnomes of Zurich have strict banking laws these days. Customers have to be identified. You have to convince the bank that what you are depositing isn't the proceeds of a crime. Various money-laundering scandals have led to stringent legislation being introduced. These days you can't open a numbered account, as you once could, without identifying yourself. The beneficial owners of accounts have to be declared. As they should.'

'Agreed,' I said, uncertain where this was leading.

'They've also tightened up on withdrawals. The whole point of using Switzerland is that every account is rigidly protected. Great Uncle Edward dies and leaves you everything and there's a rumour that he was stashing away money in a Swiss account. Can you find out from the bank? No. All you get is a petrifying glare and a reminder that they are bound by their banking codes. In another twenty years, the bank can claim the money. There are said to be tens of billions locked away in dormant accounts in Switzerland. The gnomes bide their time and then collect.'

'What a racket,' I said.

'Yes, and as soon as any of the big names gets in trouble and questions are asked about the funds they salted away, the banks freeze the accounts. Noriega, Marcos, Ceausescu, Sukarno. But I don't care about monsters like that. It's Great Uncle Edward I feel sore about. I won't say the little people, because we're talking serious money here. Let's say family money, Mike. It should stay in the family, right?'

'Right.'

'Well, I'm uniquely placed to help out people like the family of Great Uncle Edward. My dad – the banker – had a contact in one of the great Swiss banks. Someone he trusted, a man of honour who had a conscience about these unfortunate families trying to get information. His hands were tied. There was nothing he could do within the Swiss banking system. But he knew the magic numbers the families needed, you see. He passed the numbers to Dad, who passed them to me. Then it was just a matter of matching the right families to the money that rightly belonged to them. It involved some basic research. Anyone can look at a will in most countries of the world. You find the beneficiaries and you offer to help.'

'For a fee?'

'A small commission.'

'A small percentage of a big sum?'

He smiled. 'You're getting the idea, Mike.'

'So you pass on the information about the account numbers?'

'And the sums involved. Dad's friend listed the balances

with the numbers. So I'm the bearer of good news. I've made a big difference to some people's lives.'

Including your own, I thought. Not bad.

I said, 'I guess some of this money is ill-gotten gains.'

'I never enquire,' he said. 'If Great Uncle Edward was a train robber, or painted fake Van Goghs, it's no concern of mine. The way I see it, the family has more right to it than the bank. Are you with me?'

'I think so,' I said.

'I'm only mentioning this because I think you can help me.'

I hesitated. 'How?'

'Well, I still have details of a few accounts I haven't been able to follow up, and time is running out. The twenty-year rule means that the banks will scoop the pool if something isn't done. I begrudge them that. I feel I owe it to the memories of my old dad and his friend – who also died about the same time – to recover that money. These are families I haven't traced yet. I've found the wills, but the beneficiaries are more elusive.'

'You want someone to do the research, track them down?'

He shook his head. 'There isn't the time. What I need is someone I can trust to approach the bank and show them the documentation and claim the money for the estate.'

'What – go to Switzerland?'

'That isn't necessary. They have a City of London branch. I'd do it myself, but they know my face from a previous claim.'

'You want me to pretend I'm acting for the family?'

'Pretend? You *will* be acting for them, Mike. I've opened an executors' account. You show them the copy of the will and the death certificate and they verify that the names match. You give them the account details, which they confirm with Zurich. They write you a cheque, and bingo!'

'Why should they deal with *me*?'

'To keep them happy, you say you're one of the executors.'

'I don't like the sound of that.'

'Don't worry, Mike. I'll give you proof of identity.'

'No, this isn't right.'

'Would five per cent make it right?'

I didn't speak.

'Think it over,' he said. 'Let me know tomorrow, or the next day. No sweat.'

Plenty of sweat. Another night of disturbed sleep. This time I was wrestling with my conscience. It was a scam and a clever scam. But the only loser would be a bank that was about to get a fortune that didn't belong to it.

Much neater than pointing a gun at a cashier. This was beating them at their own game, with account numbers and cheques.

Could I trust Willy Plumridge? He had the lifestyle that backed his story. Good suits, a Porsche, usually parked outside the pub. I hadn't seen his house, but Sally had told me he had two, and they were both big places.

In the morning my credit card statement arrived. I owed them three grand and some more.

'If I did this,' I said to Willy, 'how much would I make out of it?'

He took out a calculator and pressed some buttons. 'Give or take a few pence, fifty-five grand.'

I tried to sound unimpressed. 'So it's a sizeable inheritance?'

'You can work it out.'

'And there won't be any problem with the family?'

He grinned. 'The beauty of it is that we don't know where they are. And when we trace them – if we do – they're going to be so delighted by this windfall that they won't begrudge us our commission. Believe me, Mike, this isn't the first such deal I've negotiated.'

I had my doubts whether Willy's efforts to trace the family would yield a quick result. Maybe, like the bank, he reckoned the money should come to him after a passage of time.

Fifty-five grand would set me up for a couple of years at least. I could do some real painting for a change, get off the treadmill of cute teddy-bears and badgers dressed as postmen.

'Would this be a one-off?'

'Has to be,' Willy said. 'I couldn't use you again. I have to find some other guy I can trust.'

'So we can draw a line under it?'

'You'll never hear from me again. It'll be as if we never met.'

'I'd prefer the money in cash, if that's possible.'

'No problem.'

He was efficient. He'd done this before. A packet arrived at my house two days later. Inside were the details of the Swiss bank account of the late James Alexander Connelly, standing at £1,106,008, his death certificate and his last will and testament, including the names of two executors, Harry and Albert Smith. I was to be Albert. There was a letter from Harry giving me authority to act on his behalf, and another from an English bank confirming that an executors' account had been opened. A birth certificate in Albert Smith's name was included as proof of identity.

Willy had told me to make an appointment. Banks don't like people coming in off the street and making big withdrawals. I was to say I was an executor for James Connelly's estate enquiring about the possibility of a bank account in his name. No more than that.

I called the bank and spoke to someone who listened without much show of interest and invited me in the next morning at eleven-thirty.

After another uneasy night I put on the only suit I owned, dropped my documents into a briefcase and took the train to London. Sitting there shoulder to shoulder with the businessmen who commuted daily, I felt isolated, one of another species about to venture into their territory.

The bank was right in the City of London, a massive building with grey pillars. Unlike my own suburban bank, this one had a security guard and a receptionist. I mentioned my appointment and was shown to a seat. The décor was intended to intimidate: marble, mahogany and murals. Don't let them get you down, I told myself. They're the crooks.

They kept me waiting ten minutes, and it felt like an hour.

'Mr Smith.'

I almost forgot to respond.

'This way, please.'

The young woman showed me upstairs, where it was Persian carpets and embossed wallpaper. She opened a door. 'Please go in and sit down. Mr Schmidt will be with you shortly.'

Schmidt. One of the family? I said to myself, trying to stay loose. I sat back in a large leather chair and patted my thighs. I wasn't going to cross my legs in case I looked nervous.

Schmidt entered through another door. He looked younger than I expected, dark, with tinted glasses. 'How can I help?'

I gave him the spiel, stressing that Uncle James had repeatedly spoken about his special account with the bank. After his death there had been a delay of some years before we – the executors – found his notes with the account details. 'His filing system was non-existent,' I said. 'We came across the note in a book of hand-written recipes. We almost threw it out. As a cook, he was a dead loss.'

'May I see?'

'I didn't bring the recipe book,' I said. 'I copied the figures.'

'And do you have other evidence with you?'

I removed everything from the briefcase and passed it across.

Schmidt spent some minutes studying the documents. 'It seems to be in order,' he said. 'Would you mind if I showed the papers to a colleague? We have to verify anything so major as this.'

'I understand.'

When he left the room I found I'd crossed my legs after all. I took deep breaths.

The wait tested me to the limit. Just in case there was a hidden camera, I tried to give an impression of calm, but pulses were beating all over my body.

When Schmidt returned, there was a cheque in his hand. 'This is what you were waiting for, Mr Smith, a cheque for a million and just over two hundred thousand pounds. The account accrued some interest. All I require is your signature on the receipt.'

Resisting the urge to embrace the man, I scribbled a signature.

'Your documents.' He handed them across. 'And now I'll show you out.' He opened the door.

Slipping the cheque into an inner pocket, I stuffed the rest of the paperwork into the briefcase and went through that door walking on air.

Some people were in the corridor outside. I wouldn't have given them a second glance had not one of them said, 'Mr Michael Hawkins.'

My own name? I froze.

'I'm DI Cavanagh, of the Serious Fraud Squad.'

I didn't hear the rest. I believe I fainted.

Three months into my sentence, I was transferred to an open prison in Norfolk. There, in the library one afternoon, I met Arthur, and we talked a little. He seemed more my sort than some of the prisoners. As you do, I asked him what he was in for.

'Obtaining money by deception.'

'Snap,' I said.

'Only I was caught with the cheque in my pocket,' he said.

'Me, too. I was caught in a Swiss bank, of all places.'

'How odd,' he said. 'So was I.'

It didn't take long to discover we had both been talked into the same scam by Willy Plumridge.

'What a bastard!' I said. 'And he's still at liberty.'

'Waiting to find another mug to tease some money out of the bank,' Arthur said. 'I bet I wasn't the first.'

'Well, he got rich by doing it himself, I gather,' I said.

'True, but with less risk. In the early days of this racket, he traced the families and advised them. They made the approach to the bank, and it worked. They paid him well for the information. Later, he was left with the account numbers he couldn't link to a family, so he thought up this idea of finding people to pose as executors. Maybe it worked a few times, but banks aren't stupid.'

'So I discovered. What I can't understand is why they haven't pulled him in. He's Mr Big. You and I are small fry.'

'They won't touch him,' Arthur said.

'Why?'

'He's the man who jumped for England.'

That again. 'Give me a break!' I said. 'How does that make a difference?'

'Don't you know?' Arthur said. He glanced to right and left to make sure no one could overhear him. 'One of those account numbers he got from his father belonged to someone pretty important. A former prime minister, in fact.'

'No! Which one?'

'I never found out, except they're dead. Supposed to have been a model of honesty when in fact they were salting away millions in bribes. Willy got on to the family and offered to liberate the money without anyone finding out. The next generation had some heavy expenses to meet, so they hired him. The bank, of course, was utterly discreet and totally duped. Willy pulled it off and was handed the cheque. Then I don't know if his concentration went, or he was light-headed with his success, but he slipped on the stairs at Bank tube station, fell to the bottom and suffered severe bruising and concussion. He was rushed to hospital and no one knew who he was.'

'Except that he was carrying the cheque?'

'Right. And various documents linking him to the family. The police called them. They panicked and said they knew nothing about Willy. He had to be an impostor and all the documents must be faked. After a night in the cells, he was charged with obtaining money by deception and brought before the magistrate at Bow Street. They put him on bail, pending further investigation. Only it never came to trial.'

'Why?'

'The secret service intervened to avert the scandal. If it had ever got to court it would have destroyed a prime minister's reputation. They decided the best way to deal with it was for Willy to jump bail and go into hiding. No attempt was made to find him and the matter was dropped. The family cashed the cheque, Willy got his commission, and the good name of a great prime minister was saved from disgrace. That's why you and I are locked in here and Willy Plumridge is sitting in the Nag's Head enjoying his vodka and tonic. He did the decent thing and jumped for England.'

Peter Lovesey's short stories have been honoured with a number of awards, including the CWA Veuve Clicquot prize, the Ellery Queen Readers' Award and the Mystery Writers of America Golden Mysteries Prize celebrating their fiftieth anniversary. Five collections of his stories have been published, the latest, The Sedgemoor Strangler, *in 2001. Many have also been read on radio and adapted for TV in the* Tales of the Unexpected *series and the BBC Schools Service. As a crime novelist, he began with historical mysteries set in the Victorian age and has more recently concentrated on contemporary police novels featuring an unorthodox detective, Peter Diamond. Lovesey has been the recipient of the Silver, Gold and (in 2000) Diamond Daggers of the CWA.*

ED McBAIN

The Interview

Sir, ever since the Sardinian accident, you have refused to grant any interviews . . .

I had no desire to join the circus.

Yet you are not normally a man who shuns publicity.

Not normally, no. The matter on Sardinia, however, was blown up out of all proportion, and I saw no reason for adding fuel to the fire. I am a creator of motion pictures, not of sensational news stories for the press.

There are some 'creators of motion pictures' who might have welcomed the sort of publicity the Sardinian . . .

Not I.

Yet you will admit the accident helped the gross of the film.

I am not responsible for the morbid curiosity of the American public.

Were you responsible for what happened in Sardinia?

On Sardinia. It's an island.

On Sardinia, if you will.

I was responsible only for directing a motion picture. Whatever else happened, happened.

297

You were there when it happened however . . .

I was there.

So certainly . . .

I choose not to discuss it.

The actors and technicians present at the time have had a great deal to say about the accident. Isn't there anything you'd like to refute or amend? Wouldn't you like to set the record straight?

The record is the film. My films are my record. Everything else is meaningless. Actors are beasts of burden and technicians are domestic servants, and refuting or amending anything either might care to utter would be a senseless waste of time.

Would you like to elaborate on that?

On what?

On the notion that actors . . .

It is not a notion, it is a simple fact. I have never met an intelligent actor. Well, let me correct that. I enjoyed working with only one actor in my entire career, and I still have a great deal of respect for him – or at least as much respect as I can possibly muster for anyone who pursues a profession that requires him to apply make-up to his face.

Did you use this actor in the picture you filmed on Sardinia?

No.

Why not? Given your respect for him . . .

I had no desire to donate fifty per cent of the gross to his already swollen bank account.

Is that what he asked for?

At the time. It may have gone up to seventy-five per

298

cent by now, I'm sure I don't know. I have no intention of ever giving a ploughhorse or a team of oxen fifty per cent of the gross of a motion picture I created.

If we understand you correctly . . .

You probably don't.

Why do you say that?

Only because I have never been quoted accurately in any publication, and I have no reason to believe your magazine will prove to be an exception.

Then why did you agree to the interview?

Because I would like to discuss my new project. I have a meeting tonight with a New York playwright who will be delivering the final draft of a screenplay upon which we have laboured long and hard. I have every expectation that it will now meet my requirements. In which case, looking ahead to the future, this interview should appear in print shortly before the film is completed and ready for release. At least, I hope the timetable works out that way.

May we know who the playwright is?

I thought you were here to talk to me.

Well, yes, but . . .

It has been my observation that when Otto Preminger or Alfred Hitchcock or David Lean or even some of the fancy young *nouvelle vague* people give interviews, they rarely talk about anyone but themselves. That may be the one good notion any of them has ever contributed to the industry.

You sound as if you don't admire too many directors.

I admire some.

Would you care to name them?

I have admiration for Griffith, DeMille, Eisenstein, several others.

Why these men in particular?

They're all dead.

Are there no living directors you admire?

None.

None? It seems odd that a man known for his generosity would be so chary with praise for other acknowledged film artists.

Yes.

Yes, what?

Yes, it would seem odd, a distinct contradiction of personality. The fact remains that I consider every living director a threat, a challenge, and a competitor. There are only so many motion picture screens in the world, and there are thousands of films competing to fill those screens. If the latest Hitchcock thriller has them standing on line outside Radio City, the chances are they won't be standing on line outside my film up the street. The theory that an outstanding box-office hit helps *all* movies is sheer rubbish. The outstanding hit helps only itself. The other films suffer because no one wants to see them, they want to see only the big one, the champion, the one that has the line outside on the sidewalk. I try to make certain that all of my films generate the kind of excitement necessary to sustain a line on the sidewalk. And I resent the success of any film but my own.

Yet you have had some notable failures.

Failures are never notable. Besides, I do not consider any of my films failures.

Are we talking now about artistic failures or box-office failures?

I have never made an artistic failure. Some of my films were mildly disappointing at the box office. But not very many of them.

When the Sardinian film was ready to open last June . . .

July. It opened on the Fourth of July.

Yes, but before it opened, when . . .

That would have been June, yes. July is normally preceded by June.

There was speculation that the studio would not permit its showing.

Rubbish.

The rumours were unfounded? That the studio would suppress the film?

The film opened, didn't it? And was a tremendous success, I might add.

Some observers maintain that the success of the film was due only to the publicity given the Sardinian accident. Would you agree to that?

I'll ask *you* a question, young man. Suppose the accident on Sardinia had been related to a film called *The Beach Girl Meets Hell's Angels*, or some such piece of trash? Do you think the attendant publicity would have insured the success of *that* film?

Perhaps not. But given your name and the stellar quality of . . .

You can stop after my name. Stars have nothing to do with any of my pictures. I could put a trained seal in one of my films, and people would come to see it. I could put you in a film, and people would come to see it.

Don't you believe that films are a collaborative effort?

Certainly not. I tell the script writer what I want, and he writes it. I tell the set designer what to give me, and he gives it to me. I tell the cameraman where to aim his camera and what lens to use. I tell the actors where to move and how to speak their lines. Does that sound collaborative to you? Besides, I resent the word 'effort'.

Why?

Because the word implies endeavour without success. You've tried to do something and you've failed. None of my films are 'efforts'. The word 'effort' is like the word 'ambitious'. They both spell failure. Haven't you seen book jackets that proudly announce 'This is So-and-So's most ambitious effort to date'? What does that mean to you? To me, it means the poor bastard has set his sights too high. And failed.

Are you afraid of failure?

I cannot abide it.

Do you believe the Sardinian film was a success? Artistically?

I told you earlier . . .

Yes, but many critics felt the editing of the film was erratic. That the sequences filmed before the drowning were inserted piecemeal into . . .

To begin with, whenever critics begin talking about editing or camera angles or dolly shots or anything technical, I instantly fall asleep. They haven't the faintest notion of what filmmaking is all about, and their pretentious chatter about the art may impress maiden ladies in Flushing Meadows, but it quite leaves me cold. In reality, *none* of them know what's going on either behind the camera or up there on the screen. Do you know what a film critic's sole requirement is? That he has seen a lot of movies, period. To my way of thinking, *that* qualifies him as an expert on popcorn, not on celluloid.

In any event, you were rather limited, were you not, in editing the final portion of the film?

Limited in what way?

In terms of the footage you needed to make the film a complete entity?

The film *was* a complete entity. Obviously, I could not include footage that did not exist. The girl drowned. That was a simple fact. We did not shoot the remainder of the film as originally planned, we *could* not. But the necessary script revisions were made on the spot – or rather in Rome. I flew to Rome to consult with an Italian screenwriter, who did the work I required.

He did not receive credit on the film.

He *asked* that his name be removed from the picture. I acceded to his wishes.

But not without a struggle.

There was no struggle.

It was reported that you struck him.

Nonsense.

On the Via Veneto.

The most violent thing I've ever done on the Via Veneto was to sip a Campari-soda outside Doney's.

Yet the newspapers . . .

The Roman press is notoriously inaccurate. In fact, there isn't a single good newspaper in all Italy.

But, sir, there was some dispute with the screenwriter, wasn't there? Surely, the stories about it couldn't all have been . . .

We had some words.

About what?

Oh my, we *must* pursue this deadly dull rot, mustn't we? All right, all right. It was *his* allegation that when he accepted the job, he had no idea the publicity surrounding the girl's death would achieve such hideous proportions. He claimed he did not wish his good Italian name – the little opportunist had written only one film prior to my hiring him, and that an Italian Western starring a second-rate American television actor – did not wish his name associated with a project that had even a *cloud* of suspicion hanging over it. Those were his exact words. Actually, quite the opposite was true. Which is why I resisted his idiotic ploy.

Quite the opposite? What do you mean?

Rather than trying to *avoid* the unfortunate publicity, I felt he was trying to capitalise on it. His move was really completely transparent, the pathetic little bastard. I finally let him have his way. I should have thought he'd be proud to have his name on one of my pictures. As an illuminating sidelight, I might add he did not return the five thousand dollars a week I'd paid for the typing he did. Apparently, my *money* did not have a similar 'cloud of suspicion' hanging over it.

'Typing', did you say?

Typing. The ideas for changing the script to accommodate the . . . to allow for a more plausible resolution were all mine.

A resolution to accommodate the drowning?

To explain the absence of the girl in the remainder of the film. I'm reluctant to discuss this, because it has a ghoulish quality I frankly find distasteful. The girl *did*, after all, drown; she *did* die. But that was a simple fact, and we must not lose sight of another simple fact. However cold-blooded this may sound, and I am well aware that it may be an unpopular observation, there had already been an expenditure of three million dollars on that film. Now I'm sure you know that leading players *have* taken ill, *have* suffered heart attacks, *have* died during the filming of other pictures. To my knowledge, such events have never caused a picture to halt production, and neither do I know of a single instance in which a film was entirely scrapped, solely because of the death of one of the leading players. Yet this was the very pressure being brought to bear on me immediately following the drowning, and indeed up to the time of the film's release.

Then the studio did try to suppress the film?

Well . . . at first, they only wanted to stop production. I refused. Later, when they saw the rough cut – this was when all the publicity had reached its peak – they sent in a team of strong-armed Executive Producers, and Production Chiefs, and what-have-you, all know-nothings with windy titles, who asked me to suppress the film. I told them exactly where to go. And then later on, when the film had been edited and scored, the same thing happened. I finally threatened suit. My contract called for a large percentage of the gross of that film, and I had no intention of allowing it to crumble unseen in the can.

You did not feel it was a breach of good taste to exhibit the film?

Certainly not. The girl met with an accident. The accident was no one's fault. She drowned. If a stunt man had died riding a horse over a cliff, would there have been all that brouhaha about releasing the film? I should say not.

But you must agree the circumstances surrounding the drowning . . .

The drowning was entirely accidental. We were shooting in shallow water.

The reports on the depth of the water vary from ten feet to forty feet. Neither of which might be considered shallow.

The water was no higher than her waist. And she was a tall girl. Five feet seven, I believe. Or eight. I'm not sure which.

Then how did she drown, sir?

I have no idea.

You were there, were you not?

I was on the camera barge, yes.

Then what happened?

I suppose we must set this to rest once and for all, mustn't we? I would much rather discuss the present and/or the future, but apparently we cannot do that until we've dealt *ad nauseam* with the past.

As you wish, sir.

I wish the accident had never happened, sir, that is what *I* wish. I also wish I would not be pestered interminably about it. The Italian inquest determined that the drowning was entirely accidental. What was good enough for the Italian courts is damn well good enough for me. But there is no satisfying the American appetite for scandal, is there? Behind each accident or incident, however innocuous, however innocent, the American public *must* insist upon a plot, a conspiracy, a cabal. Nothing is permitted to be exactly what it appears to be. Mystery, intrigue must surround everything. Nonsense. Do you think any of us *wanted* that girl to drown? I've already told you how much money we'd spent on the picture before the accident. I would estimate now that the delay in completion, the cost of revisions, the necessity for bringing in a second girl to resolve the love story added at least a million dollars to the proposed budget. No one wanted the drowning. If for business reasons *alone*, no one wanted it.

Yet it happened.

It happened.

How?

The exact sequence of events is still unclear to me.

Your assistant director . . .

Yes.

Testified at the inquest . . .

Yes, yes.

That the girl pleaded not to go into the water.

The water was unusually cold that morning. There was nothing we could do about *that*. It was a simple fact. The light was perfect, we had our set-up, and we were prepared to shoot. Actors are like children, you know. If I had allowed her to balk at entering the water, the next thing I knew she'd have balked at walking across a lawn.

The writer of the original screenplay claims that the scene you were shooting that morning . . .

Where the girl swims in to the dock? What about it?

He claims he did not write that scene. He claims it was not in the original script.

Well, let him take that up with the Writers Guild.

Was it in the original script?

I have no idea. If there were no innovations during the shooting of a film . . . really, does anyone expect me to follow a script precisely? What then is my function as director? To shout 'Louder' or 'Softer' to an actor? Let the writers direct their own scripts, in that case. I assure you they would not get very far.

Was the scene an innovation? The scene in the water?

It might have been. I can't recall. If it was not in the original shooting script, as our Hollywood hack claims, then I suppose it was an innovation. By definition, yes, it would have been an innovation, isn't that so?

When was it added to the script?

I don't recall. I will sometimes get ideas for scenes the night before I shoot them. In which case, I will call in the technicians involved, and describe the set-up I will need the next day, and I will have it in the morning. If there is additional dialogue involved, I'll see to it that the actors and the script girl have the necessary pages, and I'll ask the actors to study them overnight. If there is no additional dialogue . . .

Was there any dialogue in this scene?

No. The girl was merely required to swim in to the dock from a speedboat.

What do you do in such a case? In an added scene where there's no dialogue?

Oh, I'll usually take the actor aside and sketch in the scene for him. The gist of it. This was a particularly simple scene. She had only to dive over the side of the boat and swim in to the dock.

In shallow water?

Well, not so shallow that she was in any danger of hitting the bottom, if that's what you mean.

Then perhaps the estimates of the water's depth . . .

The water's depth was no problem for anyone who knew how to swim.

Did the girl know how to swim?

Of course she did. You certainly don't think I'd have allowed her to play a scene in water . . .

I merely wondered if she was a good swimmer or . . .

Adequate. She was neither Eleanor Holm nor Esther Williams, but the part didn't call for an Olympic champion, you know. She was an adequate swimmer.

When did you explain the gist of the scene to her?

That morning, I believe. If memory serves me . . . yes, I believe the idea came to me the night before, and I called in the people involved and told them what I would need the following morning. Which is when I explained the scene to her. At least, that's usually the way it works; I assume it worked the same way concerning this particular scene.

You explained that she would have to dive over the side of the boat and swim in to the dock?

Which is all she had to do.

Did she agree to do this?

Why, of course. She was an inexperienced little thing, this was her first film. Of course she agreed. There was never any question of her not agreeing. She'd been modelling miniskirts or what-have-you for a teenage

309

fashion magazine when I discovered her. This was an enormous opportunity for her, this film. Look at the people I surrounded her with! Do you know what we had to pay her leading man? Never mind. It still irritates me.

Is it true he threatened to walk off the picture after the girl drowned?

He has said so in countless publications across the length and breadth of the world. I'm surprised he hasn't erected a billboard on the moon, but I imagine he's petitioning NASA for the privilege this very moment.

But did he threaten to walk off?

He did. I could not allow it, of course. Neither would his contract allow it. An actor will sometimes be deluded into believing he is something more than a beast of the field. Even with today's largely independent production structure, the studio serves as a powerful steamroller flattening out life's annoying little bumps for any second-rate bit player who's ever seen his own huge face grinning down idiotically from a screen. The *real* head sometimes gets as big as the fantasy head up there. Walk off the picture? I'd have sued his socks from under him.

Why did he threaten to walk off?

We'd had difficulty from the start. I think he was searching for an excuse, and seized upon the girl's drowning as a ripe opportunity.

What sort of difficulty?

I do not believe I need comment on the reputation of the gentleman involved. It has been adequately publicised, even in the most austere family publications.

Is it true, then, that a romance was developing between him and the girl?

310

I have never yet worked on a film in which a romance did not develop between the girl and her leading man. That is a simple fact of motion picture production.

Was it a simple fact of this motion picture?

Unfortunately, yes.

Why do you say 'unfortunately'?

The girl had a brilliant career ahead of her. I hated to see her in a position that . . . I hated to see her in such a vulnerable position.

Vulnerable?

The Italian press would have enjoyed nothing better than to link her romantically with someone of his reputation. I warned her against this repeatedly. We'd spent quite a lot of money grooming this girl, you know. Stardom may happen overnight, but it takes many days of preparation for that overnight event.

Did she heed your warnings?

She was very young.

Does that mean to say . . . ?

Nineteen, very young.

There were, of course, news stories of a developing romance between them. Despite your efforts.

Yes, despite them. Well.

Yes?

The young are susceptible. And yet, I warned her. Until the very end, I warned her. The night before she drowned, there was a large party at the hotel, given in my honour. We had seen the rushes on the shooting we'd done the day before, and we were all quite pleased, and I, of course, was more than ever certain that the girl was going to be a tremendous smash. That I had found someone, developed someone, who would most certainly become one of the screen's enduring personalities. No question about it. She had . . . she had a luminous quality that . . . it's impossible to explain this to a layman. There are people, however, who are bland, colourless, insipid, until you photograph them. And suddenly, the screen is illuminated with a life force that is positively blinding. She had that quality. And so I told her again, that night of the party, I took her aside, and we were drinking quietly, and I reminded her of what she had been, an unknown model for a juvenile fashion magazine, and of what she would most certainly become once this film was released, and I begged her not to throw this away on a silly flirtation with her leading man, a man of his reputation. The press was there, you know this was quite an occasion – I had met the host on the Riviera, oh years ago, when I was doing another film, and this was something of a reunion. Well. Well, I suppose none of it matters quite, does it? She's dead. She drowned the next day.

What happened? At the party?

They managed to get some photographs of her. There is a long covered walk at the hotel, leading to the tower apartments that overlook the dock. The *paparazzi* got some pictures of the two of them in a somewhat, shall we say, compromising attitude. I tried to get the cameras, I struggled with one of the photographers . . .

Were these the photographs that were later published? After the accident?

Yes, yes. I knew even then, of course. When I failed to get those cameras, I knew her career was ruined. I knew

that everything I'd done, all the careful work, the preparation – and all for *her*, you know, all to make the girl
a star, a person in her own right – all of it was wasted.
I took her to her room. I scolded her severely, and
reminded her that make-up call was for six a.m.

What happened the next morning?

She came out to the barge at eight o'clock, made up
and in costume. She was wearing a bikini, with a robe
over it. It was quite a chilly day.

Was she behaving strangely?

Strangely? I don't know what you mean. She seemed
thoroughly chastised, as well she might have. She sat
alone and talked to no one. But aside from that, she
seemed perfectly all right.

No animosity between you?

No, no. A bit of alienation perhaps. I had, after all,
been furious with her the night before and had soundly
reprimanded her. But I *am* a professional, you know, and
I *did* have a scene to shoot. As I recall, I was quite cour-
teous and friendly. When I saw she was chilled, in fact,
I offered her my thermos.

Your thermos?

Yes. Tea. A thermos of tea. I like my tea strong, almost
to the point of bitterness. On location, I can never get
anyone to brew it to my taste, and so I do it myself,
carry the thermos with me. That's what I offered to her.
The thermos of tea I had brewed in my room before
going out to the barge.

And did she accept it?

Gratefully. She was shivering. There was quite a sharp
wind, the beginning of the mistral, I would imagine.

She sat drinking the tea while I explained the scene to her. We were alone in the stern, everyone else was up forward, bustling about, getting ready for the shot.

Did she mention anything about the night before?

Not a word. Nor did I expect her to. She only complained that the tea was too bitter. I saw to it that she drank every drop.

Why?

Why? I've already told you. It was uncommonly cold that day. I didn't want to risk her coming down with anything.

Sir . . . was there any other reason for offering her the tea? For making certain that she drank every drop?

What do you mean?

I'm only reiterating now what some of the people on the barge have already said.

Yes, and what's that?

That the girl was drunk when she reported for work, that you tried to sober her up, and that she was still drunk when she went into the water.

Nonsense. No one drinks on my sets. Even if I'd worked with W. C. Fields, I would not have permitted him to drink. And I respected him highly. For an actor, he was a sensitive and decent man.

Yet rumours persist that the girl was drunk when she climbed from the camera barge into the speedboat.

She was cold sober. I would just love to know how such rumours start. The girl finished her tea and was sitting *alone* with me for more than three hours. We were having some colour difficulty with the speedboat, I didn't like the way the green bow was registering and

314

I asked that it be repainted. As a result, preparation for the shot took longer than we'd expected. I was afraid it might cloud up and we'd have to move indoors to the cover set. The point is, however, that in all that time not a single soul came anywhere near us. So how in God's name would anyone know whether the girl was drunk or not? Which she wasn't, I can definitely assure you.

They say, sir . . .

They, they, who the hell are *they*?

The others on the barge. They say that when she went forward to climb down into the speedboat, she seemed unsure of her footing. They say she appeared glassy-eyed . . .

Rubbish.

. . . that when she asked if the shooting might be postponed . . .

All rubbish.

. . . her voice was weak, somehow without force.

I can tell you definitely and without reservation, and I can tell you as the single human being who was with that girl from the moment she stepped on to the barge until the moment she climbed into the speedboat some three-and-a-half hours later, that she was at all times alert, responsive, and in complete control of her faculties. She did not want to go into the water because it was cold. But that was a simple fact, and I could not control the temperature of the ocean or the air. Nor could I reasonably postpone shooting when we were in danger of losing our light, and when we finally had everything including the damn speedboat ready to roll.

So she went into the water. As instructed.

Yes. She was supposed to swim a short distance

underwater, and then surface. That was the way I'd planned the scene. She went into the water, the cameras were rolling, we . . . none of us quite realised at first that she was taking an uncommonly long time to surface. By the time it dawned upon us, it was too late. *He*, of course, immediately jumped into the water after her . . .

He?

Her leading man, his heroic move, his hairy-chested *star* gesture. She was dead when he reached her.

What caused her to drown? A cramp? Undertow? What?

I haven't the foggiest idea. Accidents happen. What more can I say? This was a particularly unfortunate one, and I regret it. But the past is the past, and if one continues to dwell upon it, one can easily lose sight of the present. I tend not to ruminate. Rumination is only stagnation. I plan ahead and in that way the future never comes as a shock. It's comforting to know, for example, that by the time this appears in print, I will be editing and scoring a film I have not yet begun to shoot. There is verity and substance to routine that varies only slightly. It provides a reality that is all too often lacking in the motion picture industry.

This new film, sir . . .

I thought you'd never ask.

What is it about?

I never discuss the plot or theme of a movie. If I were able to do justice to a story by capsulising it into three or four paragraphs, why would I then have to spend long months filming it? The synopsis, as such, was invented by Hollywood executives who need so-called 'story analysts' to provide simple translations because they themselves are incapable of reading anything more difficult than 'Run, Spot, Run'.

What can you tell us about your new film, sir?

I can tell you that it is set in Yugoslavia, and that I will take full cinematic advantage of the rugged coastal terrain there. I can tell you that it is a love story of unsurpassing beauty, and that I have found an unusually talented girl to play the lead. She has never made a film before, she was working with a little theatre group on La Cienega when I discovered her, quite by chance. A friend of mine asked me to look in on an original the group was doing, thought there might be film possibilities in it, and so forth. The play was a hopeless botch, but the girl was a revelation. I had her tested immediately, and the results were staggering. What happens before the cameras is all that matters, you know, which is why some of our important stage personalities have never been able to make a successful transition to films. This girl has a vibrancy that causes one to forget completely that there are mechanical appliances such as projectors or screens involved. It is incredible, it is almost uncanny. It is as though her life force transcends the medium itself, sidesteps it so to speak; she achieves direct uninvolved communication at a response level I would never have thought existed. I've been working with her for, oh, easily six months now, and she's remarkably receptive, a rare combination of intelligence and incandescent beauty. I would be foolish to make any sort of prediction about the future, considering the present climate of Hollywood, and the uncertain footing of the entire industry. But if this girl continues to listen and to learn, if she is willing to work as hard in the months ahead as she has already worked, then given the proper vehicle and the proper guidance – both of which I fully intend to supply – I cannot but foresee a brilliant career for her.

Is there anything you would care to say, sir, about the future of the industry in general?

I never deal in generalities, only specifics. I feel that so long as there are men dedicated to the art of making good motion pictures – and I'm not talking now about pornography posing as art, or pathological disorders posing as humour – as long as there are men willing to make the sacrifices necessary to bring quality films to the public, the industry will survive. I intend to survive along with it. In fact, to be more specific, I intend to endure.

Thank you, sir.

Ed McBain *is a pseudonym of Evan Hunter, a New Yorker who became in 1998 the first American to win the CWA Cartier Diamond Dagger. Hunter has written notable novels under his own name, such as* The Blackboard Jungle *and* Lizzie, *which offers an intriguing explanation of the celebrated Lizzie Borden murder case. But it is as McBain that he is probably best known, in particular for the long and continuing series of books about the cops of the 87th Precinct.* Cop Hater, *published in 1956, was the first of these classic police procedurals. McBain's other books include a series about the Florida lawyer Matthew Hope, with titles taken from nursery rhymes and fairy tales.*

VAL McDERMID

The Consolation Blonde

Awards are meaningless, right? They're always political, they're forgotten two days later and they always go to the wrong book, right? Well, that's what we all say when the prize goes somewhere else. Of course, it's a different story when it's our turn to stand at the podium and thank our agents, our partners and our pets. Then, naturally enough, it's an honour and a thrill.

That's what I was hoping I'd be doing that October night in New York. I had been nominated for Best Novel in the Speculative Fiction category of the US Book Awards, the national literary prizes that carry not only prestige but also a $50,000 cheque for the winners. *Termagant Fire*, the concluding novel in my *King's Infidel* trilogy, had broken all records for a fantasy novel. More weeks in the *New York Times* bestseller list than King, Grisham and Cornwell put together. And the reviews had been breathtaking, referring to *Termagant Fire* as 'the first novel since Tolkien to make fantasy respectable'. Fans and booksellers alike had voted it their book of the year. Serious literary critics had examined the parallels between my fantasy universe and America in the defining epoch of the sixties. Now all I was waiting for was the imprimatur of the judges in the nation's foremost literary prize.

Not that I was taking it for granted. I know how fickle judges can be, how much they hate being told what to think by the rest of the world. I understood only too well that the *succès d'estime* the book had enjoyed could be the very factor that would snatch my moment of glory from my grasp. I had already given myself a stiff talking-to in my hotel bathroom mirror, reminding myself of the dangers of hubris. I needed to keep my feet on the ground, and maybe failing to win the golden prize would be the best thing that could happen to me. At least it would be one less thing to have to live up to with the next book.

But on the night, I took it as a good sign that my publisher's table at the awards dinner was right down at the front of the room, smack bang up against the podium. They never like the winners being seated too far from the stage just in case the applause doesn't last long enough for them to make it up there ahead of the silence.

My award was third from last in the litany of winners. That meant a long time sitting still and looking interested. But I could only cling on to the fragile conviction that it was all going to be worth it in the end. Eventually, the knowing Virginia drawl of the MC, a middle-ranking news anchorman, got us there. I arranged my face in a suitably bland expression, which I was glad of seconds later when the name he announced was not mine. There followed a short, stunned silence, then, with more eyes on me than on her, the victor weaved her way to the front of the room to a shadow of the applause previous winners had garnered.

I have no idea what graceful acceptance speech she came out with. I couldn't tell you who won the remaining two categories. All my energy was channelled into not showing the rage and pain churning inside me. No matter how much I told myself I had prepared for this, the reality was horrible.

At the end of the apparently interminable ceremony, I got to my feet like an automaton. My team formed a sort of flying wedge around me; editor ahead of me, publicist to one side, publisher to the other. 'Let's get you out of here. We don't need pity,' my publisher growled, head down, broad shoulders a challenge to anyone who wanted to offer condolences.

By the time we made it to the bar, we'd acquired a small support crew, ones I had indicated were acceptable by a nod or a word. There was Robert, my first mentor and oldest buddy in the business; Shula, an English SF writer who had become a close friend; Shula's girlfriend Caroline; and Cassie, the manager of the city's premier SF and fantasy bookstore. That's what you need at a time like this, people around who won't ever hold it against you that you vented your spleen in an unseemly way at the moment when your dream turned to ashes. Fuck nobility. I wanted to break something.

But I didn't have the appetite for serious drinking, especially when my vanquisher arrived in the same bar with her celebration in tow. I finished my Jack Daniels and pushed off from the enveloping sofa. 'I'm not much in the mood,' I said. 'I think I'll just head back to my hotel.'

'You're at the InterCon, right?' Cassie asked.

'Yeah.'

'I'll walk with you, I'm going that way.'

'Don't you want to join the winning team?' I asked, jerking my head towards the barks of laughter by the bar.

Cassie put her hand on my arm. 'You wrote the best book, John. That's victory enough for me.'

I made my excuses and we walked into a ridiculously balmy New York evening. I wanted snow and ice to match my mood, and said as much to Cassie.

Her laugh was low. 'The pathetic fallacy,' she said. 'You writers just never got over that, did you? Well, John, if you're going to cling to that notion, you better change your mood to match the weather.'

I snorted. 'Easier said than done.'

'Not really,' said Cassie. 'Look, we're almost at the InterCon. Let's have a drink.'

'OK.'

'On one condition. We don't talk about the award, we don't talk about the asshole who won it, we don't talk about how wonderful your book is and how it should have been recognised tonight.'

I grinned. 'Cassie, I'm a writer. If I can't talk about me, what the hell else does that leave?'

She shrugged and steered me into the lobby. 'Gardening? Gourmet food? Favourite sexual positions? Music?'

We settled in a corner of the bar, me with Jack on the rocks, she with a Cosmopolitan. We ended up talking about movies, past and present, finding to our surprise that in spite of our affiliation to the SF and fantasy world, what we both actually loved most was film noir. Listening to Cassie talk, watching her push her blonde hair back from her eyes, enjoying the sly smiles that crept out when she said something witty or sardonic, I forgot the slings and arrows and enjoyed myself.

When they announced last call at midnight, I didn't want it to end. It seemed natural enough to invite her up to my room to continue the conversation. Sure, at the back of my mind was the possibility that it might end with those long legs wrapped around mine, but that really wasn't the most important thing. What mattered was that Cassie had taken my mind off what ailed me. She had already provided consolation enough, and I wanted it to go on. I didn't want to be left alone with my rancour and self-pity or any of the other uglinesses that were fighting for space inside me.

She sprawled on the bed. It was that or an armchair which offered little prospect of comfort. I mixed drinks, finding it hard not to imagine sliding those tight black trousers over her hips or running my hands under that black silk tee, or pushing the long shimmering overblouse off her shoulders so I could cover them with kisses.

I took the drinks over and she sat up, crossing her legs in a full lotus and straightening her spine. 'I thought you were really dignified tonight,' she said.

'Didn't we have a deal? That tonight was off limits?' I lay on my side, carefully not touching her at any point.

'That was in the bar. You did well, sticking to it. Think you earned a reward?'

'What kind of reward?'

'I give a mean backrub,' she said, looking at me over the rim of her glass. 'And you look tense.'

'A backrub would be . . . very acceptable,' I said.

Cassie unfolded her legs and stood up. 'OK. I'll go into the bathroom and give you some privacy to get undressed. Oh, and John – strip right down to the skin. I can't do your lower back properly if I have to fuck about with waistbands and stuff.'

I couldn't quite believe how fast things were moving. We hadn't been in the room ten minutes, and here was Cassie instructing me to strip for her. OK, it wasn't quite like that sounds, but it was equally a perfectly legitimate description of events. The sort of thing you could say to the guys and they would make a set of assumptions from. If, of course, you were the sort of sad asshole who felt the need to validate himself like that.

I took my clothes off, draping them over the armchair without actually folding them, then lay face down on the bed. I wished I'd spent more of the spring working out than I had writing. But I knew my shoulders were still respectable, my legs strong and hard, even if I was carrying a few more pounds around the waist than I would have liked.

I heard the bathroom door open and Cassie say, 'You ready, John?'

I was very, very ready. Somehow, it wasn't entirely a surprise that it wasn't just the skin of her hands that I felt against mine.

How did I know it had to be her? I dreamed her hands. Nothing slushy or sentimental; just her honest hands with their strong square fingers, the palms slightly callused from the daily shunting of books from carton to shelf, the play of muscle and skin over blood and bone. I dreamed her hands and woke with tears on my face. That was the day I called Cassie and said I had to see her again.

'I don't think so.' Her voice was cautious, and not, I believed, simply because she was standing behind the counter in the bookstore.

'Why not? I thought you enjoyed it,' I said. 'Did you think it was just a one-night stand?'

'Why would I imagine it could be more? You're a married man, you live in Denver, you're good-looking and successful. Why on earth would I set myself up for a let-down by expecting a repeat performance? John, I am so not in the business of being the Other Woman. A one-night stand is just fine, but I don't do affairs.'

'I'm not married.' It was the first thing I could think of to say. That it was the truth was simply a bonus.

'What do you mean, you're not married? It says so on your book jackets. You mention her in interviews.' Now there was an edge of anger, a 'don't fuck with me' note in her voice.

'I've never been married. I lied about it.'

A long pause. 'Why would you lie about being married?' she demanded.

'Cassie, you're in the store, right? Look around you. Scope out the women in there. Now, I hate to hurt people's feelings. Do you see why I might lie about my marital status?'

I could hear the gurgle of laughter swelling and

bursting down the telephone line. 'John, you are a bastard, you know that? A charming bastard, but a bastard nevertheless. You mean that? About never having been married?'

'There is no moral impediment to you and me fucking each other's brains out as often as we choose to. Unless, of course, there's someone lurking at home waiting for you?' I tried to keep my voice light. I'd been torturing myself with that idea ever since our night together. She'd woken me with soft kisses just after five, saying she had to go. By the time we'd said our farewells, it had been nearer six and she'd finally scrambled away from me, saying she had to get home and change before she went in to open the store. It had made sense, but so too did the possibility of her sneaking back into the cold side of a double bed somewhere down in Chelsea or SoHo.

Now, she calmed my twittering heart. 'There's nobody. Hasn't been for over a year now. I'm free as you, by the sounds of it.'

'I can be in New York at the weekend,' I said. 'Can I stay?'

'Sure,' Cassie said, her voice somehow promising much more than a simple word.

That was the start of something unique in my experience. With Cassie, I found a sense of completeness I'd never known before. I'd always scoffed at terms like 'soulmate', but Cassie forced me to eat the words baked in a humble pie. We matched. It was as simple as that. She compensated for my lacks, she allowed me space to demonstrate my strengths. She made me feel like the finest lover who had ever laid hands on her. She was also the first woman I'd ever had a relationship with who miraculously never complained that the writing got in the way. With Cassie, everything was possible and life seemed remarkably straightforward.

She gave me all the space I needed, never minding that my fantasy world sometimes seemed more real to me than what was for dinner. And I did the same for her, I thought. I didn't dog her steps at the store, turning up for every event like an autograph hunter. I only came along to see writers I would have gone to see anyway; old friends, new kids on the block who were doing interesting work, visiting foreign names. I encouraged her to keep up her girls' nights out, barely registering when she rolled home in the small hours smelling of smoke and tasting of Triple Sec.

She didn't mind that I refused to attempt her other love, rock climbing; forty-year-old knees can't learn that sort of new trick. But equally, I never expected her to give it up for me, and even though she usually scheduled her overnight climbing trips for when I was out of town on book business, that was her choice rather than my demand. Bless her, she never tried taking advantage of our relationship to nail down better discount deals with my publishers, and I respected her even more for that.

Commuting between Denver and New York lasted all of two months. Then in the same week, I sold my house and my agent sold the *King's Infidel* trilogy to Oliver Stone's company for enough money for me actually to be able to buy a Manhattan apartment that was big enough for both of us and our several thousand books. I loved, and felt loved in return. It was as if I was leading a charmed life.

I should have known better. I am, after all, an adherent of the genre of fiction where pride always, always, always comes before a very nasty fall.

We'd been living together in the kind of bliss that makes one's friends gag and one's enemies weep for almost a year when the accident happened. I know that Freudians claim there is never any such thing as accident, but it's hard to see how anyone's subconscious could have felt the world would end up a better or more moral place because of this particular mishap.

My agent was in the middle of a very tricky negotiation with my publisher over my next deal. They were horse-trading and haggling hard over the money on the table, and my agent was naturally copying me in on the e-mails. One morning, I logged on to find that day's update had a file attachment with it. 'Hi, John,' the e-mail read.

You might be interested to see that they're getting so nitty-gritty about this deal that they're actually discussing your last year's touring and miscellaneous expenses. Of course, I wasn't supposed to see this attachment, but we all know what an idiot Tom is when it comes to electronics. Great editor, cyber-idiot. Anyway, I thought you might find it amusing to see how much they reckon they spent on you. See how it tallies with your recollections . . .

I wasn't much drawn to the idea, but since the attachment was there, I thought I might as well take a look. It never hurts to get a little righteous indignation going about how much hotels end up billing for a one-night stay. It's the supplementaries that are the killers. Fifteen dollars for a bottle of water was the best I came across on last year's tour. Needless to say, I stuck a glass under the tap. Even when it's someone else's dime, I hate to encourage the robber barons who masquerade as hoteliers.

I was drifting down through the list when I ran into something out of the basic rhythm of hotels, taxis, air fares, author escorts. *Consolation Blonde, $500*, I read.

I knew what the words meant, but I didn't understand their linkage. Especially not on my expense list. If I'd spent it, you'd think I'd know what it was.

Then I saw the date.

My stomach did a back flip. Some dates you never forget. Like the US Book Awards dinner.

I didn't want to believe it, but I had to be certain. I called Shula's girlfriend Caroline, herself an editor of mystery fiction in one of the big London houses. Once we'd got the small talk out of the way, I cut to the chase. 'Caroline, have you ever heard the term "consolation blonde" in publishing circles?'

'Where did you hear that, John?' she asked, answering the question inadvertently.

'I overheard it in one of those chi-chi midtown bars

where literary publishers hang out. I was waiting to meet my agent, and I heard one guy say to the other, "He was OK after the consolation blonde." I wasn't sure what it meant but I thought it sounded like a great title for a short story.'

Caroline gave that well-bred middle-class English-woman's giggle. 'I suppose you could be right. What can I say here, John? This really is one of publishing's tackier areas. Basically, it's what you lay on for an author who's having a bad time. Maybe they didn't win an award they thought was in the bag, maybe their book has bombed, maybe they're having a really bad tour. So you lay on a girl, a nice girl. A fan, a groupie, a publicity girlie, bookseller, whatever. Somebody on the fringes, not a hooker as such. Tell them how nice it would be for poor old what's-his-name to have a good time. So the sad boy gets the consolation blonde and the consolation blonde gets a nice boost to her bank account plus the bonus of being able to boast about shagging a name. Even if it's a name that nobody else in the pub has ever heard before.'

I felt I'd lost the power of speech. I mumbled something and managed to end the call without screaming my anguish at Caroline. In the background, I could hear Bob Dylan singing 'Idiot Wind'. Cassie had set the CD playing on repeat before she'd left for work and now the words mocked me for the idiot I was.

Cassie was my Consolation Blonde.

I wondered how many other disappointed men had been lifted up by the power of her fingers and made to feel strong again? I wondered whether she'd have stuck around for more than that one-night stand if I'd been a poor man. I wondered how many times she'd slid into bed with me after a night out, not with the girls, but wearing the mantle of the Consolation Blonde. I wondered whether pity was still the primary emotion that moved her when she moaned and arched her spine for me.

I wanted to break something. And this time, I wasn't going to be diverted.

I've made a lot of money for my publisher over the years. So when I show up to see my editor, Tom, without an appointment, he makes space and time for me.

That day, I could tell inside a minute that he wished for once he'd made an exception. He looked like he wasn't sure whether he should just cut out the middle man and throw himself out of the twenty-third-floor window. 'I don't know what you're talking about,' he yelped in response to my single phrase.

'Bullshit,' I yelled. 'You hired Cassie to be my consolation blonde. There's no point in denying it, I've seen the paperwork.'

'You're mistaken, John,' Tom said desperately, his alarmed chipmunk eyes widening in dilemma.

'No. Cassie was my consolation blonde for the US Book Awards. You didn't know I was going to lose, so you must have set her up in advance, as a stand-by. Which means you must have used her before.'

'I swear, John, I swear to God, I don't know . . .' Whatever Tom was going to say got cut off by me grabbing his stupid preppie tie and yanking him out of his chair.

'Tell me the truth,' I growled, dragging him towards

the window. 'It's not like it can be worse than I've imagined. How many of my friends has she fucked? How many five-hundred-buck one-night stands have you pimped for my girlfriend since we got together? How many times have you and your buddies laughed behind my back because the woman I love is playing consolation blonde to somebody else? Tell me, Tom. Tell me the truth before I throw you out of this fucking window. Because I don't have any more to lose.'

'It's not like that,' he gibbered. I smelled piss and felt a warm dampness against my knee. His humiliation was sweet, though it was a poor second to what he'd done to me.

'Stop lying,' I screamed. He flinched as my spittle spattered his face. I shook him like a terrier with a rat.

'OK, OK,' he sobbed. 'Yes, Cassie was a consolation blonde. Yes, I hired her last year for you at the awards banquet. But I swear, that was the last time. She wrote me a letter, said after she met you she couldn't do this again. John, the letter's in my files. She returned her fee for being with you. You have to believe me. She fell in love with you that first night and she never did it again.'

The worst of it was, I could tell he wasn't lying. But still, I hauled him over to the filing cabinets and made him produce his evidence. The letter was everything he'd promised. It was dated the day after our first encounter, two whole days before I called her to ask if I could see her again.

Dear Tom, Thanks for transferring the $500 payment to my bank account. However, I'm enclosing a refund check *for $500. It's not appropriate for me to accept money this time. I won't be available to do close author escort work in future. Meeting John Treadgold has changed things for me. I can't thank you enough for introducing us. Good luck. Cassie White.*

I stood there, reading her words, every one cutting me like the wounds I'd carved into her body the night before.

I guess they don't have awards ceremonies in prison. Which is probably just as well, given what a bad loser I turned out to be.

Val McDermid, a former journalist, has created three distinct series characters: Lindsay Gordon, Kate Brannigan and Tony Hill. Gordon is a journalist, Brannigan a private eye based in Manchester, and Hill a criminal profiler whose first recorded case, The Mermaids Singing, *earned McDermid the CWA Gold Dagger in 1995. The Hill books have recently been adapted for television with Robson Green in the lead role. McDermid has also written a study of female private eyes,* A Suitable Job for a Woman.

SARA PARETSKY

At the 'Century of Progress'

23 May 1933
Mrs Ben Milder
The Vicarage, St Clement-sur-Mare

*Now that we are finally arrived in Chicago I have leisure
to write you a proper letter. My nephew may have been
foolish enough to lose a fortune to a plausible rogue, but
he is gentleman enough to know how to look after a
dithery elderly woman. From the moment he met my
train at Paddington until I was ensconced today in the
Stevens Hotel, every attention that could be paid to my
comfort was paid. He even had champagne waiting for
me shipboard! And when I gave him a gentle scold for
his extravagance, he reminded me that our American
cousins still practise their absurd Prohibition and that it
would be some time before I could partake of alcohol
again. Of course, I do not drink aside from the occasional sherry, but even my respected father saw nothing
amiss in a glass of champagne for women on very special
occasions. On the dear Queen's Golden Jubilee – well,*

that was long ago, and I was a foolish girl of eighteen, and those reminiscences are not the news you are hoping to read here.

We arrived here only this morning, so I have had no time to look around me. At the station poor Eric could not make any of the porters understand him: the Oxford accent does not translate well in this city of immigrants. When I thought we might have to spend the entire day on the platform, a rude man from the second-class car shoved his way past us. I was about to utter a sharp rebuke when he obligingly carried all of our cases to a taxi! He disappeared before I could thank him. Although he was gruff in manner, I suppose one must label him a diamond in the rough.

How extraordinary that Eric should be your cousin on your mother's aunt's side, as well as my own sister's grandson. Life is filled with these most curious coincidences, but I am frankly glad that I have an intimate at home with whom to share my dismay at our relation's stupidity!

The city is in a great bustle with the World's Fair about to open, certainly an ideal setting for a confidence artist. Whether the man who 'fleeced' Eric (I believe that is the police term for taking someone's money through a confidence trick) will be bold enough to show his face here, I cannot say. But Eric seems convinced such a man will want to 'work' this exposition; he says a venue like this is irresistible to the confidence artist.

Miss Palmer did not add that she thought Eric had a letter that had persuaded him to come to the Century of Progress exhibition. Every time she brought up the matter, he patted his jacket where his leather pocketbook resided. Whenever she taxed him with why he thought his swindler would be in Chicago, he would laugh.

'Oh, Aunt Mary! You're just as prim-seeming as Granny's other sisters on the outside, but you're very jolly underneath. Anyway, Chicago's just a notion I took into my head.'

She had let it go, but she was convinced the man had either said something when Eric gambled away his father's rubber plantation or had written her nephew subsequently to lure him to Chicago: Eric had been absolutely set on coming.

An indiscreet young man, even if quite charming, Eric must have told their plans to all the world and its wife. Miss Palmer thought back. When had she received her own extraordinary letter? After they had booked their tickets, not before; she was sure of that. For a brief, idiotic moment she thought she could return to the scenes of her youth, perhaps even—

Miss Palmer clipped off the thought and continued writing.

Meanwhile, it is a beautiful day, and our hotel overlooks the great lake of Michigan, which sparkles in the sunlight. I can also see the north end of the fairgrounds; indeed, your cousin has rented an entire suite for me. If I can persuade someone to make me a proper cup of tea, I will feel quite ready to start exploring. The city has changed a great deal in the forty years since I was last here.

337

Miss Palmer crossed out that last sentence and laid down her pen. The fatigue of her long journey was making her garrulous. It was one thing to act the dithering maiden lady in public – one of Sir Nevil Burdock's 'old pussies', as she'd overheard him call her – but quite another to start doing it in private.

She'd been twenty-three when she first saw the great White City on the Midway. She and Papa had travelled to Chicago on the cars from Arizona, where they'd left Mother to try the desert cure. A London specialist had recommended it for lung disorders, and Mother had come home two years later perfectly cured. During her own time in Chicago with Papa, he was tied up with some tedious business about railroad investments. As for her, for a few months she thought she had opened a new book on life, but it turned out to be a closed chapter.

Miss Palmer looked at the offending sentence. It was still quite legible behind the strong line she'd drawn over it. She would have to copy the whole letter again from the beginning. It would take a spill of ink to cover the line, and Mother would never have allowed her to send a letter with such an unsightly blot on it. Even in her seventh decade, Miss Palmer could not go against the teachings of that scrupulous educationist.

The Twentieth Century Limited blows me into Union Station at 2.08 on the dot. I pick up my hat and my overnighter from the rack and saunter off the train, only to find my way blocked by an old lady with enough luggage to sink the *Titanic*. She has a young whippersnapper with her who's trying to grab a porter. I oblige just so the rest of us poor saps can get moving. They don't know me in Chicago yet, but anyone in New York could tell you Race Williams don't have a heart, or manners either.

Compared to Gotham, this burg is strictly a small potato, but you see the same guys lying on park benches and the same pathetic fools trying to cadge two bits for dope. They're about to open a World's Fair here that they're calling 'A Century of Progress'. We're like a bunch of apes walking backward into the sea, and they want the mugs to believe we're in a century of progress! There's thirty bucks trying to keep each other warm in my wallet, and they're all that's separating me from the boys on the corners with their cans full of pencils, so I walk across town until I find a place on Harrison Street where I can flop for a couple of bucks a night. It was those thirty slender dollars that persuaded me to leave the great city on the ocean for the small pretender by the lake.

If you're from west of the Hudson, you may not know the name Race Williams – may not know I'm the first and the best of the private investigators. Still, I hesitated when a gent calling himself Lionel Maitland waltzed into my office on Monday telling me he wanted to nail Jimmy 'Red Dog' Glazer.

Now, Red Dog never did anyone a day's harm that didn't have money to lose. He's not the kind of guy who'd as soon plug you as look at you, and taking things altogether, I'd just as soon go after the uglier customers. Your true hoods are in oversupply, to use the economists' lingo, and there's no demand for 'em, whereas a skilled con artist is doing a hard day's work and getting paid for it. But I'd had to swallow my pride. My last thirty bucks were limiting my options.

So this Maitland comes in, very British, down to the cane, the gloves, the thin moustache and of course the accent. But he sees he's dealing with a professional, and he don't try any tricks on me. He just tells me that Red Dog bilked him of five million in a phony bottling scheme, and if he don't get it back, well, he'll have to sell off the ancestral home. Which would make his ancestors rise from their graves and haunt him, I suppose. Anyway, he had enough left to buy me a ticket to Chicago, enough left to promise me a thousand when I spot the Dog and twenty if I get the dough back. And he thinks Red Dog will turn up at the Fair – partly because it's filled with mugs and partly because Chicago's Red Dog's hometown.

It was my hometown too, once upon a time, if you can call that orphanage down on Cottage Grove a home. I had hoped never to see this dim-bulb burg again after I hightailed it to the Great City in '07, but here I am – a fish out of water, so to speak.

4 June 1933

We have been in a positive whirlwind of activity since the opening of the Fair last Saturday. Our second night, Eric struck up acquaintance with a compatriot, a Colonel Townsend, who is here with the British Industrial Council. We all had dinner together after the formal

340

opening, but I am not entirely at ease with this new acquaintance. Colonel Townsend reminds me of Major Thorndike, who settled in St Clement-sur-Mare shortly before the Great War and persuaded poor Arnold Huxtable to open that garage with all his mother's savings. When Arnold discovered he had been defrauded, Thorndike broke Arnold's shoulder by flinging him from the roof of the garage. I always thought Thorndike meant to murder Arnold to keep him from talking, and I could only be happy that the police were on hand.

Now I can't help wondering why this Colonel Townsend has so much time to spend in bars with young men like Eric. The two of them have derived vast amounts of fun from watching the celebrated fan dancer Sally Rand appear from her boat as Lady Godiva every night. I have had several conversations with this young woman, and despite the risqué nature of her entertainment, I believe Miss Rand is actually quite intelligent.

Of course, because of Prohibition, the Stevens Hotel does not have a bar, so the gentlemen retire to other parts of town where they can imbibe in private. Eric and Colonel Townsend have been joined by several Americans, including the man who was so kind as to help us with our luggage when we arrived. They play a game called poker, at which I fear my nephew has his usual ill luck.

Since ladies do not frequent such places — called speakeasies — you may be wondering how I have acquired such knowledge. It comes from the Negro woman who cleans my room. We fell into conversation the day after the Fair opened when I asked if she had attended the ceremonies.

341

'No, ma'am. That place is for white people, not Negroes.'

'Excuse me, my dear, but surely in the North there are no laws forbidding members of your race to enter public places?'

She continued dusting the furniture without speaking for a moment or two, then said in a cold, clipped voice, 'How many jobs do you think that Fair has brought the out-of-work Negro in this city? If I told you seventy-five out of the many thousands working there, would you think it was because no Negro applied for work?'

When I didn't answer she said, 'I haven't been there, nor will I go.' Noting the bitterness in her tone, I left her alone to clean the room.

After attending church, I walked over to the Fair. It had not struck me before that in this city of many million people, with many hundreds of thousands of African descent, how few were at the fairgrounds. Indeed, the only ones I saw were employed as janitors in the public lavatories.

My eyes have since been opened to the many injustices here. No Negroes may stay as guests in this fine hotel or eat in any of its restaurants. Nor are they allowed to shop at Chicago's most magnificent store, Marshall Field's.

The list goes on, but to return to matters of more moment to you: when the maid saw I was sympathetic to the plight of her people, she came to warn me of the bad company my nephew has fallen into. Her uncle, it seems, plays poker at the same speakeasy Eric frequents and has talked to her of the gullible young Englishman who seems a prey for any passing card shark, to use her uncle's term.

342

I tried to remonstrate with Eric, but he only laughed at me. He comes in very late now and sleeps until noon. When he gets up, he does not look refreshed. But when I suggest that we go home to England, he protests vehemently and says not until he has found the man who robbed him of his inheritance!

I can't help worrying that Eric may be compounding his problems by associating with Mr Williams – for such is the name of our 'diamond in the rough' – and another American named Mr Redmond, who has lately joined them. Mr Redmond represents a South American mining company and is in Chicago to find investors among the wealthy attending the Fair. Our diamond in the rough, however, reminds me of someone . . .

The memory was elusive. Miss Palmer stared sightlessly out the window at the light dancing on the lake as she tried to capture the fugitive resemblance. When it came, she gasped softly. She stared at the paper, then picked up her pen again and quickly continued:

. . . but not anyone who would be known to you in St Clement-sur-Mare.

Well, Mr Redmond has offered to take me to church with him this morning, although I fear the sermon will not be as interesting as those I am accustomed to hearing from your dear husband.

Miss Palmer signed the letter and took it with her to the hotel's front desk. She had selected a number of gauzy scarves to drape around her neck and shoulders, which, with the widebrimmed hat, should keep the worst of the sun from scorching her. The cool weather of her first week in the city had suddenly changed to a stifling damp heat that she had never known at home. Dear Mother had suffered greatly from sunburn while she took the desert cure.

After their return to England, Miss Palmer had never been able to submit to her mother's parental authority again. After her father died, they had lived as uneasy strangers in the house in St Clement-sur-Mare, attending divine service together twice every Sunday and again on Wednesdays. Everyone said what a devoted daughter Miss Palmer remained, as twenty turned to thirty, then somehow to forty-four, and she spent middle age nursing wounded men sent back to the village from the trenches.

But a deeper, more complicated feeling tied Mary Palmer to her mother. Anger and resentment, yes – but it was a vindictive desire to prove she could be more upright, more thoroughly moral than Mrs Palmer that had given them twenty-five exhausting years together and had taught Miss Palmer that even in a small village, the pond's surface hides more than it reveals.

Mr Redmond thought she seemed a little fragile and was concerned about her walking more than a mile to divine worship, but the air, humid though it was, seemed to do her good. It happened to be Whitsunday, and Miss Palmer was struck by the Collect, with its prayer 'to have a right judgment in all things and evermore rejoice in the Spirit's Holy Comfort'. Only God, of course, had a right judgment in all things, but surely, if she avoided the sin of pride, she might find her reason properly guided.

On the way back to the hotel, she was willing to let Mr Redmond hail a cab. 'Too much mortification of the flesh is as bad as not enough,' she commented.

'I'm glad you think like that, Miss Palmer. Young Master Eric would be mighty upset if you gave up your beautiful suite in the Stevens to stay in a lesser hotel. He's a relation, I take it?'

'My sister's grandson, Mr Redmond, and my own godson, which makes me feel a special interest in his welfare.'

Redmond eyed the fluttering scarves thoughtfully. 'I only wondered, ma'am, because – well, not to put it too bluntly. I shouldn't like to think he was guiding your investments.'

'Investments! Now you are asking me to speak of finance, Mr Redmond, and my dear father held that women's brains could not encompass such a subject. I must say I am inclined to agree, although when one sees the sad squandering of family fortunes on the most injudicious investments, one cannot help asking whether the male brain is always suited for such deep subjects, either. Dear Eric . . . he is so impulsive. You will think this is most foolish, perhaps insulting to a young man of twenty-four, but he cannot sign any documents abroad without my cosignature. Still, it might keep him from pursuing some foolish-sounding venture to begin with, because of course it would be beyond me to unravel it.'

In the earnestness of her discourse, Miss Palmer managed to spill the entire contents of her pocketbook on the floor of the cab. Despite her protests, Mr Redmond got down on the floor in his clean linen suit and gathered up all the component parts. By the time he had presented them to her, the taxi had let them out in front of the Stevens Hotel. He walked away with a thoughtful frown.

The next day, Miss Palmer, carefully following the directions of the head porter, walked across downtown Chicago to the City-County Building. As she crossed the Loop – and why 'Loop', she wondered, then decided it must be the elevated train circling the central business district – she fell prey to an unaccustomed melancholy. So much had changed since 1893 – all these hotels and office buildings had been nonexistent then. And State Street, now jammed with cars and buses, had then been jammed with horse-drawn wagons, carriages and foot traffic. Even the City-County Building, which was old enough to show some signs of wear, had not been thought of on her previous visit. And she – she had changed as well, settling into the rut of one of Sir Nevil's well-mannered, interfering pussies.

She fluttered earnestly from one official to another until she was finally able to consult the birth and death registers. She looked under every name she could think of but turned up nothing to the point. Of course, that was not conclusive proof – but something cold clutched around her heart. Why had she not done this years ago? Illness was never an excuse for feebleness of mind or purpose: dear Mother had taught her that by precept as well as example. And she might have spared herself much grief.

★　★　★

I can't figure the dame and the kid. I spotted him for a mark right from the get-go, and if you're looking for Red Dog Glazer, the best thing to do is hang out by a mark. Now the dame, she flutters around waving her veils and whatnot, so I do my best to calm her down, get her to take a sight-seeing trip or go to church or whatever old English dames do when they're overseas, and she stares at me with those china-doll eyes and says, 'Oh, too kind of you, Mr Williams, but – now I know you wouldn't think it to look at me – I'm well able to take care of myself, so please don't worry about needing to entertain me.' And on she hangs for dear life.

But getting the kid to a speakeasy did the trick. Miss China Doll Palmer may want to hold on to him twenty-four hours a day, but she's not about to follow him drinking on Rush Street, much less on to the 'Streets of Paris' for Sally Rand's show. Although, peculiarly, I could swear I saw her leaving Miss Rand's dressing room – or should I say *un*dressing room? – after the performance the other night, when all the sex-starved boys of Chicago were hanging around panting.

Sure enough, two days after I detach the boy from his aunt, we start to draw a group for poker. A breezy American with more luck at cards than is good for him, name of Doug Redmond. A large, middle-aged Negro named Sam Leyden who works as a stevedore during the day and has the devil's own skill at cards. And damn me if who doesn't turn up but my client Lionel Maitland, gloves, cane, accent, everything just like it was in New York except his name. He's calling himself Colonel

Townsend. I take advantage of young Eric's excitement at winning a hand to haul Maitland outside.

'What the hell's your game, Maitland? You hired me to find Red Dog Glazer, and now you've blown into town to do the job yourself! You afraid to part with your money?'

'My dear chap! I can scarcely blame you for being distressed, but – can you kindly remove your hands from my weskit?'

'Not until I've had a look at your wallet, my friend.' And I pull it out of his vest pocket – or weskit, as he calls it. He wants to grab it back, but I never travel without my gun, and it's casually pointing at his watch pocket while I flip the contents of his wallet with my left hand. He's got cards in every name under creation – Colonel Townsend, Lionel Maitland and three or four more besides. And enough cash to put me up in the Stevens for the rest of the summer. I pull out four fifties and tuck them into my inside jacket pocket before stuffing the wallet into his weskit again.

'I need some walking-around money, Colonel Townsend-Maitland. It'll help me draw Red Dog to my side. You can hold the rest until I've executed my mission. But what the hell are you doing here?'

He looks at my face, doesn't like what he sees, and transfers his affections to the gun. Father's helper is still pointing at his chest.

'It just seemed to me, old chap, that this feller Glazer being a master of disguise, it might be handy if I was on the spot, see if I recognise him, what?'

'He's much more likely to recognise *you* and spoil

your game.' I let go of his lapels and shove him backward, not gently, toward the alley. 'Leave the detecting to me. If you can't trust me to do the job right, why did you hire the best investigator in New York?'

'No offence, old man, but what have you been doing besides tagging along with that milk-fed youth?'

'If you haven't seen me at work, that means I'm doing a good job,' I snarl.

And I hadn't been idle. My first stop in town had been the *Chicago American*, where I met a reporter named Reuben Levine, who was interested in the Dog. I got what pix there were of him and a basketful of tales of his doings. Around the time of the Great War, Red Dog'd posed as a wealthy German looking for Americans to invest in land devalued by the war. He found plenty of suckers, all right, just as he had for running a shady betting scheme on some horses he controlled. His main gig lately, though, has been the one Maitland says he got caught on. Seems Glazer likes to pretend he's a bumbling idiot with a booze factory he can't handle, finds a mark who wants to make a fast buck on the shady side. He rents a warehouse, fills it for twenty-four hours with actors pretending to be bootleggers, gets a still, bottles, the works, and sells the lot, including the distribution routes. When the mug shows up the next day to take over, he finds an empty warehouse!

And I'd found the speakos Glazer liked to hang at when he was home – one of them being the very place I'd just pulled Colonel Townsend-Maitland from. But it's not my policy to let the client know what I'm up to. Keep an air of mystery and they think you're all-powerful. Let them in on your secrets and they always think you haven't done enough.

'I've done some digging,' was all I told Maitland-Townsend. 'And I've found out more than you realise.'

He gives me a sceptical look, but he heads up the alley and away from me. I go back into the speako.

Young Eric, after his big victory ten minutes ago, is managing to lose a few bills, but he keeps joking around in his usual good-natured way. He may be a fool, but at least he's a well-behaved fool. Redmond is dealing, which kind of makes me wonder.

Redmond looks mighty uncomfortable when I come back in, which has me even more curious about his system for marking cards. But he asks after Townsend-Maitland, and when I say the limey's taken a hike, he relaxes and orders a round for everyone at the table.

Meanwhile, I take advantage of the lull to exchange my own deck for the one Redmond was using. The big Negro gives me a long, hard look and demands a fresh deck from the houseman. We all take a turn inspecting the cards and play begins again. Pretty soon the luck has evened out, and Redmond is looking peevish. He breaks up the party a little after two and saunters into the night.

Now anyone who knows Race Williams will tell you I am not a sap, so don't think I'd turned into a soft touch when I took young Eric by the hand to lead him back to his auntie and his hotel. The old lady drives me crazy, but there's something about how she looks at me with those china-doll eyes that makes me think the way to minimise trouble is bring her little boy home and tuck him into bed, that's all.

On the way I try to pry into how Maitland–Townsend and Redmond act around each other – what kind of clues are they dropping about their past relationship. Of course the kid's never noticed anything. But just as I'm about to give up on him, Eric adds, in that accent I can hardly make out, 'Now the funny thing is, Williams, I think I know Townsend myself from someplace. It's how he deals cards that makes me think it, but when I asked him if we'd ever met, he got quite huffy. He says he's spending his time working night and day for the Empire. Although I can't see how playing poker in speakeasies does the Empire much good.'

Which just shows that even an innocent like young Eric isn't totally stupid. I deliver him into the care of the night man at the Stevens and hoof it back to my own flop. He calls after me to pick him up in time for Sally's entrance tomorrow night.

7 June 1933
Cable from Miss Mary Palmer, Stevens Hotel, Chicago
To Chlotilde Milder, The Vicarage, St Clement-sur-Mare

See no point in your crossing Atlantic. Will arrange for Eric's body to be sent home for funeral as soon as police complete investigation. Letter follows.

7 June 1933

I cannot tell you how remiss I feel, for how laden with remorse I am over this tragedy. Had I the least notion

of his being in danger, I would have overridden his
protests about leaving Chicago. And then for his body to
be found by the janitors as they cleaned up the 'Streets
of Paris' venue early yesterday morning!

The police have arrested Samuel Leyden, a Negro
who had played cards with Eric at the speakeasy they
both frequented. In fact, Mr Leyden is the uncle of my
Negro maid, the one I wrote you about. I went to visit
the unfortunate man in prison. I cannot believe him to
be the perpetrator of this crime.

Mr Williams, who brought me the news, seemed to
think the murder had to do with a row over cards. Such
a sad way to die, if true, although how Eric happened
to be in Miss Rand's pavilion without anyone the wiser,
I do not know. When they took me to identify the body—

Miss Palmer broke off here. No need to distress poor
Chlotilde with details. Or with the matter that had troubled Miss Palmer for the last twenty-four hours: the fact
that Eric's pocketbook had been rifled. As far as Miss
Palmer could tell, no money had been stolen, yet except
for his passport, he had no papers in it. What had he
kept hidden there all these weeks?

She could not believe the Negro, Mr Leyden, would
have murdered Eric over a dispute at cards and stolen
his papers while leaving his money intact. The papers
could be of no use to a third party unless there were
something in them worth committing blackmail over.
Miss Palmer felt suddenly chilly, despite the oppressive
humidity of the June day.

Then, too, if the dispute had been over cards, why

was Eric's body found at the pavilion? He had been murdered elsewhere and taken there. Even Captain Oglesby, the arresting officer, who had scarcely been civil enough to take his cigar out of his mouth when speaking to Miss Palmer, could acknowledge that. 'Had there been bloodstains at the speakeasy where Eric played cards?' she asked of him.

'The police know what they're doing, lady. If you'll take my advice, you'll mind your own business and leave me to mind mine.'

'But the murder of my nephew must *be* my own business, Captain, and I cannot believe Mr Leyden did this deed.'

'Woman's intuition?' Oglesby's mouth curled in an ugly sneer. 'We've had our eyes on this Leyden for some time. He's uppity, a commie, an agitator, and God knows what else besides. Leave the police work to those who know how to do it.'

She knew when it was futile to argue. But she was certain Eric had not been killed over cards. It had to be about the confidence artist he had come to Chicago to find. For a time, Miss Palmer wondered whether Mr Redmond was the man. He was certainly American. He was a rogue, but not cruel. Now if it had been Colonel Townsend . . . but the colonel was so very definitely British, and the man who had fleeced Eric in Malaysia was American.

Miss Sally Rand, a keen observer behind her ostrich-feather fans, had taken a fancy to Miss Palmer. Looking into those blue eyes, the dancer had seen a kindred spirit and a soul of steel, and had taken to inviting Miss Palmer into her dressing room after her shows, past the crowds of men who clamoured for her attention. So on Monday night Miss Palmer had looked for Eric at his usual seat in the pavilion. When she couldn't spot him, she had searched the crowd through her opera glasses, without finding him or the men who were usually in his company.

Miss Palmer finished her letter with a brief description of Leyden's arrest and her own determination to stay in Chicago until all matters relating to Eric's death had been resolved. She pondered what steps to take. There was no point in telling Captain Oglesby that Sir Nevil Burdock at New Scotland Yard would vouch for her. The police captain hated the English with all the usual passion of the Irish in America. Certainly he had no use for Scotland Yard. No, she would have to use her wits.

Eventually she put on a hat with a veil long enough to protect her face from the sun. Swathing her shoulders in voile, she gave the bellman a dime to find her a taxi.

I never should have left New York for this two-bit dump. The mark gets himself bumped off, and Leyden is arrested for the crime. A coloured man killing a visiting Brit is bad for business, so he'll fry before the end of the year.

And what about my fee? Since the kid's body surfaced, there's been no sign of Doug Redmond, although my client, Maitland-Townsend, is hovering around, officious enough. Of course, I'd figured Redmond for Red Dog Glazer even before I saw Reuben Levine's pix. The name itself tipped me – not much of a disguise, almost as if he was flirting with discovery. But I didn't unmask him, and now the slicko's hoofed it. Why didn't I finger him and at least get my thousand, you want to know. Because I wondered what game he was playing and how much of my client's story about the booze-factory scam to believe.

And since there's no fee waiting for me, I might as well get back on the Twentieth Century Limited. I've parlayed the Brit's four fifties into eight hundred cool ones at the poker table, so I can swank it with the rich folks in the sleepers going home.

I'm lying on my bed with only a flask to keep me company when a knock on my door is followed by the arrival of – of all people – Miss China Doll. Of course, I have my gun pointed at the door before the knocking stops. Does this make her jump? About as much as if it had been a silver platter for her to put her visiting card in.

'You come to chew me out for your nephew getting iced? Forget it. You want my condolences, you got them. Now take off. This flop is no place for a lah-ti-dah lady, so you'd better go where they can get you a cup of tea when you come all-over faint.'

'Perhaps you could put the gun away, Mr Williams. I assure you I am not going to shoot you.'

And with that, seeing the dump doesn't run to chairs, she sits on the end of the bed. I lower the gun but keep hold of it while I swing my legs past her head and sit up on the side.

She keeps on nattering. 'I know there are people, Mr Williams – and doubtless you like to think you are one of them – who think human life consists of kill or be killed. But I do have to confess that I doubt very much whether you truly believe that deep down. You remind me too much of a man I knew many years ago, a Mr Guillaume, who, like you, was a diamond in the rough but a gentle man at heart. I would like to know how Eric came to be killed. *Where* he came to be killed, for that matter. I'm hoping you can tell me whether on Monday night he was at that drinking establishment you and he frequented.'

I feel the blood rush to my head. 'Ever since you blocked my path getting off the train two weeks ago, you've been slowing me down – you and your nephew between you. Now you want me to hang around this burg to clean up after him?'

She shakes her head. 'Eric was an adult, even if not very wise, Mr Williams. I truly regret his death, but I hold you no more responsible than I hold myself – less, if the truth be known, since his dear grandmother had entrusted him to my care. Of course, between ourselves, Eric had got into trouble in the Far East before return-ing to England in March. He had been sent there to look after his father's rubber plantation in Kuala Lumpur – or do I mean Rangoon? So much alike, these Asian places – but instead, he took up with a plausible rogue and lost the entire plantation at cards. I feared the worst when he began going to the speakeasy with you and—'

I interrupt her roughly. 'You may be an old lady, but you're not the innocent you'd like everyone to believe. I've seen you hanging out in Sally Rand's dressing room, and no virtuous maiden aunt carries on like that. And I've seen a look in those china-doll eyes of yours that could stop a charging elephant.'

'You are right, Mr Williams, I am not a total fool. Only' – she makes a helpless, fluttering gesture that sends her scarves flying across the bed – 'when the head of New Scotland Yard refers to one as an "old pussy", even though one has been most helpful in solving several murders, it seems easier to play that role than to make people uncomfortable by acting differently from what they expect.'

I pick her scarves out of my hair and hand them back to her. 'So why are you here?'

'I find it impossible to think of Mr Leyden as a murderer.'

I cut in before she can go on. 'You think he's a general in the Salvation Army, saving the down-and-outs? He's a Wobbly. Know what that is, lady? A labour agitator who ain't afraid to beat up someone who gets in his way.'

'But does he cheat at cards, Mr Williams? Has he murdered anyone in cold blood?'

'Cheating at cards – that'd be more Red Dog's game.' Then I have to interrupt myself to explain to her about Doug Redmond really being Red Dog Glazer, and all about his phony bootleg warehouses, his fixed horse races, and fuzzing the cards. 'A dyed-in-the-wool con man, and the top skinner of all time.'

'Red Dog? What a fascinating and most unusual alias. I'm not doubting he is a highly skilled confidence artist, Mr Williams. But is he a murderer? I fancy' – and here she coughs a little, as though what she is saying doesn't really count – 'I fancy that if someone discovered what Mr Glazer was doing, he would smile and find another ... another mug. You see, I am *au fait* with the language of the criminal world! But I don't think Mr Glazer would be concerned to murder his unmasker. Now if it had been Colonel Townsend – but Eric was convinced his scoundrel was American.'

'One thing about Townsend: it's not the only name he uses. Maybe not the only nationality, either.' I tell her what I know about my client, and what I don't know – which is a whole lot more.

'So either he is an American assuming a British accent, or an Englishman who can speak with a strong American accent,' she says. 'Now I incline to the latter. I would be able to tell if his British accent were spurious, but I doubt whether poor Eric could have detected a false American accent. Our job is to find out who he really is. And whether he murdered Eric.'

'The cops have arrested Eric's murderer. It's an open-and-shut case, Oglesby says.'

'But don't you think, Mr Williams, that if a Negro of Mr Leyden's size had come into the pavilion, the number of witnesses would have been very great? Most Negroes are boycotting the Fair because of its very unfair anti-African policies. The few that show up are instantly remarkable.' She fiddles with the catch on her handbag for a minute, then says, 'I'm assuming that they arrested Mr Leyden because he was with Eric at the ... the speakeasy where you and he played poker. I'm wondering whether Colonel Townsend was there Monday night as well.'

358

'Can't tell you, lady. I had other fish to fry.'

I don't see any need to tell her about my fish, but it came in the form of an anonymous letter suggesting that the dame who'd cold-bloodedly laid me in that orphanage thirty-nine years ago was in town wanting to see me. Well, I figured I have a score or two to settle with any dame who'd leave her kid to the kind of treatment I got, but when I showed up at that place down on Cottage Grove, it was a bust. The orphanage was gone, see, and there was a gas station and a furniture store on the spot, but no dame waiting to meet me.

'But you know,' I say to Miss China Doll as the idea comes to me, 'now I have to wonder if someone was getting me out of the way deliberate. No one's going to mess with the kid with me around to see fair play done, so they had to ditch me. If it wasn't Leyden, then it had to be either Townsend or Red Dog.'

She shakes her head. 'I doubt very much that it was Mr Redmond – or Mr Glazer, as I suppose I should say. How hard it is to keep track of all these people and their different names! Mr Glazer is so like – well, like a man in my village at home. If you stopped him from trying to defraud you, he wouldn't hurt you – just give you a cheerful bow and move on to someone else. But Colonel Townsend, now he is very like – well, another, much uglier man, who did try to murder a man once. No, if I had to choose from among the men with whom poor Eric associated here in Chicago, it would be Colonel Townsend.'

'Why'd Townsend want to kill the kid?'

'If I knew that, Mr Williams, I would be at the police

359

station, not in your room. But no one is asking that question about Mr Leyden. No, they arrested him without even really thinking.'

She paused. 'The first thing to do is to find out who Colonel Townsend really is. I can do that readily through friends at the British consulate. Perhaps you could use your knowledge of weapons to find out about the gun that killed my nephew. Was it recovered? Did it have Mr Leyden's fingerprints on it? And do they know *where* Eric was killed? Perhaps you can talk to men in the police department or the newspapers, maybe even go to the speakeasy yourself. Why don't you come to my hotel tomorrow for lunch so that we can compare notes?'

She gathers her scarves together and flutters out the door. Now, I'm flopping in a part of town where they take dames like that apart and put them together in their soup. So I follow her down four flights of stairs and make sure she gets into a cab without being molested. Don't go thinking that makes me a softy. Just common sense. If she's right, and it's a mighty big if, then she's going to help me nail a guy who sucker-punched me. So it's in my interest to keep her in one piece, see.

After I get back to my room and commune with my flask, I start to wonder if she's playing me for the biggest sucker of all. So I call my friend Reuben Levine over at the *Chicago American* and ask him to cable London, get his pals there to say whether this Palmer dame really knows the head of Scotland Yard, get someone there to cable back a description of her. I'm tired of Brits waltzing into my life pretending they're person 'X' – Maitland-

Townsend, say — and popping up in Chicago as 'Y' — Miss Palmer, say.

Reuben Levine pulled his chair closer to Sally Rand's. 'You what?'

'I stayed late after my show Monday night. I do sometimes, just to have some privacy. If I leave right away, I waltz into a crowd of mashers. Well, Monday I must have fallen asleep, because the pavilion was deserted and the Fair was closed when a loud noise woke me up. Now are you interested, or am I still just a crazy exhibitionist?'

Levine threw up a hand. 'Sorry! Sorry I once wrote that about you, Miss Rand! I must've had some cheap bootleg and it went to my brain.'

Sally Rand beamed at him and tapped his arm with an ostrich feather. 'Listen, I know Sam Leyden didn't kill that kid because I saw the guy dumping the body.'

Levine sat bolt upright. 'You . . . *what?* Who was it?'

Sally shrugged. 'I couldn't make him out that clearly. After all, I was seeing him by moonlight. Which was definitely not romantic. But he was a white man — that much I'm sure of. And I bet I'd know him again.'

'Why are you coming up with this story now?' Levine asked.

'Because I only just found out that they arrested Sam for the murder. I don't care what all those sharks do to each other, but Sam Leyden helped me load my horse on to the boat the first night I came here. He's always willing to help a working girl, and one good turn deserves another.'

After the reporter left, the dancer called out, 'How'd I do?'

'You were perfect, my dear.' Miss Palmer emerged from behind the famous fans and helped Race Williams to his feet. 'And now I think you'd better let Mr Williams stay near you for protection until we flush our murderer.'

'Who do you think it will be?' Miss Rand asked.

'I'm assuming either Colonel Townsend or Mr Redmond – Mr Glazer, I mean. But we could be surprised. It might be someone who is a stranger to both of us.'

I straighten up from my position behind the dancer's costumes and try to brush the dust from my knees. 'Miss Palmer likes people to think she's a lady, so she won't say we have a bet on the action. I think it's Red Dog Glazer; she's betting on the colonel.'

Not that I'm going to reveal the stakes in front of Sally Rand, however much her curves appeal to my eyes. No, that all came up in Miss China Doll's and my luncheon conversation. I showed her my cable: 'There is no detective in England equal to a spinster lady of uncertain age with plenty of time on her hands,' the head of Scotland Yard said, 'and Miss Palmer is the best of the bunch.' She seemed tickled I'd suspected her of masterminding an international criminal gang, but in my line of work you see plenty of stranger things.

So we get down to brass tacks. I go to the speako last night and talk to some of the boys, but everyone is clamming up, and that gets me suspicious. I'm the outsider, see, the tough from New York, and they're

362

going to protect their own from me. Townsend is an outsider too, but Red Dog is a hometown boy, and that makes me think they're protecting him. Where is he, I ask, and pretty soon the bouncer is trying to show me the outside of the door. So I leave and nose around the alley in back, and I see some signs of blood, all right.

In the morning I go back to Reuben Levine at the *Chicago American* and get the lowdown on the police investigation. It seems pretty clear they nailed Sam Leyden without looking too hard for evidence. There was a big punch-up at the speako Monday night. From what the reporter says, no one knows who started it or why, but the smart money is on my client, Maitland-Townsend, trying to get ugly with Red Dog. The kid gets in the middle of it, trying to break it up, the Negro turns ugly, and the next thing they know, the boy is dead. I tell all this to the Palmer dame, and suggest the kid got plugged by mistake.

'I fear not, Mr Williams,' she says, throwing her scarves all over the table for some poor waiter to come and sort out. 'You see, I have received some definitive information from New Scotland Yard.'

And damn me if the dame hasn't collected all our fingerprints from the first night we ate dinner with her and the kid at the hotel! She bribed the waiter not to clear the table, came back and collected our water glasses, packed them up as neat as you please and shipped them back to home-sweet-home. And it turns out that Townsend-Maitland's real name is Thorndike. He's the son of a man Palmer hounded out of her home village fifteen years ago, and he and his old man have been bearing a grudge against her all these years.

So when they run into her nephew out in the jungle and see what a sap he is, well, they promptly set out to rob him of his life's savings. But they're not content with that: they lure him and the Palmer dame to Chicago.

'You see,' Miss Palmer says, 'I found an anonymous letter in Eric's room when I searched it last night. I knew some kind of missive had brought him here, because whenever I queried him, "Why Chicago?" he unconsciously patted his breast pocket. As you know, all personal papers were missing from his pocketbook when his body was found, but I knew what a careless young man he was and hoped he might have left something in his luggage. And although the search took me some hours, I was ultimately rewarded. He had put an earlier missive in his trunk when he left England. I recognised the type – an *e* badly out of alignment – from a similar document I had received myself, so I knew the same hand was drawing us here for no good purpose.'

And that's when my blood goes cold. Because that was the same type on the letter that lured me down to Eighty-ninth and Cottage Grove on Monday night.

So the dame sees I know something, and I see she's got the same correspondence, and the upshot is this: the person who's wrong about who'll show up to croak Miss Rand has to show the other their letter first.

Levine's scoop merits an early-afternoon extra, and long before Miss Rand is ready to load her horse on to the boat and head for the pavilion, we've got every

364

reporter in America wanting to ask her questions. I sort them out, let her put her spiel on radio and make the others go away: Miss Rand is an artiste and needs her rest before she performs, see.

Of course Oglesby comes nosing around, but I tell him she's asleep. 'I need to talk to her,' he says. 'If you don't let me question her, I'll arrest her as a material witness in the murder.'

'You and who else? You got Leyden under lock and key. You're too right to make a mistake, like confusing a white man and a coloured, or an Englishman with an American, so what do you need Miss Rand for?'

He don't like it, and he threatens to come the heavy over me, but Miss China Doll flutters her scarves over him and he vamooses. But we can be sure he's going to have a front-row seat at the 'Streets of Paris' tonight, my goodness, yes.

It all works out according to plan. We get Sally and her horse loaded on the boat, she makes her entrance at the pavilion right on schedule, begins her act, and the crowd goes wild. They don't care that reporters have flown in all the way from New York City and Los Angeles to see if someone kills her mid-dance.

At the height of her performance, a shot sounds out above the band, and so does a woman's scream. I muscle my way to the centre of the mêlée. Miss Palmer is sitting next to the colonel, all right. She beaned him with her handbag as he was taking aim.

She stunned him for a minute, but he's got his hands around her throat now. Ladies in the mob are screaming. I knock them out of my way and take a shot, cool as you please, that sends him to the deck. Then Oglesby shows up and tries to show some authority.

Townsend-Maitland-Thorndike isn't dead yet – I couldn't get a clean shot at him without winging Miss China Doll in the bargain. He's writhing on the floor, calling Miss Palmer every name in the book.

'You bitch! You got my father by a dirty trick, and now you're trying to get me too! Yes, I killed that precious nephew of yours, and I wish to God I'd killed you too. Hounding my father out of town, costing him his commission, leaving us to a life of poverty while you lorded it over creation. Well, you smug old biddy, your mother talked about you plenty. Plenty, I mean, and I heard it all from my father. I bided my time, but . . . but . . .'

And here his howls became incoherent and mixed with the great rattle of death itself.

Miss China Doll is looking mighty pale, but she is trying to ignore my client's outburst. Instead, she's breathlessly thanking people for retrieving her everlasting scarves. Miss Rand? Well, she just keeps dancing through it all.

Of course, the cops don't like having to let Leyden go. They never want to give up a body once they've got it locked up. And when it's the body of a Negro labour agitator, it just about takes an act of Congress. In the end, though, they release him to his niece, the hotel maid. I think I saw Red Dog in the crowd earlier, but he's melted. I never do learn whether Townsend-Maitland-Thorndike really had anything against him, whether he actually did get taken in by Red Dog's booze-factory scam. After Miss Palmer and I go off to share our mail, I have to guess my ex-client just wanted some excuse to bring me to Chicago.

Miss Palmer — well, she leaves for England and I go to Union Station for the train to New York. I hope to God I never see her again, or Chicago either. I belong in the great city. I plan to stay there.

10 June 1933

I know I will never mail this letter, but writing to you has become the easiest way for me to organise my thoughts during this long trip to Chicago — by far the longest journey of my life, for it has taken me back in time, as well as exhausting my spirit in the present.

I had buried my past so deeply that I came to believe myself remote from the passions that actuate others. It is certainly true that strong passion impedes judgment; perhaps I judge more accurately than most because I have subdued such violent emotions within myself. But forty years ago it was a far different story.

My mother told me the baby had died shortly after birth. I was prepared to stay in America and raise him, far from the censorious eyes of her village intimates, giving her full permission to say I had drowned or disappeared in some other way, but I suppose my situation was far too shocking for her. 'A lady must never show either shock or surprise,' she often told me. So the shock she felt was something she kept buried deep within herself. Or perhaps it was her rage at my having stepped outside her tight bonds of confinement that led her to act as she did.

She must have stolen my baby from his cot while I was still too weak to notice what she was doing, and taken him to the orphanage. She translated poor Robert's last name into English and told the nuns the boy's name was Williams, that the mother had died in childbirth – I suppose that had been her hope for me! – and the nuns gave him the first name Race as a representative of the human race.

Thorndike insinuated himself into the homes of numbers of old ladies before the Great War, and Mother's mind tended to wander in those days. She might well have shared her – and my – secret with him.

Robert had disappeared before he knew I was expecting a baby. He was an itinerant showman who took shooting galleries around the country to different fairs. At least his son inherited his marksmanship! And perhaps my instincts as an investigator. The loner detective on the edge of society – not the life one would choose for one's child. I had planned to look for Robert Guillaume once I got back on my feet, to show him his son and see if he wanted to make a life with us, but thinking my child dead, I saw no point in searching for his father.

Race and I had no touching reunion such as you find in novels or motion pictures. He is angry with me for abandoning him. 'You're a better investigator than that,' he said, 'to take the word of your mother, an old lady who wants you and your kid dead. You looked at the death certificates last week and saw that no child named Palmer or Guillaume had died that winter. Well, if you'd really wanted to know, you would have looked years ago, before ever leaving Chicago. In the end, your conventional

English morality made it convenient for you to believe your mother and return to your cosy little village.'

Perhaps he is right.

'O cleanse thou me from secret faults,' says the Psalmist in this morning's lesson. 'Keep thy servant from presumptuous sins, lest they get dominion over me.' I hope when I return to St Clement-sur-Mare I can remember the havoc my secret faults have wrought in others' lives, and try not to judge too presumptuously when I see the failings of my fellow men.

Sara Paretsky *made effective use of her knowledge of the world of commerce (she once worked in the insurance sector) in creating Chicago-based private eye V.I. Warshawski. V.I.'s cases, starting with* Indemnity Only *(1982), focus on white-collar crime and often result in her uncovering corruption in a major institution. Paretsky was one of the founders of Sisters in Crime and served as its first president. In 1988 she was awarded the CWA Silver Dagger and this was followed in 2002 when she became only the second American crime writer to be honoured with the CWA Cartier Diamond Dagger.*

GUIDE TO DOOM

Ellis Peters

This way down, please. Mind your heads in the door-way, and take care on the stairs, the treads are very worn. And here we are in the courtyard again.

That concludes our tour, ladies and gentlemen. Thank you for your attention. Please keep to the paths as you cross to the gatehouse.

Yes, madam, it *is* a very little castle. Properly speaking, it's a fortified manorhouse. But it's the finest of its kind extant, and in a unique state of repair. That's what comes of being in the hands of the same family for six centuries. Yes, madam, that's how long the Chastelays have been here. And in these very walls until they built the Grace House at the far end of the grounds a hundred and fifty years ago.

The well, sir? You'll see the well as you cross the courtyard there. What was that sir? I didn't quite catch—

Not that well? The *other* one?

Now I wonder, sir, what should put it into your head that a small household like this—

The one where Mary Purcell drowned herself!

371

Hush, sir, please! Keep your voice down. Mr Chastelay doesn't like that affair remembered. Yes, sir, I know, but we don't show the well-chamber. He wants it forgotten. No, I can't make exceptions, it's as much as my job's worth. Well, sir – very handsome of you, I'm sure. Were you, indeed? I can understand your being interested, of course, if you were one of the reporters who covered the case. You did say *Mary Purcell*?

Oh, no, sir, I wasn't in this job then. But I read the papers, like everybody else. Look, sir, if you'll wait just a moment, till I see this lot out—

That's better, now we can talk. I'm always glad to get the last party of the day through this old door, and drop the latch on 'em. Nice to hear the cars driving away down the avenue. Notice how the sound vanishes when they reach the turn where the wall begins. Quiet, isn't it? Soon we shall begin to hear the owls.

Now, sir, you want to see the well. The *other* well. The one where the tragedy occurred. I shouldn't do it, really. Mr Chastelay would be very annoyed if he knew. No, sir, that's right, of course, he never need know.

Very well, sir, it's through here – through the great hall. After you, sir! There, fancy you turning in the right direction without being told! Mind your step, the floor's very uneven in places.

You mustn't be surprised at Mr Chastelay not wanting that old affair dragged up again. It very nearly wrecked his life. Everybody had him down for the lover, the fellow who drove her to it. Her being his farm foreman's wife, you see, and him having been noticeably took with her, and on familiar terms with the two of them. I daresay it was only natural people should think it was him. If he could have run the rumours to their source he'd have sued, but he never could. For a year it was touch and go whether his wife divorced him, but they're over it now. After all, it's ten years and more. Nobody wants to start the tongues wagging again. No, sir, I'm sure *you* don't, or I wouldn't be doing this.

She was very beautiful, they say, this Mrs Purcell. Very young, only twenty-one, and fair. They say the photographs didn't do justice to her colouring. Wonderful blue eyes, I believe. *Green*, were they, you say? Not blue? Well, I wouldn't argue with you, sir, you were reporting the affair, you should know. Watch out for the bottom step here, it's worn very hollow. *Green* eyes!

Oh, no, sir, I wouldn't dispute it. Wonderful trained memory you have.

Well, at any rate she was young and very pretty, and I dare say a bit simple and innocent, too, brought up country-style as she was. She was the daughter of one of the gardeners. I don't suppose you ever met him? No, he wouldn't have anything to say to the press, would he? He had a stroke afterwards, and Mr Chastelay pensioned him off with a light job around the place. But that's neither here nor there. Mind the step into the stone gallery. Here, let me put on the lights.

Yes, gives you quite a turn, doesn't he, that halberdier standing there, with his funny-shaped knife on a stick? I keep him all burnished up like that specially, it gives the kids a thrill. Tell you the truth, when I've been going round here at night, locking up and seeing all's fast after the folks have gone, I've often borrowed his halberd and carried it round with me, just for company, like. It gets pretty eerie here after dark. Makes me feel like one of the ghosts myself, trailing this thing. If it's all the same to you, sir, I'll take it along with us now.

They put a heavy cover on the well after that fatality. There's a ring in the middle, and the haft of the halberd makes a very handy lever. You'd like to look inside, I dare say. There are iron rungs down the shaft like a ladder. Her husband went down, you know, and got her out. More than most of us would like to do, but then, he felt responsible, I suppose, poor soul.

Where's her husband now? Did you never hear, sir? He cracked up, poor lad, and they had to put him away. He's still locked up.

The way I heard it, this affair of hers had been going on some time, and when she found she was expecting a child it fairly knocked her over. Made her turn and look again at what she'd let this fellow persuade her into. She went to him, and asked what to do.

And he told her not to be a fool, why should she want to do anything? She'd got a husband, hadn't she? All she had to do was hold her tongue. But he could see she didn't see it that way; she felt bad about her husband and couldn't let him father the child with his eyes shut. She was hating herself, and wanting to be honest, and wanting her lover to stand by her even in that. And wanting her husband back on the old terms, too, because I don't suppose she ever really stopped loving him, she only lost sight of him in the excitement. So this fellow put her off and said they'd talk about it again, after they'd considered it.

And he lit out the next day for I don't know where, and left her.

No, sir, you're right, of course, I wasn't in this job then, how would I know? Just reconstructing in my own mind. Maybe it wasn't like that. No, as you say, if it was Mr Chastelay he didn't light out for anywhere; he stayed right here and got the muck thrown at him. But a lot of people think now it wasn't him, after all.

Anyhow, she went to her husband and told him the truth. All but the name, she never told anyone that. Very nearly killed him, I shouldn't wonder, if he was daft about her, as they say. He didn't rave or anything, just turned his back on her and went away. And when she followed him, crying, he couldn't bear it; he turned round and hit her.

Yes, sir, a very vivid imagination I've got, I don't deny it. So would you have if you lived in this place alone. I fairly see 'em walking, nights.

And the way I see it, she was too young and inexperienced to understand that you don't hit out at somebody who means nothing to you. She thought he was finished with her. And if he was gone, everything was gone. She didn't know enough to wait, and bear it, and hope. She ran along here, crying, and jumped into the well.

Five minutes, and he was running after her. By that time it was too late. When he got her out she was dead. Her fair hair all smeared with scum, and slime in her beautiful green eyes.

★ ★ ★

375

Right here, where we're standing. There's the cover they've put over it, since. Good and heavy, so's nobody can shift it easily. But if you'll stand back, sir, and let me get some leverage on this halberd—

There you are. Nobody knows quite how deep. Let's have a little more light, shall we? There, now you can see better. A girl would have to be at the end of her tether, wouldn't she, to go that way?

My sweet Mary, my little lamb!

No, sir, I didn't say anything. I thought *you* were about to speak.

What am I doing, sir? Just turning the key in the lock. Just seeing how smoothly it works. A lot of keys and wards to look after, you know, and Mr Chastelay is very particular about this room being kept closed. No one's been here for more than three years, except me. Not until tonight. I don't suppose there'll be anyone else for the next three years, either, and if they did they wouldn't lift the well-cover. I do all the cleaning myself, you see. I'm a great one for keeping things in perfect order. Look at this halberd, now. Sharp as a butcher's knife. Here; look.

Oh, sorry, sir, did I prick you?

Mad, sir? No, sir, not me. That was her husband, remember? They put him away. All that happened to me was a stroke, and it didn't affect my co-ordination. Pensioned off with a light job I may be, but you'd be surprised how strong I still am. So I shouldn't try to rush me, if I were you, sir. It wouldn't do you any good.

It's always a mistake to know too much, sir. *Mary*

Purcell, you said. Alice was her first name, the one all the papers used, did you know that? It was only her family and her intimates who called her Mary. And then, *how did you know her eyes were green?* They were shut fast enough before ever the press got near her. But her lover knew.

Yes, sir, I know you now, you were the young man who was staying with the Lovells at the farm that summer. We must have a talk about Mary. Sorry poor Tim Purcell couldn't be here to make up the party; it might have done him a power of good. But we'll spare him a thought, won't we? Now, while there's time.

Funny, isn't it? Providential, when you come to think, you walking out here from the farm, without a car or anything. And I'd stake this key and this halberd – I don't have to tell you how much I value them, do I? – that you never told a soul where you were going.

But you couldn't keep away, could you?

And I don't suppose either you or I will ever really know why you came – never dreaming you'd meet Mary's father. So I can believe it was because I've wanted you so much – *so much!*

Oh, I shouldn't scream like that, if I was you, sir, you'll only do yourself an injury. And nobody'll hear you, you know. There's nobody within half a mile but you and me. And the walls are very thick. Very thick.

Ellis Peters was the pseudonym of Edith Mary Pargeter (1913–95). She wrote many historical novels and detective stories (the latter often featuring members of the Felse family) before publishing a 'medieval whodunit', A Morbid Taste for Bones, in 1977 when she was sixty-four. This book introduced an unlikely detective in Brother Cadfael, a twelfth-century Benedictine monk with a taste for sleuthing. The Cadfael books, which were televised with Sir Derek Jacobi cast as Cadfael, earned their author worldwide acclaim – and contributed significantly to the rise in popularity of the historical mystery novel. She was awarded the CWA Cartier Diamond Dagger in 1993.

IAN RANKIN

Tell Me Who to Kill

Saturday afternoon, John Rebus left the Oxford Bar after the football results and decided that he would try walking home. The day was clear, the sun just above the horizon, casting ridiculously long shadows. It would grow chilly later, maybe even frost overnight, but for now it was crisp and bright – perfect for a walk. He had limited himself to three pints of IPA, a corned beef roll and a pie. He carried a large bag with him – shopping for clothes his excuse for a trip into the city centre, a trip he'd known would end at the Ox. Edinburgh on a Saturday meant day-trippers, weekend warriors, but they tended to stick to Princes Street. George Street had been quieter, Rebus's tally finally comprising two shirts and a pair of trousers. He'd gone up a waist size in the previous six months, which was reason enough to cut back on the beer, and for opting to walk home.

He knew his only real problem would be The Mound. The steep slope connected Princes Street to the Lawnmarket, having been created from the digging out of the New Town's foundations. It posed a serious climb. He'd known a fellow cop – a uniformed sergeant – who'd cycled up The Mound every day on his way to work, right up until the day he'd retired. For Rebus, it had often proved problematical, even on foot. But he would give it a go, and if he failed, well, there was a bus-stop he could beat a retreat to, or taxis he could flag down. Plenty of cabs about at this time of day, ferrying spent shoppers home to the suburbs, or bringing revellers into town at the start of another raucous evening. Rebus avoided the city centre on Saturday nights, unless duty called. The place took on an aggressive edge, violence spilling on to the streets from the clubs on Lothian Road and the bars in the Grassmarket. Better to stay at home with a carry-out and pretend your world wasn't changing for the worse.

A crowd had gathered at the foot of Castle Street. Rebus noticed that an ambulance, blue lights blinking, was parked in front of a stationary double-decker bus. Walking into the middle of the scene, Rebus overheard muttered exchanges of information.

'Just walked out . . .'

'. . . right into its path . . .'

'Wasn't looking . . .'

'Not the first time I've seen . . .'

'These bus drivers think they own the roads, though . . .'

The victim was being carried into the ambulance. It didn't look good for him. One look at the paramedics' faces told Rebus as much. There was blood on the roadway. The bus driver was sitting in the open doorway of his vehicle, head in his hands. There were still passengers on the bus, reluctant to admit that they would need to transfer, loaded down with shopping and unable to

380

think beyond their own concerns. Two uniformed officers were taking statements, the witnesses only too happy to fulfil their roles in the drama. One of the uniforms looked at Rebus and gave a nod of recognition.

'Afternoon, DI Rebus.'

Rebus just nodded back. There was nothing for him to do here, no part he could usefully play. He made to cross the road, but noticed something lying there, untouched by the slow crawl of curious traffic. He stooped and picked it up. It was a mobile phone. The injured pedestrian must have been holding it, maybe even using it. Which would explain why he hadn't been paying attention. Rebus turned his head towards the ambulance, but it was already moving away, not bothering to add a siren to its flashing lights: another bad sign, a sign that the medics in the back either didn't want or didn't feel the need of it. There was either severe trauma, or else the victim was already dead. Rebus glanced down at the phone. It was unscathed, looked almost brand new. Strange to think such a thing could survive where its owner might not. He pressed it to his ear, but the line wasn't open. Then he looked at it again, noting that there were words on its display screen. Looked like a text message.

TELL ME WHO TO KILL

Rebus blinked, narrowed his eyes. He was back on the pavement.

TELL ME WHO TO KILL

He scrolled up and down the message, but there wasn't any more to it than those five words. Along the top ran the number of the caller; looked like another mobile phone. Plus time of call: 16.31. Rebus walked over to the uniformed officer, the one who'd spoken to him.

'Larry,' he said, 'where was the ambulance headed?'

'Western General,' the uniform said. 'Guy's skull's split open, be lucky to make it.'

'Do we know what happened?'

'He walked straight out into the road, by the look of it. Can't really blame the driver . . .'

Rebus nodded slowly and walked over to the bus driver, crouched down in front of him. The man was in his fifties, head shaved but with a thick silvery beard. His hands shook as he lifted them away from his eyes.

'Couldn't stop in time,' he explained, voice quavering. 'He was right there . . .' His eyes widened as he played the scene again in his head. Shaking his head slowly. 'No way I could've stopped . . .'

'He wasn't looking where he was going,' Rebus said softly.

'That's right.'

'Busy on his phone maybe?'

The driver nodded. 'Staring at it, aye . . . Some people haven't got the sense they were born with. Not that I'm . . . I mean, I don't want to speak ill or anything.'

'Wasn't your fault,' Rebus agreed, patting the man's shoulder.

'Colleague of mine, same thing happened not six months past. Hasn't worked since.' He held up his hands to examine them.

'He was too busy looking at his phone,' Rebus said. 'That's the whole story. Reading a message maybe?'

'Maybe,' the driver agreed. 'Doing something anyway, something more important than looking where he was bloody well going . . .'

'Not your fault,' Rebus repeated, rising to his feet. He walked to the back of the bus, stepped out into the road, and waved down the first taxi he saw.

Rebus sat in the waiting area of the Western General Hospital. When a dazed-looking woman was led in by a nurse, and asked if she wanted a cup of tea, he got to his feet. The woman sat herself down, twisting the handles of her shoulder-bag in both hands, as if wringing the life out of them. She'd shaken her head, mumbled something to the nurse, who was now retreating.

'As soon as we know anything,' were the nurse's parting words.

Rebus sat down next to the woman. She was in her early thirties, blonde hair cut in a pageboy style. What make-up she had applied to her eyes that morning had been smudged by tears, giving her a haunted look. Rebus cleared his throat, but she still seemed unaware of his close presence.

'Excuse me,' he said. 'I'm Detective Inspector Rebus.' He opened his ID, and she looked at it, then stared down at the floor again. 'Has your husband just been in an accident?'

'He's in surgery,' she said.

Rebus had been told as much at the front desk. 'I'm sorry,' he said. 'I don't even know his name.'

'Carl,' she said. 'Carl Guthrie.'

'And you're his wife?'

She nodded. 'Frances.'

'Must be quite a shock, Frances.'

'Yes.'

'Sure you don't want that tea?'

She shook her head, looked up into his face for the first time. 'Do you know what happened?'

'Seems he was starting to cross Princes Street and didn't see the bus coming.'

She squeezed shut her eyes, tears glinting in her lashes. 'How is that possible?'

Rebus shrugged. 'Maybe he had something on his mind,' he said quietly. 'When was the last time you spoke to him?'

'Breakfast this morning. I was planning to go shopping.'

'What about Carl?'

'I thought he was working. He's a physiotherapist, sports injuries mostly. He has his own practice in Corstorphine. He gets some work from the BUPA hospital at Murrayfield.'

'And a few rugby players too, I'd guess.'

Frances Guthrie was dabbing at her eyes with a paper tissue. 'How could he get hit by a bus?' She looked up at the ceiling, blinking back tears.

'Do you know what he was doing in town?'

She shook her head.

'This was found lying in the road,' Rebus said, holding up the phone for her to see. 'There's a text message displayed. You see what it says?'

She peered at the screen, then frowned. 'What does it mean?'

'I don't know,' Rebus admitted. 'Do you recognise the caller's number?'

She shook her head, then reached out a hand and took the phone from Rebus, turning it in her palm. 'This isn't Carl's.'

'What?'

'This isn't Carl's phone. Someone else must have dropped it.'

Rebus stared at her. 'You're sure?'

She handed the phone back, nodding. 'Carl's is a silver flip-top sort of thing.' Rebus stared at the black, one-piece Samsung.

'Then whose is it?' he asked, more to himself than to her. She answered anyway.

'What does it matter?'

'It matters.'

'But it's a joke surely.' She nodded at the screen. 'Someone's idea of a practical joke.'

'Maybe,' Rebus said. The same nurse was walking towards them, accompanied by a surgeon in green scrubs. Neither of them had to say anything. Frances Guthrie was already keening as the surgeon began his speech.

'I'm so sorry, Mrs Guthrie . . . we did everything we could.'

Frances Guthrie leaned in towards Rebus, her face against his shoulder. He put his arm around her, feeling it was the least he could do.

★　★　★

Carl Guthrie's effects had been placed in a large cardboard box. His blood-soaked clothes were protected by a clear polythene bag. Rebus lifted them out. The pockets had been emptied. Watch, wallet, small change, keys. And a silver flip-top mobile phone. Rebus checked its screen. The battery was low, and there were no messages. Rebus told the nurse that he wanted to take it with him. She shrugged and made him sign a docket to that effect. He flipped through the wallet, finding banknotes, credit cards, and a few of Carl Guthrie's own business cards, giving an address in Corstorphine, plus office and mobile numbers. Rebus took out his own phone and punched in the latter. The silver telephone trilled as it rang. Rebus cancelled the call. He nodded to the nurse to let her know he was finished. The docket was placed in the box, along with the polythene bag. Rebus pocketed all three phones.

The police lab at Howdenhall wasn't officially open at weekends, but Rebus knew that someone was usually there, trying to clear a backlog, or just because they'd nothing better to do. Rebus got lucky. Ray Duff was one of the better technicians. He sighed when Rebus walked in.

'I'm up to my eyes,' he complained, turning away to walk back down the corridor.

'Yes, but you'll like this,' Rebus said, holding out the mobile. Duff stopped and turned, stared at it, then ran his fingers through an unruly mop of hair.

'I really am up to my eyes . . .'

Rebus shrugged, arm still stretched out. Duff sighed again and took the phone from him.

'Discovered at the scene of an accident,' Rebus explained. Duff had found a pair of spectacles in one of the pockets of his white lab-coat and was putting them on. 'My guess is that the victim had just received the text message, and was transfixed by it.'

'And walked out in front of a car?'

'Bus actually. Thing is, the phone doesn't belong to the victim.' Rebus produced the silver flip-top. 'This is his.'

'So whose is this?' Duff peered at Rebus over the top of his glasses. 'That's what you're wondering.' He was walking again, heading for his own cubicle, Rebus following.

'Right.'

'And also who the caller was.'

'Right again.'

'We could just phone them.'

'We could.' They'd reached Duff's work-station. Each surface was a clutter of wires, machines and paperwork. Duff rubbed his bottom lip against his teeth. 'Battery's getting low,' he said, as the phone uttered a brief chirrup.

'Any chance you can recharge it?'

'I can if you like, but we don't really need it.'

'We don't?'

The technician shook his head. 'The important stuff's on the chip.' He tapped the back of the phone. 'We can transfer it . . .' He grew thoughtful again. 'Of course, that would mean accessing the code number, so we're probably better off hanging on to it as it is.' He reached down into a cupboard and produced half a dozen mains adaptors. 'One of these should do the trick.'

Soon, the phone was plugged in and charging. Meantime, Duff had worked his magic on the keypad, producing the phone number. Rebus punched it into his own phone, and the black mobile trilled.

'Bingo,' Duff said with a smile. 'Now all we do is call the service provider . . .' He left the cubicle and returned a couple of minutes later with a sheet of numbers. 'I hope you didn't touch anything,' he said, waving a hand around his domain.

'I wouldn't dare.' Rebus leaned against a work-bench as Duff made the call, identified himself, and reeled off the mobile phone number. Then he placed his hand over the mouthpiece.

'It'll take a minute,' he told Rebus.

'Can anyone get this sort of information?' Rebus asked. 'I mean, what's to stop Joe Public calling up and saying they're a cop?'

Duff smiled. 'Caller recognition. They've got a screen their end. IDs the caller number as Lothian and Borders Police Forensic Branch.'

'Clever,' Rebus admitted. Duff just shrugged. 'So how about the other number? The one belonging to whoever sent that message.'

Duff held up a finger, indicating that he was listening to the person at the other end of the line. He looked around him, finding a scrap of paper. Rebus provided the pen, and he started writing.

'That's great, thanks,' he said finally. Then: 'Mind if I try you with something else? It's a mobile number . . .' He proceeded to reel off the number on the message screen, then, with his hand again muffling the mouthpiece, he handed the scrap of paper to Rebus.

'Name and address of the phone's owner.'

Rebus looked. The owner's name was William Smith, the address a street in the New Town. 'What about the text sender?' he asked.

'She's checking.' Duff removed his hand from the mouthpiece, listening intently. Then he started shaking his head. 'Not one of yours, eh? Don't suppose you can tell from the number just who is the service provider?' He listened again. 'Well, thanks anyway.' He put down the receiver.

'No luck?' Rebus guessed. Duff shrugged.

'Just means we have to do it the hard way.' He picked up the sheet of telephone numbers. 'Maybe nine or ten calls at the most.'

'Can I leave it with you, Ray?'

Duff stretched his arms wide. 'What else was I going to be doing at half past six of a Saturday?'

Rebus smiled. 'You and me both, Ray.'

'What do you reckon we're dealing with? A hit-man?'

'I don't know.'

'But if it is . . . then Mr Smith would be his employer, making him someone you might not want to mess about with.'

'I'm touched by your concern, Ray.'

Duff smiled. 'Can I take it you're headed over to that address anyway?'

'Not too many gangsters living in the New Town, Ray.'

'Not that we know of,' Duff corrected him. 'Maybe after this, we'll know better . . .'

★ ★ ★

The streets were full of maroon-scarved Hearts fans, celebrating a rare victory. Bouncers had appeared at the doors of most of the city-centre watering-holes: an unnecessary expense in daylight, but indispensable by night. There were queues outside the fast-food restaurants, diners tossing their empty cartons on to the pavement. Rebus kept eyes front as he drove. He was in his own car now, having stopped home long enough for a mug of coffee and two paracetamol. He guessed that a breath test might just about catch him, but felt OK to drive nonetheless.

The New Town, when he reached it, was quiet. Few bars here, and the area was a dead end of sorts, unlikely to be soiled by the city-centre drinkers. As usual, parking was a problem. Rebus did one circuit, then left his car on a double-yellow line, right next to a set of traffic lights. Doubled back on himself until he reached the tenement. There was an entryphone, a list of residents printed beside it. But no mention of anyone called Smith. Rebus ran a finger down the column of names. One space was blank. It belonged to Flat 3. He pushed the button and waited. Nothing. Pushed it again, then started pressing various bells, waiting for someone to respond. Eventually, the tiny loudspeaker grille crackled into life.

'Hello?'

'I'm a police officer. Any chance of speaking to you for a minute?'

'What's the problem?'

'No problem. It's just a couple of questions concerning one of your neighbours . . .'

There was silence, then a buzzing sound as the door unlocked itself. Rebus pushed it open and stepped into the stairwell. A door on the ground floor was open, a man standing there. Rebus had his ID open. The man was in his twenties, with cropped hair and Buddy Holly spectacles. A dishtowel was draped over one shoulder.

'Do you know anyone called William Smith?' Rebus asked.

'Smith?' The man narrowed his eyes, shook his head slowly.

'I think he lives here.'

'What does he look like?'

'I'm not sure.'

The man stared at him, then shrugged. 'People come and go. Sometimes they move on before you get to know their names.'

'But you've been here a while?'

'Almost a year. Some of the neighbours I know to say hello to, but I don't always know their names.' He smiled apologetically. Yes, that was Edinburgh for you: people kept themselves to themselves, didn't want anyone getting too close. A mixture of shyness and mistrust.

'Flat 3 doesn't seem to have a name beside it,' Rebus said, nodding back towards the main door.

The man shrugged again.

'I'm just going to go up and take a look,' Rebus said.

'Be my guest. You know where I am if you need me.'

'Thanks for your help.' Rebus started climbing the stairs. The shared space was well maintained, the steps clean, smelling of disinfectant mixed with something else, a perfume of sorts. There were ornate tiles on the walls. Flats 2 and 3 were on the first floor. There was a buzzer to the right of Flat 3, a typed label attached to it. Rebus bent down for a closer look. The words had faded, but were readable: LT Lettings. While he was down there, Rebus decided he might as well take a look through the letter-box. All he could see was an unlit hallway. He straightened up and pressed the bell for Flat 2. Nobody was home. Rebus took out one of his business cards and a ballpoint pen, scribbled the words 'Please call me' on the back, and pushed the card through the door of Flat 2. He thought for a moment, but decided against doing the same for Flat 3.

Back downstairs again, he knocked on the door of the young man with the dishtowel. Smiled as it was opened.

'Sorry to bother you again, but do you think I could take a look at your phone book . . . ?'

Rebus went back to his car and made the call from there. An answering machine played its message, informing him that LT Lettings was closed until ten o'clock on Monday morning, but that any tenant with an emergency should call another number. Rebus jotted it down and called. The person who answered sounded like he was stuck in traffic. Rebus explained who he was.

'I need to ask about one of your properties.'

'I'm not the person you need to speak to. I just mend things.'

'What sorts of things?'

'Some tenants aren't too fussy, know what I mean? Place isn't their own, they treat it like shit.'

'Until you turn up and sort them out?'

The man laughed. 'I put things right, if that's what you mean.'

'And that's all you do?'

'Look, I'm not sure where you're going with this . . . It's my boss you need to speak to. Lennox Tripp.'

'Okay, give me his number.'

'Office is shut till Monday.'

'His home number, I meant.'

'I'm not sure he'd thank me for that.'

'This is a police matter. And it's urgent.'

Rebus waited for the man to speak, then jotted down the eventual reply. 'And your name is . . . ?'

'Frank Empson.'

Rebus jotted this down, too. 'Well, thanks for your help, Mr Empson. You heading for a night out?'

'Absolutely, Inspector. Just as soon as I've fixed the heating in one flat and unblocked the toilet in another.'

Rebus thought for a moment. 'Ever had cause to visit Gilby Street?'

'In the New Town?'

'Number 26, Flat 3.'

'I moved some furniture in, but that was months back.'

'Never seen the person who lives there?'

'Nope.'

'Well, thanks again . . .' Rebus cut the call, punched in the number for Lennox Tripp. The phone was answered on the fifth ring. Rebus asked if he was speaking to Lennox Tripp.

'Yes.' The voice hesitant.

'My name's John Rebus. I'm a detective inspector with Lothian and Borders Police.'

'What seems to be the problem?' The voice more confident now, an educated drawl.

'One of your tenants, Mr Tripp, 26 Gilby Street.'

'Yes?'

'I need to know what you know . . .'

Rebus was smoking his second cigarette when Tripp arrived, driving a silver Mercedes. He double-parked outside number 26, using a remote to set the locks and alarm.

'Won't be long, will we?' he asked, turning to glance at his car as he shook Rebus's hand. Rebus flicked the half-smoked cigarette on to the road.

'Wouldn't imagine so,' he said. Lennox Tripp was about Rebus's age – mid-fifties – but had worn considerably better. His face was tanned, hair groomed, clothes casual but classy. He stepped up to the door and let them in with a key. As they climbed the stairs, he said his piece.

'Only reason William Smith sticks in my head is that he pays cash for the let. A wad of twenties in an envelope, delivered to the office on time each month. This is his seventh month.'

'You must have met him, though.'

Tripp nodded. 'Showed him the place myself.'

'Can you describe him?'

Tripp shrugged. 'White, tallish . . . nothing much to distinguish him.'

'Hair?'

Tripp smiled. 'Almost certainly.' Then, as if to apologise for the glib comeback: 'It was six months ago, Inspector.'

'And that's the only time you've seen him?'

Tripp nodded. 'I'd have called him the model tenant . . .'

'A model tenant who pays cash? You don't find that a mite suspicious?'

Tripp shrugged again. 'I try not to pry, Inspector.' They were at the door to Flat 3. Tripp unlocked it and motioned for Rebus to precede him inside.

'Was it rented furnished?' Rebus asked, walking into the living room.

'Yes.' Tripp took a look around. 'Doesn't look like he's added much.'

'Not even a TV,' Rebus commented, walking into the kitchen. He opened the fridge. There was a bottle of white wine inside, open and with the cork pushed back into its neck. Nothing else: no butter, milk . . . nothing. Two tumblers drying on the draining-board, the only signs that anyone had been here in recent memory.

There was just the one bedroom. The bedclothes were mostly on the floor. Tripp bent to pick them up, draping them over the mattress. Rebus opened the wardrobe, exposing a single dark-blue suit hanging there. Nothing in any of the pockets. In one drawer: underpants, socks, a single black T-shirt. The other drawers were empty.

'Looks like he's moved on,' Tripp commented.

'Or has something against possessions,' Rebus added. He looked around. 'No phone?'

Tripp shook his head. 'There's a wall-socket. If a tenant wants to sign up with BT or whoever, they're welcome to.'

'Too much trouble for Mr Smith, apparently.'

'Well, a lot of people use mobiles these days, don't they?'

'They do indeed, Mr Tripp.' Rebus rubbed a thumb and forefinger over his temples. 'I'm assuming Smith provided you with some references?'

'I'd assume he did.'

'You don't remember?'

'Not off-hand.'

'Would you have any records?'

'Yes, but it's by no means certain . . .'

Rebus stared at the man. 'You'd rent one of your flats to someone who couldn't prove who they were?'

Tripp raised an eyebrow by way of apology.

'Cash upfront, I'm guessing,' Rebus hissed.

'Cash does have its merits.'

'I hope your tax returns are in good order.'

Tripp was brought up short. 'Is that some kind of threat, Inspector?'

Rebus feigned a look that was between surprise and disappointment. 'Why would I do a thing like that, Mr Tripp?'

'I wasn't meaning to suggest . . .'

'I would hope not. But I'll tell you what . . .' Rebus laid a hand on the man's shoulder. 'We'll call it quits, once we've been to your office and checked those files . . .'

★　★　★

But there was precious little in the file relating to Flat 3, 26 Gilby Street – just a signed copy of the lease agreement. No references of any kind. Smith had put his occupation down as 'market analyst' and his date of birth as 13 January 1970.

'Did you ask him what a market analyst does?'

Tripp nodded. 'I think he said he worked for one of the insurance companies, something to do with making sure their portfolios didn't lose money.'

'You don't recall which company?'

Tripp said he didn't.

In the end, Rebus managed a grudged 'thank you', headed out to his car, and drove home. Ray Duff hadn't called, which meant he hadn't made any progress, and Rebus doubted he would be working Sunday. He poured himself a whisky, stuck John Martyn on the hi-fi, and slumped into his chair. A couple of tracks passed without him really hearing them. He slid his hand into his pocket and came out with both phones, the silver and the black. For the first time, he checked the silver flip-top, finding messages from Frances Guthrie to her husband. There was an address book, probably listing clients and friends. Rebus laid this phone aside and concentrated on the black one. There was nothing in its memory: no phone numbers stored, no messages. Just that one text: TELL ME WHO TO KILL. And the number of the caller.

Rebus got up and poured himself another drink, then took a deep breath and pushed the buttons, calling the sender of the text message. The ringing tone sounded tremulous. Rebus was still holding his breath, but after twenty rings he gave up. No one was about to answer. He decided to send a text instead, but couldn't think what words to use.

Hello, are you a hired killer?

Who do you think I want you to kill?

Please hand yourself in to your nearest police station . . .

He smiled to himself, decided it could wait. Only half past nine, the night stretching ahead of him. He surfed all five TV channels, went into the kitchen to make some coffee, and found that he'd run out of milk. Decided on a walk to the corner shop. There was a video store almost next door to it. Maybe he'd rent a film, something to take his mind off the message. Decided, he grabbed his keys, slipped his jacket back on.

The grocer was about to close, but knew Rebus's face, and asked him to be quick. Rebus settled for a packet of sausages, a box of eggs, and a carton of milk. Then added a four-pack of lager. Settled up with the grocer and carried his purchases to the video store. He was inside before he remembered that he'd forgotten to bring his membership card; thought the assistant would probably let him rent something anyway. After all, if William Smith could rent a flat in the New Town, surely Rebus could rent a three-quid video.

He was even prepared to pay cash.

But as he stared at the rack of new releases, he found himself blinking and shaking his head. Then he reached out a hand and lifted down the empty video box. He approached the desk with it.

'When did this come out?' he asked.

'Last week.' The assistant was in his teens, but a good judge of Hollywood's gold dust and dross. His eyes had gone heavy-lidded, letting Rebus know this film was the latter. 'Rich guy's having an affair, hires an assassin. Only the assassin falls for the wife and tops the mistress instead. Rich guy takes the fall, breaks out of jail with revenge in mind.'

'So I don't need to watch it now?'

The assistant shrugged. 'That's all in the first fifteen minutes. I'm not telling you anything they don't give away on the back of the box.'

Rebus turned the box over and saw that this was largely true. 'I should never have doubted you,' he said.

'It got terrible reviews, which is why they end up quoting from an obscure radio station on the front.'

Rebus nodded, turning the box over in his hands. Then he held it out towards the assistant. 'I'll take it.'

'Don't say I didn't warn you.' The assistant turned and found a copy of the film in a plain box. 'Got your card?'

'Left it in the flat.'

'Surname's Rebus, right? Address in Arden Street.' Rebus nodded. 'Then I suppose it's OK, this one time.'

'Thanks.'

The assistant shrugged. 'It's not like I'm doing you a favour, letting you walk out with that film.'

'Even so . . . you have to admit, it's got a pretty good title.'

'Maybe.' The assistant studied the box for *Tell Me Who to Kill*, but seemed far from convinced.

★ ★ ★

Rebus had finished all four cans of lager by the time the closing credits rolled. He reckoned he must have dozed off for a few minutes in the middle, but didn't think this had affected his viewing pleasure. There were a couple of big names in the main roles, but they, too, tended towards drowsiness. It was as if cast, crew and writers had needed a decent night's sleep.

Rebus rewound the tape, ejected it, and held it in his hand. So it was a film title. That was all the text message had meant. Maybe someone had been choosing a film for Saturday night. Maybe Carl Guthrie had found the phone lying on the pavement. William Smith had dropped it, and Guthrie had found it. Then someone, maybe Smith's girlfriend, had texted the title of the film they'd be watching later on, and Guthrie had opened the message, hoping to find some clue to the identity of the phone's owner.

And he'd walked out under a bus.

TELL ME WHO TO KILL.

Which meant Rebus had wasted half a day. Half a day that could have been better spent . . . well, spent differently anyway. And the film had been preposterous: the assistant's summary had only just scratched the surface. Starting off with a surfeit of twists, there'd been nowhere for the film to go but layer on more twists, deceits, mixed identities, and conspiracies. Rebus could not have been more insulted if the guy had woken up at the end and it had all been a dream.

He went into the kitchen to make some coffee. The place still held the aroma of the fry-up he'd amassed before sitting down to watch the video. Over the sound of the boiling kettle, he heard his phone ringing. Went back through to the living room and picked it up.

'Got a name for you, sorry it took so long.'

'Ray? Is that you?' Rebus checked his watch: not far short of midnight. 'Tell me you're not still at work.'

'Called a halt hours ago, but I just got a text message from my friend who was doing some cross-checking for me.'

'He works odder hours than even we do.'

'He's an insomniac, works a lot from his house.'

'So I shouldn't ask where he got this information?'

'You can ask, but I couldn't possibly tell you.'

'And what is it I'm getting?'

'The text message came from a phone registered to Alexis Ojiwa. I've got an address in Haddington.'

'Might as well give it to me.' Rebus picked up a pen, but something in his voice had alerted Ray Duff.

'Do I get the feeling you no longer need any of this?'

'Maybe not, Ray.' Rebus explained about the film.

'Well, I can't say I've ever heard of it.'

'It was news to me, too,' Rebus didn't mind admitting.

'But for the record, I do know Alexis Ojiwa.'

'You do?'

'I take it you don't follow football.'

'I watch the results.'

'Then you'll know that Hearts put four past Aberdeen this afternoon.'

'Four-one, final score.'

'And two of them were scored by Alexis Ojiwa . . .'

★ ★ ★

Rebus's mobile woke him an hour earlier than he'd have liked. He blinked at the sunshine streaming through his uncurtained windows and grabbed at the phone, dropping it once before getting it to his ear.

'Yes?' he rasped.

'I'm sorry, is this too early? I thought maybe it was urgent.'

'Who is this?'

'Am I speaking to DI Rebus?'

'Yes.'

'My name's Richard Hawkins. You put your card through my door.'

'Did I?'

Rebus heard a soft chuckle. 'Maybe I should call back later . . .'

'No, wait a sec. You live at Gilby Street?'

'Flat 2, yes.'

'Right, right.' Rebus sat down on his bed, ran his free hand through his hair. 'Thanks for getting back to me.'

'Not at all.'

'It was about your neighbour, actually.'

'Will Smith?'

'What?'

Another chuckle. 'When he introduced himself, we had a laugh about that coincidence. Really, it was down to me. He called himself "William", and it just clicked: Will Smith, same as the actor.'

'Right.' Rebus was trying to gather himself. 'So you've met Mr Smith, talked to him?'

'Just a couple of times. Passing on the stairs . . . He's never around much.'

'Not much sign of his flat being lived in either.'

'I wouldn't know, never been inside. Must have something going for him though.'

'Why do you say that?'

'Absolute cracker of a girlfriend.'

'Really?'

'Just saw her the once, but you always know when she's around.'

'Why's that?'

'Her perfume. It fills the stairwell. Smelled it last night actually . . .'

Yes, Rebus had smelt it, too. He moistened his lips, feeling sourness at the corners of his mouth. 'Mr Hawkins, can you describe William Smith to me?'

Hawkins could, and did.

Rebus turned up unannounced at Alexis Ojiwa's, reckoning the player would be resting after the rigours of the previous day. The house was an unassuming detached bungalow with a red Mazda sports car parked in the driveway. It was on a modern estate, a couple of neighbours washing their cars, watching Rebus with the intensity of men for whom his arrival was an event of sorts, something they could dissect with their wives over the carving of the afternoon sirloin. Rebus rang the doorbell and waited. A woman answered. She seemed surprised to see him.

He showed his ID as he introduced himself. 'Mind if I come in for a minute?'

'What's happened?'

'Nothing. I just have a question for Mr Ojiwa.'

She left the door standing open and walked back through the hall and into an L-shaped living area, calling out: 'Cops are here to put the cuffs on you, baby.' Rebus closed the door and followed her. She stepped out through French windows into the back garden, where a tiny, bare-chested man stood, nursing a drink that looked like puréed fruit. Alexis Ojiwa was wiry, with thick-veined arms and a tight chest. Rebus tried not to think about what the neighbours thought. Scotland was still some way short of being a beacon of multiculturalism, and Ojiwa, like his partner, was black. Not just coffee-coloured, but as black as ebony. Still, probably the only question that would count in most local minds was whether he was Protestant black or Catholic black.

Rebus held out a hand to shake, and introduced himself again.

'What's the problem, officer?'

'I didn't catch your wife's name.'

'It's Cecily.'

Rebus nodded. 'This is going to sound strange, but it's about your mobile phone.'

'My phone?' Ojiwa's face creased in puzzlement. Then he looked to Cecily, and back again at Rebus. 'What about my phone?'

'You do have a mobile phone, sir?'

'I do, yes.'

'But I'm guessing you wouldn't have used it yesterday afternoon? Specifically not at 16.31. I think you were still on the pitch at that time, am I right?'

'That's right.'

'Then someone else used your phone to send this

message.' Rebus held up William Smith's mobile so Ojiwa could read the text. Cecily came forward so she could read it, too. Her husband stared at her.

'What's this all about?'

'I don't know, baby.'

'You sent this?' His eyes had widened. She shook her head.

'Am I to assume that you had your husband's phone with you yesterday, Mrs Ojiwa?' Rebus asked.

'I was shopping in town all day . . . I didn't make any calls.'

'What the hell is this?' It appeared that the footballer had a short fuse, and Rebus had touched a match to it.

'I'm sure there's a reasonable explanation, sir,' Rebus said, raising his hands to try to calm Ojiwa.

'You go spending all my money, and now this!' Ojiwa shook the phone at his wife.

'I didn't do it!' She was yelling too now, loud enough to be heard by the car-polishers. Then she dived inside, producing a silver mobile phone from her bag. 'Here it is,' she said, brandishing the phone. 'Check it, check and see if I sent any messages. I was shopping all day!'

'Maybe someone could have borrowed it?' Rebus suggested.

'I don't see how,' she said, shaking her head. 'Why would anyone want to do that, send a message like that?'

Ojiwa had slumped on to a garden bench, head in hands. Rebus got the feeling that theirs was a relationship stoked by melodrama. He seated himself on the bench next to the footballer.

'Can I ask you something, Mr Ojiwa?'

'What now?'

'I was just wondering if you'd ever needed physio?'

Ojiwa looked up. 'Course I need physio! You think I'm Captain Superman or something?' He slapped his hands against his thighs.

If anything, Rebus's voice grew quieter as he began his next question. 'Then does the name Carl Guthrie mean anything to you . . . ?'

'You've not committed any crime.'

These were Rebus's first words to Frances Guthrie when she opened her door to him. The interior of her house was dark, the curtains closed. The house itself was large and detached and sited in half an acre of grounds in the city's Ravelston area. Physios either earned more than Rebus had counted on, or else there was family money involved.

Frances Guthrie was wearing black slacks and a loose, low-cut black top. Mourning casual, Rebus might have termed it. Her eyes were red-rimmed, and the area around her nose looked raw.

'Mind if I come in?' Rebus asked. It wasn't really a question. He was already making to pass the widow. Hands in pockets, he walked down the hallway and into the sitting room. Stood there and waited for her to join him. She did so slowly, perching on the arm of the red leather sofa. He repeated his opening words, expecting that she would say something, but all she did was stare at him, wide-eyed, maybe a little scared.

He made a tour of the room. The windows were large, and even when curtained there was enough light to see by. Rebus stopped by the fireplace and folded his arms.

'Here's the way I see it. You were out shopping with your friend Cecily. You got to know her when Carl was treating her husband. The pair of you were in Harvey Nichols. Cecily was in the changing room, leaving her bag with you. That's when you got hold of her phone and sent the message.' He paused to watch the effect his words were having. Frances Guthrie had lowered her head, staring down at her hands.

'It was a video you'd watched recently. I'm guessing Carl watched it, too. A film about a man who cheats on his wife. And Carl had been cheating on you, hadn't he? You wanted to let him know you knew, so you sent a text to his other phone, the one registered to his fake name – William Smith.' Smith's neighbour had given Rebus a good description of the man, chiming with accident victim Carl Guthrie. 'You'd done some detective work of your own, found out about the phone, the flat in town . . . the other woman.' The one whose perfume had lingered in the stairwell. Saturday afternoon: Carl Guthrie heading home after an assignation, leaving behind only two glasses and an unfinished bottle of wine.

Frances Guthrie's head jerked up. She took a deep breath, almost a gulp.

'Why use Cecily's phone?' Rebus asked quietly.

She shook her head, not blinking. Then: 'I never wanted this . . . Not this . . .'

'You weren't to know what would happen.'

'I just wanted to do something.' She looked up at

him, wanting him to understand. He nodded slowly. 'What . . . what do I do now?'

Rebus slipped his hands back into his pockets. 'Learn to live with yourself, I suppose.'

That afternoon, he was back at the Oxford Bar, nursing a drink and thinking about love, about how it could make you do things you couldn't explain. All the passions – love and hate and everything in between – they all made us act in ways that would seem inexplicable to a visitor from another planet. The barman asked him if he was ready for another, but Rebus shook his head.

'How's the weekend been treating you?' the barman asked.

'Same as always,' Rebus replied. It was one of those little lies that went some way towards making life appear that bit less complicated.

'Seen any good films lately?'

Rebus smiled, stared down into his glass. 'Watched one last night,' he said. 'Let me tell you about it . . .'

Ian Rankin was Chairman of the CWA in 1999–2000. He is renowned as the creator of Inspector John Rebus, who has appeared in such novels as the CWA Gold Dagger-winning Black and Blue, The Hanging Garden and Set in Darkness. His short stories have also won CWA Daggers, most recently for 'Herbert In Motion', which appeared in the CWA anthology Perfectly Criminal. Rankin's other publications include thrillers written under the name of Jack Harvey.

RUTH RENDELL

When the Wedding Was Over

'Matrimony,' said Chief Inspector Wexford, 'begins with
dearly beloved and ends with amazement.'

His wife, sitting beside him on the bridegroom's side
of the church, whispered, 'What did you say?'

He repeated it. She steadied the large floral hat which
her husband had called becoming but not exactly
conducive to *sotto voce* intimacies. 'What on earth makes
you say that?'

'Thomas Hardy. He said it first. But look in your
Prayer Book.'

The bridegroom waited, hangdog, with his best man.
Michael Burden was very much in love, was entering
this second marriage with someone admirably suited to
him, had agreed with his fiancée that nothing but a religious ceremony would do for them, yet at forty-four
was a little superannuated for what Wexford called 'all
this white wedding gubbins'. There were two hundred
people in the church. Burden, his best man and his
ushers were in morning dress. Madonna lilies and
stephanotis and syringa decorated the pews, the pulpit

and the chancel steps. It was the kind of thing that is properly designed for someone twenty years younger. Burden had been through it before when he *was* twenty years younger. Wexford chuckled silently, looking at the anxious face above the high white collar. And then as Dora, leafing through the marriage service, said, 'Oh, I *see*,' the organist went from voluntaries into the opening bars of the *Lohengrin* march and Jenny Ireland appeared at the church door on her father's arm.

A beautiful bride, of course. Seven years younger than Burden, blonde, gentle, low-voiced, and given to radiant smiles. Jenny's father gave her hand into Burden's and the Rector of St Peter's began:

'Dearly beloved, we are gathered together . . .'

While bride and groom were being informed that marriage was not for the satisfaction of their carnal lusts, and that they must bring up their children in a Christian manner, Wexford studied the congregation. In front of himself and Dora sat Burden's sister-in-law, Grace, whom everyone had thought he would marry after the death of his first wife. But Burden had found consolation with a red-headed woman, wild and sweet and strange, gone now God knew where, and Grace had married someone else. Two little boys now sat between Grace and that someone else, giving their parents a full-time job keeping them quiet.

Burden's mother and father were both dead. Wexford thought he recognised, from one meeting a dozen years before, an aged aunt. Beside her sat Dr Crocker and his wife, beyond them and behind were a crowd whose individual members he knew either only by sight or not

410

at all. Sylvia, his elder daughter, was sitting on his other side, his grandsons between her and their father, and at the central aisle end of the pew, Sheila Wexford of the Royal Shakespeare Company. Wexford's actress daughter, who on her entry had commanded nudges, whispers, every gaze, sat looking with unaccustomed wistfulness at Jenny Ireland in her clouds of white and wreath of pearls.

'I, Michael George, take thee, Janina, to be my wedded wife, to have and to hold from this day forward . . .'

Janina. *Janina*? Wexford had supposed her name was Jennifer. What sort of parents called a daughter Janina? Turks? Fans of Dumas? He leaned forward to get a good look at these philonomatous progenitors. They looked ordinary enough, Mr Ireland apparently exhausted by the effort of giving the bride away, Jenny's mother making use of the lace handkerchief provided for the specific purpose of crying into it those tears of joy and loss. What romantic streak had led them to dismiss Elizabeth and Susan and Anne in favour of – Janina?

'Those whom God hath joined together, let no man put asunder. Forasmuch as Michael George and Janina have consented together in holy wedlock . . .'

Had they been as adventurous in the naming of their son? All Wexford could see of him was a broad back, a bit of profile, and now a hand. The hand was passing a large white handkerchief to his mother. Wexford found himself being suddenly yanked to his feet to sing a hymn.

'O, Perfect Love, all human thought transcending, Lowly we kneel in prayer before Thy throne . . .'

These words had the effect of evoking from Mrs Ireland audible sobs. Her son – hadn't Burden said he was in publishing? – looked embarrassed, turning his head. A young woman, strangely dressed in black with an orange hat, edged past the publisher to put a consoling arm round his mother.

'O Lord, save Thy servant and Thy handmaid.'

'Who put their trust in Thee,' said Dora and most of the rest of the congregation.

'O Lord, send them help from Thy holy place.'

Wexford, to show team spirit, said, 'Amen,' and when everyone else said, 'And evermore defend them,' decided to keep quiet in future.

Mrs Ireland had stopped crying. Wexford's gaze drifted to his own daughters, Sheila singing lustily, Sylvia, the Women's Liberationist, with less assurance as if she doubted the ethics of lending her support to so archaic and sexist a ceremony. His grandsons were beginning to fidget.

'Almighty God, who at the beginning did create our first parents, Adam and Eve . . .'

Dear Mike, thought Wexford with a flash of sentimentality that came to him perhaps once every ten years, you'll be OK now. No more carnal lusts conflicting with a puritan conscience, no more loneliness, no more worrying about those selfish kids of yours, no more temptation-of-St-Anthony stuff. For is it not ordained as a remedy against sin, and to avoid fornication, that such persons as have not the gift of continency may marry and keep themselves undefiled?

'For after this manner in the old time the holy women who trusted in God . . .'

412

He was quite surprised that they were using the ancient form. Still, the bride had promised to obey. He couldn't resist glancing at Sylvia.

'. . . being in subjection to their own husbands . . .'

Her face was a study in incredulous dismay as she mouthed at her sister 'unbelievable' and 'antique'.

'. . . Even as Sarah obeyed Abraham, calling him Lord, whose daughters ye are as long as ye do well, and are not afraid with any amazement.'

At the Olive and Dove hotel there was a reception line to greet guests, Mrs Ireland smiling, re-rouged and restored, Burden looking like someone who has had an operation and been told the prognosis is excellent, Jenny serene as a bride should be.

Dry sherry and white wine on trays. No champagne. Wexford remembered that there was a younger Ireland daughter, absent with her husband in some dreadful place – Botswana? Lesotho? No doubt all the champagne funds had been expended on her. It was a buffet lunch, but a good one. Smoked salmon and duck and strawberries. Nobody, he said to himself, has ever really thought of anything better to eat than smoked salmon and duck and strawberries unless it might be caviare and grouse and syllabub. He was weighing the two menus against one another, must without knowing it have been thinking aloud, for a voice said:

'Asparagus, trout, apple pie.'

'Well, maybe,' said Wexford, 'but I do like meat. Trout's a bit insipid. You're Jenny's brother, I'm sorry I don't remember your name. How d'you do?'

'How d'you do? I know who you are. Mike told me. I'm Amyas Ireland.'

So that funny old pair hadn't had a one-off indulgence when they had named Janina. Again Wexford's thoughts seemed revealed to this intuitive person.

'Oh, I know,' said Ireland, 'but how about my other sister? She's called Cunegonde. Her husband calls her Queenie. Look, I'd like to talk to you. Could we get together a minute away from all this crush? Mike was going to help me out, but I can't ask him now, not when he's off on his honeymoon. It's about a book we're publishing.'

The girl in black and orange, Burden's nephews, Sheila Wexford, Burden's best man and a gaggle of children, all carrying plates, passed between them at this point. It was at least a minute before Wexford could ask, 'Who's we?' and another half-minute before Amyas Ireland understood what he meant.

'Carlyon Brent,' he said, his mouth full of duck. 'I'm with Carlyon Brent.'

One of the largest and most distinguished of publishing houses. Wexford was impressed. 'You published the Vandrian, didn't you, and the de Coverley books?'

Ireland nodded. 'Mike said you were a great reader. That's good. Can I get you some more duck? No? I'm going to. I won't be a minute.' Enviously Wexford watched him shovel fat-rimmed slices of duck breast on to his plate, take a brioche, have second thoughts and take another. The man was as thin as a rail too, positively emaciated.

'I look after the crime list,' he said as he sat down

again. 'As I said, Mike half-promised ... This isn't fiction, it's fact. The Winchurch case?'

'Ah.'

'I know it's a bit of a nerve asking, but would you read a manuscript for me?'

Wexford took a cup of coffee from a passing tray. 'What for?'

'Well, in the interests of truth. Mike was going to tell me what he thought.' Wexford looked at him dubiously. He had the highest respect and the deepest affection for Inspector Burden but he was one of the last people he would have considered as a literary critic. 'To tell me what he thought,' the publisher said once again. 'You see, it's worrying me. The author has discovered some new facts and they more or less prove Mrs Winchurch's innocence.' He hesitated. 'Have you ever heard of a writer called Kenneth Gandolph?'

Wexford was saved from answering by the pounding of a gavel on the top table and the beginning of the speeches. A great many toasts had been drunk, several dozen telegrams read out, and the bride and groom departed to change their clothes before he had an opportunity to reply to Ireland's question. And he was glad of the respite, for what he knew of Gandolph, though based on hearsay, was not prepossessing.

'Doesn't he write crime novels?' he said when the enquiry was repeated. 'And the occasional examination of a real-life crime?'

Nodding, Ireland said, 'It's good, this script of his. We want to do it for next spring's list. It's an eighty-year-old murder, sure, but people are still fascinated by it. I think this new version could cause quite a sensation.'

'Florence Winchurch was hanged,' said Wexford, 'yet there was always some margin of doubt about her guilt. Where does Gandolph get his fresh facts from?'

'May I send you a copy of the script? You'll find all that in the introduction.'

Wexford shrugged, then smiled. 'I suppose so. You do realise I can't do more than maybe spot mistakes in forensics? I did say maybe, mind.' But his interest had already been caught. It made him say, 'Florence was married at St Peter's, you know, and she also had her wedding reception here.'

'And spent part of her honeymoon in Greece.'

'No doubt the parallels end there,' said Wexford as Burden and Jenny came back into the room.

Burden was in a grey lounge suit, she in pale blue sprigged muslin. Wexford felt an absurd impulse of tenderness towards him. It was partly caused by Jenny's hat which she would never wear again, would never have occasion to wear, would remove the minute they got into the car. But Burden was the sort of man who could never be happy with a woman who didn't have a hat as part of her 'going-away' costume. His own clothes were eminently unsuitable for flying to Crete in June. They both looked very happy and embarrassed.

Mrs Ireland seized her daughter in a crushing embrace.

'It's not for ever, Mother,' said Jenny. 'It's only for two weeks.'

'Well, in a way,' said Burden. He shook hands gravely with his own son, down from university for the weekend, and planted a kiss on his daughter's forehead. Must have been reading novels, Wexford thought, grinning to himself.

'Good luck, Mike,' he said.

The bride took his hand, put a soft cool kiss on to the corner of his mouth. Say I'm growing old but add, Jenny kissed me. He didn't say that aloud. He nodded and smiled and took his wife's arm and frowned at Sylvia's naughty boys like the patriarch he was. Burden and Jenny went out to the car which had Just Married written in lipstick on the rear window and a shoe tied on the back bumper.

There was a clicking of handbag clasps, a flurry of hands, and then a tempest of confetti broke over them.

It was an isolated house, standing some twenty yards back from the Myringham road. Plumb in the centre of the façade was a plaque bearing the date 1896. Wexford had often thought that there seemed to have been positive intent on the part of late-Victorian builders to design and erect houses that were not only ugly, complex and inconvenient, but also distinctly sinister in appearance. The Limes, though well maintained and set in a garden as multi-coloured, cushiony and floral as a quilt, nevertheless kept this sinister quality. Khaki-coloured brick and grey slate had been the principal materials used in its construction. Without being able to define exactly how, Wexford could see that, in relation to the walls, the proportions of the sash windows were wrong. A turret grew out of each of the front corners and each of these turrets was topped by a conical roof, giving the place the look of a cross between Balmoral castle and a hotel in

Kitzbuehl. The lime trees which gave it its name had been lopped so many times since their planting at the turn of the century that now they were squat and misshapen.

In the days of the Winchurches it had been called Paraleash House. But this name, of historical significance on account of its connection with the ancient manor of Paraleash, had been changed specifically as a result of the murder of Edward Winchurch. Even so, it had stood empty for ten years. Then it had found a buyer a year or so before the First World War, a man who was killed in that war. Its present owner had occupied it for half a dozen years, and in the time intervening between his purchase of it and 1918 it had been variously a nursing home, the annexe of an agricultural college and a private school. The owner was a retired brigadier. As he emerged from the front door with two Sealyhams on a lead, Wexford retreated to his car and drove home.

It was Monday evening and Burden's marriage was two days old. Monday was the evening of Dora's pottery class, the fruits of which, bruised-looking and not invariably symmetrical, were scattered haphazardly about the room like windfalls. Hunting along the shelves for G. Hallam Saul's *When the Summer is Shed* and *The Trial of Florence Winchurch* from the Notable British Trials series, he nearly knocked over one of those rotund yet lopsided objects. With a sigh of relief that it was unharmed, he set about refreshing his memory of the Winchurch case with the help of Miss Saul's classic.

Florence May Anstruther had been nineteen at the time of her marriage to Edward Winchurch and he forty-seven.

418

She was a good-looking fair-haired girl, rather tall and Junoesque, the daughter of a Kingsmarkham chemist – that is, a pharmacist, for her father had kept a shop in the High Street. In 1895 this damned her as of no account in the social hierarchy, and few people would have bet much on her chances of marrying well. But she did. Winchurch was a barrister who, at this stage of his life, practised law from inclination rather than from need. His father, a Sussex landowner, had died some three years before and had left him what for the last decade of the nineteenth century was an enormous fortune, two hundred thousand pounds. Presumably, he had been attracted to Florence by her youth, her looks and her ladylike ways. She had been given the best education, including six months at a finishing school, that the chemist could afford. Winchurch's attraction for Florence was generally supposed to have been solely his money.

They were married in June 1895 at the parish church of St Peter's, Kingsmarkham, and went on a six-month honeymoon, touring Italy, Greece and the Swiss Alps. When they returned home Winchurch took a lease of Sewingbury Priory while building began on Paraleash House, and it may have been that the conical roofs on those turrets were inspired directly by what Florence had seen on her alpine travels. They moved into the lavishly furnished new house in May 1896, and Florence settled down to the life of a Victorian lady with a wealthy husband and a staff of indoor and outdoor servants. A vapid life at best, even if alleviated by a brood of children. But Florence had no children and was to have none.

Once or twice a week Edward Winchurch went up to London by the train from Kingsmarkham, as commuters had done before and have been doing ever since. Florence gave orders to her cook, arranged the flowers, paid and received calls, read novels and devoted a good many hours a day to her face, her hair and her dress. Local opinion of the couple at that time seemed to have been that they were as happy as most people, that Florence had done very well for herself and knew it, and Edward not so badly as had been predicted.

In the autumn of 1896 a young doctor of medicine bought a practice in Kingsmarkham and came to live there with his unmarried sister. Their name was Fenton. Frank Fenton was an extremely handsome man, twenty-six years old, six feet tall, with jet black hair, a Byronic eye and an arrogant lift to his chin. The sister was called Ada, and she was neither good-looking nor arrogant, being partly crippled by poliomyelitis which had left her with one leg badly twisted and paralysed.

It was ostensibly to befriend Ada Fenton that Florence first began calling at the Fentons' house in Queen Street. Florence professed great affection for Ada, took her about in her carriage and offered her the use of it whenever she had to go any distance. From this it was an obvious step to persuade Edward that Frank Fenton should become the Winchurches' doctor. Within another few months young Mrs Winchurch had become the doctor's mistress.

It was probable that Ada knew nothing, or next to nothing, about it. In the eighteen-nineties a young girl could be, and usually was, very innocent. At the trial it was stated by Florence's coachman that he would be sent to the Fentons' house several times a week to take Miss Fenton driving, while Ada's housemaid said that Mrs Winchurch would arrive on foot soon after Miss Fenton had gone out and be admitted rapidly through a French window by the doctor himself. During the winter of 1898 it seemed likely that Frank Fenton had performed an abortion on Mrs Winchurch, and for some months afterwards they met only at social gatherings and occasionally when Florence was visiting Ada. But their feelings for each other were too strong for them to bear separation and by the following summer they were again meeting at Fenton's house while Ada was out, and now also at Paraleash House on the days when Edward had departed for the law courts.

Divorce was difficult but by no means impossible or unheard-of in 1899. At the trial Frank Fenton said he had wanted Mrs Winchurch to ask her husband for a divorce. He would have married her in spite of the disastrous effect on his career. It was she, he said, who refused to consider it on the grounds that she did not think she could bear the disgrace.

In January 1900 Florence went to London for the day and, among other purchases, bought at a grocer's two cans of herring fillets marinaded in a white wine sauce. It was rare for canned food to appear in the Winchurch household, and when Florence suggested that these herring fillets should be used in the preparation of a dish called *Filets de hareng marinés à la Rosette*, the recipe for which she had been given by Ada Fenton, the cook, Mrs Eliza Holmes, protested that she could prepare it from fresh fish. Florence, however, insisted, one of the cans was used, and the dish was made and served to Florence and Edward at dinner. It was brought in by the parlourmaid, Alice Evans, as a savoury or final course to a four-course meal. Although Florence had shown so much enthusiasm about the dish, she took none of it. Edward ate a moderate amount and the rest was removed to the kitchen where it was shared between Mrs Holmes, Alice Evans and the housemaid, Violet Stedman. No one suffered any ill-effects. The date was 30 January 1900.

Five weeks later on 5 March Florence asked Mrs Holmes to make the dish again, using the remaining can, as her husband had liked it so much. This time Florence too partook of the marinaded herrings, but when the remains of it were about to be removed by Alice to the kitchen, she advised her to tell the others not to eat it as she 'thought it had a strange taste and was perhaps not quite fresh'. However, although Mrs Holmes and Alice abstained, Violet Stedman ate a larger quantity of the dish than had either Florence or Edward.

Florence, as was her habit, left Edward to drink his port alone. Within a few minutes a strangled shout was heard from the dining room and a sound as of furniture breaking. Florence and Alice Evans and Mrs Holmes went into the room and found Edward Winchurch lying on the floor, a chair with one leg wrenched from its socket tipped over beside him and an overturned glass of port on the table. Florence approached him and he went into a violent convulsion, arching his back and baring his teeth, his hands grasping the chair in apparent agony.

John Barstow, the coachman, was sent to fetch Dr Fenton. By this time Florence was complaining of stomach pains and seemed unable to stand. Fenton arrived, had Edward and Florence removed upstairs and asked Mrs Holmes what they had eaten. She showed him the empty herring fillets can, and he recognised the brand as that by which a patient of a colleague of his had recently been infected with botulism, a virulent and usually fatal form of food poisoning. Fenton immediately assumed that it was *bacillus botulinus* which had attacked the Winchurches, and such is the power of suggestion that Violet Stedman now said she felt sick and faint.

Botulism causes paralysis, difficulty in breathing and a disturbance of the vision. Florence appeared to be partly paralysed and said she had double vision. Edward's symptoms were different. He continued to have spasms, was totally relaxed between spasms, and although he had difficulty in breathing and other symptoms of botulism, the onset had been exceptionally rapid for any form of food poisoning. Fenton, however, had never seen a case of botulism, which is extremely rare, and he supposed that the symptoms would vary greatly from person to person. He gave jalap and cream of tartar as a purgative and, in the absence of any known relatives of Edward Winchurch, he sent for Florence's father, Thomas Anstruther.

If Fenton was less innocent than was supposed, he had made a mistake in sending for Anstruther, for

Florence's father insisted on a second opinion, and at ten o'clock went himself to the home of that very colleague of Fenton's who had recently witnessed a known case of botulism. This was Dr Maurice Waterfield, twice Fenton's age, a popular man with a large practice in Stowerton. He looked at Edward Winchurch, at the agonised grin which overspread his features, and as Edward went into his last convulsive seizure, pronounced that he had been poisoned not by *bacillus botulinus* but by strychnine.

Edward died a few minutes afterwards. Dr Waterfield told Fenton that there was nothing physically wrong with either Florence or Violet Stedman. The former was suffering from shock or 'neurasthenia', the latter from indigestion brought on by over-eating. The police were informed, an inquest took place, and after it Florence was immediately arrested and charged with murdering her husband by administering to him a noxious substance, to wit *strychnos nux vomica*, in a decanter of port wine.

Her trial took place in London at the Central Criminal Court. She was twenty-four years old, a beautiful woman, and was by then known to have been having a love affair with the young and handsome Dr Fenton. As such, she and her case attracted national attention. Fenton had by then lost his practice, lost all hope of succeeding with another in the British Isles, and even before the trial his name had become a by-word, scurrilous doggerel being sung about him and Florence in the music halls. But far from increasing his loyalty to Florence, this seemed to make him the more determined to dissociate himself from her. He appeared as the prosecution's principal witness, and it was his evidence which sent Florence to the gallows.

Fenton admitted his relationship with Florence but said that he had told her it must end. The only possible alternative was divorce and ultimately marriage to himself. In early January 1900 Florence had been calling on his sister Ada, and he had come in to find them looking through a book of recipes. One of the recipes called for the use of herring fillets marinaded in white wine sauce, the mention of which had caused him to tell them about a case of botulism which a patient of Dr Waterfield was believed to have contracted from eating the contents of a can of just such fillets. He had named the brand and advised his sister not to buy any of that kind. When, some seven weeks later, he was called to the dying Edward Winchurch, the cook had shown him an empty can of that very brand. In his opinion, Mrs Winchurch herself was not ill at all, was not even ill from 'nerves' but was shamming. The judge said that he was not there to give his opinion, but the warning came too late. To the jury the point had already been made.

Asked if he was aware that strychnine had therapeutic uses in small quantities, Fenton said he was but that he kept none in his dispensary. In any case, his dispensary was kept locked and the cupboards inside it locked, so it would have been impossible for Florence to have entered it or to have appropriated anything while on a visit to Ada. Ada Fenton was not called as a witness. She was ill, suffering from what her doctor, Dr Waterfield, called 'brain fever'.

The prosecution's case was that, in order to inherit

his fortune and marry Dr Fenton, Florence Winchurch had attempted to poison her husband with infected fish, or fish she had good reason to suppose might be infected. When this failed she saw to it that the dish was provided again, and herself added strychnine to the port decanter. It was postulated that she obtained the strychnine from her father's shop, without his knowledge, where it was kept in stock for the destruction of rats and moles. After her husband was taken ill, she herself simulated symptoms of botulism in the hope that the convulsions of strychnine poisoning would be confused with the paralysis and impeded breathing caused by the bacillus.

The defence tried to shift the blame to Frank Fenton, at least to suggest a conspiracy with Florence, but it was no use. The jury were out for only forty minutes. They pronounced her guilty, the judge sentenced her to death, and she was hanged just twenty-three days later, this being some twenty years before the institution of a Court of Appeal.

After the execution Frank and Ada Fenton emigrated to the United States and settled in New England. Fenton's reputation had gone before him. He was never again able to practise as a doctor but worked as the travelling representative of a firm of pharmaceutical manufacturers until his death in 1932. He never married. Ada, on the other hand, surprisingly enough, did. Ephraim Hurst fell in love with her in spite of her sickly constitution and withered leg. They were married in the summer of 1902 and by the spring of 1903 Ada Hurst was dead in childbirth.

By then Paraleash House had been re-named The

Limes and lime trees planted to conceal its forbidding yet fascinating façade from the curious passer-by.

The parcel from Carlyon Brent arrived in the morning with a very polite covering letter from Amyas Ireland, grateful in anticipation. Wexford had never before seen a book in this embryo stage. The script, a hundred thousand words long, was bound in red, and through a window in its cover appeared the provisional title and the author's name: *Poison at Paraleash, A Reappraisal of the Winchurch Case* by Kenneth Gandolph.

'Remember all that fuss about Gandolph?' Wexford said to Dora across the coffee pot. 'About four years ago?'

'Somebody confessed a murder to him, didn't they?'

'Well, maybe. While a prison visitor, he spent some time talking to Paxton, the bank robber, in Wormwood Scrubs. Paxton died of cancer a few months later, and Gandolph then published an article in a newspaper in which he said that during the course of their conversations, Paxton had confessed to him that he was the perpetrator of the Conyngford murder in 1962. Paxton's widow protested, there was a heated correspondence, MPs wanting the libel laws extended to libelling the dead, Gandolph shouting about the power of truth. Finally, the by then retired Detective Superintendent Warren of Scotland Yard put an end to all further controversy by issuing a statement to the press. He said Paxton couldn't have killed James Conyngford because on the day of Conyngford's death in Brighton Warren's sergeant and a constable had had Paxton under constant surveillance in London. In other words, he was never out of their sight.'

'Why would Gandolph invent such a thing, Reg?' said Dora.

'Perhaps he didn't. Paxton may have spun him all sorts of tales as a way of passing a boring afternoon. Who knows? On the other hand, Gandolph does rather set himself up as the elucidator of unsolved crimes. Years ago, I believe, he did find a satisfactory and quite reasonable solution to some murder in Scotland, and maybe it went to his head. Marshall, Groves, Folliott used to be his publishers. I wonder if they've refused this one because of the Paxton business, if it was offered to them and they turned it down?'

'But Mr Ireland's people have taken it,' Dora pointed out.

'Mm-hm. But they're not falling over themselves with enthusiasm, are they? They're scared. Ireland hasn't sent me this so that I can check up on the police procedural part. What do I know about police procedure in 1900? He's sent it to me in the hope that if Gandolph's been up to his old tricks I'll spot what they are.'

The working day presented no opportunity for a look at *Poison at Paraleash*, but at eight o'clock that night Wexford opened it and read Gandolph's long introduction.

Gandolph began by saying that as a criminologist he had always been aware of the Winchurch case and of the doubt which many felt about Florence Winchurch's guilt. Therefore, when he was staying with friends in Boston, Massachusetts, some two years before and they spoke to him of an acquaintance of theirs who was the niece of one of the principals in the case, he had asked to be introduced to her. The niece was Ada Hurst's daughter, Lina, still Miss Hurst, seventy-four years old and suffering from a terminal illness.

Miss Hurst showed no particular interest in the events of March 1900. She had been brought up by her father and his second wife and had hardly known her uncle. All her mother's property had come into her possession, including the diary which Ada Fenton Hurst had kept for three years prior to Edward Winchurch's death. Lina Hurst told Gandolph she had kept the diary for sentimental reasons but that he might borrow it and after her death she would see that it passed to him.

Within weeks Lina Hurst did die and her stepbrother, who was her executor, had the diary sent to Gandolph. Gandolph had read it and had been enormously excited by certain entries because in his view they incriminated Frank Fenton and exonerated Florence Winchurch. Here Wexford turned back a few pages and noted the author's dedication: *In memory of Miss Lina Hurst, of Cambridge, Massachusetts, without whose help this reappraisal would have been impossible.*

More than this Wexford had no time to read that evening, but he returned to it on the following day. The diary, it appeared, was a five-year one. At the top of each page was the date, as it might be 1 April, and beneath that five spaces each headed 18 . . . There was room for the diarist to write perhaps forty or fifty words in each space, no more. On the 1 January page in the third heading down, the number of the year, the eight had been crossed out and a nine substituted, and so it went on for every subsequent entry until March 6, after which no more entries were made until the diarist resumed in December 1900, by which time she and her brother were in Boston.

Wexford proceeded to Gandolph's first chapters. The story he had to tell was substantially the same as Hallam Saul's, and it was not until he came to chapter five and the weeks preceding the crime that he began to concentrate on the character of Frank Fenton. Fenton, he suggested, wanted Mrs Winchurch for the money and property she would inherit on her husband's death. Far from encouraging Florence to seek a divorce, he urged her never to let her husband suspect her preference for another man. Divorce would have left Florence penniless and homeless and have ruined his career. Fenton had known that it was only by making away with Winchurch and so arranging things that the death appeared natural, that he could have money, his profession and Florence.

There was only his word for it, said Gandolph, that he had spoken to Florence of botulism and had warned her against these particular canned herrings. Of course he had never seriously expected those cans to infect Winchurch, but that the fish should be eaten by him was necessary for his strategy. On the night before Winchurch's death, after dining with his sister at Paraleash House, he had introduced strychnine into the port decanter. He had also, Gandolph suggested, contrived to bring the conversation round to a discussion of food and to fish dishes. From that it would have been a short step to get Winchurch to admit how much he had enjoyed *Filets de hareng marinés à la Rosette* and to ask

Florence to have them served again on the following day. Edward, apparently, would have been highly likely to take his doctor's advice, even when in health, even on such a matter as what he should eat for the fourth course of his dinner, while Edward's wife did everything her lover, if not her husband, told her to do.

It was no surprise to Frank Fenton to be called out on the following evening to a man whose spasms only he would recognise as symptomatic of having swallowed strychnine. The arrival of Dr Waterfield was an unlooked-for circumstance. Once Winchurch's symptoms had been defined as arising from strychnine poisoning there was nothing left for Fenton to do but shift the blame on to his mistress. Gandolph suggested that Fenton attributed the source of the strychnine to Anstruther's chemist's shop out of revenge on Anstruther for calling in Waterfield and thus frustrating his hopes.

And what grounds had Gandolph for believing all this? Certain entries in Ada Hurst's diary. Wexford read them slowly and carefully.

For 27 February 1900, she had written, filling the entire small space: *Very cold. Leg painful again today. FW sent round the carriage and had John drive me to Pomfret. Compton says rats in the cellars and the old stables. Dined at home with F who says rats carry leptospiral jaundice, must be got rid of.* 28 February: *Drove in FW's carriage to call on old Mrs Paget. FW still here, having tea with F when I returned. I hope there is no harm in it. Dare I warn F?* 29 February: *F destroyed twenty rats with strychnine from his dispensary. What a relief!* 1 March: *Poor old Mrs Paget passed away in the night. A merciful release. Compton complained about the rats again. Warmer this evening and raining.* There was no entry for 2 March. 3 March: *Annie gave notice, she is getting married. Shall be sorry to lose her. Would not go out in carriage for fear of leaving FW too much alone with F. To bed early as leg most painful.* 4 March: *My birthday. 26 today and an old maid now, I think. FW drove over, brought me beautiful Indian shawl. She is always kind. Invited F and me to dinner tomorrow.* There was no entry for 5 March, and the last entry for nine months was the one for 6 March: *Dined last night at Paraleash House, six guests besides ourselves and the Ws. F left cigar case in the dining room, went back after seeing me home. I hope and pray there is no harm.*

Gandolph was evidently basing his case on the entries for 29 February and 6 March. In telling the court he had no strychnine in his dispensary, Fenton had lied. He had had an obvious opportunity for the introduction of strychnine into the decanter when he returned to Paraleash House in pursuit of his mislaid cigar case, and when he no doubt took care that he entered the dining room alone.

The next day Wexford re-read the chapters in which the new information was contained and he studied with concentration the section concerning the diary. But unless Gandolph were simply lying about the existence of the diary or of those two entries – things which he would hardly dare to do – there seemed no reason to differ from his inference. Florence was innocent, Frank Fenton the murderer of Edward Winchurch. But still Wexford wished Burden were there so that they might have one of their often acrimonious but always fruitful discussions. Somehow, with old Mike to argue against him and put up opposition, he felt things might have been better clarified.

And the morning brought news of Burden, if not the inspector himself, in the form of a postcard from Agios Nikolaios. The blue Aegean, a rocky escarpment, green pines. Who but Burden, as Wexford remarked to Dora, would send postcards while on his honeymoon? The post also brought a parcel from Carlyon Brent. It contained books, a selection from the publishing house's current list as a present for Wexford, and on the compliments slip accompanying them, a note from Amyas Ireland. *I shall be in Kingsmarkham with my people at the weekend. Can we meet? AI.* The books were the latest novel about Regency London by Camilla Barnet; *Put Money in Thy Purse*, the biography of Vassili Vandrian, the financier; the memoirs of Sofya Bolkinska, Bolshoi ballerina; an omnibus version of three novels of farming life by Giles de Coverley; the *Cosmos Book of Stars and Calendars*; and Vernon Trevor's short stories, *Raise me up Samuel*. Wexford wondered if he would ever have time to read them, but he enjoyed looking at them, their handsome glossy jackets, and smelling the civilised, aromatic, slightly acrid print smell of them. At ten he phoned Amyas Ireland, thanked him for the present and said he had read *Poison at Paraleash*.

'We can talk about it?'

'Sure. I'll be at home all Saturday and Sunday.'

'Let me take you and Mrs Wexford out to dinner on Saturday night,' said Ireland.

But Dora refused. She would be an embarrassment

to both of them, she said, they would have their talk much better without her, and she would spend the evening at home having a shot at making a coil pot on her own. So Wexford went alone to meet Ireland in the bar of the Olive and Dove.

'I suppose,' he said, accepting a glass of Moselle, 'that we can dispense with the fiction that you wanted me to read this book to check on police methods and court procedure? Not to put too fine a point on it, you were apprehensive Gandolph might have been up to his old tricks again?'

'Oh, well now, come,' said Ireland. He seemed thinner than ever. He looked about him, he looked at Wexford, made a face, wrinkling up nose and mouth. 'Well, if you must put it like that — yes.'

'There may not have been any tricks, though, may there? Paxton couldn't have murdered James Conyngford, but that doesn't mean he didn't tell Gandolph he did murder him. Certainly the people who give Gandolph information seem to die very conveniently soon afterwards. He picks on the dying, first Paxton, then Lina Hurst. I suppose you've seen this diary?'

'Oh, yes. We shall be using prints of the two relevant pages among the illustrations.'

'No possibility of forgery?'

Ireland looked unhappy. 'Ada Hurst wrote a very stylised hand, what's called a *ronde* hand, which she had obviously taught herself. It would be easy to forge. I can't submit it to handwriting experts, can I? I'm not a policeman. I'm just a poor publisher who very much wants to publish this reappraisal of the Winchurch case if it's genuine – and shun it like the plague if it's not.'

'I think it's genuine.' Wexford smiled at the slight lightening in Ireland's face. 'I take it that it was usual for Ada Hurst to leave blanks as she did for March 2nd and March 5th?'

Ireland nodded. 'Quite usual. Every month there'd have been half a dozen days on which she made no entries.' A waiter came up to them with two large menus. 'I'll have the *bouillabaisse* and the lamb *en croûte* and the *médaillon* potatoes and french beans.'

'Consommé and then the parma ham,' said Wexford austerely. When the waiter had gone he grinned at Ireland. 'Pity they don't do *Filets de hareng marinés à la Rosette*. It might have provided us with the authentic atmosphere.' He was silent for a moment, savouring the delicate tangy wine. 'I'm assuming you've checked that 1900 genuinely was a Leap Year?'

'All first years of a century are.'

Wexford thought about it. 'Yes, of course, all years divisible by four are Leap Years.'

'I must say it's a great relief to me you're so happy about it.'

'I wouldn't quite say that,' said Wexford.

They went into the dining room and were shown, at Ireland's request, to a sheltered corner table. A waiter brought a bottle of Château de Portets 1973. Wexford looked at the basket of rolls, croissants, little plump brioches, miniature wholemeal loaves, Italian sticks, swallowed his desire and refused with an abrupt shake of the head. Ireland took two croissants.

'What exactly do you mean?' he said.

'It strikes me as being odd,' said the chief inspector, 'that in the entry for February 29th Ada Hurst says that her brother destroyed twenty rats with strychnine, yet in the entry for March 1st that Compton, whom I take to be the gardener, is still complaining about the rats. Why wasn't he told how effective the strychnine had been? Hadn't he been taken into Fenton's confidence about the poisoning? Or was twenty only a very small percentage of the hordes of rats which infested the place?'

'Right. It is odd. What else?'

'I don't know why, on March 6th, she mentions Fenton's returning for the cigar case. It wasn't interesting and she was limited for space. She doesn't record the name of a single guest at the dinner party, doesn't say what any of the women wore, but she carefully notes that her brother had left his cigar case in the Paraleash House dining room and had to go back for it. Why does she?'

'Oh, surely because by now she's nervous whenever Frank is alone with Florence.'

'But he wouldn't have been alone with Florence, Winchurch would have been there.'

They discussed the script throughout the meal, and later pored over it, Ireland with his brandy, Wexford with coffee. Dora had been wise not to come. But the outcome was that the new facts were really new and sound and that Carlyon Brent could safely publish the book in the spring. Wexford got home to find Dora sitting with a wobbly-looking half-finished coil pot beside her and deep in the *Cosmos Book of Stars and Calendars*.

'Reg, did you know that for the Greeks the year began on Midsummer Day? And that the Chinese and Jewish calendars have twelve months in some years and thirteen in others?'

'I can't say I did.'

'We avoid that, you see, by using the Gregorian Calendar and correct the error by making every fourth year a Leap Year. You really must read this book, it's fascinating.'

But Wexford's preference was for the Vassili Vandrian and the farming trilogy, though with little time to read he hadn't completed a single one of these works by the time Burden returned on the following Monday week. Burden had a fine even tan but for his nose which had peeled.

'Have a good time?' asked Wexford with automatic politeness.

'What a question,' said the inspector, 'to ask a man who has just come back from his honeymoon. Of course I had a good time.' He cautiously scratched his nose. 'What have you been up to?'

'Seeing something of your brother-in-law. He got me to read a manuscript.'

'Ha!' said Burden. 'I know what that was. He said something about it but he knew Gandolph'd get short shrift from me. A devious liar if ever there was one. It beats me what sort of satisfaction a man can get out of the kind of fame that comes from foisting on the public stories he *knows* aren't true. All that about Paxton was a pack of lies, and I've no doubt he bases this new version of the Winchurch case on another pack of lies. He's not interested in the truth. He's only interested in being known as the great criminologist and the man who shows the police up for fools.'

'Come on, Mike, that's a bit sweeping. I told Ireland I thought it would be OK to go ahead and publish.'

Burden's face wore an expression that was almost a caricature of sophisticated scathing knowingness. 'Well, of course, I haven't seen it, I can't say. I'm basing my objection to Gandolph on the Paxton affair. Paxton never confessed to any murder and Gandolph knows it.'

'You can't say that for sure.'

Burden sat down. He tapped his fist lightly on the corner of the desk. 'I *can* say. I knew Paxton, I knew him well.'

'I didn't know that.'

'No, it was years back, before I came here. In Eastbourne, it was, when Paxton was with the Garfield gang. In the force down there we knew it was useless ever trying to get Paxton to talk. He *never* talked. I don't mean he just didn't give away any info, I mean he didn't answer when you spoke to him. Various times we tried to interrogate him he just maintained this total silence. A mate of his told me he'd made it a rule not to talk to policemen or social workers or lawyers or any what you might call establishment people, and he never had. He talked to his wife and his kids and his mates all right. But I remember once he was in the dock at Lewes Assizes and the judge addressed him. He just didn't answer – he wouldn't – and the judge, it was old Clydesdale, sent him down for contempt. So don't tell me Paxton made any sort of confession to Kenneth Gandolph, not *Paxton*.'

The effect of this was to reawaken all Wexford's former doubts. He trusted Burden, he had a high opinion of his opinion. He began to wish he had advised Ireland to have tests made to determine the age of the ink used in the 29 February and 6 March entries, or to have the writing examined by a handwriting expert. Yet if Ada Hurst had had a stylised hand self-taught in adulthood . . . What good were handwriting experts anyway? Not much, in his experience. And of course Ireland couldn't suggest to Gandolph that the ink should be tested without offending the man to such an extent that he would refuse publication of *Poison at Paraleash* to Carlyon Brent. But Wexford was suddenly certain that those entries were false and that Gandolph had forged them. Very subtly and cunningly he had forged them, having judged that the addition to the diary of just thirty-four words would alter the whole balance of the Winchurch case and shift the culpability from Florence to her lover.

Thirty-four words. Wexford had made a copy of the diary entries and now he looked at them again. 29 February: *F destroyed twenty rats with strychnine from his dispensary. What a relief!* 6 March: *F left cigar case in the dining room, went back after seeing me home. I hope and pray there is no harm.* There were no anachronisms – men certainly used cigar cases in 1900 – no divergence from Ada's usual style. The word 'twenty' was written in letters instead of two figures. The writer, on 6 March, had written not about that day but about the day before. Did that amount to anything? Wexford thought not, though he pondered on it for most of the day.

That evening he was well into the last chapter of *Put*

Money in Thy Purse when the phone rang. It was Jenny Burden. Would he and Dora come to dinner on Saturday? Her parents would be there and her brother.

Wexford said Dora was out at her pottery class, but yes, they would love to, and had she had a nice time in Crete?

'How sweet of you to ask,' said the bride. 'No one else has. Thank you, we had a lovely time.'

He had meant it when he said they would love to, but still he didn't feel very happy about meeting Amyas Ireland again. He had a notion that once the book was published some as yet unimagined Warren or Burden would turn up and denounce it, deride it, laugh at the glaring giveaway he and Ireland couldn't see. When he saw Ireland again he ought to say, don't do it, don't take the risk, publish and be damned can have another meaning than the popular one. But how to give such a warning with no sound reason for giving it, with nothing but one of those vague feelings, this time of foreboding, which had so assisted him yet run him into so much trouble in the past? No, there was nothing he could do. He sighed, finished his chapter and moved on to the farmer's fictionalised memoirs.

Afterwards Wexford was in the habit of saying that he got more reading done during that week than he had in years. Perhaps it had been a way of escape from fretful thought. But certainly he had passed a freakishly slack week, getting home most nights by six. He even read Miss Camilla Barnet's *The Golden Reticule*, and by Friday night there was nothing left but the *Cosmos Book of Stars and Calendars*.

* * *

It was a large party, Mr and Mrs Ireland and their son, Burden's daughter Pat, Grace and her husband and, of course, the Burdens themselves. Jenny's face glowed with happiness and Aegean sunshine. She welcomed the Wexfords with kisses and brought them drinks served in their own wedding present to her.

The meeting with Amyas Ireland wasn't the embarrassment Wexford had feared it would be – had feared, that is, up till a few minutes before he and Dora had left home. And now he knew that he couldn't contain himself till after dinner, till the morning, or perhaps worse than that – a phone call on Monday morning. He asked his hostess if she would think him very rude if he spoke to her brother alone for five minutes.

She laughed. 'Not rude at all. I think you must have got the world's most wonderful idea for a crime novel and Ammy's going to publish it. But I don't know where to put you unless it's the kitchen. And you,' she said to her brother, 'are not to eat anything, mind.'

'I couldn't wait,' Wexford said as they found themselves stowed away into the kitchen where every surface was necessarily loaded with the constituents of dinner for ten people. 'I only found out this evening at the last minute before we were due to come out.'

'It's something about the Winchurch book?'

Wexford said eagerly, 'It's not too late, is it? I was worried I might be too late.'

'Good God, no. We hadn't planned to start printing before the autumn.' Ireland, who had seemed about to disobey his sister and help himself to a macaroon from a silver dish, suddenly lost his appetite. 'This is serious?'

'Wait till you hear. I was waiting for my wife to finish dressing.' He grinned. 'You should make it a rule to read your own books, you know. That's what I was doing, reading one of those books you sent me, and that's where I found it. You won't be able to publish *Poison at Paraleash*.' The smile went and he looked almost fierce. 'I've no hesitation in saying Kenneth Gandolph is a forger and a cheat and you'd be advised to have nothing to do with him in future.'

Ireland's eyes narrowed. 'Better know it now than later. What did he do and how do you know?'

From his jacket pocket Wexford took the copy he had made of the diary entries. 'I can't prove that the last entry, the one for March 6th that says, *F left cigar case in the dining room, went back after seeing me home,* I can't prove that's forged, I only think it is. What I know for certain is a forgery is the entry for February 29th.'

'Isn't that the one about strychnine?'

'*F destroyed twenty rats with strychnine from his dispensary. What a relief!*'

'How do you know it's forged?'

'Because the day itself didn't occur,' said Wexford. 'In 1900 there was no February 29th, it wasn't a Leap Year.'

'Oh yes, it was. We've been through all that before.' Ireland sounded both relieved and impatient. 'All years divisible by four are Leap Years. All century years are divisible by four and 1900 was a century year. 1897 was the year she began the diary, following 1896 which was a Leap Year. Needless to say, there was no February 29th in 1897, 1898 or 1899 so there must have been one in 1900.'

'It wasn't a Leap Year,' said Wexford. 'Didn't I tell you I found this out through that book of yours, the *Cosmos Book of Stars and Calendars*? There's a lot of useful information in there, and one of the bits of information is about how Pope Gregory composed a new civil calendar to correct the errors of the Julian Calendar. One of his rulings was that every fourth year should be a Leap Year except in certain cases . . .'

Ireland interrupted him. 'I don't believe it!' he said in the voice of someone who knows he believes every word.

Wexford shrugged. He went on, 'Century years were not to be Leap Years unless they were divisible not by four but by four hundred. Therefore, 1600 would have been a Leap Year if the Gregorian Calendar had by then been adopted, and 2000 will be a Leap Year, but 1800 was not and 1900 was not. So in 1900 there was no February 29th and Ada Hurst left the space on that page blank for the very good reason that the day following February 28th was March 1st. Unluckily for him, Gandolph, like you and me and most people, knew nothing of this as otherwise he would surely have inserted his strychnine entry into the blank space of March 2nd and his forgery might never have been discovered.'

Ireland slowly shook his head at the man's ingenuity and perhaps his chicanery. 'I'm very grateful to you. We should have looked fools, shouldn't we?'

'I'm glad Florence wasn't hanged in error,' Wexford said as they went back to join the others. 'Her marriage didn't begin with dearly beloved, but if she was afraid at the end it can't have been with any amazement.'

Ruth Rendell, *under her own name and as Barbara Vine, has won both critical and popular acclaim for her achievement in showing the rich potential of the crime novel. Her first book about the Kingsmarkham policeman Reg Wexford*, From Doon With Death, *appeared in 1964. Her non-series novels under her own name include* A Demon in my View, *which won the CWA Gold Dagger in 1976, and* A Judgement in Stone. Lake of Darkness *won the Arts Council National Book Award for Genre Fiction in 1981. The much-praised Vine novels include* A Fatal Inversion *(another CWA Gold Dagger winner) and* The Brimstone Wedding. *She was awarded the CWA Cartier Diamond Dagger in 1991.*

JULIAN SYMONS

The Tigers of Subtopia

It began with the telephone call from Miriam. 'Bradley,' she said, 'there are some boys outside.'

Bradley Fawcett recognised in his wife's voice the note of hysteria that was occasionally discernible nowadays. It's the menopause, Dr Brownlow had said, you must be patient with her. So now his voice took on a consciously patient tone, a talking-to-Miriam tone it might have been called, although he did not think of it in that way.

'Friends of Paul's, you mean?'

'No. Oh, no. Beastly boys. Louts. They took his sweets.'

'Took his sweets,' Brad echoed stupidly. He stared at the contract on the desk in front of him.

'They asked him for them and he gave them one or two, and then they knocked them out of his hand.' She ended on a rising note.

Had she telephoned the office simply to tell him this? Patiently he said, 'Calm down now, Miriam. Is Paul upset?'

'No, he's – but they're outside, you see, they're still outside.' There was a sound that could have been

445

interpreted as a kind of tinkling crack and then he heard her shriek, 'They've broken the glass!'

'What glass?'

'The living room – our beautiful living-room window.'

Brad put down the telephone a couple of minutes later, feeling hot and angry. He had not rung the police because they would have come round and talked to Miriam, and he knew that would upset her. The window itself was not important, although he would have to put in a large and expensive sheet of plate glass, but this was not the first trouble they had had with hooligans in The Oasis.

Geoff Cooper's garage wall had been daubed one night with filthy phrases, and on another occasion the flowers in the middle of one of the green areas had been uprooted and strewn around as though by some great animal; on a third occasion the sandpit in the children's playground had been filled with bits of broken glass, and one little boy had cut his foot quite badly.

It was the senselessness of such acts that irritated Brad, as he said to his companions in the train, on the way back from the city to Dunkerley Green. The journey was a short one, no more than twenty minutes, but there were four of them who always made it together. The trains they caught – the 9.12 in the morning and the 6.18 at night – were never crowded, and they preferred the relaxation of sitting in the train to the tension of driving through the traffic.

Geoff Cooper, Peter Stone, and Porky Leighton all lived in The Oasis, and they had other things in common. Cooper was an accountant, Stone ran a travel agency,

Porky Leighton was in business as a builder's merchant, and Brad himself was one of the directors of an engineering firm. They all dressed rather similarly for going into the city, in suits of discreet pinstripe or of plain clerical grey. Porky, who had been a rugger international in his youth, wore a striped tie, but the neckwear of the other three was sober.

They all thought of themselves as professional men, and they all appreciated the civilised amenities of life in The Oasis. Brad, who had passed the age of fifty, was the oldest of them by a decade. He liked to feel that they looked to him for counsel, that he was the elder statesman of their little group. He felt the faintest twinge of annoyance that it should have been Geoff Cooper who mentioned the idea of a Residents' Committee. The others took it up so enthusiastically that it seemed incumbent on him to express doubts.

'Forgive me for saying it, Geoff, but just how would it help?'

'Look, Brad, let's start from the point that we're not going to put up with this sort of thing any longer. Right?' That was Porky. He wiped his red face with a handkerchief, for it was hot in the carriage. 'And then let's go on to say that the police can't do a damned thing to help us.'

'I don't know about that.' Brad was never at ease with Porky. It seemed to him that there was an unwelcome undercurrent of mockery in the man-to-man straightforwardness with which Porky spoke to him.

'You know what the police were like when Geoff had that trouble with his garage wall.'

447

'Told me that if I could say who'd done it they would take action.' Geoff Cooper snorted. 'A lot of use that was.'

'The fact is, The Oasis is a private estate and, let's face it, the police don't mind too much what happens. If you want something done, do it yourself, that's my motto.' That was Porky again.

'Half the trouble is caused by television,' Peter Stone said in his thin fluting voice. 'There are programmes about them every night, these young toughs. They get puffed up, think they're important. I saw one this week – do you know what it was called? *The Tigers of Youth.*'

Geoff snorted again. Porky commented, 'You can tame tigers.'

'Nevertheless,' Brad said. It was a phrase he often used when he wanted to avoid committing himself.

'Are you against it? A Committee, I mean,' Geoff asked.

'I believe there must be some other way of dealing with the problem. I feel sure it would be a good idea to sleep on it.'

Did he catch an ironic glance from Porky to the others? He could not be sure. The train drew into Dunkerley Green. Five minutes' walk, and they had reached The Oasis.

There were gates at the entrance to the estate, and a sign asking drivers to be careful because children might be playing. There were green strips in front of the houses, and these strips were protected by stone bollards with chains between them. The houses were set back behind small front lawns, and each house had a rear garden. And

448

although the houses were all of the same basic construction, with integral garages and a large through room that went from front to back, with a picture window at each end, there were delightful minor differences – like the basement garden room in Brad's house, which in Geoff's house was a small laundry room, and in Porky's had been laid out as a downstairs kitchen.

Brad's cousin, an architect from London, had once burst into a guffaw when he walked round the estate and saw the bollards and chains. 'Subtopia in Excelsis,' he had said, but Brad didn't really mind. If this was Subtopia, as he said to Miriam afterwards, then Subtopia was one of the best places in England to live.

He had expected to be furiously angry when he saw the broken window, but in fact the hole was so small, the gesture of throwing a stone seemed so pathetic, that he felt nothing at all. When he got indoors, Miriam was concerned to justify her telephone call. She knew that he did not like her to phone him at the office.

'I told them to go away and they just stood there, just stood laughing at me.'

'How many of them?'

'Three.'

'What did they look like?'

'The one in the middle was big. They called him John. He was the leader.'

'But what did they—'

'Oh, I don't know,' she said impatiently. 'They all looked the same – you know those ghastly clothes they wear, tight trousers and pointed shoes. I didn't go near them. I called out that I was going to phone the police, and then I came in and spoke to you. Why should they *do* such a thing, Bradley, that's what I don't understand.'

She was the only person who called him by his full Christian name, and he had sometimes thought that it typified the nature of their relationship, without knowing quite what that meant. It always seemed, too, that he talked rather more pontifically than usual in Miriam's presence, as though she expected it of him.

'It's a natural youthful impulse to defy authority,' he said now. 'And when you told them you were going to call the police – why, then they threw the stone.'

She began to cry. It did not stop her talking. 'You're making it sound as if *I* were in the wrong. But I did nothing, *nothing*!'

'Of course you're not in the wrong. I'm just explaining.'

'What harm have we ever done to them?'

'No harm. It's just that you may find it easier if you try to understand them.'

'Well, I can't. And I don't *want* to understand.' She paused, and said something that astonished him. 'Paul knows them. They're his friends.'

That was not strictly true, as he discovered when he talked to Paul. They sat in the boy's bedroom, which was full of ingenious space-saving devices, like a shelf which swung out to become a table top. Paul was sitting at this now, doing school work. He seemed to think the whole thing was a fuss about nothing.

'Honestly, Dad, nothing would have happened. We were playing around and Fatty knocked the sweets out of my hand, and it just so happened that Mum had come to the door and saw it. You know what she's like – she let fly.'

'Fatty? You know them?'

'Well, they come and play sometimes down on the common, and they let us play with them.'

The common was a piece of waste ground nearby, on which Paul sometimes played football and cricket. There was no provision in The Oasis for any kind of ball game.

'Are they friends of yours?'

Paul considered this. He was a handsome boy, rather small for his thirteen years, compact in body and curiously self-contained. At least, Brad thought it was curious; he was intermittently worried by the fact that he could not be sure what Paul was thinking.

Now, after consideration, Paul replied, 'I shouldn't say friends. Acquaintances.'

'They don't sound like the sort of boys your mother and I would welcome as your friends.' Paul said nothing to this. 'You were playing with them this afternoon?'

It was all wrong, Brad felt, that he should have to drag the information out of Paul by asking questions. A boy and his father should exchange confidences easily and naturally, but it had never been like that with them.

By direct questioning, of the kind that he felt shouldn't be necessary, he learned that they had been playing football. When they had finished these three boys walked back with Paul to The Oasis. On the way Paul had bought the sweets. Why had they walked back? he asked. Surely they didn't live in Dunkerley Green? Paul shook his head.

451

'They live in Denholm.'

Brad carefully avoided comment. Denholm was a part of the city that he had visited only two or three times in his life. It contained the docks and a good many factories, and also several streets of dubious reputation.

It would have been against Brad's principles to say that he did not want his son going about with boys from Denholm. Instead, he asked, 'Why did they come up here with you? I don't understand that.' Paul muttered something, and Brad repeated rather sharply, 'Why, Paul, why?'

Paul raised his head and looked his father straight in the face. 'John said, "Let's have another look at Snob Hill".'

'Snob Hill,' Brad echoed. 'That's what they call The Oasis?'

'Yes. He said, "Let's see if they've put barbed wire round it yet".'

'Barbed wire?'

'To keep them out.'

Brad felt something – something that might have been a tiny bird – leap inside his stomach. With intentional brutality he went on, 'You live here. On Snob Hill. I'm surprised they have anything to do with you.'

Paul muttered again, so that the words were only just audible.

'They think I'm OK.'

Brad gripped his son's shoulder, felt the fine bones beneath his hand. 'You think it's all right for them to throw stones, to break windows?'

'Of course I don't.'

'This John, what's his last name?'

'Baxter.'

'Where does he live?'

'I don't know.' Paul hesitated, then said, 'I expect he'll be in The Club.'

'The Club?'

'They go there most nights.'

'Where is it?'

'East Street.'

A horrifying thought occurred to Brad. 'Have you been there?'

'They say I'm too young.' Paul stopped, then said, 'Dad.'

'Yes?'

'I shouldn't go there. It won't do any good.' With an effort, as though he were explaining, saying something that made sense, he added, 'You won't like it.'

In the time that it took to drive to Denholm, the bird that had been fluttering in Brad's stomach had quieted down. He was, as he often said, a liberal with a small 'l'. He believed that there was no problem which could not be solved by discussion round a table, and that you should always make an effort to see the other fellow's point of view.

The trip by car gave him time to think about his own attitude, and to admit that he had been a bit unreasonable. He could understand that these boys held a sort of glamour for Paul; could even understand to a certain extent their feelings about The Oasis. And just because he understood, it would be silly, it would even be cowardly not to face them and talk to them.

Much of Denholm was dark, but East Street blazed with neon light. There seemed to be a dozen clubs of various kinds, as well as several cafés, and he had to ask for The Club. He did so at first without success, then a boy giggled and said that he was standing almost in front of it.

As Brad descended steps to a basement and advanced towards a wall of syncopated sound, he felt for the first time a doubt about the wisdom of his mission.

The door was open, and he entered a low-ceilinged cellar room. At the far end of it four boys were singing or shouting on a raised platform. In front of him couples moved, most of them not holding each other, but gyrating in strange contortions that he had never seen before except in one or two television programmes.

The atmosphere was remarkably clear. Well, at least most of them are non-smokers, he thought, and was pleased that he hadn't lost his sense of humour. He spoke to a boy who was standing by a wall.

'Can you tell me where to find John Baxter?'

The boy stared at him, and Brad repeated the question.

'John?' The boy gave Brad a long deliberate look, from face to shoes. Then somebody tapped Brad's shoulder from behind. He turned to face a fat boy wearing a purple shirt, jeans, and elastic-sided shoes.

The fat boy muttered something lewd.

His other shoulder was tapped. A boy with bad teeth grinned at him. 'You want the john?'

The first boy, not the fat one, tapped him, repeating the lewd remark.

The fat boy tapped him again. 'It's just looking at you. This way.' He walked slowly round Brad, staring at him. ''Cause we never seen nothing so square before, get it?'

As Brad looked at the clothes of the three boys around him, clothes that were different in several ways and yet were identical in the brightness of their shirts, the tightness of their jeans, and the pointedness of their shoes, he had the ridiculous feeling that it was he and not they who was outraging orthodoxy, that his neat dark suit and well-polished square-toed shoes were badges of singularity, the clothing of an outlaw.

The sensation lasted for only a moment. Then he shouted – he had to shout, because the tribal music rose suddenly to a louder beat – 'I want John Baxter.'

The boy with the bad teeth tapped him. 'You ask for the john, then you don't pay attention. I don't like that, not polite. I'm John.'

Brad faced him. 'You are? You're the John who—'

The fat boy said, 'You heard that, he said you're the john. You going to take that?'

The three of them had closed in so that they were now almost touching him, and he thought incredulously: they're going to attack me. Then a voice said, 'Break it up, come on now, break it up.'

The three boys moved back, and a stocky man with thick eyebrows and arms like marrows said, 'Whatcher want?' Brad found it hard to speak. The man went on, 'They're blocked. You don't want to get mixed up with 'em when they're blocked.'

'Blocked?' It was a new country, a new language.

'I'm here if there's trouble, but they're no trouble – it's you that's making trouble, mister.'

'I didn't – that's not true.'

'So they're blocked, they feel good, have fun, what's the harm? You don't belong, mister. They don't like you so why don't you just get out?'

He could just hear himself say *all right, all right.* Then there was a small scream from the dance floor, and a girl cried, 'He hit me!' The bouncer began to push his way through the crowd on the dance floor.

Brad stumbled away, eager to go, and had almost reached the outer door when there was one more tap on his shoulder. He turned again, putting up his fists. A tall dark boy he had not seen before asked, 'Want me?'

The boy was dressed like the others, but there was something different about him – a kind of authority and even arrogance.

'You're John Baxter?'

'What do you want?'

Behind him was the fat boy who said now, with a hint of silly irrational laughter in his voice, 'He says he wants John, see, so we're—'

'Shut it, Fatty,' the dark boy said. The fat boy stopped talking.

'I'm Bradley Fawcett.'

'Should I care?'

'I'm the father of the boy—' He stopped, began again. 'You threw a stone and broke our window.'

'I did?' The boy sounded politely surprised. 'Can you prove it?'

'You did it, isn't that so? My wife would recognise you.'

'I tell you what,' the dark boy said. 'You got a suspicious mind. You don't want to go around saying things like that – might get you into trouble.'

A fair-haired girl came up, pulled at the tall dark boy's arm. 'Come on, John.'

'Later, Jean. Busy.' He did not stop looking at Brad.

In Brad's stomach the bird was fluttering again, a bird of anger. He said carefully, 'I believe you call the place where I live Snob Hill—'

The boy laughed. 'It's a good name for it.'

'I've come to warn you and your friends to keep away from it. And keep away from my son.'

Fatty crowed in a falsetto voice, 'Don't touch my darling boy.'

'Do I make myself clear?'

'John,' the girl said, 'Don't let's have any trouble. Please.'

The tall dark boy looked Brad up and down. Then smiled. 'We do what we like. It's a free country, they say, and if we want to come up to Snob Hill, see your son, we do it. But I'll tell you what – we'd like to make you happy. If you haven't got the money to pay for the window' – Brad raised a hand in protest, but it was ignored – 'we'll have a whip-round in The Club here. How's that?'

He laughed, and behind him came the sound of other laughter, sycophantic and foolish. They were all laughing at Brad, and it was hard now to control the bird that leaped inside him. He would have liked to smash the sneering face in front of him with his fist.

But what he did in fact was to run up the steps to

the street, get into his car, slam it into gear, and drive hurriedly away. It was as though some fury were pursuing him; but there was no fury, nothing worse than the sound – which he continued to hear in his ears during most of the drive home – of that mocking laughter.

When he opened the living-room door their faces were all turned to him – Porky's, Geoff's, Peter's, eager and expectant. He stared at the three of them with a kind of hostility, even though they were his friends. Geoff was their spokesman.

'We were talking again, Brad, about that idea.'

'Idea?' He went over and poured whisky.

'The Residents' Committee. We all think it's pretty good, something we should have done a long while ago. We came to ask if you'd let us nominate you for chairman.'

'Brad!' That was Miriam, who had come in from the kitchen with coffee on a tray. 'Whatever are you doing?'

'What?' Then he realised that he had poured whisky for himself without offering it to his guests. He said, 'Sorry,' and filled their glasses. Porky was watching him with the ironical gaze.

'Hear you bearded the tigers on your own, Brad. How did it go?'

Miriam asked in a high voice, 'Did you see them? Are they going to pay for the window?'

'I saw them. They're louts, hooligans.'

'Of course they are,' Peter fluted.

'I told them some home truths, but it's impossible to talk to them. They—' But he found that he could not go into the humiliating details. 'They've got a kind of club. I saw them there, and I met the ringleader. I shall go to the police tomorrow morning.'

Porky stared at him, but said nothing. Geoff threw up his hands. 'You won't get anywhere with the police.'

Miriam came over to him. 'They *will* do something? Surely we've got a right to protection. We don't have to let them do what they like, do we? They frighten me, Bradley.'

'The best form of protection is self-protection,' Porky said, and expanded on it. 'We've got the nucleus of a Residents' Committee right here. We can easily get another dozen to join us, mount guard at night, look after our own properties. And if we find these tigers, we'll know how to deal with them.'

Miriam looked at Brad inquiringly. It seemed to him that they all waited on his judgement. Just for a moment a picture came into his mind – the picture of a tiger with the dark sneering face of John Baxter, a tiger being hunted through the gardens of The Oasis. Then the picture vanished as though a shutter had been placed over it. What was all this nonsense about tigers?

Brad Fawcett, a liberal with a small 'l', began to speak. 'I think we should be extremely careful about this. I'm not saying it isn't a good idea; I think it is, and I'm inclined to agree that it should have been set up long ago. But I do say we ought to think more carefully about ways and means. There are lots of aspects to it, but essentially it's a community project, and since you've been good enough to come to me, may I suggest that the first step is to sound out our fellow residents and see how many of them like the idea . . .'

As he went on he found that verbalisation brought him self-assurance, as it did when he got up to speak as chairman of the Rotary Club. He was not disturbed by the unwinking stare of Porky's little eyes, and if Geoff Cooper looked bored and Peter Stone disappointed, he pretended not to notice it.

They talked for another half hour and drank some more whisky, and by the time the others said good night, see you on the 9.12, the recollection of the visit to Denholm had become no more than a faint disturbance inside him, like indigestion. It did not become urgent again even when Miriam, gripping him tightly in bed, whispered, 'You *will* go to the police in the morning, won't you?'

Sleepily he said that he would – before he caught his train.

At 11.30 the following morning he was preparing with his secretary, Miss Hornsby, an intricate schedule for a conference to begin at noon. The conference was about the installation of new boilers, and his mind was full of maintenance costs when he picked up the telephone.

Miriam's voice asked, 'What did they say?'

For a moment he did not know what she was talking about, so utterly had he shut away that unsatisfactory interview at the police station. Then he remembered.

'The police? They seemed to think we were making a mountain out of a molehill. Perhaps they were right.'

'But what did they *say*?'

'They said if we could identify the boy who broke the window—'

'We can,' she said triumphantly. 'Paul can. He knows them.'

'They explained that it would mean Paul being the chief witness. He would be examined, perhaps cross-examined, in court. We don't want that, do we?'

In her high voice she said, 'I suppose not.'

'Of course we don't. At the moment he's taken it quite calmly. I can't think of anything worse than dragging him through the courts.'

'No.' There was silence. Miss Hornsby raised her eyebrows, pointed at her watch. With the note of hysteria in her voice, Miriam said, 'I'm sorry to bother you—'

'It's all right. I should have phoned you, but I've had a lot of work piled up, still have.'

'Isn't there *anything* the police can do?'

'I've told you what they said.' He was patient; he kept the irritation out of his voice. 'We'll talk about it later.'

'What time will you be home? Can you come home early?'

Still patiently, speaking as though to a child, he said, 'I have to go into conference at noon, and I don't know when I shall be free. I won't be able to take any phone calls. Pull yourself together, Miriam, and stop worrying.'

As he put down the receiver he saw Miss Hornsby's eyes fixed speculatively on him. He felt guilty, but what had he said that was wrong or untrue? Paul had been tremendously cheerful at breakfast, and had gone off in high spirits. As for the police, the Sergeant had as good as said they had more important crimes to worry about than a broken window. Brad sighed, and returned to the schedule.

He came out of the conference six hours later, feeling tight and tense all over. The client had queried almost everything in the estimate, from the siting of the boilers to the cost of the material used for lining them. He had finally agreed to revise the whole plan. Miss Hornsby had sat in, making notes, but when he got back to his room her assistant, a scared-looking girl, came in.

'Your wife telephoned, Mr Fawcett. Three times. She said it was very important, but you'd said nothing at all must be put through, so—'

'All right. Get her for me.'

'I hope I did right.'

'Just get her for me, will you?'

Half a minute later Miriam's voice, in his ear, was crying, 'They've got him, they've got him, Bradley – he's gone!'

'What are you talking about?'

'Paul. He's not come home from school. He's an hour and a half late.'

'Have you called the school?'

'Oh, yes, yes,' she cried, as though eager to get as quickly as possible through all such silly questions and force on him realisation of what had happened. 'I've spoken to them. He left at the usual time. I've been down to the common, he hasn't been there, I've done everything. Don't you see, Bradley, those boys have *taken* him. After you went to see them last night, this is their – their revenge.'

He saw again John Baxter's face, dark and sneering;

he remembered the things that had been said in The Club; he knew that the words she spoke were true. Heavily he said, 'Yes. Leave it to me.'

'Bradley, what are they doing to my little boy?'

'He's my boy too,' he said. 'I'll get him back. Leave it to me.'

When he had hung up he sat for a moment, and felt the bird leaping in his belly again. You try to treat them decently, he thought, you try to be reasonable and discuss things with them, and this is what you get. They are like animals, and you have to treat them like animals. He dialled Porky Leighton's number.

Porky wasted no time in saying, 'I told you so.' He was brisk. 'This calls for action, old man. Agreed?'

'Yes.'

'Right, then. This is what we do . . .'

A thin rain was falling as they pulled up outside The Club. They grouped on the pavement, and Brad pointed down the steps. Porky led the way, the others followed. The door was closed, but it opened when Porky turned the handle. There was no sound of music inside and the room seemed to be empty.

'Nobody here,' Geoff Cooper said disgustedly. Then two figures came out from the other end of the room, behind the band platform.

Brad cried out, 'There he is.'

The four of them advanced on the boy. Porky brought him crashing to the floor with a rugger tackle. There was a short scuffle and then, in a moment it seemed, the boy's hands were tied behind his back.

The boy's companion launched herself at Porky. It was the fair-haired girl who had been with Baxter the previous night. Geoff and Peter held her. She was wearing jeans and a boy's shirt.

'Hard to know if it's a boy or girl,' Peter said. He put his hand on her and laughed on a high note. 'You can just about tell.'

The girl cried out, and Porky turned on Peter. 'Cut it out. None of that – you know what we're here for. We've got no quarrel with you, you aren't going to get hurt,' he said to the girl. He spoke to Baxter. 'You know why we're here.'

The boy spoke for the first time. 'You're off your beat, fatso. Shove off.'

They had gone to The Oasis before coming down here, and changed into the old clothes they wore on weekends for gardening or cleaning the car – clothes so different from their neat daily wear as to be in themselves a kind of uniform. Porky's thick jersey made him look fatter than usual. He was wearing gym shoes, and he balanced himself carefully on his toes.

'Just a few questions, Baxter. Answer them and we won't have any trouble. Where's the gang? Why is the place empty?'

'It's not club night.'

'Why are you here?'

'Cleaning up for tomorrow. What's it to you?'

Porky stuck his red face close to the boy's dark one, jerked a thumb at Brad. 'Know him?'

'That drip. He was in here last night.'

'You know his son. Where is he?'

464

Baxter looked at him with a half sneer, half smile. 'Tucked up in bed – would that be the right answer?'

Brad saw Porky's hand, large as a knuckle of ham, swing back and slap Baxter's face. The bird leaped inside him, throbbed so violently that his chest was tight. There was a ring on Porky's finger, and it had cut the boy's cheek.

'Not the right answer,' Porky said. 'The boy's been kidnapped. By your friends, while you've fixed yourself a pretty little alibi to keep out of trouble. We want to know where he is.'

'I'll tell you what to do.'

'What?'

Baxter sneered. 'Ask a policeman.'

The bird fluttered up into Brad's throat. He moved toward Baxter with his fist raised. He wanted to speak, but he was breathing so hard he could say nothing intelligible.

After that it was all dreamlike. He participated in what was done – binding up the girl's mouth so that she could not cry out, locking the basement door, bundling the boy out into the car; but it did not seem to him that Bradley Fawcett was doing these things. Another person did them – somebody who had been released from Bradley Fawcett's habitual restraints. In this release there was freedom, some kind of freedom.

They had come in his car, and as he drove back he took a hand from the driving wheel and passed it over his face. He was not surprised to find the skin damp, cold, unfamiliar. He absented himself from the presence of the others in the car, and thought about Miriam –

how she had clung to him when he returned, and had begged him to go back to the police.

No, we're going to deal with it ourselves, he had told her quietly and patiently, as he took off his city clothes and put on his weekend ones. Who were 'we'? Porky and the others who had come to the house last night.

'What are you going to do?'

'See them. Find out what they've done with Paul. Get him back.'

'You really think that's best?' Without waiting for him to say yes, she went on, 'You won't do anything to make them hurt Paul, will you?'

The very thought of Paul being hurt had made him feel sick and angry. 'What do you think I am?' he asked, and as he repeated the words he was aware that they were a question – and one to which he could provide no simple answer, as he could have done a few days or even a few hours earlier.

As he was leaving she had come up and held him close to her. 'It's all our fault, isn't it?'

'*Our* fault?'

'Something to do with us. People like us.'

He had stared at her, then disengaged her arms, and left the house.

They took the boy into the garage. His arms were still tied behind his back. The small cut on his cheek had dried. He made no attempt to call for help, or even to speak, but simply looked at them.

'All right,' Porky said. 'That saw bench over there is just the job, Geoff. Agreed?' He had brought in with him from the car a small leather attaché case, and now

466

he took out of it a length of rope. Geoff and Peter bent Baxter over the saw bench.

'Stop,' Bradley Fawcett said. 'What are you doing?'

'He needs a lesson. All agreed on that, aren't we? Let's give him one. Here's teacher.' And now Porky took something else from the attaché case and held it up, laughing. It was a thick leather strap.

As the bird inside him fluttered and leaped and hammered on his chest trying to get out, Bradley Fawcett said in a strange voice, 'We must ask him first. Don't do anything without asking him again first.'

Porky's glance at him was amused, contemptuous, tolerant. 'We've asked already, but let's do it according to Hoyle.' Casually he said to Baxter, 'Where's Paul? What have you done with him?'

Baxter spat out an obscenity. 'If I knew, d'you think I'd tell you?' And he spat out another obscenity.

'Very nice.' Porky savoured the response almost with pleasure. 'You see what we're up against, Brad. He's a tiger. We must show him we're tigers too.'

Brad took no part in stretching the boy over the bench and securing his feet. Instead, he considered wonderingly the garage in which everything was stacked tidily – the mower in one corner with its small bag of spanners beside it; the hoe, rake, garden shears, standing in racks; the packets of grass seed and weed-killer on a shelf; Paul's canoe suspended by pulleys. Surely this was the apparatus of a harmless and a decent life?

Yet he knew that he would never again be able to look at these things without thinking of the intrusion among them of this boy with his insolent manner and

467

his strange clothing – the boy who was now bent over the saw bench with his trousers down around his ankles and some of his flesh visible, while Porky stood to the right of him holding the strap and Geoff tucked the boy's head firmly under his arm.

Brad took no part, but he found himself unable to move or to speak while the bird leaped within him, was quiet, then leaped again in its anxiety to escape as the belt descended and a red mark showed on the white flesh. The bird leaped violently at the sight of that red mark and Brad jerked a hand up in the air – but what did he mean to say with that outstretched hand? Was it a gesture of encouragement or of rejection?

He wondered about this afterwards and was never able to know if the answer he gave was honest; but at the time he could not wonder what the gesture meant for the garage door opened, Paul stood framed in it, and Brad was the first to see him. Brad said nothing, but he made a noise in his throat and pointed, and Porky half turned and lowered the strap.

'Dad,' Paul said. 'Mr Leighton. I saw a light. What are you doing?'

In his voice there was nothing but bewilderment. He had his school cap on, he looked handsome and detached, as an adult might look who had discovered children playing some ridiculous secret game.

Bradley Fawcett ran forward, grabbed his son's arm and shook it, trying to shake him out of that awful detachment, and said in a voice which he was horrified to hear come out as high and hysterical as his wife's, 'Where have you been? What's happened to you?'

'Happened? I went to Ainslie's party. Ainslie Evans, you know him.'

'Why didn't you tell anybody? You've got no right—' He could not think what it was that Paul had no right to do.

'But I did tell – I told Mummy yesterday morning. She must have forgotten.'

Paul took his arm away from his father's hand. He was looking beyond Brad to where Geoff and Peter were untying John Baxter, who drew up his trousers. 'Why were you beating John? Have you kidnapped him or something? Is this your idea of a joke?'

Porky gave a short snarl of laughter.

Paul went on. 'It's something to do with that broken window, isn't it?' Now he faced his father and said deliberately, 'I'll tell you something. I'm glad they broke that window.'

'Paul,' Brad cried out. He held out his hand to his son, but the boy ignored it. Paul stood in the doorway and seemed about to say something decisive, irrevocable. Then the door closed behind him.

John Baxter had his trousers zipped. He looked from one to the other of them. 'It was assault. I could make a case out of it. If I wanted.'

'It was a mistake.' Geoff cleared his throat. 'I don't know about the others, but I don't suppose you'd say no to a fiver.' He took out his wallet.

Peter already had his wallet out.

Porky said, 'Don't be silly.' They stared at him.

'Have you forgotten who he is? He's the little punk who daubs garages and breaks windows. What are you

469

giving him fivers for – to come back and do it again?'
When he spoke to John Baxter, the cords of his thick
neck showed clearly. 'You were lucky. You just got a little
taste of what's good for you. Next time it might be more
than a taste, eh, Brad?'

'It's done now,' Brad said mechanically. He was not
thinking of the boy, but of the look on Paul's face.

'Don't worry,' Baxter said. 'You can stuff your money.
But next time you come our way, look out.'

'We won't—' Geoff began to say.

'Because next time we'll be ready for you, and we'll
cut you. So look out.'

Then the garage door closed behind him too, and
Porky was saying with a slight laugh, as he snapped his
attaché case, 'All's well that ends well, no harm done,
but you certainly want to be careful of what your wife
says, Brad old man.'

The bird fluttered again within him, and he found
relief in shouting, 'Shut up!'

Peter Stone fluted at him, 'I think you're being
unreasonable. We were doing it for you.'

'Get out!' Brad held open the door. Outside was
darkness.

'You're overwrought.' Porky was smiling. 'A good
night's sleep's what you need, Brad old man.'

They walked away down the path, Porky with a slight
swagger, Peter Stone with an air of being the injured
party. Geoff Cooper was last. He gave Brad's arm a slight
squeeze and said, 'You're upset. I don't blame you. See
you on the 9.12.'

I never want to see you again; you have made me do things

470

I never intended – things I know to be unworthy: those were the words he cried out in his mind, but they remained unspoken.

He stood there for some minutes after the sound of their footsteps faded, and looked at the light in the house which showed that Miriam was waiting to receive him in a gush of apologetic tears; and as he stood there he came slowly to the realisation that Porky was right in saying no harm had been done.

A young tough had got a stripe on his backside, and very likely it would do him good. And as for Paul, it was absurd to think that what he had seen would affect him, or their relationship, permanently.

Bradley Fawcett's thoughts drifted away, and suddenly he found that instead of being concerned with Paul he was reliving that moment in which leather struck flesh and the bird had leaped violently, passionately, ecstatically, within him.

As he dismissed these thoughts and walked over to the house and the lighted window, he reflected that of course he would catch the 9.12 in the morning. There was for him, after all, no other train to take.

Julian Symons (1912–94), *who was awarded the CWA Cartier Diamond Dagger in 1990, achieved excellence not only as a crime novelist but also as a critic, biographer and historian.* The Colour of Murder *won the CWA Gold Dagger in 1957, and many of his later books showed a mastery of the psychological crime novel: examples include* The Man Whose Dreams Came True, The

Players and the Game *and* Death's Darkest Face. *Of his historical mysteries,* Sweet Adelaide *(1980) is noteworthy, but it may be that his most lasting contribution to the genre is* Bloody Murder, *a history of the genre which ran into three editions and has never been surpassed.*

MARGARET YORKE

Mugs

He was such a nice young man.

Mildred Cox had been instructed by Tricia, her daughter, never to let anyone she didn't know into her house,
but Mr Bryan – Nick, as later he asked her to call him
– was different. He wasn't 'anyone'. For one thing, he
wore a suit, a dark grey one like her son-in-law wore
to the office. His tie was prettily floral – so modern, just
like those of some newscasters on television and not at
all gaudy.

She didn't tell Tricia about Nick's visits, not even
when Tricia noticed the small green Worcester bowl had
gone from the top of the tallboy, nor that she no longer
used her Georgian teaspoons which had been a wedding
present.

The first time he came, she thought he must be someone she ought to recognise – a childhood friend of her
son's, perhaps, or someone who'd been with him on his
last trek from which he never returned. She'd welcomed
him in that spirit, sitting him down with a cup of tea,
hoping a clue to his identity would be revealed without

her asking. They'd discussed the weather, which was not very good that day, raw and windy, and he'd said how nice it was to see a real coal fire. She'd asked where he'd come from and he mentioned Brighton. That was a long way. It must have taken him several hours, she'd remarked.

'Only two,' he'd said, smiling. He had a charming smile. 'The M25, you know.'

She'd not been on it herself, but she knew about it. Choked with traffic it was, every day. You saw that on television.

'You must be tired, then,' she'd said.

He said he was glad of the tea. Two sugars, he took. She used her good Crown Derby cups and saucers, and he admired them.

'You don't often see such fine porcelain being used these days,' he said.

'No,' she agreed. 'It's all mugs, isn't it? But I like to get my better things out now and then.'

'I expect you've got a lot of china you've had a long time,' he suggested, and as soon as he had finished his tea she was showing him her Coalport plates and an engraved spoon that was even older than her teaspoons. He said it might be worth quite a bit. 'Even a tenner,' he said, handing it back. 'I know someone who might like it — a friend of mine's just had a daughter and I'm her godfather. It would make a perfect christening present.' He picked it up again and turned it over, his admiration obvious.

'Take it,' said Mildred, and if he was a friend of Jack's he could have it for nothing.

But he disclaimed Jack. He'd found it didn't do to

pretend acquaintance unless you were sure of your facts, and he didn't know who Jack was.

'I do a bit of collecting myself,' he confided. 'It's my hobby. Sometimes I buy in things I like and sell them on to other collectors, so that I can build up my own special interest — that's porcelain,' he explained. 'But I can place anything good.'

'What a nice hobby,' said Mildred, and poured him out more tea.

By the time he left she had sold him the Worcester bowl and two Staffordshire plates, as well as the spoon, and had received £35 which she put in a Toby jug on the dresser. He'd admired that, too; it bore the face of Sir Winston Churchill, and he said people built up collections, acquiring as many varieties as they could. She'd use the money for something special.

He left, promising to come back if he was in the area again, and he did, several times.

Mildred never discovered exactly what brought him to the locality, since he hadn't come specifically to visit her. She still felt he must somehow be connected with Jack. Maybe he'd tell her eventually.

In December she went to town on the bus. It was a pleasant ride — twenty minutes if the traffic was not too bad. She stepped aboard behind a young man in his early twenties — a nice-looking fellow with well-cut fair hair, spotless jeans and a fresh face. He had only a £20 note for his fare and the driver hadn't got enough change. How lucky he was to have plenty of ready cash, thought Mildred.

'How much is your fare?' she asked, and was told it was £1.60.

'I'll pay,' she said, smiling. If she had a grandson – if Jack had had a son – he might be like this young man.

'I travel free,' she added, showing the driver her pass.

'Are you sure?' The young man was astonished. 'It's very good of you. Thanks.'

'It's your lucky day,' she said.

'It certainly is,' he replied. He couldn't believe it.

'You'll do the same for someone else one day, won't you?' she said, and he nodded.

'Yes – yes, I will,' he agreed, and repeated, 'Thanks,' then swiftly ran up the stairs to the upper floor of the bus.

Millicent sat near the front, watching the road. What a delightful young man. They weren't all yobbos and louts or car thieves and drug addicts. Of course, in terms of charity there were many more deserving cases, but it lay in his power to aid one of them and she hoped he would.

She had come into town to do her Christmas shopping. She had a list with Tricia's name at the top, followed by that of Susie, Tricia's daughter. There were other gifts to buy: presents for friends at the day centre where Mildred, though seventy-nine, was a helper, and the kind librarian who always mentioned it when the latest Maeve Binchy or Rosamund Pilcher was on the returns trolley. They were such good writers, Mildred thought, with characters you would like to meet, unlike those in some of the other novels she had tried. Tricia was easy: a new book about birds, for she was a keen bird-watcher, never happier than when out with binoculars on some bleak hill. Mildred had once given her a beautiful silk blouse in a shade of peacock blue, which would set off her glowing auburn hair and pink-and-white skin, but Tricia seldom wore it; she went to few dressy occasions, preferring to be in tracksuit and trainers. Tricia worked for a building society where, by day, she wore their uniform; personal clothes didn't interest her. Mildred always gave Gerry, her son-in-law, a bottle of whisky; it was an annual joke as he opened it on Christmas Day and poured her the first tot. Mildred always stayed with them for Christmas, just overnight; they lived only ten miles away.

The problem present was Susie's. When she was younger it hadn't been difficult, and even recently she'd wanted tapes for her stereo. She wore it plugged into her ears as she cycled to work in the mornings – a dangerous habit, her father said, as she couldn't then hear traffic coming up from behind. Susie said that, in the rush hour, she knew it was there anyway. Mildred wished she had a car. Perhaps, when Nick came again, she could discuss with him the possibility of raising enough money to buy her one. It needn't be new, after all. Nick might even know of a reliable one that was for sale.

Thinking of Susie, Mildred sighed. She had fond parents and a secure home, and a job with prospects in the council offices where she spent her days before a computer. When she had reached five foot, Susie stopped growing upwards but continued to expand sideways, despite Tricia's efforts to feed her on salads and fruit. She got hungry riding her bike; and no one could say she lacked exercise. Chocolates and cake were what she most enjoyed eating.

Susie sometimes came over on her own to see Mildred,

and even occasionally stayed the night. In summer she cycled the distance but usually she travelled on the bus, and, rarely, borrowed her mother's car. She was always cheerful and would tell her grandmother stories about life at work, making it sound so amusing. Once, for several months, she had had a boyfriend called Jason, and in those weeks she bloomed, even losing half a stone. She brought him to meet Mildred, who did not warm to him because he addressed her as 'dear' and made no attempt to help clear away the meal she provided. She felt patronised, and she hadn't cared for the pointed manner in which he squeezed past Susie when moving around, exaggerating her bulk. If she wasn't so short, she wouldn't seem so stout.

Mildred was pleased when the romance was over, though Tricia was upset.

'He seemed so nice,' she said. 'She's had no other boyfriends since Colin in Year Seven at school.'

'You can't have wanted her to marry him,' Mildred said. 'He wasn't a kind man, Tricia.'

'What other chance will she get?' Tricia asked. 'She loves children.'

'She might go far in local government,' Mildred declared. 'I'm sure she's good at her job.'

'Oh yes,' Tricia said. 'She's bright and conscientious. I'm sure she is.' But she looked like a joke, her mother thought. The hair that in Tricia was richly auburn was, in Susie, vivid red, so that she had been called 'Ginger' and 'Carrots' as a child – and might still be, at work, for all Tricia knew. At college she had dyed it black in an effort to avert the teasing she attracted, but that ended when she joined the dramatic society and was given a comic role for which her red hair was an asset. She survived there by being a bit of a card, playing up the humour, most of it at her own expense, and because she was such a kind girl. She became an excellent cook, which earned her popularity. Mildred thought that perhaps she ought to have gone into catering, but she hadn't seemed drawn to the prospect. Maybe she was simply too small to lift heavy pots and pans around.

She should wear blue, Mildred thought: a misty blue sweater with a mauve tinge in that soft shaded wool you saw. That would be as becoming to her as the silk blouse was to her mother. It would have to be large, even very large. Mildred herself was still a neat size twelve and bought bargains in the sales, much envied by her daughter who was almost Junoesque.

Mildred went round the shops until she grew quite tired. She found the bird book. She'd get the whisky from the local pub, to save carrying it far. She bought soap and bath oil and a small purse, and other such things, for the day centre people, and a scarf for the librarian. Then she went home. She'd got wrapping paper, too; she could get ahead with her preparations.

On the bus, tired but content, she wondered how the young man whose ticket she had paid for had spent the day. Where had he been going? Had things worked out well for him?

At home, she put on the kettle and eased her feet into comfortable slippers, a thing she never did during the day. That would betray her standards. Only when, once, she had a sprained ankle had she stooped so low.

You mustn't let things slide, Mildred always said; if you did, it was difficult to retrieve them.

She picked up the paper and glanced at the crossword, which she did each day, annoyed when she couldn't finish it. Later, she turned on the television for the news, and was watching it when the doorbell rang.

It was Susie. She'd come in her mother's car, and had brought a lasagne from the supermarket, apologising because she had not had time to make it herself, a bottle of red wine, and a chocolate gâteau. She had come to supper.

Mildred roused herself, kissed Susie warmly and bustled her into the warm sitting-room.

Susie was full of the news that, in an office raffle, she had won two tickets to the mayor's Christmas Ball which was held in aid of a charity.

'It's amazing,' she said. 'It's not like the office party. Much grander.' She hated the annual office party, at which the men all seemed to think she was fair game, desired by none and therefore deprived and panting for sex.

She had learned how to walk away, spending time in the ladies' cloakroom. She had endured crude fumblings and lewd suggestive comments, and had been pressed against the wall by sweating heavy drunken men, most of them married. They should have been ashamed of themselves, she thought, but did not say, because she had to work with them later. It never occurred to her that, in the light of their morning's hangover, some of them were.

But now, though excited, she was also despairing.

'Who can I ask to come with me?' she exclaimed. 'And what shall I wear?'

Mildred thought immediately of Nick. He was a bit old for her, perhaps, but he was so charming. If he came to see her soon, she might lead the conversation round to ask if he was married – he probably was – and, if he was not, to sound him out as a possibility.

'I'll give you your dress,' she said. 'It can be your Christmas present.'

'Oh no, Gran, I couldn't let you,' said Susie. 'I'll hire one. After all, I'll never need it again.'

What a pity, thought Mildred, but it might be true. Anyway, fashions changed.

'Well, I'll pay for the hire, then,' she said, adding, 'I had a little windfall the other day, and there's more to come.'

'Did you? Have you been backing the horses, Gran?' Susie asked, laughing. When she was happy she was so pretty, Mildred thought.

'Not that,' Mildred said. 'Let's just say luck went my way. Perhaps you're right to hire. Choose something good, though. Something to set off your hair.' Blue, she thought, but I won't suggest it. She knows I think blue suits her:

'I will,' said Susie. 'Now, let's fix our lasagne, and then you can tell me what you've been up to lately.'

At the office, Susie's win was envied by her colleagues, who thought any one of them was more deserving and better equipped to appreciate the prize. She was mysterious about her partner, saying they would see who it was on the night, but in reality, Susie was desperate. There was no one she could possibly ask. She could give the tickets to someone else. Perhaps that would be the best solution. She could even raffle them again, in aid of some good cause. But that would mean admitting defeat. She felt like Cinderella in reverse, invited to the ball but without a prince.

She could go to an escort agency. They worked for women, not just men; she'd seen their advertisements when she was reading the lonely hearts columns in the local paper, feeling tempted to answer one. Perhaps she should advertise herself. No one except her partner would know.

How was she to solve the problem?

Two days later, Nick returned to Mildred's house.

On his last visit – he'd been several times now, on each occasion buying a pot or bowl or a piece of glass – he'd admired a bureau she had, walnut, once her father's. He'd offered her £250 for it, but she had said she didn't want to sell it.

'It's too big for most modern houses,' Nick pointed out. 'I'd be doing you a favour, really. You don't need it, do you? And your daughter won't have room for it.'

That was true, and £250 would come in very useful for Susie – help her towards a holiday, or the car she was saving up for.

'Are you married?' Mildred asked him.

'No.' Nick was startled at the inconsequence of her question.

'Are you busy on December the ninth?' she asked. 'It's a Friday.'

'Why do you ask?' What could she be leading up to?

'It's my granddaughter,' said Mildred. 'She's going to the mayor's ball, and her partner's – er – in hospital with a broken leg. She won the tickets, you see.' Once launched on her specious explanation, Mildred rattled on, embarrassed. 'Would you escort her? I know you can be trusted.'

Nick had noticed the bureau on his first visit. His whole aim had been to nurse his victim to the yielding point, to soften her with attention. It was worth a cool fifteen K at least, he knew, and he could place it: a genuine gem, unappreciated because it had been in its owner's possession so long. It was in perfect condition, as far as he could tell. By now he knew about Mildred's daughter Tricia, and her son Jack who had been killed on a scientific expedition in South America. He'd heard of Susie, too. Now he was being offered a deal: take Susie to the ball and get the bureau. Well, what had he to lose? Only an evening. He might even be able to remove the bureau first and then stand the girl up.

But that idea didn't work. The old girl forestalled him.

'You could take the bureau away after you bring Susie back from the ball,' she said. 'She can stay here that night.' Then she'd see Susie in her lovely dress.

Nick agreed to it all. He agreed, too, to meet Susie before then; her grandmother would ask her round to supper. He deplored the waste of time, but if he got the bureau, that would compensate.

He'd done well in this area. He'd picked up a lot of nice bits of porcelain, and some silver, and he'd tipped a mate off who wanted paintings. He came back as planned, some days later, and met Susie.

Could he possibly go through with it? Nick, who spoke the truth when he said he wasn't married, had a girlfriend who helped him in his knocking business; sometimes she went with him. She did the books, such as they were, and minded the shop where he put out stuff for sale.

Nick's girlfriend was twenty-nine, five feet eight inches tall, and very slim. She had black hair permed into wiry ringlets, and wore very short skirts. Her fingernails were long and red; her lips were full. She was experienced, and looked it. Susie was her complete opposite, even down to bitten fingernails.

He used his charm, however.

'I'm so fond of your grandmother,' he said.

Susie wondered how they'd met, but neither of them told her. Mildred was not going to confess to any of her sales.

Nick arranged to fetch her on the evening of the ball. He'd come to her grandmother's at eight o'clock. He couldn't stay now, he said.

'Must dash,' he declared, remembering to smile at both of them, meanwhile busy scheming. He'd had an idea.

He couldn't get the bureau out of the house unaided; it was much too big and heavy. He'd take Susie to the ball, pretend he was going to the cloakroom and abandon her. She'd simply be bewildered, and he'd be back again before she became suspicious. Meanwhile, he'd have nicked the bureau, tying the old girl up if necessary, but she might already be asleep – old folk notoriously went to bed early. It'd be easy. Jimmy Fox would help him, for a consideration; he'd helped Jimmy out before now, on similar jobs. He'd use his car and Jimmy could bring the van. He'd tell the old woman he'd collect the bureau on Sunday. It'd be like robbing a baby.

Most of the time, Nick did straightforward knocking, calling at houses and picking up good pieces for trifling sums from unsuspecting pensioners. Many old people had something worth a good few pounds more than he offered them and now and then he came upon a real find, like Mildred's desk, and her mugs: she had a full run of coronation and other celebratory mugs ranging from George VI's coronation to the marriage of the Prince of Wales. They were to be another prize, he'd decided. He knew where they were; he'd take them when he took the bureau. And he'd take the Toby jugs. She had others, besides Winston Churchill.

Susie was delighted by Nick, but also frightened. He was a good deal older than she was, and seemed quite a man of the world. She'd given him her telephone number at work; he already had her grandmother's. He'd ring her before the ball, he said, to make a final plan.

Dinner was not included in the ticket deal. People made their own plans to eat, some having dinner parties, others dining out, but Susie, who had never been to such a smart event, did not know that. She'd told Nick that dress was formal; that meant a dinner suit, she said. She'd heard some people in the office mention hiring them.

Nick said he'd got one. It was true.

Friday the ninth arrived, and in the morning Susie received a telephone call. It was Nick. He said he was going to be delayed and could not arrive in time to fetch her from her grandmother's. He would meet her at the Town Hall. She could wait for him in the foyer, or, if she went in to the reception, she could leave his ticket with the doorman.

Susie's heart sank. She'd imagined making quite an entrance on his arm.

'That's all right,' she said, however. 'Don't worry.'

She rang her grandmother to tell her of the change of plan. She'd go home to change, she said.

'So I won't see your lovely dress,' said Mildred.

'You will when Nick brings me back,' said Susie. But then she had a thought. 'Perhaps I'd better get him to take me home,' she said. 'I don't want to wake you up, and it's nearer.'

In the end, her grandmother agreed. It made sense, and Susie's parents would be at the house; they'd know when she had been delivered safely, after, Mildred hoped, a lovely evening.

'I'll come and tell you all about it tomorrow,' Susie promised. 'I'll take the dress back after I've shown it to you.'

She'd not been sure about it, as it wasn't blue, but the girl in the shop had talked her into it, saying it and her hair made a striking combination.

The other women in the department had heard the conversation Susie had with Nick, and one of them felt sorry for her. Several of them were also going to the ball, not by luck but because it was a good annual event, and beforehand a group of them – three couples – were joining more from the office for a Christmas dinner at The Anchor Hotel. Those going to the ball would go on to the Town Hall, while the rest made a night of it. Susie, naturally enough, had not been included in these plans, but now her department head suggested she should join them all for dinner.

'Pity about your date,' she said. 'Still, we'll meet him later.' They were intrigued by the mystery man who was going to be her partner. She'd told them nothing about him except to say that he was very good-looking, and about six feet tall.

Susie, rescued, accepted. She'd pay her way, she said, and that was agreed. It would be all right because she had Nick to look forward to.

There were a few grumbles about this plan when Susie went off to the washroom, but on the whole people felt magnanimous about her; after all, it was Christmas and her man had been held up. It could happen to anyone.

'I suppose he does exist,' said Margery, and was shushed as Susie returned.

They were to meet at The Anchor, a stone's throw from the Town Hall.

Susie took hours to get ready, bathing, doing what she could about her bitten nails, rubbing cream on her hands. Her newly washed hair stood out around her head in a ginger cloud, and she stepped into her dress, somehow managing to zip it up the back. Her parents had gone out to a different Christmas celebration, so there was no one to help her or to admire her in her finery.

Her dress had such a bouffant skirt that she could not wear a coat over it; she dug out the old cape her mother had had years ago when they were fashionable. Then she was ready. She rang for a taxi and waited till it came; it took only five minutes to drive to The Anchor.

Susie left her cape in the cloakroom. Then she made her way into the bar, where she had been told to meet the others in her party. Afraid of being early, she was, in fact, one of the last arrivals. Without meaning to, she seemed to make an entrance as she hesitated, shyly, in the doorway, looking round for them. She seldom entered bars alone; even as a student, she had not done so, and this one, bedecked with Christmas decorations, was crowded.

Her group was in a corner, and they looked up as she approached. Then, without exception, they all broke into near hysterical laughter, for Susie's dress was the exact shade of her hair. Its satin bodice moulded her plump breasts and revealed pale skin above; its skirt, made of many-layered net, billowed out around her like an overgrown tutu, as one witness later said, describing it as a ballroom dancing costume.

'Susie dear, you look just like an orange,' someone said, and so she did, except for her face, which had been flushed with eagerness but now turned pale.

It took her a few moments to realise that they were all laughing at her, that she looked a sight. She'd been doubtful in the cloakroom, but had reassured herself as she remembered the encouragement of the dress agency assistant.

Susie never learned that one girl in the office, jealous of the promotion Susie had recently gained, and knowing she planned to hire a dress, had gone along to the shop and chosen this one, promising the assistant ten pounds if she succeeded in getting Susie to select it.

Now she caught a glimpse of herself in the sheet looking-glass behind the bar. All she saw was garish colour. There had been a green dress that fitted her, very plain, cut straight and loose enough to hide her bulges. She had liked it, really wanted it, but been dissuaded. Wrong! Tears filled her eyes and she turned and fled, not even pausing to collect her cape.

She rushed into the road, saw a bus, and leapt on it, still in her gaudy dress, the tears pouring down her face. The driver gazed at her, expectant, quite unmoved by her grief and by her raiment.

'Where to?' he asked, but she was diving past him to the nearest seat.

'Finchbury,' she gulped.

A young man got on behind her.

'I'll pay for her,' he said. 'Two, please.'

He paid, accepting change and tickets, then removed his coat, a padded anorak, quite large, for he was a tall young man. 'Put this on,' he told her, and he bundled her into it, holding her small gold handbag while he made her insert her arms. 'Now, where are you going?' he asked.

'To my gran's,' she said, beginning to calm down.

He tried again.

'Where were you going?'

'To the mayor's ball. My dress is ridiculous,' she said.

'Your hair's gorgeous,' he told her. 'Try not to cry.'

'I ought to be going home,' she said. 'To change.'

'Where's home?'

'Here. In Sinclair Road,' she said.

'Well, we're on the way to Finchbury,' he said. 'Is that where your gran lives?'

'Yes.'

'We'll go there, then,' he said. 'I'll take you.'

She went on crying for a while, but at last grew quiet, blowing her nose on a small tissue which she found in her bag, along with the two tickets for the ball.

'I'm meant to meet Nick at the Town Hall,' she said.

'We'll telephone,' he answered, unperturbed.

When the bus stopped near Mildred's street, she said, 'This is where I get off.'

'Keep the coat on,' he advised. 'I'm coming too.'

They left the bus together, and he loped down the road beside her, a tall young man in black trousers and wearing a blue sweater. In her gold slippers with their high heels, Susie was teetering along, and he seized her arm and tucked it through his.

'Where's your gran's house?' he asked.

'It's at the end of the road,' she answered. 'Where the big tree is.'

They walked on together silently, and then, nearing the house, she slowed up, pulling her companion to a halt.

'What's wrong?' he asked.

'There's someone there. At my gran's,' she said. 'Oh, look! It's burglars!' and she put her hand to her mouth in a gasp of horror.

Her saviour looked at her sharply.

'Are you sure?' he said, but it was obvious. A van had been reversed into the short driveway outside the house. Its doors were open, and the front door of the house was also open.

'My grandmother!' she cried.

'Stay there,' he said. 'No – go back a few houses and bang on the door and ask them to call the police. And stay there,' he warned her.

'What are you going to do?'

'See if the keys are in the van for a start,' he said. 'If not, try to let down the tyres or at least take the number. No heroics,' he added, and then, 'Get going.'

She took off her slippers and ran back up the road in her stockinged feet, turning in three doors down at her grandmother's friend Mrs Wilson's house, where she was known.

Ten minutes later the police caught Nick and Jimmy Fox carrying the bureau – its drawers, the contents crudely tipped on to the sitting-room floor, now loaded with the mug collection, carefully wrapped. Mildred had been tied up and gagged, with a pillowslip placed over her head to act as a blindfold. She was not hurt, but she was very shaken. The two robbers had worn black woollen Balaclava hoods and she had not recognised Nick. He hadn't touched her; Jimmy Fox had done the tying up.

The story of his deal with Mildred was never revealed; greed had been his undoing, loving folly hers. He did not want to humiliate himself by confessing to the plan, and she would not betray what she had tried to do to help her granddaughter.

When she had been untied, Mildred knew her rescuer at once. And he knew her.

'You paid my bus fare,' said the young man. 'And today I paid Susie's. You said to do it for someone else another day.'

'But why did you?' Susie asked him later, when her grandmother had gone round to spend the night with Mrs Wilson.

'I saw what happened in the bar,' he said. 'I was there, waiting to meet my sister. She's the mayoress. Our mother is the mayor. Look – these are my dinner suit trousers; I was going to put my tie and jacket on later. I think you ought to tell me your side of the story while we return to the ball. You must face your friends. My sister will have a dress that you can borrow. Even if we only get there in time for the last waltz, I think you need to do it, Susie.'

'You keep saying my name. You knew it before the police asked me what it was,' said Susie.

'I couldn't forget your gorgeous hair,' he said. 'Do you remember Colin, in Year Seven? I used to carry your recorder for you.'

Before they left Colin made some telephone calls and said his sister had an appropriate dress. They'd go to her house at once, in a taxi. When they arrived, she was waiting for them, having rushed there from the Town Hall. There was no need for Susie to be told that the flowing royal blue gown was a maternity dress, calf length on the sister, full length when worn by Susie. She and Colin danced several numbers together before the ball ended, watched in astonishment by her colleagues. She had said her mystery partner was good-looking, and he was: no wonder she'd kept quiet about his being the mayor's son. Strange, though, about the change of dress: perhaps she had planned it as a joke.

After the ball, Susie went back with him to supper in his mother's kitchen, for both of them were hungry, having missed their dinner. Then he took her home.

Colin was a botanist, back for Christmas from Canada where he was working on a five-year project. He thought there might be an opening there for Susie, since she was so expert at analysing statistics on her computer.

By the time she flew out, in the spring, she had lost two stone.

Nick was sent to prison for two years: his knocking offences were more difficult to pin down, since money had been handed over, but at least he was removed from circulation for a while. It was no good his pleading that Mildred had agreed to sell her bureau, as she had agreed to sell her other things; why had he needed to wear a mask and tie her up, if that were true?

'He'll find more mugs to fall for his sweet talk, when he comes out,' was the rueful comment of the prosecuting counsel.

Alas, it was doubtless true. Mildred, however, never fell victim again to a con man.

Margaret Yorke was awarded the CWA Cartier Diamond Dagger in 1999. After writing a series of detective novels in the traditional vein featuring the sleuthing don Patrick Grant, she turned her *attention to stand-alone novels of psychological suspense, many of which benefit from her abiding interest in penology and the criminal mind.* No Medals for the Major *made an immediate impact and later titles include* The Cost of Silence *and* Devil's Work. Pieces of Justice *collects together her incisive short stories.*